W9-DCF-059

COLLISION OF LIES

COLLISION OF LIES

TOM THREADGILL

Revell

a division of Baker Publishing Group
Grand Rapids, Michigan

© 2020 by Thomas D. Threadgill

Published by Revell
a division of Baker Publishing Group
PO Box 6287, Grand Rapids, MI 49516-6287
www.revellbooks.com

Printed in the United States of America

Library of Congress Cataloging-in-Publication Data
Names: Threadgill, Tom, 1961– author.
Title: Collision of lies / Tom Threadgill.
Description: Grand Rapids : Revell, a division of Baker Publishing Group, 2020.
Identifiers: LCCN 2019028419 | ISBN 9780800736507 (paperback)
Subjects: LCSH: School bus accidents—Texas—San Antonio. | Criminal
    investigations—Texas—San Antonio.
Classification: LCC HE5614.4.S32 T57 2020 | DDC 363.12/59—dc23
LC record available at https://lccn.loc.gov/2019028419

ISBN 978-0-8007-3785-6 (casebound)

Published in association with the Hartline Literary Agency, LLC.

20 21 22 23 24 25 26   7 6 5 4 3 2 1

Thirty seconds.

If they were still arguing, she'd call the cops then. Let the professionals deal with them.

Amara Alvarez leaned her athletic frame outside the diner's booth to get in the man's line of sight. He glanced up and she shot her best death stare his way. Clenched jaw, narrowed eyes, the works.

No effect. The man and woman continued their argument or breakup or whatever was happening. He bounced between whispers and shouts. She alternated between screaming and sobbing.

The couple, both appearing to be Hispanic and around thirty years old, had been at it for nearly an hour. Of all the restaurants in San Antonio, did they have to come here? Today? Her initial empathy toward the pair had faded a long time ago. Most folks would've recognized the impact of their outbursts on others. Not these two.

As a result, Amara's mood had risen to level-ten irritation. Her Saturday morning ritual of a quiet meal at the Breakfast Bodega was ruined, thanks to them. Was it so much to ask? That people keep their personal matters *personal*?

Ronnie, the heavyset weekend manager of the diner, had stopped by their table twice with little impact on the theatrics. Most of the other customers had shoveled their meals into Styrofoam containers and fled the scene. Not Amara. This wasn't her first battle of wills.

The red second hand on the wall clock hit the 12. She grabbed her phone, sighed, and laid it back on the table. Five more minutes. If they were still going, she'd call the police then.

Her heart leaped as a metallic bang echoed throughout the area. Something in the kitchen, dropped or thrown, clattered a few more times, followed by muffled shouting, which may or may not have been sprinkled with a few choice expletives. The door from back there flung open and Ronnie made a beeline for her, his face steaming. An image of herself as a matador sprang to mind and she shook her head as he sat opposite her.

"Uh-uh," she said. "Don't come over here with that attitude."

He gestured over his shoulder at the contentious couple. "They're killing our business. You going to sit there and do nothing?"

She raised her phone. "Getting ready to call the cops."

"You *are* a cop."

Yeah, and she mostly loved the job. But her Saturday plans didn't include arbitrating personal conflicts. Armed robbery, home break-in, even a shoplifter couldn't ruin her day off. But this was asking too much for too little. She shrugged and bit into a thick piece of bacon. "A little overcooked today. Tell Ruby there's a difference between crispy and charcoal."

He slapped his hands together into a praying position. "Please? I'll bring out some fresh pancakes for you. And the meal's on the house this morning."

She leaned to the side and studied the couple. The woman wept while the man held her hand across the table.

"You know the rules," Amara said. "Can't take anything free. I'll leave the usual and you can do what you want with it. Give it to Ruby for bacon-cooking lessons."

"Deal," he said. "Just go now, before we lose more business."

"Next time, call the cops." She tapped her elbow on the weapon in her belt holster and walked to the couple's table. "Everything okay here?"

The man glared at her before turning his attention back to the woman across from him. "Sorry. My wife's a little emotional this morning."

Yeah? Well, me too. She focused on his spouse. Her dark shoulder-length hair had faint traces of blonde highlights, and bright red lipstick expanded her full lips. Swollen bags under her eyes added to the pudginess of her face. "Ma'am, everything okay?"

"No, it's not." Tears trickled down her face and she pulled her hand from her partner's, then dabbed her cheeks with a napkin.

The man straightened. "Now, honey, let's not—"

Amara held up her hand. "Let her talk."

The corners of his mouth dropped, and he shifted his body to face the newcomer. "Who do you—"

"Detective Amara Alvarez. San Antonio PD." She showed her ID. "I don't know what's going on here and, honestly, don't need to know. As long as I'm certain your wife's not in any danger, I'll let you get back to your breakfast. But you have to keep the noise down."

"In danger?" the woman said. "From who?"

Amara tilted her head toward the husband. "From him."

The woman's mouth hung open and she blinked several times. "What? No. I mean . . . no. Why would you think that?"

"Police, remember?"

The woman cleared her throat and sipped her water to compose herself, then slid over and patted the seat. "Would you mind sitting for a moment, Officer? I'm Marisa Reyes and he's my husband, Enzo."

"Detective. And I really don't want to get involved unless this is a police matter."

Mr. Reyes crumpled his napkin and deep wrinkles lined his forehead. "It's not."

His wife's shoulders spasmed as another wave of hysterics neared. "How can you say that? Of course it is."

"Honey, you have to let it go."

"Do I?" The woman's voice shook. "*You* sure let it go in a hurry, didn't you?"

Amara's shoulders sagged, and she sat and angled herself toward Mrs. Reyes. "Tell me what's going on."

"She got a text this morning," the husband said, "and it has her all stressed out. I told her to ignore it. Either a prank or wrong number. Not worth getting all worked up over."

His wife brushed her hand under her eyes. "How can you be so sure? You can't know it wasn't him."

Amara turned to face the woman beside her. "Tell me about the text."

"A message came about two hours ago from a number I didn't recognize. 'Help me, Mom.' That's all it said. When I tried to respond, my phone said the number was no good." She flattened her palms on the table and took a deep breath. "I know it's from Benjamin, our son. I can't explain it, but the text is from him."

Amara dangled her arm across the back of the seat. "Have you called your son to see if he's okay?"

"Detective"—Mr. Reyes grabbed his wife's hand and squeezed—"there's no point. Benjamin's been dead for three years."

2

Sunday mornings in the office weren't good for much besides playing catch-up. Amara shuffled through the paperwork covering her desk. The Reyeses would be coming by sometime this morning. Meantime, she planned to get her notes from the prior week into the computer. A rash of burglaries in Leon Valley consumed her working hours. Lots of paperwork, lots of interviews, lots of angry homeowners, and zero leads.

Another thirty minutes or so and it'd be time for a late breakfast. Mama's leftover vegetable enchiladas, covered in chili sauce to jump-start her taste buds. Her stomach rumbled in anticipation and she hunched forward, covering her belly with her arms in a futile attempt to disguise the sound.

One of the other detectives eyeballed her. "Hey, Alvarez. Do you mind? Trying to work over here."

"Whatever, Dotson. Not like I haven't heard any noises from your direction. Keep it over there, okay?"

He chuckled. "More room on the outside, right?"

She threw a paper clip at him. "What are you, like, six? Grow up already."

Another detective joined in. "She's right, Wylie. Lay off the late-night burritos, for all our sakes."

Dotson stood and hitched his pants up around his waist. "And risk losing this figure? No thanks. After my tours, I promised myself that when I left the service, I'd eat whatever and whenever I wanted.

Oh, and Alvarez, fifty-eight years young come next Thursday. Be sure and buy me something nice."

"Case of Pepto?"

He laughed and plopped back into his chair. "Eh, I'll settle for whatever you brought for lunch."

"Sorry to disappoint you, but no leftovers from last night." *At least not enough for both of us. And if he gets to the food first . . .*

"Uh-huh. Never known Mama not to send food home with you. Everybody must've been extra hungry."

She shrugged. "The nieces and nephews brought friends. I was lucky to scavenge enough scraps for Larry."

He leaned around his monitor to get a better look at her. "I can't believe you took care of your iguana instead of me."

"Larry's nicer to me. Smells better too."

Dotson rubbed his chin and nodded. "Point taken. What have you got going today?"

"Got to head out to Leon Valley later. Paperwork till then. You?"

He scratched the back of his neck. "Got a B&E at a Best Buy over by North Star."

"They get much?"

"Don't know yet. Probably a bunch of VCRs and stuff."

She grinned and turned back to her computer. "VCRs. Yep. They're the hottest thing on the black market these days. Hey, while you're there, see if they've got any good deals on record players. Honestly, you're the lead detective. You could at least make an effort to stay in the right century."

Her desk phone buzzed and the lobby receptionist announced that Enzo and Marisa Reyes were here. Great. She shouldn't have offered to meet with them, but it seemed the polite thing to do at the time. No surprise that they'd taken her up on the suggestion. The pain of losing a child must be unbearable. Whether cruel joke or wrong number, the text message flared new hope in the mother, and the woman would do anything to turn that hope into reality.

She asked the front desk to escort the Reyeses to a meeting room and tell them she'd join them in a moment. Mama's enchiladas would have to wait a bit, unless Dotson found them first. After a stop in the break room to hide her breakfast under a container of some sort of pasta that had transitioned to a science experiment, she took the stairs down two flights and paused.

Keep it short. No commitments. She pasted on a smile and stepped inside. "Mr. and Mrs. Reyes. Thank you for coming in."

Enzo Reyes stood and extended his hand. "Thank you for meeting with us, Detective."

"Of course. Mrs. Reyes, how are you feeling today?"

The woman clutched a tissue in her hands. "About the same. Sorry to be such a problem yesterday."

"Nonsense," Amara said. "I understand completely. The death of a child is—"

"He's not dead," Mrs. Reyes said.

Her husband placed his arm around her shoulders. "Honey, you're making this worse on yourself. Don't dredge it all up again. We have to keep moving forward. You know Benjamin wouldn't want you to suffer like this."

"He texted us, Enzo. Why can't you accept that?"

Amara shifted in her seat. "Mrs. Reyes, your son was one of the children killed in the accident down in Cotulla, isn't that right?"

"Yes. I mean, no. We thought he was, but then we got this text and . . ." She dabbed at her eyes, took a deep breath, and stared at her hands.

Amara pushed a box of Kleenex across the table and waited for the woman to recover. Cotulla. Seventeen kids on the school bus. All dead. The train had been traveling at full speed, and if the impact didn't kill them, the subsequent explosion and fire did. Counting the bus driver and two engineers on the train, twenty people dead.

The president called the incident a national tragedy when he visited the site. For the families of those who died, "tragedy" seemed far too weak a word. Mrs. Reyes was a living testimony of that fact.

Amara cleared her throat. "Ma'am, every detail of the incident was scrutinized to the nth degree. DNA tests confirmed the remains of all the children on the school bus, including Benjamin's. Remember?"

Mrs. Reyes pulled a clean tissue from the box. "Mistakes happen."

"Sure they do." Her heart ached for the woman, but giving her false hope would only add to the pain. "There's overwhelming proof Benjamin died that day along with the other kids. There's absolutely nothing to indicate he didn't. I'm sorry. I wish I could help."

"What about the text message?"

Mr. Reyes squeezed his wife's shoulder. "Wrong number. Cruel prank. Who knows? You have to let it go, baby. You have to."

"I can't. If there's the tiniest hope, I'll always wonder."

Amara clasped her hands together. "Mrs. Reyes, your son was six years old at the time of the accident. Would he even know your phone number?"

"He knew our full names, address, and phone number. We used to make him recite them to us. The school recommended all parents do that in case their child got lost, or worse."

Smart. Sad, but smart. "I see." Amara studied the mother as her thoughts battled one another. *Don't offer. Don't.* "Tell you what. How about I get our tech guys to take a look at your phone? See if they can figure out anything on the text. Would that make you feel better? Maybe put this all behind you?"

Mrs. Reyes reached her hand across the table and clutched Amara's. "Would you do that? We'd be so grateful."

"We would," her husband said. "I know how busy you must be."

"It's no problem. Really." Amara forced a smile. *This is going to be a huge problem.*

The woman slid her phone across the table. "How long will you need it?"

Amara rubbed the back of her neck. "A day or two probably. Will that be an issue?"

"No," she said. "Of course not. Anything for Benjamin."

"Okay. We won't answer the phone or any texts while it's in our possession. Did you disable the lock screen?"

Her husband grunted. "It's always disabled. I tell her that's not safe, but she says it's a headache to always have to unlock the thing."

Amara stood and tucked the phone in her pocket. "Well then, if there's nothing else . . . ?"

The Reyeses glanced at each other and shook their heads.

"Fine. I'll get this right to the lab and give you a call when I hear from them. Oh, one more thing. The cell provider will contact you to get your signature on a couple of forms. You'll be giving us approval to look at the history of your incoming calls and messages. Are you okay with that?"

"Certainly," Mrs. Reyes said. "Thank you again, Detective. I can't tell you what a relief it is to have someone working on this for us."

Working on this? The poor woman must think we're opening an investigation. Hard to do with no evidence of a crime. She placed her hand on the mother's arm. "Please don't get your hopes up. I don't want to mislead you. I'm assigned to the Property Crimes Division. I typically do burglaries, robberies, that kind of stuff. I'm happy to help, but I firmly believe your son passed away. I'm not investigating his death. I'm simply seeking an explanation for the text you received so you can have peace about it."

Mr. Reyes placed his hand under his wife's elbow and guided her to her feet. "We understand, don't we, honey? And Detective Alvarez, *gracias*."

"*De nada.*" She held the door for the couple and pointed the way out of the building. "I'll call you when I know something."

She remained staring as the couple wandered from view. Had the pain of their son's death faded at all over the past three years? Or at least moved into the realm of acceptance? And now, the grieving would begin anew. Emotional scars would be ripped open and nothing she did would heal them.

The dead remained dead.

Hope couldn't change that.

"You're sure?" Amara said. It'd been four days since her meeting with the Reyeses. Four days and seven phone messages from Benjamin's mom.

The crime lab tech handed her Mrs. Reyes's phone.

"Hundred percent certain? No. But unless I pass this on to the next level, I'm as sure as I can be."

"The next level?"

"The Feds. They've got better tools than we do. 'Course, there's a lot of paperwork that goes along with having them take a look."

She slipped the phone into her pocket. The powers that be weren't about to give the okay on getting other agencies involved, especially when she couldn't even convince herself it was worth the effort. "No way I'd get approval for that without some evidence that a crime was committed. But I appreciate you doing this for me."

"No problem. Oh, and the guys said thanks for the pizza."

No better bribe than food, and it paid to keep the lab guys happy. Wasn't the first time—and wouldn't be the last—she'd needed a favor done off the books. She'd make a quick call to Mr. Reyes, tell him what they both already knew, and move on to whatever waited on top of the stack on her desk. She'd done her best and that was all anyone could ask.

So why did the text still bother her? Mrs. Reyes was convincing. Who wouldn't empathize with her and hope that, by some miracle, her son was still alive?

Let it go, Amara. Move on to actual crimes. She dialed Mr. Reyes's number, crossing her fingers she'd get voice mail. The easy way out. Leave a message, tell them the phone would be at the front desk, and—

"Hello?"

Not her day. "Oh, hello, Mr. Reyes. This is Detective Alvarez with the San Antonio Police Department."

"Yes, Detective. How are you today?"

She pressed the phone against her ear as the vending machine guy rattled past her in the hallway. "Fine, thanks. Listen, I wanted to let you know we're done with your wife's phone. As I expected, we didn't learn anything. Whoever sent the text used a bogus number and Wi-Fi instead of a cell network. Impossible to trace. The tech guys said there are dozens of apps that will do that."

"I see. Well, I can't say I'm surprised."

"Sorry I couldn't be more help. I'll leave the phone at the front desk and you can pick it up at your convenience."

"Detective, would you mind telling my wife what you told me? I think this would have more, um, finality coming from you. I'd really appreciate it."

She tilted her head back against the wall and closed her eyes. "I'm pretty busy, Mr. Reyes. I mean, I guess I could spare a couple of minutes, but—"

"Wonderful. What time should we be there?"

"I'll be doing paperwork most of the afternoon, so anytime before six. Please give me a call before you come to make sure I'm still here."

"Will do. Again, thank you so much. I can't tell you what a help you've been to us."

She frowned and headed toward her desk. "Glad to do it."

* * *

"Got a live one, don't you?" Dotson asked.

Amara looked up from her keyboard. "Nope. This'll be the end of it. Give her the phone and we both move on."

"Not likely. I've seen this before. It's like dessert at a lunch buffet." She leaned back and crossed her arms. "I'm going to hate myself for asking, but what's that supposed to mean?"

He scooted his chair to the right and rested his elbows on his desk. "See, you tell yourself you'll be happy with only one piece of apple pie. Toss in a cookie too. But when you finish them, you start to wonder if there's more. Maybe the kitchen's holding out on you. Waiting for you to move on so they can put out the chocolate meringue. But your wife's nagging you to hurry up because her show starts in twenty minutes. Oh no, can't miss *Downtown Abbey*, whoever she is. Pretty sure I arrested her once over in vice."

She massaged her forehead. "You know that makes no sense, right? And it's *Downton Abbey*. It's a place, not a person."

"You watch that stuff? Didn't have you pegged as a girly-girl, Alvarez."

She threw another paper clip his direction. "I don't watch it, but I'm not an idiot."

He leaned forward, squinted, and turned his head side to side. "You *do* watch it, don't you?"

"No, but even if I did, what difference would it make? It's not like you couldn't stand a little culture in your life."

"Hey, I get all the culture I need from yogurt. Mostly frozen with sprinkles and chocolate chips."

"It all comes back to food with you, doesn't it, Dotson? I'd be happy to get you a guest pass to my gym. An hour of kickboxing would let you work up a real appetite, plus it'd be nice to have a live target for a change."

He stood and bowed, grunting as his belly pressed against his thighs. "As you wish, Lady Downtown Amara."

Her suppressed laugh erupted as a snort. "*Que idiota!* I should—"

The phone beeped and the front desk alerted her that the Reyeses had arrived. She took a deep breath and exhaled a slow, steady stream of dread.

"Wish me luck."

* * *

The overpowered air conditioner had the small meeting room at near-subzero temperatures. The joys of living in Texas. A hundred ten degrees outside, sixty degrees inside.

Mr. Reyes had obviously already shared the results with his wife. Her watery eyes and nearly blank expression gave her away. The tears remained, but the hope was gone.

Amara nodded to the couple, slid a chair closer to the grieving mother, and did her best to smile. "Mrs. Reyes, I'm sorry, but there's nothing on the phone to indicate the text was anything other than what we suspected. Wrong number most likely. Could've been a prank, but I don't think so. If someone wanted to hurt you, seems like they'd have been more deliberate. Sign your son's name even."

The woman brushed the back of her hand under her nose. "But that doesn't make sense. Who else would send a message like that? 'Help me mom.' If it's not Benjamin, then who? And if it wasn't for me, who needed help?"

Mr. Reyes placed his hand on his wife's arm. "Marisa, she's told you everything she knows. You have to let it go. Isn't that right, Detective?"

"I'm afraid so. Our lab was quite thorough. They considered the possibility the text might be from a person who was actually in trouble, but there's really no way to know. There have been no new reports of missing children in the last week or so."

Mr. Reyes patted his wife's back. "We need to let the detective get back to her work, Marisa."

Amara handed her the phone and reached to shake her hand,

but the woman stood and hugged her. "Thank you for your help. You'll call if you get any updates?"

"Um, I'm not—"

Mrs. Reyes stepped back and handed a wallet-size photo to Amara. "That's our Benjamin. We took the picture at the park about two weeks before . . ."

Amara studied the photo of the six-year-old boy. Strands of dark brown hair drooped across his forehead, almost reaching his jet-black eyes. A dab of blue face paint covered his nose, and cat whiskers had been drawn around his mouth. "Oh, what a cutie."

"Yes, he was. Is."

Is? Dotson was right. Mrs. Reyes wanted the chocolate meringue pie.

Mr. Reyes rubbed the back of his neck and sighed. "Marisa, baby, don't—"

"Enzo, please. Detective Alvarez, you'll call if you get any updates?"

She lifted her hand, paused, and let it drop to her side again. *Give her a couple of weeks to let the hope die again.* "Um, yes. Absolutely."

Amara poked at what was left of her two pancakes, rubbed her palms on her pants, then glanced toward the entrance of the Breakfast Bodega. Three weeks since she'd spoken to Mrs. Reyes, but the woman had phoned an hour ago and begged to meet. Said she had information that would help the investigation and would be here by eight.

Amara shifted in her seat and focused on slowing her breathing. She had enough stress without adding Mrs. Reyes's fictions to the pile. There'd been another burglary in Leon Valley this week, and the neighborhood demanded action, as if she wasn't already doing everything she could. Hard as it might be, if the woman did show up, it was time to shut her down forcefully. Make her understand there was no investigation and holding out hope could only cause more pain.

The ancient Coca-Cola clock on the wall said it was eight thirty, but the thing constantly ran ten minutes slow. Maybe Mrs. Reyes's husband finally got through to her and she wasn't coming. Amara downed the last of her orange juice and dug through her purse for a few dollar bills. She always tipped extra here, often as much as the total check. The waitstaff knew her by name and kept the coffee hot, the table clean, and the pancakes just right.

"*Buenos días*, Detective."

Amara glanced up and smiled. Great. "Mrs. Reyes. I didn't think you were coming."

The woman slid into the booth across from her. "Sorry. Was digging through a stack of old newspapers and lost track of time."

"Sure. Well, I can give you a few minutes, but then I really need to go."

"Absolutely, but I felt it was important to show you this." The woman passed a blank, unsealed manila envelope across the table.

Amara reached inside and pulled out a Ziploc bag containing a scrap of paper. "What is this?"

"I put it in the bag because I figured you'd want to check the paper for fingerprints. You'll need mine and Daniella Delacruz's too. We both touched it."

"So . . . what is this? And who is Daniella Delacruz?"

She shifted forward and placed her forearms on the table. "That's a note Daniella found on her car at work. Her daughter Caterina died in the bus accident. Same one that supposedly killed Benjamin."

Supposedly. There was no convincing this woman. Amara turned the bag over and read the two words scribbled on the note. "It says 'I'm sorry.' Is that supposed to mean something?"

Wrinkles deepened on Mrs. Reyes's forehead. "Isn't it obvious?"

"Um, not to me."

"It's got to be connected to my text from Benjamin. It's too big a coincidence. Two mothers getting messages?"

Let her down easy but be firm. "This could be anything. Maybe they backed into her car. Cut her off on the interstate. Who knows, but to say it's somehow related to—"

The woman slapped the table. "It's connected! It has to be. Our children—" She buried her head in her hands.

"I'm sorry." Three years had passed, and for some, including the woman across the table, the suffering continued. "I know you're hurting, and if I could make things right, I would."

Amara stared at the piece of paper, turning the clear bag over repeatedly to stall the words she had to say. "But this isn't a clue and there is no case. We are not investigating Benjamin's death."

She lowered her voice. "Mrs. Reyes, the department has access to several wonderful doctors. I'd be happy to put you in touch with one. They could help you move on with your life."

The woman jerked back in her seat. "Move on with my life? What do you think I'm doing? Can't you understand that as long as there's hope, I have to chase it? I pray you never know the grief of losing a child. But the text message, the note, they came to me. I didn't go looking for them."

"Yes, ma'am. I understand the—"

"Can I get you ladies anything?" Ronnie stopped at the table and reached down to refill Amara's water glass.

Both shook their heads.

"The bacon okay this morning?"

Amara glanced at her plate. "What? Yeah, great."

"Really? 'Cause Ruby thought—"

"Can you give us a minute, Ronnie?"

His shoulders sagged and he nodded. "Oh, yeah. Sure. I'll leave you two alone."

She waited until he'd moved away, then continued. "Mrs. Reyes, I'm sorry, but I have to ask this. Did you send the text and write the note?"

Her eyes widened and her mouth flew open. She started to speak, paused, then sighed. "I did not. And to answer your next question, I don't know who did."

Amara slid the paper back across the table. "Yes, ma'am. I didn't mean to accuse, but I had to ask. And my offer stands. If you want me to put you in touch with one of our doctors, I'd be happy to help. Otherwise . . ."

"Otherwise you're done with me." She straightened, sniffled, and blinked several times. "I won't stop, Detective. Until I know for sure one way or the other, I won't stop. I can't."

Amara reached and placed her hand on the woman's. "How will you know, Mrs. Reyes? As long as you let the possibility in, you'll always wonder. You'll catch a glimpse of a kid and think it could be Benjamin. Your phone will ring and they'll hang up before you answer and you'll wonder if it might have been him. You've seen the DNA results and you've buried your son. I'm sorry, but there's nothing else we can do."

The woman's head dipped and she pulled her hand away. "Do you know who Caterina Delacruz is—was?"

"One of the kids on the bus with your son that morning. If you hadn't told me, I wouldn't have known, though."

"Sí, she was on the bus. Sitting near the back, they think. But she wasn't supposed to be."

"Wasn't supposed to be what?"

"On the bus. Caterina only lived half a block from the school. Every morning, her mother would walk her to her classroom, but not that day. Caterina had spent the night with her friend, so she rode the bus with her."

"Okay?"

"Do you not think it's strange that the note went to the mother of the only child who wasn't supposed to be on the bus that day?"

Amara arched her back. Nothing she could say would change the woman's mind. Granted, it *was* an interesting coincidence, and in most cases she didn't believe in such chance events, but c'mon. This was stretching the boundaries of belief. "The note could mean a thousand different things that have nothing to do with her daughter or your son. Mrs. Reyes, please don't take this the wrong way, but how's your relationship with your husband?"

Her eyes narrowed and the corners of her lips drooped. "He's not doing this."

"No, I don't think he is either, but I have to ask."

"Our relationship is like any other. We have our problems, especially since Benjamin—well, anyway, lately more good days than bad, *gracias a Dios*. My husband suffers no less than I do."

"Of course. Again, I had to ask. I'm sorry I wasn't able to help more, but there's nothing there for law enforcement to get involved with. I hope you understand."

She nodded and did her best to smile. "I do. Thank you for your time. And please, let me buy your breakfast."

Amara stood and dropped a ten on the table. "Thank you, but that's not necessary. And I know it doesn't mean much, but I can't imagine what you're going through. You're a strong woman, Mrs. Reyes."

"Persistent too."

"You are that." Amara's mind flashed to the photo of Benjamin. Eternally six years old. She leaned over and wrapped her arms around the boy's mother. "I wish I could help."

❊ ❊ ❊

Amara hit the button on her watch as she started the second loop around the park. She passed a couple of joggers and picked up her pace. No chance of beating her personal best today. Too hot. She circled the pond, dodging a few ducks seeking handouts, and ran toward the playground. As usual, the area was packed this morning. The slides and swings were prime real estate. And it was about to get worse.

A pair of bright yellow buses from the Austin Independent School District pulled in the parking lot and began disgorging their young passengers. A few adults trailed after them, toting coolers and grocery sacks. The kids looked like kindergartners, around

Benjamin's age when he died. Here on a weekend field trip, then on to the Alamo most likely.

So many children. One of her mother's favorite topics, and one certain to come up again at dinner tonight. Can never have enough grandkids, Mama would say. By the time your brothers and sisters were your age, they all had children. Time's running out. Thirty-two is at the upper end of medical science's abilities. Of course, she'd add, nothing is impossible with God, but why risk it?

She quickened her pace and rounded a bend, leaving the playground mayhem behind her. One more lap. Her mind blanked to all but the *thwap-thwap-thwap* of her running shoes against the trail. One foot in front of the other. Sweat dripping from her face.

Pass the old couple strolling hand in hand. Dodge the three kids veering her direction on their skateboards. Ignore the teenagers making out on their blanket. Around the pond. Jump over a duck. Back toward the overcrowded playground and the laughing parents and rowdy kids and . . . an image of Benjamin Reyes she couldn't shake.

She slowed to a walk and stood behind an empty bench overlooking the area. Benjamin was dead. But the text and the note *were* an odd coincidence. If the two were linked, what did it mean? Why would anyone want to hurt the Reyes family? She squeezed the back of the seat. It didn't make sense. There was nothing to gain from dragging them through this torture.

She jogged back to her car. Time to head home for a shower. Let Larry wander the apartment for a while. Maybe see if the lizard could answer the question that knocked louder with each minute.

Marisa Reyes believed her son was alive. That could not be true. Every fact supported the one inescapable conclusion that Benjamin Reyes died in a horrid accident.

But the itch was there, slowly creeping forward in her thoughts. The Cotulla investigation was long over. Multiple law enforcement agencies had their say and closed the case.

So why, despite everything, could Amara not turn loose of the deepening notion the woman might be right?

5 **Monday morning traffic** on I-10 moved at an unusually good pace. Amara flicked her turn signal, took the Huebner Road exit, and checked the clock. Didn't want to get there too early.

Daniella Delacruz was employed as a receptionist for a law firm in northwest San Antonio. Finding the woman's information had taken all of five minutes. Where she lived and worked. What she drove. Cell phone number. No prior arrests. If her story about the note was true, and Amara had no reason to believe it wasn't, Mrs. Delacruz had found the piece of paper while at work. According to Google, the office was in a six-story building with outside parking. If the company had halfway decent security, there'd be cameras around the perimeter. Maybe one of them caught something useful.

She cruised through the lot until she spotted Mrs. Delacruz's vehicle two rows back from the front of the building. If she was like most people, the woman parked near the same place every day.

The visitors' spaces were full, so Amara found a spot near the back. Nice morning for a walk anyway. Unfortunately, no cameras were mounted on the parking lot's lights, but the brick building did have two cameras on each visible corner, though they were older models from the looks of them. Big and white. Probably not on a digital backup system.

She identified herself at the front desk, and the security manager escorted her to his office. After she explained what she needed in the vaguest possible terms, he agreed to allow her to view the recording of the day in question. Thankfully, they'd upgraded their system a couple of years back, and she would be able to review a digital copy. Even better, he'd leave her alone while she watched. Nothing worse than a person looking over her shoulder while she worked.

The images on the screen weren't exactly sharp, and the farther from the building, the fuzzier the picture. Amara located the woman's car within a few spaces of where she'd parked today. Only one camera, E3, covered the area.

She fast-forwarded the recording and watched as people scurried to and fro like ants that had stumbled into a puddle of an energy drink. At lunchtime, Mrs. Delacruz left for twenty-five minutes and returned to the same spot. No indication that anything was wrong.

A short time later—1:27 p.m., assuming the video's clock was accurate—a figure entered the lot from a side street. Amara clicked the rewind button and played the footage at normal speed. The person was most likely a man, based on height, shape, and gait. He wore jeans, a short-sleeved blue T-shirt, and a green baseball cap with no logo. He shuffled as much as walked and made no effort to hide his face. Not that it made any difference. The recording's quality didn't offer much hope of identifying the man.

He made a beeline for Mrs. Delacruz's vehicle and stopped, pointed at the car, and looked back over his shoulder. After a moment's pause, he slipped something under the driver's-side windshield wiper and returned the way he came.

Amara ran the footage back a few frames and watched again. The man needed confirmation this was the correct car. Someone in the background, out of sight of the camera, must have been watching to make sure the note went on the right vehicle. She paused the video, pursed her lips, and tapped her index fingers together. *Why not do it yourself? Afraid of being identified? There's no law against leaving notes on windshields.*

She watched the sequence three more times, then fast-forwarded to when Mrs. Delacruz left work. The woman unlocked her door and got into her car before noticing the paper, then stepped out and read the note. She looked around the parking lot, then reread the message before sliding back into the vehicle and driving off.

Amara leaned back in her chair and chewed on her cheek. A man, possibly homeless based on his appearance, left the note on behalf of an anonymous third party. So what? Nothing illegal had been done. There were plenty of real crimes demanding her attention. She'd already cut her losses with Mrs. Reyes, and nothing she'd seen this morning would change anything.

No. She was finished with it. Time to let the whole ordeal become a memory.

On her way out of the building, she stopped to thank the security manager. He asked if she wanted a copy of the recording.

Her quick response overwhelmed her prior determination. "Yes, please."

* * *

Amara reviewed the off-the-record report from the lab's dissection of the video. The job had cost her another couple of pizzas, a cheap price to pay for the crew to stay late and review the footage. Nothing she didn't already know. Definitely male, between five foot ten and six foot one. Approximately one hundred fifty pounds, give or take a dozen. No luck finding anyone in the background.

Unfortunately, real life didn't work like the crime shows on TV. No pointing at the video and saying, "Clean this up a little right here" and having the suspect's face become crystal clear. No looking in the reflection of someone's eyes and making out a license plate halfway down the street. Images could be enhanced considerably, but technology could only do so much.

She sighed and ran the report through the office shredder. None of it made any difference. A dead end in a dead investigation.

"Alvarez, you're up." Sergeant Alan Norwood stood in his office doorway and held out a manila folder.

Her heart shrank and she fought not to frown. "Let me guess," she said. "Burglary in Leon Valley?"

Norwood smacked his ever-present bubble gum. "It's like you're one of those psychics. 'Course, the fact that we've had a slew of burglaries over there you haven't solved yet could account for your keen sense of deduction."

"Working on it, Sarge." She took the folder and headed for her desk without opening it.

"Hang in there, Alvarez. Another five, six years, you'll get your chance."

She sank into her chair and dropped the folder on her desk. "My chance?"

Norwood blew a small pink bubble, popped it, and grinned. "Hey, Dotson. What's Alvarez want?"

The detective stood and straightened his shirt. "Aw, come on, Sarge. Don't make it worse for her. She knows I'm not looking to get married again. Man like me's got to play the field."

Amara chucked a paper clip in his direction and dodged the return fire.

"You kids knock it off," Norwood said. "I'm not filling out the paperwork when one of you loses an eye. Dotson, besides you, what does Alvarez want more than anything else?"

"Easy. A transfer to Homicide. Or Special Victims. Maybe even Vice or Narcotics. Definitely not Financial Crimes, though. Too much desk time."

"Uh-huh," the sergeant said. "And how would you know that?"

Dotson shrugged. "Been a detective for a long time. I can read people. Know what they're like. What they want. That and the fact she tells us two or three times a week how much she'd like to transfer to—"

"I get it," Amara said. "You boys have your fun. Some of us have work to do."

* * *

She spent the better part of the afternoon working on the residential break-in. The intruders had kicked the back door until it splintered in half. The top section remained secured with a deadbolt. The bottom half lay in the kitchen floor. A reverse Dutch door.

The mother had come home for lunch and discovered the damage, then called 911 from the driveway and waited for a patrol unit to arrive before going inside. The place was remarkably clean, except for the teenage daughter's bedroom, but the mom assured Amara it always looked like that.

Whoever had broken in didn't appear to have stayed long. Grabbed whatever they could find and left. So far, jewelry, a laptop computer, and two boxes of Ding Dongs from the freezer were all that seemed to be missing. Either kids, druggies, or both. Same as all the others in the area.

Amara tried to reassure the family and gave the generic "We'll do our best" response when asked if she thought they'd catch the culprits. She offered vague promises of increasing patrols in the area. Said they'd notify pawnshops of the stolen items. Told them not to worry. To call their insurance company. Maybe look into a security system. As she left, she handed them her card, wished them a good day, and said she'd let them know if anything turned up.

She had the routine down pat. The couple knew as well as she did there was virtually no chance they'd catch the burglars without a break of some kind. Still, everyone played their part well. And pawnshops? Thieves had quit using them long ago. Too dangerous. Most store owners would report anything suspicious rather than risk being accused of accepting stolen property.

Back in her car, she sighed and tossed her notes into the passenger seat. Another day, another frustration. Follow the procedures, fill out the reports, move on to the next case.

She glanced at the car's clock. No point in heading back today. Get an early start tomorrow and clean up the paperwork on this one. For now, a kickboxing workout, then grab a salad, then home for much-needed downtime. Maybe check out the new series on Netflix.

* * *

Amara flicked on the kitchen light, opened the refrigerator, and after a heartbeat's hesitation, tossed her leftover salad in the trash. Lettuce didn't hold up, and with its lack of nutritional value, no point in feeding it to Larry. She grabbed a cold drink and carried it to her bedroom, stopping to check on her roommate first.

The lizard lounged on a branch at the top of his floor-to-ceiling enclosure. The cage took up most of her second bedroom and nearly all of her electric bill. The heat lamps ran almost constantly, but she didn't mind. Larry had been with her since a couple of years after the divorce. From one reptile to another. An upgrade, really, since Larry would never cheat on her.

Back then he was the size of her hand, and if he lived long enough, he would more than double in length from his current three feet. On her days off, she let him wander the apartment. He'd follow her like a puppy, his tail sliding side to side and making patterns in the carpet. Not tonight, though. She checked his water supply and tossed in several spinach leaves. *Good night, buddy.*

She stopped by the bathroom to scrub her hands, as she did

every time she came near Larry. Salmonella lived naturally in his intestines, and though lizards rarely passed the bacteria to humans, better safe than sorry. After slipping into her oversize Spurs T-shirt, she propped a couple of pillows against the headboard and sat on the bed. Her three evening essentials rested on the nightstand beside her: a cold drink, the TV remote, and her Glock 19, not necessarily in that order.

Netflix gave three stars for the new show, so their formula figured it was slightly more probable she'd enjoy the series than not. Four minutes in, she decided the algorithm had guessed wrong. She deleted the series from her queue and scanned the other recommendations. The only possibilities were in the Watch It Again section, and reruns didn't fit her mood.

She sighed, slid out of bed, and padded into the living room to grab her laptop. The AC was cranked down—couldn't sleep if she was hot—and her feet were cold, so she hurried back to bed and slipped under the covers.

She took another sip of her drink. She could always catch up on Facebook. See all the happy news from the friends she'd grown up with. Like a perpetual *Día de los Muertos*, the Day of the Dead, most of them never removed their masks. When you dealt with people as much as she did, you understood the truth. Everyone had problems, no matter how rosy a picture they tried to paint.

Reading the news would only depress her. Maybe she'd play around on YouTube until she got sleepy.

Or . . . she clicked the address bar and typed in "Caterina Delacruz."

**Cotulla. Say the word** and most Texans would immediately know. Little town, about ninety miles southwest of San Antonio. Nothing to separate it from the thousands of other small settlements spread all over the state like oversize tumbleweeds captured by cacti.

Nothing except the accident just over three years back.

Amara's internet search pulled up article after article about the incident. Choose your theory on Bradley Gingham, the bus driver. Depressed and angry due to his mother's recent death. PTSD-afflicted from his time in the Gulf War. Maybe even delusional. Whichever it was, that morning Gingham intentionally drove his vehicle into the path of an oncoming freight train. The collision was horrifying. The explosion far worse. Three tanker cars of propane burst in the derailment. The fireball could be seen from dozens of miles away. Windows were shattered for over a mile in all directions.

Seventeen kids dead. Two engineers on the train, plus Gingham. National news for a week or so, until the next catastrophe struck.

She didn't need to go to Cotulla to know the locals remembered. There would still be crosses at the scene of the accident with faded, rotting stuffed animals propped against them. A few washed-out plastic flowers wilting in the oppressive Texas sun sprinkled around. Sparse brush returning to the heat-blasted landscape. The railroad had probably installed crossing bars in addition to the lights. Not that they'd have stopped a man bent on dying and taking a busload of kids with him.

Caterina Delacruz shouldn't have died. Like dominoes falling, a series of events led to her demise. Her dad worked as an over-the-road trucker. It was his day off, but the company had called and asked him to fill in for a sick coworker. A quick run to Oklahoma and back. The overtime was welcome, and he'd agreed, after making sure Caterina's mother could leave her job early enough to pick up their daughter from school. Their home was too close to be on the bus route.

The mom worked as a cashier at Walmart and took college courses on the internet at night. Wanted to be a teacher. She verified she'd be able to leave work and pick up their daughter. No problem. At least not until the fender bender in the parking lot. An old man backed out of a handicapped space into the side of her vehicle. He seemed confused and the police were called. The minor mishap was going to take a while to resolve, so Mom phoned a friend with a daughter in the same class. Asked her if she could pick up Caterina from school and bring her to Walmart.

As friends do, the other mom had not only agreed to pick up Catrina but volunteered to let the little girl spend the night. Not much more work keeping two kids than one, she said. The girls could ride the bus together in the morning. They'd love it.

Amara massaged her forehead. So many trivial things led to Caterina's death. So many ifs that could've saved her but didn't. Seventeen kids died that day instead of sixteen. And now, a sympathetic note showed up on the little girl's mother's windshield. Left there by an unknown man for an unknown reason.

Amara skimmed through more articles about the child. Construction paper hearts. A baby sister. A grieving family.

All the usual quotes. A special girl. Always smiling. Made everyone happy. Loved to sing.

Photos of the funeral. First child to be identified. First one buried.

Overflow crowd outside the church. A tiny casket carried to a black hearse.

Amara pushed the laptop away, debated the odds of falling asleep, then turned the TV back on.

* * *

"Mornin', Alvarez," Dotson said.

Amara glanced up from her monitor. "Glad you could make it in today. If you can't get here on time, get here when you can, right?"

"Yeah, forgot to iron my shirt last night. Had to do it this morning."

She crinkled her nose and pinched it shut for a couple of seconds before both laughed. Amara shook her head. "I hope I never have to hook you up to a polygraph."

He shrugged. "It's a gift. Got a big day?"

"Yeah. This Leon Valley mess is killing me. Why?"

"Thinking you might want to do a bit of extra pa—"

"I'm not doing your paperwork, Dotson. Take a class. Learn to type with something besides your index fingers."

He settled into his chair and massaged his chin. "A class, huh? Learn to type with a bunch of college girls. I could handle that."

"Hate to burst your bubble, but kids learn to type at birth these days. Look in a mirror. That's who takes typing classes."

"Life's not fair, Alvarez."

"Yeah, I know." She focused on her computer screen. Something she read had nagged at her all night. Maybe it was a coincidence. Just a fluke. But how many times had she said that lately?

The text to Benjamin's mother. The note to Caterina's mom. Both petty incidents not worth wasting more time on, so why couldn't she let it go?

The accident had been investigated by every possible agency.

If there'd been the slightest indication of anything other than a deliberate act of murder-suicide, they'd have found it. Yet here she was, trying to explain away another quirk in what little she knew of Cotulla.

Caterina had been the only nonregular on the bus that morning. Like most kids, she'd probably sat beside her friend on the ride to school. Giggled and whispered about whatever it was young girls giggled and whispered about. Right up to the impact.

The photos of the collision showed a scene straight out of a war zone. No chance for survival. Chaos. Mangled fragments of bus and train and bodies, each piece smaller than the last.

So what were the odds Caterina Delacruz, the only child not supposed to be on that bus, would be the first one identified?

7   **Amara scanned the long** list of agencies who participated in the crash investigation. It'd be easier to name who *wasn't* involved. The National Transportation Safety Board had coordinated the inquiry, but the FBI and virtually every state and local resource had been active as well. With fewer than ten thousand people in Cotulla's county, their limited resources meant they needed all the help they could get. Because the bus driver was a veteran, even the Department of Defense had stepped into the fray.

When everybody'd had their say, the crash boiled down to one finding: suicide-murder. No charges were filed since the lone culprit was already dead. The Feds promised to do more for PTSD victims. The railroad put up crossing gates at every intersection in the county. The elementary school students planted seventeen trees in memory of their friends. The community grieved.

And the Reyeses still mourned. All the families probably did. Amara dragged her finger across the screen and leaned closer. Who'd done the body IDs?

She jerked when Sergeant Norwood popped his bubble gum. "Whatcha working today, Alvarez?"

"Paperwork on the Leon Valley burglaries mostly." She shrank her internet window and grabbed a pen. "Then I've got to go out later and meet with the parents of a couple of juvies arrested for shoplifting."

"Don't forget about that Neighborhood Watch meeting tonight."

"I don't know anything about—"

"You do now." Norwood grinned. "I'll shoot you the address later. The usual stuff. Lock your cars. Keep your garage doors closed. Make a note of any suspicious vehicles. Oh, and remember to look serious and nod a lot when they talk about their problems. They like that."

She leaned back and stared at the ceiling. "Can't you send Dotson? It's not like he has anything to do at night."

A paper clip ricocheted off her monitor. "I'm right here, you know."

"Yeah, I know." She sat straighter, tilted her head, and arched her eyebrows. "Probably be some single women there. Always are. Worried about their safety and all. No man in the house to protect them. What do you say? Want to cover for me?"

Dotson rubbed his chins and nodded. "No. Wait . . . yeah, still no."

Norwood popped his gum again. "Looks like you win, Alvarez. I'll text you the address later. Seven p.m. sharp. Take cookies."

"Looking forward to it, Sarge." She sighed and turned back to her monitor.

Due to the scope of the Cotulla incident, the Bexar County medical examiner's office in San Antonio had responsibility for identifying the victims. They'd released a statement when Caterina Delacruz's remains were confirmed, and after that, it'd taken nearly five days for the next child to be identified. Why such a big time gap? She didn't know the ME, but she was friendly enough with several of the homicide detectives. Could she ask them to talk to the ME about a closed case from three years back? Homicide had plenty to do without her creating work for them. Plus, it wouldn't help her chances for a transfer if people knew she tended to go on wild-goose chases.

She clicked the link for the ME's contact info and fired off a quick email identifying herself and asking one question: was there a specific reason Caterina Delacruz's remains had been identified so much earlier than any of the other kids'? She thanked the ME for his time, apologized for any inconvenience, and hit the send button.

Done. The burden passed on to someone else who'd probably— hopefully?—never respond. And even if he did, the answer would be enough to relieve her curiosity. *It won't pacify Marisa Reyes, but the woman needs more help than—*

Her computer beeped as an email appeared in her inbox. She glanced at the sender. The ME. Great. Probably an autoreply saying he was on vacation or he was busy and would respond as soon as possible. She clicked the message and read it.

She confirmed the sender and studied the words again.

And again.

Detective Alvarez, curious why a property crimes officer wants to know. 2:30 this afternoon in my office.

Douglas Pritchard, ME

⁂

Amara sat in one of the red leather guest chairs and waited for the doctor to finish his paperwork. Her guess that the ME's office would be cluttered, his desk crammed with paper, piles of books stacked everywhere, was dead wrong. Too many reruns of *Quincy* and *Psych* had tainted her, she supposed. If anything, the place was too neat. And instead of the scraggly doctor with half-glasses on the end of his nose, as she'd expected, Dr. Pritchard was meticulously dressed and groomed. No wedding ring, but not her type. His goatee wasn't doing him any favors.

The ME finished signing a few papers, tapped them on the desk to make sure they were straight, then stapled the top left corner before placing the pile into a basket. "Now then, Detective. What can I do for you?"

She scooted forward in her seat and placed her hands in her lap. "Thank you for seeing me, Dr. Pritchard. I hope I won't take too much of your time."

"Can't." He glanced at his watch. "I've got four minutes. Strict schedule and all that. Corpses won't wait." He angled his head to the side. "Correction. They *will* wait, but I can't be late or we'll fall behind. You can stay as long as you want, but in four minutes I'm leaving."

Well, okay then. "Yes, sir. I'll get right to it. Can you explain to me why Caterina Delacruz's body was the first to be identified? In layman's terms, of course."

He opened a desk drawer and pulled out a box of green breath refreshers. "Did you know most people get their Tic Tacs the wrong way?"

"I'm not sure I—"

"They do. Most people open the container and then turn it upside down and shake the thing. The result is too many Tic Tacs. They go everywhere. Horrible."

Did he actually shudder? "Yes, well—"

"Allow me to demonstrate the proper method." He brandished the breath mints with the grace and flair of a model on *The Price Is Right*. "Don't open the container. Turn it upside down and give a few gentle side-to-side shakes. *Then* you can open it, keeping the tab level while you tilt the container back. And voilà. One Tic Tac served up on a platter." He popped the mint into his mouth and laid the plastic box beside a notepad, carefully aligning the container so it was square with the desk's edge.

She glanced at her watch. Two minutes. "I'll keep that in mind. Now if you could please . . . ?"

"Certainly. But first, I'd like to understand why you want the information. That case is long closed, and even if it wasn't, I wouldn't think Property Crimes would be involved."

"Honestly, sir—"

He snapped his fingers. "Always best to be honest."

"Uh-huh. Well, a mother whose son died on the bus is having some, um, issues dealing with her child's passing."

"Not surprising, even after so long. Though I fail to see how your question will do anything to alleviate those issues."

She coughed lightly into her fist. "Well, it—"

He waved his hand at her. "We don't have time to get into all that. Per your request, in layman's terms Caterina Delacruz was the first to be identified simply because her body sustained less damage than the other children. We were able to use dental records rather than DNA. Though, to be clear, we did later confirm the DNA match with her parents'."

"I see. When you say her body wasn't as badly damaged, can you give me an idea of the difference between her corpse and the other children's?"

"Of course I can. Her remains were roughly thirty percent as damaged. She was the only child with any tangible flesh remaining. The others were nothing but bone matter."

"And do you have a theory as to why?"

He stood and straightened his tie. "I do. Her injuries were consistent with the driver's. I believe she was at the front of the bus when the accident occurred. For whatever reason, those two took less damage."

"Did something on the bus—"

"Detective, were you at the scene?"

"No, I wasn't."

He walked toward his office door. "I was, and I can tell you there were no scraps of the bus left that were larger than a two-foot square. A collision with a freight train, followed by a gas explosion, tends to do that. Now, I apologize but I must leave. Feel free to remain if you'd like. And if you take a Tic Tac, please leave the box as you found it."

The gym's parking lot was already crowded. Six a.m. and the MMA wannabes were going at it. Amara frowned and turned her car toward the office. At least she'd beat the traffic. Might be time to set up a bag at home. Work out when she wanted without the hassle of others nearby. Nobody but her and Larry.

She switched the radio to the local news station and listened through traffic and weather reports. No accidents so far. Going to be hot today. Possible pop-up thunderstorm this afternoon. The easiest job in the world had to be a San Antonio meteorologist. The headlines cycled back around and she turned up the volume.

The lead story was a double murder downtown last night. Two unidentified bodies turned up near a popular nightclub. Couple of tourists found them. No details so far, at least none that were released to the press. The detectives in Homicide would be busy today. Processing evidence. Interviewing people. Searching databases.

Meanwhile, she'd be taking notes at whatever house was broken into last night. Empathizing with the homeowners. Assuring them the PD was doing everything it could to recover the stolen items. All good stuff. Important stuff. But not Homicide.

Unlike the gym, the parking area at the police department HQ had tons of spots open. Plenty of cops would be here, but the administrative staff didn't clock in until eight. She parked at the back of the lot anyway. Might as well get some exercise.

She debated changing in the car but decided against it. If anyone saw her, she'd never hear the end of it. Nobody beats a story into the ground like a cop. Besides, she'd learned long ago to keep an extra set of clothes at the office.

Inside, she stepped into the restroom, changed, and dabbed on a touch of makeup. Light red lipstick, little bit of eyeliner. Good enough.

The lights were still off in Property Crimes and she paused before rounding the corner and stepping into Homicide. As expected, several detectives were already there, doubtless called in early to assist on last night's murders. At least one would remain at the scene, waiting for CSI to finish and hoping they'd get a quick clue from them.

"Morning, Alvarez. Surprised to see you in here at this hour." A redheaded man, early forties with his suit jacket looking a couple of sizes too big on his lanky frame, toasted her with his coffee cup. Detective Jeremiah Peckham, better known as Starsky. No idea why. She'd looked up the series online and even watched a few of the old shows, and still had no clue. And the ones who did know weren't sharing the information. Maybe it was because he didn't look like a Jeremiah. One day she'd ask.

"Hey, Starsky. Too many people at the gym. Skipped it and figured I'd get this place to myself until I heard the news on the radio. A double, huh? Your case?"

"No, Bledsoe was on tap for this one. Still, going to be one of those days. Doesn't help that a couple of tourists found the bodies. You-know-who's going to be all over this."

"The chief, the mayor, or Lieutenant Spelling?"

"The LT's the only one I care about. Already called me. Said he'd be assisting Bledsoe and would personally—how did he phrase it?—'expedite the investigation.' You know, because we normally drag our feet on homicides. Give it around eighty percent effort.

Guess we're going to have to ratchet up to the nineties if we want to keep our jobs."

She laughed and tilted her head toward the coffeepot. "Mind if I grab a cup? You guys get the good stuff. Norwood buys store-brand. Says it's all the same anyway."

"Help yourself. One of the perks of getting called in at all hours. Decent joe." He pursed his lips and scratched his forehead. "Now that I think about it, probably the only perk."

"You're forgetting the biggest benefit. Same one I've got."

Starsky raised his almost-invisible eyebrows. "Yeah? What's that?"

"Job security. Always have thieves and killers."

"You got that right. Can't have the good guys without the bad guys."

"Surprised Lieutenant Spelling didn't throw a couple more of you guys on this if there's so much visibility. Thought you paired up on the big ones?"

"Short-staffed. LT's trying to hit his budget, I suppose. Not that I mind. Plenty of advantages to working with a partner, but I prefer going solo. Not like we can't ask for help if we get stuck."

She leaned against a file cabinet and sipped her coffee, then coughed. "Strong stuff. This'll keep me going all day."

The corners of his mouth drooped. "Might get me to second breakfast."

"Yeah? You must have a cast-iron stomach. Got any scoop on the killings?"

He shrugged. "Both shot at close range. Street robbery probably. Saw some of the pics from CSI but couldn't tell much. Bledsoe will have his hands full, especially if the LT's hanging all over him."

"Got an ID on the two dead yet?"

He rubbed a hand over the spotty stubble on his face. "One's a homeless guy. Figured that out pretty quick. The other? No idea. No wallet, prints aren't on file."

"Going public with it?"

"Might. Not my call, though."

"Mind if I take a peek at what you've got?"

He turned his monitor toward her. "Stays in here, right?"

She smiled and tugged a chair to his desk. "As always."

"Fair warning. This one's grisly. I'm going to hit the head. Don't change anything, okay?"

"Look but don't touch. Got it." She clicked through the pictures. Her gut churned as the stout coffee, her stomach acid, and the crime scene photos combined and sent burning gas up her throat. Both men had probably died instantly. Would Pritchard do the autopsy or pass it off to someone else? Might be too mundane for him. Single gunshot wound to the side of the head on each. Not quite execution style, but close.

One man was dressed neatly in khakis and a button-down blue shirt. The other wore torn jeans and a faded white T-shirt from a blood donor center. The first had a graying mustache and closely cropped beard, the other, stringy brown hair. A straight, pointed nose versus a crooked, flat one. Their only commonality seemed to be that both men were very dead.

Of course, pictures didn't tell the whole story. The men could be related somehow. Could've served in the military together. Had the same kindergarten teacher. Eaten at the same restaurant. All that would take time to figure out. If she was in Homicide, she'd start by—

"Got the case solved yet?" Starsky was back.

"Pretty much. Just don't want to make you look bad."

He laughed and topped off his coffee mug. "Feel free. Everyone else does."

"These all the photos?"

"Far as I know. A couple of real opposites, huh? Felix and Oscar."

"Who?"

"Thanks, Alvarez. Like my knees weren't already reminding me of my age."

She focused on the image on the monitor. "What's this in the background?"

He walked over, started to lean over her shoulder, then paused. "Uh, can you scoot over a little?"

She smiled and shifted to the side. "Sure."

"Looks like a baseball cap. Probably belonged to the homeless guy."

"That's what I thought. Can you tell what color it is?"

"Hard to say. Those lights they use can play games with the images. Always better to wait until you can see the details from every angle, but if I had to guess, I'd say green. Why?"

She edged forward on her seat and fidgeted with her fingers. "I need to see the front of the cap. Are there any photos that might show a different angle?"

"What you see is all I've got. You know this guy?"

The man who left the note on Mrs. Delacruz's windshield wore a green hat. "What? No. Don't think so. Listen, Starsky. Can you find out what's on the cap and let me know? Soon as possible, *por favor?*"

He sighed and sank into his chair. "Yeah, but no more. Anything else, you've got to go through Bledsoe. Unwritten rule. Your case, your information. Easier to control things."

"Thanks. I need to satisfy my curiosity, that's all. Won't bother you with anything else."

Part of her hoped that would be the end of it. Another part, this one much larger and more spirited, wished there was more. Another coincidence to add to the list. If the cap had no logo, it'd still be a stretch to tie it to her parking lot guy. But coupled with an unknown victim? Maybe none of these things were connected, but it sure was looking interesting.

Her mind raced as she walked back to her desk. Was there something to all this, or was it only wishful thinking? Had she been tainted by Mrs. Reyes's hopes? And what was the next step if the cap *was* a match? Who should she talk to about her suspicions?

She should make a list. No, a flowchart. Organize her thoughts. Help her explain the hunch that something was off-kilter and needed investigating.

She stopped at the entrance to her assigned area and stared at her reflection in the door. Her chest tightened and she rubbed a hand over her heart. What did it say about her that she was so excited after two people were murdered?

Amara's office phone buzzed and she checked the display. Homicide. "Alvarez."

"Hey, Starsky here. Yeah, uh, on the cap you asked about. Green, no logo. That's all they could tell me."

A jolt of adrenaline shot through her. "Great, thanks. Listen, can you ask if—"

"Sorry, like I said, not my case. Talk to Bledsoe. He's got lead. Hate to be that way, but we try not to stick our noses in each other's investigations unless we're asked. Plus, the LT's already *assisting* on this one. Wants everything to go through him. That's a headache I don't need."

"No problem. I really appreciate your help. And thanks again for the coffee."

"Anytime. Later."

She pulled her mouth to the side. Had to be lots of hats like that around. Couldn't even call this a coincidence. It'd be like saying the guy in the parking lot and the murdered homeless man each had two legs.

The unidentified victim, though. Probably in the wrong place at the wrong time. A street robbery gone wrong. Maybe even a drug deal. But the gunshots to the side of the head didn't seem random. A person in a hurry to get away would have plugged them in their chests. Not been so precise. Whoever did this wanted to make sure those two men died quickly. Of course, Homicide would know all that. And if Lieutenant Spelling was involved, the higher-ups must be pushing the case. They'd solve it soon enough.

A green baseball cap. They'd laugh if she brought that to them as evidence of something amiss. No sense wasting her time dwelling on it. Maybe he was the same guy. More likely he wasn't.

She tapped the eraser end of a pencil on her desk. There was a way she could satisfy her curiosity. Go back to Mrs. Delacruz's workplace and expand her search. Check for cameras on buildings farther out. See if any of them caught the second person. The one who'd given approval for the note to be placed.

Footsteps approached from behind and she glanced back. "Hey, Sarge."

"Bucking for promotion, Alvarez?"

"Nah. Gym was crowded, so I came on in."

He blew a pink bubble and then drew the gum back into his mouth. "Don't hit me with overtime."

"You know, if I transferred to Homicide, I could get all the OT I wanted."

"No openings over there. You'll know about it when I do."

"That simple, huh?"

He popped another bubble and peeled a thin layer of pink off his chin. "Sure. All you have to do is fill out the paperwork, hope no one with higher seniority goes for the position, and agree to take Dotson with you."

She laughed and turned back to her desk. "I don't think you could drag Wylie out of here. The man knows what he likes."

"A lot to be said for low stress and decent hours."

"Yeah. Hey, listen. I may need to run out for a few hours this morning."

He tilted his head. "Police business?"

"Uh-huh."

"Then why tell me?"

"I thought, um, maybe . . ."

Sergeant Norwood straightened. "Let me clarify. Property Crimes business?"

She bit the inside of her cheek and pulled up Google Maps on her computer. "Have a good day, Sarge."

He grunted and turned to his office. "Your work here comes first. And no overtime."

* * *

The buildings around Mrs. Delacruz's workplace were dingy and half occupied. Amara stood near where the woman's car had been that day. The homeless man had wandered into the lot from a side street, then looked back over his shoulder in the direction of a two-story white brick building. She pushed her sunglasses up on her nose and walked that direction.

No cameras were mounted on the structure's exterior. The opposite side of the building faced a two-lane street, currently backed up due to some sort of construction. Water line repair from the looks of it. A police car, its lights flashing, sat parked on the curb. The cop stood in the center of the road and directed traffic. The officer dragged his arm across his forehead and licked his lips.

Amara held up her badge and hollered at the cop. "Got water in the car?"

He nodded and waved.

She grabbed a bottle from the cooler in the front seat, carried it to him, and glanced at his nameplate. "Officer Rogerson, I'm Detective Alvarez, Property Crimes. Miserable out here, huh?"

"They've got us on two-hour shifts. Those guys don't finish the construction soon, might need to cut back to an hour."

"I don't—"

He grabbed her arm and pulled her closer to the construction.

"Watch the cars, Detective. This job would be boring if it weren't for nearly getting run over at least once or twice a shift."

"Thanks. How long they been digging in that hole?"

"Week and a half. Couldn't work for a few days because of rain. Said they'd be done by the end of this week, though. Hope so."

"Yeah, me too. Hey, you guys are still required to keep your dash cams on all the time, right?"

He nodded and waved a line of vehicles past. "Yep. Turn it off and someone will be waiting for you when you get back to the station. Make you fill out a stack of paperwork. Why?"

"Nothing big. Trying to dig up footage on a guy who may have been around here recently."

"Hope you can narrow down the date and time. Otherwise you're going to be searching a lot of video."

She smiled and peered around him at the traffic. "Got to run. Gracias, Rogerson. Stay cool."

* * *

Back at the station, Amara accessed the video database and found the time in question. One to two p.m. on the date the note had been left on the windshield. Rogerson wasn't on duty then, but the officer who was had followed protocol. Not much foot traffic had passed the vehicle. No surprise. Not a lot of places to eat or shop around there.

Her search didn't take long. She froze the image, reversed the video, and watched it again. The man strode past the police car, his back to the camera. When he was several feet in front of the vehicle, a loud pop came from the construction site. Probably an air hose blowing. The man ducked and whipped his head to the right toward the sound.

Amara zoomed in on the profile of his face. Older-looking man.

Mustache and short beard. Straight, pointed nose. It was him. The other dead guy. No question. White dress shirt, blue tie with red stripes, black slacks, black suit jacket folded over his arm. Fancy dresser. Different clothes, same face.

She printed the photo and held it up to study. *Who are you? What do—did—you want with Daniella Delacruz?*

And is Marisa Reyes right about her son?

10

Amara pulled in front of the Reyeses' home in Karnes City, a good hundred miles from their old home in Cotulla. No distance could erase the memories, but at least the family didn't have to see daily reminders of the tragedy. The sun would set in a few minutes, and the light in the yard was already on. Homicide had confirmed that the image from the police dash cam was of the well-dressed murder victim but had nothing else they could share with her. To the contrary. She'd spent the better part of an hour explaining to them what she knew of the man.

Sixty minutes to tell the other detectives she was kinda-sorta looking into the possibility that one of the dead kids from the Cotulla accident had texted his mother. Maybe. The looks she got from Homicide let her know it might be a rocky start if she ever managed to transfer over.

The front door of the house opened and Marisa Reyes stepped out. She emptied the contents of a clear pitcher into the three hanging baskets around her porch, then shaded her eyes and peered toward the street.

Amara sighed, grabbed the photo, and stepped out of the vehicle. "*Hola*, Mrs. Reyes. I hope I'm not stopping by too late."

"That you, Detective? Of course not. Please, come in." She placed the pitcher on the ground and brushed her hands on her shorts.

A walkway bisected the yard, ran through an arched trellis, and on to the porch. Amara hurried up the path. "Yes, ma'am. I won't keep you. I wanted to ask about—"

"Don't be silly! The mosquitoes will eat us alive out here." She motioned toward the door.

"Only for a moment. I can't stay."

The women stepped inside the house. Cool air fanned the thin layer of perspiration on Amara's face, and she paused to allow the tingling to pass. The living room was decorated with faux cowhide lampshades, a large plaque with a barbed-wire Texas, and a coffee table with several cattle brands burned into the surface.

"Benjamin loved cowboys," Mrs. Reyes said. "When we moved here after the accident, I thought about getting rid of everything. More things to remind me of him, you know? But I couldn't do it." She motioned to the leather sofa. "Would you like to sit down? I can mix up a pitcher of lemonade."

Amara held up her hand, palm toward her host. "Oh, no, thank you. Like I said, I can't stay. I wanted to show you this photo and see if you recognized the man." She handed the picture to Mrs. Reyes and waited as the woman reviewed it.

"I don't know. Maybe. I mean, he seems vaguely familiar. Like one of those guys on a TV show and you can't figure out where you've seen him before. Who is he?"

"Not sure. I thought there might be a connection to, uh, well . . ."

Mrs. Reyes's forehead wrinkled. "To Benjamin? You think this man has something to do with his disappearance?"

Great. His disappearance instead of his death. She squeezed her hands together. "What? You mean the accident? No."

"Then I'm confused. Why would you show this to me? I mean, you must think—"

"Mrs. Reyes, I stopped by the Delacruzes' and showed it to them as well. I'm following up on the possibility this man may have something to do with the note left on Mrs. Delacruz's windshield. That's all."

The woman took a step closer. "And did Daniella know him?"

"No, she didn't. And since you don't either, case closed. No point in any of us worrying about it."

"Were you worried about it?"

Good grief. She forced a smile. "No, not worried. Merely curious."

"But why would you think he—this man—had anything to do with—"

"He might have been around Mrs. Delacruz's vehicle when the note was left. I thought if he was, maybe we could put this to bed and get some closure for you." She sighed. "Unfortunately, it didn't turn out that way. I'm sorry."

"That's okay. I'm glad you came by. It means a lot that there are others thinking about Benjamin."

"Sure. Listen, I won't keep you." She turned toward the door. "Have a good night."

"You too, Detective. Maybe I can treat you to lunch sometime?"

A possible friend? Or a way to keep the non-investigation going? The woman needed both, and if Amara was honest, so did she. "Absolutely. I'd like that."

Back in her car, Amara peered at the photo again. She pushed against the headrest and closed her eyes. A heaviness filled her heart and she exhaled. She'd badly wanted there to be a connection. A reason for hope for a grieving mother. A way to get her foot into Homicide.

She should never have come out here. At least she could turn loose of the Reyes case, such as it was. Maybe even—

A series of taps on the passenger window startled her. Mrs. Reyes.

Amara hit the switch and lowered the window. "Forget something?"

The woman grabbed the photo from the seat and turned so the

light from the post in her yard reflected off the picture. "I knew he looked familiar."

Amara's pulse accelerated and she leaned toward Mrs. Reyes. "You know him?"

"No. But I've seen him. I'm sure of it."

"Where?"

"Come inside and I'll show you." The woman hustled back into the house with the photo.

Amara rolled up the window, trotted up the walkway, and stepped into the home. "Mrs. Reyes?"

"Here," she said from a back room.

Amara walked down a hallway and found the woman in a spare bedroom, rummaging through a cardboard box.

"I kept everything from the accident. Read all the newspaper clippings over and over. Here." She pulled a front-page section of the *Express-News* from the box. The top half of the sheet had a full-color photo of the Cotulla crash scene. "Look at this."

Amara studied the newspaper. The picture had been taken shortly after the accident. In the foreground was a barely recognizable fragment of the school bus, mostly charred black with a few yellow paint chips flaking off. Behind that, smoke wafted close to the ground as emergency personnel scoured the scene. "I'm sorry, but I don't see—"

Mrs. Reyes jabbed her finger at the paper. "Right there."

Amara squinted at the figure of a man standing off to the side. He wore no police or fire uniform, but neither did half of the other people there. Volunteers had flooded the area before law enforcement managed to control the scene. The image was newspaper quality, a bit grainy to save on ink. She peered at the man before shaking her head. "I don't know. Could be. I mean, the picture's not that great and—"

"It's him. I know it."

Amara pulled her bottom lip into her mouth. "Mrs. Reyes. You want this to be him. Honestly, it may or may not be. Tell you what. Tomorrow I'll check with the paper. See if they've got the original photo on file. Get a clearer image."

"You'll call me?"

She touched the woman's arm. "Of course I will. As soon as I know something either way. May I keep this copy?"

Mrs. Reyes licked her lips and rubbed her fingertips together. "Um, I'm not . . ."

Amara used her phone to snap a photo of the newspaper and handed the clipping back. "Don't worry about it. Won't be a problem finding another copy. I'll give you a call, but it might be a few days."

"Thank you, Detective. I can't tell you how much Enzo and I appreciate all your help."

"Get some rest, Mrs. Reyes."

"I will. You do the same."

The next morning, Amara contacted the *San Antonio Express-News* and requested a high-resolution copy of the image. Within minutes, the newspaper emailed the file to her. She zoomed in on the man in question and knew immediately.

It was him. The same man found dead next to the homeless guy. A photo expert would have to confirm the match, but she had no doubt. She sank back in her chair and drummed her fingers on the desk.

Who was he, and what did he know about the Cotulla accident? And did that knowledge have something to do with his death?

Homicide needed to be told. Sharing it might mean she'd be dropped from the loop, but so be it. Maybe she could swing a deal with Sergeant Norwood. Let her spend time training in Homicide in exchange for off-the-books overtime.

Timing would be everything. She had to ask when the caseload was low enough that they'd survive without her for a while. The last time that'd happened was never.

She sighed and forwarded the photo to Starsky, then wandered over to share her news. Wasn't his case, but he'd get the information to the right people. And he wouldn't treat her like a groupie. All police departments tended to be tight-knit, but Homicide carried the kinship to a higher level. Their jobs required it. Unless you'd seen and experienced what they had, you couldn't understand the toll it took. It was the reason she wanted to join them. To push herself. Prove that she could do it. Make her dad proud.

* * *

Amara strolled back to her desk and was greeted with a grunt from Sergeant Norwood. Obviously not the time to ask for a temporary transfer. Wylie nodded to her as he finished off his McDonald's sausage biscuit. When they'd started serving them all day, he nearly wept with joy.

"What's up, Dotson?" she asked.

He licked grease off his fingertips and brushed biscuit crumbs off his pants. "Another day in paradise. You?"

She shrugged. "Another home burglary over in Leon Valley. Got to swing by this morning and get the paperwork done."

"Any leads?"

"None. Doesn't seem to be related to gang activity. Not violent enough. Either kids or druggies or both."

He frowned and shook his head. "Seen this too many times. Sooner or later they're going to set foot in the wrong house and somebody's going to get shot."

"Yeah, probably. Wish I could change that, but won't happen unless new info turns up. The fingerprints didn't turn up anyone, nobody's talking, and none of the stolen stuff's shown up, so not much to do except fill out forms. What's your day look like?"

"Might have a lead on the items stolen from Best Buy. Crime Stoppers got a call last night about a rental truck parked behind a house over in Harlandale. I'll swing by and check it out. Grab a bite of lunch while I'm down that way. Great little Cuban restaurant there."

"Want backup?"

"Nah. I'll do a drive-by, and if it looks dicey, I'll get a marked unit to come over. Want me to bring you back a Cuban sandwich?"

She bit her lip. "Yes, but no. Sounds delicious, but I'll pass on the calories."

He stood and pulled on his jacket. "Suit yourself. You don't know what you're missing, though."

"Yeah, I do. Be careful, Dotson."

He rolled his eyes. "Easy, Alvarez. I told you. I'm not looking to get married again."

* * *

The Leon Valley house fit the profile. No one home all day. No alarm system. No dogs. And no witnesses.

"Yes, sir," Amara said. "We'll get this information in the system as soon as possible. Patrols have already been increased in the area until we catch these guys."

The man crossed his arms and leaned closer. At around six foot three, he towered over her. "So that's it? You just sit and wait for them to pawn my stuff? What am I supposed to tell my daughter when she gets home from cheerleading practice?"

"Like I said, we've stepped up patrols in the area. I'd recommend you consider an alarm system if you—"

"Oh, so I'm supposed to spend money because the police can't do their job?"

Her phone rang and she ignored it. "Sir, we have an active investigation in progress. There are—"

"Well, your active investigation didn't do me much good, now did it?"

She drew her mouth into a straight line and narrowed her eyes. "Mr. Rosemond, here's my card. I wrote the case number on the back. Your insurance company will want that. If you think of anything else, feel free to call. If there are any updates, I'll contact you."

He leaned close enough she could feel the heat of his breath. "*If* there are any updates? Not when? *If?*"

She flexed her fingers. "Sir, would you please take a step back?"

"Or what?"

She forced a smile. "I hope your day gets better. Please call if we can be of any more assistance."

As she turned to go, he extended his hand toward her shoulder.

"You don't want to do that," she said.

His arm froze in midair. "We're not done yet. I'm not satisfied you're doing everything you can to catch whoever broke in."

She turned and faced him directly. "I report to Sergeant Alan Norwood. If you have a problem with me, please contact him at your convenience. However, I should inform you, if you lay your hand on me, you may be arrested."

"Wouldn't be the first time."

"Maybe not, but I bet it will be the first time you have to explain to your friends how a woman a foot shorter than you managed to—"

Her phone rang again and she pulled it from her pocket. Sergeant Norwood. Perfect timing. Let him talk some sense into this idiot. "Hey, Sarge. Can you—"

"Alvarez, Dotson's down. Shot at least twice."

Her mind blanked as she struggled to process the information. "What? I—where did—"

"AirLIFE's got him. They're taking him to the trauma center at University. Should be there in a few minutes."

Confusion flashed to adrenaline as she sprinted to her vehicle. "On the way."

The back of her mind registered shouting from the homeowner. A choice expletive or two. Within seconds, her siren drowned him to nothing.

By the time Amara arrived at the hospital, a dozen police cars were already there. Sirens wailed as more closed in on the medical facility. Two TV stations had vans out front, their satellite dishes and antennas raised. She double-parked next to a marked unit and ran inside.

People packed into the emergency room waiting area, and the steady, low drone of whispered conversations added to the weight of the situation. Uniformed cops congregated near the double doors leading into the hospital's nether regions. Ethan Johnson, the chief of police, stood off to the side, his arms crossed and gray hair mussed. Several high-ranking officers from the PD surrounded him.

Amara craned her neck, seeking a familiar face. There. Sergeant Norwood fidgeted near the reception desk with a couple of other detectives from Property Crimes. She hurried over and joined their vigil. "How is he?"

Norwood took a deep breath and stared over her head. "Not good. Two shots to the chest. Fortunately, he had his vest on. The first one bruised him pretty bad. Maybe cracked a rib. The second missed the vest. Came in under his arm, most likely when he turned to, um . . ." He cleared his throat before continuing. "When he turned to avoid the next shot."

Amara's eyes watered and she clenched her teeth. "What do the doctors say?"

The sergeant shook his head. "Not much. He'll be in surgery for a while."

"If he needs blood . . ." She ran a hand under her nose.

Norwood swept his arm in a wide arc. "Get in line."

"They get the shooter yet?"

Norwood's lips turned up a millimeter. "Yeah, he's got a bed in the morgue. Dotson plugged him. Best we can piece together so far, shot the guy from the ground. Idiot must have been standing over Dotson. He was dead by the time the first officers arrived."

"Who called it in?"

"Couple of teenagers shooting hoops across the street saw the whole thing. Might even be the ones who called Crime Stoppers. Said they figured Dotson was a cop because of his suit and car. Didn't fit with the neighborhood. One of 'em dialed 911 while the other started yelling on the radio in his car. Minute and a half before a unit got there and began first aid. If it'd been much longer . . ."

Amara nodded. "Gracias a Dios. What do you need me to do?"

"Right now? Nothing. Other divisions will pick up the load if anything urgent breaks. We wait here until we hear from the surgeons. They've got a couple of tables set up over there with food and drinks. People keep coming by and dropping stuff off."

Amara brushed away a tear. "Oh, man. If Wylie could see the buffet."

Norwood placed his hand on her shoulder and angled her away from the others. "When things settle down, I'm going to need you to step up."

"Whatever you need. More hours or—"

"Alvarez, I want to move you to lead investigator, at least until Dotson's able to come back."

Lead investigator? If she accepted, there was no chance of transferring to Homicide anytime soon. Turn it down though, and be known as ungrateful and not a team player. "Listen, Sarge, I'll do whatever you want, but—"

The double doors opened and a doctor, his scrubs wrinkled and beads of sweat dotting his forehead, scanned the crowd. "Are any of Detective Dotson's family members here?"

Sergeant Norwood stepped forward. "We're all family."

The doctor ran a hand across his brow. "Yes, well, I appreciate that, but HIPAA guidelines prevent me from discussing—"

"Wylie doesn't have any family," Amara said. "His ex-wife lives out of state somewhere. No kids. That's all we know."

"I see. Is there someone here I could speak with who might have access to his employment paperwork? Emergency contact information? That kind of thing?"

Starsky spoke up from the back of the crowd. "Doc, we don't need the details. Is he going to be okay? Yes or no?"

The doctor removed his glasses and used his scrub shirt to clean them. "The regulations are very specific. If I could tell you anything, I would. But the law says Detective Dotson is entitled to keep his medical information private. Unless he has provided permission for the details to be shared, I can't—"

A commotion erupted at the emergency room's entrance as San Antonio's mayor hurried in. She paused briefly to get her bearings, then moved to the police chief. After a brief discussion, the two of them strode through the crowd and faced the surgeon for a moment before taking his arm and escorting him away from the assembly. A heated conversation, highly animated on the mayor's part, took place for all of thirty seconds before the three turned back around.

The doctor, his face now bright red, held his chin high as he spoke. "Detective Dotson is still in surgery. I expect it to be another couple of hours at least. I can tell you we've retrieved the bullet and stopped most of the internal hemorrhaging. One lung was hit, but we were able to repair it. That appears to have been the worst of the injuries, but I must caution we are still examining him. The prognosis could change as we continue with the surgery. However, his vital signs have stabilized. That's really all I can say. Anything else would be guessing."

The mayor nodded. "Thank you, Doctor. You'll let us know if Wylie needs anything?"

Wylie. Like she knew him.

"Okay," Chief Johnson said. "If you're on duty, get back on the road. For the rest of you, the hospital's setting up a room for us to wait in. You're welcome to stay, but we'll issue updates as they're available."

A half-dozen uniformed cops wandered outside to resume their patrols. No one else left.

Amara's shoulders slumped as the adrenaline seeped from her body. She wanted to put her fist through the wall, angry she hadn't insisted on going with Wylie. Frustrated she couldn't do anything to help. Furious she couldn't confront the man who'd shot her co-worker. Wylie had taken care of that. Good for him.

She squeezed her eyes shut and leaned against the reception desk. She'd nearly lost her friend. Might still.

And then the pain would return.

Losing her father so long ago still devastated her in random moments. Brought waves of emotions drowning her in sorrow.

She sniffled and straightened and thought of Marisa Reyes. How could anyone bear the agony of losing a child?

Three days since the shooting. Two cracked ribs had been added to Wylie's list of injuries, and a chest tube had been inserted to protect the damaged lung. He was still in ICU in critical condition, but the doctors seemed confident he was out of immediate danger. Recovery would be slow, and he might never return to work, but none of that mattered to Amara. As long as he survived, she'd be happy with whatever came next for him.

Sergeant Norwood had not been pleased when she turned down the promotion. Said he'd gone out on a limb for her. That it'd be a long time before another opportunity like this arose. The cynical side of her suspected he was at least partly upset because he'd lost a twofer on the personnel charts: promoting a Hispanic woman.

She'd explained her reason. Taking a promotion would tie her to Property Crimes for at least another couple of years. Not that she didn't enjoy the job, but it wasn't where she wanted to spend her career. She'd offered to work whatever hours he needed. Take any or all of Wylie's cases.

In the end, the sergeant promoted Gregory Paciorek, a quiet detective with a solid record of closing cases. If there was a candidate with a personality more unlike Wylie's, Amara didn't know who it could be. In the two days he'd been in the position, the office had become a bit more formal. Somewhat tame. Not bad. Just different. At least her paper clip stash remained secure, as well as any leftovers in the fridge.

Fortunately, Norwood's disappointment hadn't lingered beyond a day. His bubble-gum popping continued unabated and he'd taken her up on her offer to work more hours. But today was the eighteenth, and at some point she'd have to break away, if only for a few minutes, to visit her dad's grave.

Seventeen years since he'd died. His burial site had become her quiet place where she could think and refresh. Clear her mind and try to focus on the things—people—that mattered. Sometimes it worked. Sometimes.

Her cell phone rang and her stomach tensed when she saw the caller ID. Marisa Reyes. Like her life wasn't complicated enough right now. "Buenos días, Mrs. Reyes."

"Hola, Detective. I'm going to be up your way later today and wanted to see if you'd have a few minutes for the lunch I promised you. Might do you good to get out of the office. If you can spare the time, I mean."

"That's very kind, but I'm absolutely buried in work. Maybe another day?"

"Certainly. Looking forward to it. Detective, I hate to ask, but were you able to find out anything about the photo in the newspaper?"

"Lo siento. I'm sorry. It's been hectic around here lately. I should've called you and let you know I turned everything over to Homicide the next day. I did get a better copy of the photo, and I do think it's the same man. What that means, if anything, I have no idea."

"It is interesting though, don't you think?"

Maybe even a bit more than simply interesting. She glanced at her watch. "Mrs. Reyes, I think I will take you up on lunch. If the offer still stands, that is."

"Of course it does. I'd be delighted. I can pick you up if that's okay?"

"That will be fine. Say eleven thirty?"

"See you then. Remember, my treat. Come hungry."

* * *

The line at the deli was long, but most folks seemed to be getting their food to go. Amara chose a booth off to the side and smiled as Marisa Reyes scooted in across from her. "Thanks again for lunch. It's nice to get away from the office for a few minutes."

"My pleasure. After all you've done for us, I'm ashamed I didn't do this earlier."

Amara patted the woman's hand. "Nonsense. I know what it's like to lose a close family member."

"A child?"

She dropped her hands into her lap. "No, my dad. When I was fifteen."

"I'm sorry. That must've been hard."

Amara searched her purse and passed a photo to Marisa. "That's me and him about a week before he died. We were shopping for a dress for my *quinceañero*."

"Look at the way he's grinning. That man loves his little girl."

"I was his oldest child. Got two brothers and two sisters. He doted on all of us, but never let us slack. Always pushed us to do better, whether it was school or chores or whatever. We never got a day off. Had to prove ourselves, he always said. First-generation immigrant, so I suppose that's normal."

The deli's cashier slid their lunch onto the table, waited to make sure everything was okay, and left them in peace.

"Your chicken salad looks wonderful," Mrs. Reyes said.

"It does. You want my croissant? Don't need the carbs."

The woman shook her head. "If I had your figure, I wouldn't worry too much about a bit of extra bread now and then."

Amara laughed and retrieved the photo. "Another thing from my dad. His parents died young. Heart attacks, both of them. They were overweight and he blamed their lifestyles for their deaths. Said he wasn't going to let that happen to us."

"Well, good for him. I hope I'm not prying, but can I ask how your dad died?"

Amara blinked several times and inhaled deeply. "Heart attack. Ironic, right? Thin as a rail and could run circles around anyone I knew. May 18, 2001, not long after the picture was taken, on the way to my quinceañero. He had to work for a couple of hours that morning and was going to meet us at the party. He crashed his car into a parked pickup truck. The doctor said it happened quick. He was probably dead before the collision."

Mrs. Reyes widened her eyes and wiped them with her napkin. "It's hard, isn't it?"

Amara bit her lips and poked at her chicken salad with her fork. "Some days more than others. We canceled the quinceañero, of course. Dad would've been upset about that. The joy was gone, though. It took me a long time to get over it." She glanced across the table. "But you know about that."

"Detective, Enzo and I have made a decision. I wanted to share it with you, not because I expect anything in return, but because we owe it to you. If you hadn't helped us, well, I'd have spent my life wondering about Benjamin. Buried in my belief and frustration. So you deserve to know."

"It'll take time, but eventually you'll realize it's what your son would—"

She held up her hand. "We're having Benjamin's body exhumed. It's the only way to be sure."

Amara's fork clattered against her plate. "What?"

"I've looked into it. All I need to do is fill out a couple of forms to have him moved from one cemetery to another. While that's happening, I'll have someone get DNA samples and test them. You know, just to settle this one way or the other."

"It won't be that easy. The state has to approve the move first, and that won't happen unless you can give a good reason."

"Our lawyer said the same thing. Enzo and I purchased plots at a cemetery close to our new home. We want Benjamin near us. Since there are no other relatives involved, the state will have to approve it."

"They tested the DNA, Mrs. Reyes. It was Benjamin. Remember, you and your husband both had to give a blood sample so they could match it?"

The woman shrugged.

Amara pushed her plate away. "Think about it. DNA testing isn't like what you see on TV. And after three years, who knows if there's anything even there? I don't want to seem indelicate, but we're talking about bone fragments here. Many of them burned."

"We know. We've talked about that, but what do we have to lose? The worst case is they don't find any DNA and we're right back where we are now. Any other result is an improvement, right?"

Yes and no. This was literally opening up old wounds. "Have you thought about the emotional impact on you both? Digging up a grave isn't something you forget easily."

"We have to know."

Amara sighed and sipped her water. "I know you do. Have you thought this all the way through? I mean, let's say you find DNA, but it's not Benjamin's? That wouldn't necessarily prove anything. With all the bone fragments from the, um, victims, it's likely once the body was identified, they moved on to the next one. No way every fragment was tested."

The woman nodded. "So it's probable that remains from the

other children will also be in Benjamin's coffin. Yes, we've thought about that. If it's not our son's DNA, then it should match one of the other kids on the bus."

"But you don't have access to that information."

"We'll deal with that if it happens."

"Please tell me you haven't spoken with the other parents."

"No, I haven't. The last thing I want is for any of them to experience what I'm going through. Mrs. Delacruz is curious, of course, especially since your visit with the photograph, but I have told her nothing."

"Please think about this more before you commit to going through with the exhumation. Promise me."

"I will, but consider this, Detective. If you had the tiniest hope your dad might still be alive, despite all evidence to the contrary, wouldn't you do everything you could to find out one way or the other?"

Amara looked at the picture again. She was standing in front of a mirror and holding a dress against her. The gown was several inches too long, and her dad stood behind her, holding it scrunched at her waist so the hem didn't drag the floor. Mom had snapped the photo at just that moment.

Dad stared straight at the camera, a wide grin on his face. Mom focused on her daughter's reflection in the mirror, Amara's mouth squished to the side as she debated the scarlet-colored high-neck dress. The beaded bodice had seemed a bit much for her taste, but Dad loved it.

She smiled and slipped the snapshot back into her purse. "Yes, Mrs. Reyes. I'd do everything I could."

14

"Wow," Wylie said. "What did you say then?"

Amara closed the curtains in the hospital room to limit the glare on the TV. "What could I say? I mean, there's no talking her out of it even if I wanted to. And I'd be lying if I said I wasn't curious."

"Think she'll be able to get everything done? DNA testing a corpse isn't exactly something you arrange by going through the Yellow Pages."

She shifted in the uncomfortable vinyl chair. "Yellow Pages? Seriously, Wylie. You have got to get with this century."

"You know what I mean. Don't get me all riled up or I'll push my button again and tell the nurse to run you off."

"I already slipped her a five to ignore you. She gave me a twenty back and said if I was going to sit in here, I deserved it more than she did."

He lifted his head, then coughed twice and groaned. "Thank goodness for these broken ribs. If not for them, I'd only have the chest tube to drive me crazy. Doc says the thing comes out tomorrow. I told him if he didn't pull it out, I'd do it myself."

"Yeah, big talker. Do what they say or I'll see they handcuff you to the bed." She reached over, lifted his head, and straightened his pillow.

"Fine. Who's doing the DNA testing?"

"Mrs. Reyes said it could be weeks or even months before they get approval to move Benjamin's body. She's pretty determined. She'll find someone."

"And in the meantime?"

"In the meantime what?"

"What're you going to be doing on the Reyes case?"

She rolled her eyes and propped a foot on the lowered bedrail. "I'm done with everything except Property Crimes. I'm sure Mrs. Reyes will call if she gets the exhumation approved, but I've got enough of my own work, not to mention fixing all the screwups on your cases."

"Right. So you didn't leave a message for Homicide to notify you as soon as they ID'd that guy's body?"

"How did you—"

"Didn't. But wasn't hard to guess."

Her phone dinged and she checked the time. "Got to go. Trying to get a workout in tonight when it's not so crowded at the gym. Need anything?"

"Yeah, I need you to stay away from here. Let me get my rest."

She brushed a strand of hair off his forehead. "Won't happen. The only joy left in my life is annoying you."

"Then you should be very happy. But if you happen to go by my apartment, would you pick up a few things for me?"

"Of course I will. What do you need?"

"There's a stack of DVDs by my TV. No hurry, but anything's better than watching *The Price Is Right* all day." He motioned toward a small table with a bouquet on it. "Keys are over there."

"Which DVDs? All of them?"

"You'll know them when you see them. And it's our secret, okay?"

"Dotson, these aren't—"

"Please. Is that what you think of me? I keep those in the top of my closet." He smiled and winked.

She patted his hand and headed for the door. "Why do I even bother?"

* * *

The next morning, Amara reviewed her task list. Full day and then some. Three cases needed updating, pawnshop reports hadn't been checked in over a week, and a Neighborhood Watch meeting was on tap for early this evening. The other detectives in her division were just as busy. Sergeant Norwood said they'd have a new investigator transferred in within a day or two. Couldn't come soon enough. Hopefully, whoever they sent had done this before. Training a rookie would be worse than not having help. She stood to stretch and clear her head.

"Alvarez, you awake or what?"

She jerked and turned toward the voice. Starsky. "Hey. Yeah, trying to get motivated. What're you doing slummin' over here in PC?"

"Got some news for you. Stop in for the good stuff when you get a chance."

She arched an eyebrow and tilted her head.

His face turned as red as his hair. "Coffee. In Homicide." He pivoted and hurried from the room.

"Hold up," she said. "I'll walk with you."

He slowed his pace but didn't look back. His long legs meant she had to half jog to catch up.

"So what's going on? They figure out who your dead guys are?"

"The homeless dude was easy enough. Everybody in the area knew him. The other guy, though? Complete blanks on the databases. No military record. Nothing on missing persons either, whatever that's worth. John Doe's still in the morgue."

"So . . . ?"

They stepped into Homicide and stood by the coffeepot. She poured herself a full cup and sipped.

"No cream or sugar?"

She shook her head. "Take it black. Puts hair on my chest, right?"
His face flushed again and he shuffled his feet while staring over her head.

"You know," she said, "for an ex-Marine you sure are easy to embarrass."

"There are no *ex*-Marines." He lowered his chin and deepened his voice. "Only Marines. Enjoy your coffee. I've got to get to work."

She laughed and leaned against the counter. "Sorry. Won't happen again."

"Right." His voice cracked and he cleared his throat. "Tough age to go through puberty. Anyway, I thought you'd want to know there's been a break in the double homicide."

"Yeah?"

"Yeah. They found the guy who killed them."

Amara straightened. "Who killed them?"

"Probably not what you want to hear," Starsky said, "but looks like the shooter was an addict. One Eric Messer, street name Messy. That's original, huh? Most likely a random mugging. Trying to get money for his next fix."

She frowned and shifted the steaming coffee to the other hand. So much for her grand conspiracy theory. Still didn't explain the windshield note and why one of the dead men was at Cotulla, though. "Why would a homeless man be targeted in a robbery? Doesn't make sense."

He shrugged. "Homeless guy was a witness. Reason enough. Crime Stoppers got a tip. We tracked it down and found the suspect in an abandoned warehouse. Dead from an OD. Coroner puts his death last night between ten and two."

"Evidence?"

"Recovered the murder weapon and drugs at the scene. Crack mostly, but looks like heroin killed him. Got the spoon he cooked the tar in and the needle he shot up with. His prints are all over the pistol and he still has gunshot residue on his hands."

"No wallet?"

"Probably took the cash and tossed everything else in a Dumpster."

"Seems kind of flimsy, doesn't it?"

"Better than what we get on a lot of cases. We've got convictions on less. You'll see when you transfer over here. Most of the time there's no smoking gun. Best you hope for is one or two solid pieces of evidence, then enough circumstantial to round it out."

She wrinkled her nose. "Convenient, isn't it?"

"How so?"

"Everything tied up so quickly. The suspect already dead. Plus, look at the murders. Each guy shot once in the head. Clean. Ever see an addict who could pull that off? Hold his hand that steady? Seems more likely there'd have been bullets flying everywhere."

He nodded and grinned. "You'll fit right in. All that's being discussed. So is the fact the two dead guys may have had prior contact, based on what you shared."

"I don't understand. If there are questions, why are you closing the case?"

"Not my case, Alvarez."

She smiled. "Sí, you keep saying that. Not mine either, but here we are."

"True enough. I didn't say we were closing the case. I said we caught the killer."

"But aren't they the same thing?"

He glanced around the room. "Supposed to be, but there are ways to drag it out. Enough unanswered questions and we'll hang on to the file until we're forced to turn loose."

"Forced?"

"This isn't the movies. Next murder comes in, something has to be shoved to the rear. The LT wants the paperwork today so he can wrap this one up. Might even have a press conference to announce the case is solved. Get his face on the news. We'll keep a copy on hand down here to remind us. Bottom line is it'll be chalked up as a successful investigation and somebody somewhere will put a mark in the win column for us. Got to keep those numbers up, you know?"

"Tell me about it. Keep me in the loop, okay?"

"Will do. Hey, how's Dotson doing?"

"Mentally, he's back to his old self." She laughed and rolled her eyes. "Not that I think that's a good thing. Physically, it's going to be a while. I'm swinging by there at lunch if I get a chance. Pester him for a few minutes."

"Let him know we're all thinking about him. Still talking about the way he shot that guy. Drinks are on us when he's up to it."

"I'll tell him. And thanks for the info. Can I ask one more thing?"

He shrugged. "You know everything I do about the case."

"Not that," she said. "I was wondering, um, why they call you Starsky."

He grinned and headed for his desk. "All my best to Dotson."

* * *

Amara tapped on the hospital room door before nudging it open. "You awake?"

"Hey, Alvarez. Come on in. You missed all the excitement."

She stepped inside and stood at the foot of Wylie's bed. "Excitement?"

"Had to take a leak. Decided I could handle things myself, so I took a stroll."

"What? Are you trying to kill yourself?"

He chuckled. "Made it just fine, thank you. A little dizzy from the meds and some pain in my legs, but no problem. Took it slow and easy."

"Yeah, so what was the excitement?"

"Nurse caught me on the way back to bed. The mean one. You know who I'm talking about? Really short, about your height, I guess. Brunette. Pretty. She's got a nasty bite, though."

"You think I'm short? I'm average height for a woman."

"Really? Eh, you must be skewing the average lower then."

She held up a plastic Walmart bag. "Keep it up and I'll take these back to your apartment. Spread the news around the department too."

He held up a hand. "My DVDs? I surrender. Apologize. Whatever works for you."

"All of the above. I'm being generous because you made my day. I must've laughed for twenty minutes. Almost had to pull the car over a couple of times."

"Our secret, right? You promised."

"Up to you. Get out of that bed again and all deals are off."

He scowled. "Oh, come on. You ever pee in that thing they give you? Or worse?"

"Can't say as I have. Don't care, though. We have an agreement?"

"And you won't tell?"

She dropped the bag on his bedside table and laughed. "*Downton Abbey*. The complete series. Never would've guessed it."

"Don't judge me. Lots of guys watch it."

"Uh-huh. Whatever you need to tell yourself."

"You've never seen the show?"

She shook her head. "Not exactly my thing."

"Don't know that until you've tried. When you get time, drop by and watch it with me. I'll start at the first episode. You don't want any more after that, fine."

"We'll see. Can't hang today, though. Pawnshop reports this afternoon and neighborhood meeting tonight."

"Have fun with all that. Wish I was there."

She laid her hand on his arm. "That would've been sarcastic from anyone else. Do what the doctors say if you want to get out of here."

"Oh, by the way. There's a young nurse, a guy, who comes in here once a day. No wedding ring and—"

"Wylie, don't try to set me up. My social life is taking a back seat right now."

"Nothing new there."

"All right, got to run. You need anything, you call."

"No update on your case before you go?"

"Not my case. Homicide's wrapping it up. Caught the shooter. Oh, they said to tell you hey."

"Caught the guy, huh? They ID your mystery man?"

She shook her head. "Not yet. Still a John Doe. Won't be a priority for much longer. Unless somebody comes looking for him, I suppose they'll hold him in cold storage for as long as they can and then the county will bury him."

"You good with that?"

She turned her palms upward and frowned. "Does it matter?"

"You tell me."

"There's something there. I don't know what, but it's important."

"Important to who?"

"The Reyeses. They deserve some closure."

"Really? They had closure. They buried their son. You could give it to them again. All you have to do is tell them the case is closed. Your mystery man was just a victim of a street robbery. The text, the note, that stuff adds up to nothing. A series of unrelated events. And we both know the exhumation is not going to satisfy her unless it's her boy's DNA. Even then, she'll find another reason to wonder. Time to move on."

"Can't do that."

"Why not? You said it was important to them. Give them peace. You'll sleep better at night."

"No, I won't. I'll know there's something we missed. Something that might matter."

"Oh, so it's important to *you*."

"You interrogating me, Dotson?"

"It's what detectives do, right? Keep digging until we get the answer. Maybe not the one we want, but the truth, or at least the truth as we know it at that time."

She crossed her arms. "Yes, it's important to me. No, I'm not dropping the case. Happy?"

"Not until you watch *Downton Abbey* with me."

"Soon. Promise. Behave while I'm gone."

"Yes, ma'am." He pointed at her. "Be careful out there."

"Always." She squeezed his hand, then took a step toward the door and paused. "Can I ask you a question? Personal one?"

He smiled. "You already know my darkest secret, so shoot."

"Why didn't you ever transfer to Homicide? That's what everybody wants, right? Catching the killer, the one who committed the ultimate crime?"

His head sank into the pillow and he stared at the ceiling. "Iraq and Afghanistan. Saw enough bodies there. After a while, I kind of didn't even notice them anymore. Became almost routine. 'Course, if it was one of our guys, it was different, but that didn't happen too often."

"So you got used to it?"

His hand gripped the sheet and he looked away from her. "Thought I did."

She drew her lips into her mouth, patted her hand against the door, then walked over and kissed him on the forehead. "Sorry, Wylie. Get some rest."

16 The Neighborhood Watch meeting, as usual, ran longer than expected. Amara's plans for an evening jog faded as fast as her willpower to avoid the homemade cupcakes. Her phone buzzed and she slid her finger across the screen to silence the vibrating. Several seconds later, a low beep let her know she had a new voice mail.

The meeting's host wrapped up with a reminder to encourage their neighbors to leave their porch lights on all night, then thanked Amara for her time. She smiled and nodded. A few people shook her hand on the way out the door and the hostess offered her the remaining cupcakes. She accepted and assured her she'd share them around the department.

By the time she settled in for the drive home, the streetlights had flickered on as a dark dusk sank through the sky. She dialed her voice mail and moved the cupcakes to the back seat, out of temptation's way.

The message was brief. Someone named Jeremy Winter said Wylie had asked him to call. Might be able to help with her problem. Left his number and nothing more.

Help with her problem? If Wylie was setting her up on a date, he'd soon have a new batch of injuries to worry about. She scrolled to the call log and redialed the number.

A woman answered. "Hello?"

"Hi. I'm trying to get in touch with Jeremy Winter. He left me a message with this number?"

"Sure. Hang on a sec. I'll go find him."

The sound of giggling and a little girl's laughter could be heard in the background. The woman covered the phone, but not enough Amara didn't hear her admonish someone about getting the girl all wound up before her bedtime. After a moment, a breathless voice came through.

"Hello?"

"Mr. Winter?"

"Yes?"

"Hi, this is Amara Alvarez. You left me a message?"

"Oh, sure. You're Wylie's friend, right?"

"Yeah. We work together."

"Sorry to hear about what happened. Wylie's a good guy."

"He is. Listen, I'm not sure what—"

"You alone?"

She scrunched her forehead and checked the rearview. "Um, yeah. I'm about to head home and—"

"I'll call you right back. Your phone will show unknown caller, but it will be me."

The call disconnected and seconds later, her cell buzzed. "Hello?"

"Hey. Me again. Wylie called me and said you could use some help identifying a John Doe."

"Why, um, what exactly did he say?"

"Not much. Didn't need to. Wylie and I spent time together overseas. First I've talked to him since then, but I know he wouldn't ask if it wasn't important."

"I didn't know he was going to do this, but thank you. Can I ask what you do?"

"Ex-FBI. Do my own thing now, but I have access to a few contacts who come in handy on occasion. Might be able to use, shall we say, other means to identify your body."

"Mr. Winter, I don't want to waste your time. Right now my John Doe is more of a curiosity to me. Not sure he did anything illegal."

"Ms. Alvarez, the less I know about this, the better. If I can get you a name to match your guy, I will, but that's it. And if I do provide any information, I didn't. Got it?"

"Yes, absolutely. How do you want to do this?"

"Check the spam folder on your personal email. You'll find a message there saying silver's at an all-time low and now's your chance to buy. Reply to that with whatever you've got on your guy. Photos, prints, everything. Keep checking your spam. You'll get another message if I find anything. You'll know it when you see it."

"I can't tell you how much I appreciate this. Really."

"Thank Wylie. And remember, if I do find anything, a name is all you'll get. More would be too easy to trace back to me."

"I understand."

"Have a good evening, Ms. Alvarez."

"Wait. Don't you need my email address?"

He chuckled. "Be safe driving home."

* * *

Increíble! Eleven hours since she'd responded to the initial spam message and an answer already? What kind of technology does this guy have access to? This spam message had a FedEx logo and a bogus return email address.

Dear customer:

We are delighted to inform you that your package has arrived at today. Our courier is unable to deliver the parcel from Philip Dragan. Please click the link below to find direction to recover your package.

The link was to the Wikipedia page for the US Marines' Force Recon unit. Mr. Winter had gone over and above.

So their John Doe was ex-military. Not just that, but special forces. So why weren't his prints on file? Wasn't that standard procedure?

She googled his name. Nothing. Searched the FBI's NCIC database. Nothing. John Doe might have a name now, but that was all.

She scribbled *Philip Dragan* on a yellow sticky note and passed it to Starsky before hurrying back to her desk. His questions about how she'd acquired the information went unanswered. He had the wisdom not to press the issue.

A pop from behind startled her and she spun her chair around. "Morning, Sarge."

He nodded and peered over her shoulder. "NCIC?"

"Yeah, searching for a background on someone."

"Any luck?"

"Not yet."

"Hmm. Which case?"

"Which case? One from over in Leon Valley."

Norwood ripped a corner off her legal pad, dropped his bubble gum in the paper, and tossed it into the garbage. "You repeated my question. Got to come up with better stall tactics. Don't let whatever you're doing interfere with your job."

"I won't. Promise."

"You going to see Dotson today?"

"After work. Stopping by the hospital before I hit the gym."

He popped a new wad of gum into his mouth. "Tell him it's time to get off his lazy rear end and get back to work. Tired of his slacking."

"You got it."

"Could stand to see a few more closed cases from you too."

"Well, you know, just saving up for the end of the month to hit my quota."

His mouth formed a thin line. "I'm serious, Alvarez. Look, I know you want out of here. I'll do what I can, but you've got to help. Give me some ammunition."

"I know, Sarge, and I appreciate it. This other research is not distracting me from my work."

He pursed his lips, nodded, and blew a gum bubble. "I hope you're right, because now's the time to step it up. Of all the detectives on my shift, you're the only one with nothing to show this month."

"Come on. You know that isn't fair. These things run in cycles."

"Yeah, and so do job openings. Nothing I can do about either. You want to get noticed? Wrap up the Leon Valley mess."

"Job openings?"

He leaned forward and placed his palms on her desk. "Off the record, there's talk of starting a cold case team. Pull two or three guys out of Homicide."

"And you'd recommend me to transfer over?"

"Bring me Leon Valley."

"It's not that easy."

"'Course it's not. You want easy, transfer to Traffic."

17 **Wylie paused the DVD** for the third time. "Are you going to watch or are you going to talk?"

"You can't tell me anything about the guy? How you met him? Nothing?"

He motioned and she passed him the water bottle off the bedside table. "I met Jeremy Winter overseas. End of story."

She crossed her arms. "Not buying it. To get Dragan's name that fast, the guy has to—"

"End. Of. Story."

"Fine," she said. "You don't want to tell me."

"There's that detective instinct kicking in." He restarted the DVD.

"Can you turn on the subtitles?" Amara asked. "I can hardly understand what they're saying."

Wylie sighed and paused *Downton Abbey* again. "They're speaking English. The same thing we speak."

She gestured toward the TV. "They may be using the same words, but they're not using the same language."

"No subtitles. Blocks the picture. If you have a question, ask me. After a couple of episodes, you'll be calling me 'guvna' and having afternoon tea."

"Dream on. So the guy with the limp is his butler?"

Wylie pressed the button to raise the head of his bed higher. "Mr. Bates. No, he's the earl's valet."

"Valet, butler, what's the difference?"

"The valet is Earl Crawley's personal assistant. Helps him get dressed. Takes care of his errands. Stuff like that. The butler is in charge of everyone who works in the home. That's Mr. Carson, the man who always looks like he's got a stick up his, um—he looks stern."

She glanced sideways at him. "I'm a little alarmed you know all that."

"There's nothing wrong with having culture."

"For most people, I'd agree. But you?"

"Har har. You want to talk or you want to watch?"

"Finish this episode, then I've got to get out of here. Already stayed longer than I'd planned and I still have to hit the gym."

He downed the last of the water, pushed himself back against his pillows, and pulled the blanket up to his neck. "Hey, if you've got to go—"

"You okay? Your face is flushed."

"Got a little overheated, that's all."

She placed the back of her hand on his forehead. "I'm getting the nurse. You feel hot."

"I'm fine. Let's finish this episode and then you can be on your merry way."

"Uh-uh. Not until someone takes your temperature. Be right back."

She returned with the nurse a few minutes later. A low-grade fever. They'd inform the doctor and have him stop by to check.

"Stay in bed, Wylie. And don't watch the rest of the show without me."

He smiled, then coughed twice. "Knew it. You're hooked."

* * *

Amara donned her ankle supports and boxing gloves, but opted to leave off the shin guards. The Muay Thai bag would serve as her opponent this evening. The six-foot-tall bag dragged the floor, allowing her to work on her low kicks and harden her shins. She popped her mouth guard in place and threw a few jabs to loosen up.

Bap bap.

She ducked and bobbed for half a minute, then attacked again.

Bap bap poom.

The low kick sent a brief flash of pain from her ankle to knee. Openings coming up in Homicide.

Bap bap thwomp.

Her right fist landed a cross punch on the bag. Norwood was pretty clear about it.

Bap thwomp poom.

Show progress on the Leon Valley burglaries.

Thwok.

Her roundhouse kick landed head-high on the bag. Show progress. Wouldn't she have already done that if she could have?

Bap bap bap thwup.

The uppercut jarred her wrist. Watch your form.

She brushed the back of a glove across her forehead to clear away sweat.

Thwup bap bap poom.

Better. Only thing to do is start over. Nearly a dozen break-ins.

Pop bap bap.

Her hook was weak. Always had been. No way pros would risk so many burglaries in such a small area. Had to be kids or addicts, didn't it?

Bap bap bap.

She bounced on her toes, bobbing and weaving. Need to talk to Larry about the burglaries. Discuss it over some mustard greens at home.

Poom poom thwup.

She worked out for another twenty minutes, then walked on a treadmill for ten to cool down. A shower could wait until she got home. Larry never complained about her smell.

* * *

She sank onto the sofa, propped her feet on the coffee table, and smiled as Larry waddled into the room. The pale green lizard investigated a couple of spots before running to her and staring up. If she had her jeans on, she'd have let him climb up her leg. Gym shorts? No way. She reached down and plopped him on the couch beside her.

"Any ideas, buddy? Boss says we need to solve this case."

Larry closed his eyes and bobbed his head as she scratched his back.

"You're no help, you know that?" She tapped her finger on the iguana. Nothing had shown up at pawnshops or flea markets, according to the database these types of businesses were required to fill out. Not that many unique items were missing anyhow. Nothing on Craigslist or eBay either. Why steal something if you weren't going to sell it? Could be fencing the items or shipping them out of town, but that'd point to something more professional. Plus, valuables had been left in several houses. Antique silverware. A gold pocket watch inscribed with a great-grandfather's name. Even handguns in two of the homes. Why?

She lifted Larry and placed him in her lap. "Anytime you want to chime in, feel free."

The locations of the burglaries seemed random, yet confined to Leon Valley. Nice enough neighborhood. Outside of this, no real crime to speak of. Kids. Had to be. Too young to drive or no car available. Cutting classes. Knew their way around the area. No problem dodging the extra patrols.

She could check school records. Try to match up absences with the dates of the burglaries. Nothing else seemed to be working. Why do it? Electronics, sure. Laptops, video game systems. Understandable. And would a kid leave a gun? Maybe, but why? Too easy to trace? None of it made any sense.

"What am I missing, buddy?" She scraped her hand along the spikes on his back and scratched the iguana's head. "How about a Diet Coke and some mustard greens? Guess which one's for me?"

She placed him on the floor and wandered into the kitchen with Larry plodding right behind. She tore off several large leaves and waved them over him. "Hungry? Come on, let's get you to bed."

The lizard padded after her into his room and stood by the door, his tongue darting out like a dog waiting for a treat.

She dangled the greens. "Get in your cage, Larry."

He stared.

"You want your supper? Better get in here then. Mmmm, mustard greens."

He kept staring.

"You stubborn lizard. Mama's got to get her sleep. Be a good boy."

He blinked.

She sighed and dropped the greens into the cage, then took a step toward him. Larry turned and scooted away as fast as he could. She caught him behind the sofa and scooped him up, squeezing him against her chest so he couldn't scratch. "Gotcha. We'll play tomorrow. I promise. But now you've got to get in your room."

She placed him on the floor of his cage and he poked at his meal before grabbing a leaf and dragging it to the back of his enclosure.

"Go ahead and pout. Love you anyway. Night, buddy."

Back in the kitchen, she scrubbed her hands and grabbed a drink from the fridge. Last cold one. She loaded another six-pack on the bottom shelf. Had a feeling she'd better stock up. Her future held long days, high stress, and a short temper.

A note was stuck on her monitor.

Come by Homicide asap. Starsky

Something happen on the Dragan case? Had they made a connection between him and Cotulla? She hurried over and found Starsky sitting at his desk.

He held a photo in each hand and glanced between them before passing them to Amara. "Anything strike you as odd about these?"

In her left hand was Dragan at the scene of his death. In her right, the still frame of Dragan from the police car. She'd seen them dozens of times. "Fancy dresser. Meticulous about his appearance. Not to the point of vanity, I think. Didn't dye his hair. Handsome, though, for an older guy."

He turned his eyes toward the ceiling and shook his head. "Trust me. Handsome is not all it's cracked up to be. The way women constantly come on to you. Ugh. Being treated like a piece of meat gets old."

She grinned and nodded. "Get that a lot, do you?"

"You have no idea. Enough about my good looks, but I do appreciate you bringing them up. Look at the pictures again. Tell me what else you see."

She held the two photos under his desk lamp and alternated her view between them. "I see . . . what?"

He reached over and pointed at Dragan's waist. "Check out his belt."

"What about it?"

"Looks like he's wearing the same one in both pictures. Can't be sure because we can't see the buckle in the image from the dashboard camera, but I'd bet they're the same belt."

"He's wearing the same belt. So what?"

Starsky leaned back in his chair. "Think about it in relation to what you said earlier."

She tapped her finger on her lips. "You think he'd wear different belts with different clothes? I don't know. My ex only had one belt. Didn't matter what he was wearing. If he needed a belt, that was the one."

"Yeah? Your ex pay as much attention to his appearance as Dragan did?"

She laughed. "Point taken. So there's something special about this belt?"

He shook his head. "Probably not. Like Freud said, sometimes a belt is just a belt. But this guy, I don't know. The belt's either too dark for the khakis or too light for the suit. I'm with your ex on this one. Pick one belt that works with anything. Better yet, get one of those reversible ones. Black on one side, brown on the other. A silver buckle and voilà. Good to go. But Dragan's tastes seem a little more particular."

"Worth checking out."

He stood and gestured to the door. "Care to escort me to the evidence room?"

"I'd be delighted."

A uniformed officer signed them into the secured area and had them wait while he retrieved the requested container. He returned moments later and placed the cardboard box on the table, removed the lid, and did a quick inventory of the contents. After cautioning the pair not to remove anything from the room, he wandered back to his seat near the door.

Starsky emptied the box and laid everything out on the table. Dragan's clothing, dark stains evident on the blue shirt, took up most of the space. The belt was in a bag by itself and he handed it to her.

"If we need to take a closer look," he said, "we'll go to the crime lab and do it there."

She nodded and pressed the belt against the inside of the bag to get a better view. Dark brown, almost black. Somewhat thick leather, two pieces sewn together. Heavy black stitching along the top and bottom. The third hole was stretched out, indicating most frequent use by the brass buckle. She manipulated the bag until she'd seen the full length of each side of the belt.

"Anything?" Starsky asked.

"Not yet. Looks fairly new. Good quality too. Probably cost more than your whole outfit."

"Hey, come on now. That's not fair. My suits are tailor-made. Not for me, of course, but for whoever dropped them off at Goodwill."

She chuckled and inspected the belt again. Still nothing. She worked the leather between her fingers, feeling the width. When she got to the buckle, she froze.

"Find something?" he asked.

"Shhh." Amara closed her eyes and moved her hand back and forth over the belt, her fingers barely grazing the leather. The evidence bag complicated the process, but after a moment she licked her lips, opened her eyes, then bent and twisted the belt, keeping her focus on one spot. Maybe.

"Amara, what is it?"

She handed the bag to him. "Thought I felt something right before the buckle attaches. The belt's stiff there, so I can't be sure. Probably just the way it's made. A little thicker to support the added weight and stress."

He frowned. "I don't feel anything. Let's get it to the lab and out of this bag."

The crime lab consisted of an oversize room divided into several sections by shoulder-height panels. The fluorescent lights glared on the white walls, white floors, white counters, white everything. A fenced area against the back wall contained shelves with an assortment of paper bags, each with a bright yellow tag. A door to the left had signs indicating that a darkroom and ballistics testing were in that direction.

Three technicians were at work, two wearing a mask and gloves, the third sitting at a desk and using a computer. None of them looked up when the pair entered the room. Starsky approached the woman at the desk and waited while she finished typing. After a moment, she pushed her glasses up on her nose and glanced at him.

Starsky nodded. "Afternoon. Detective Peckham, Homicide. Got something here I need you to take a look at."

The woman glanced at the evidence bag. "A belt? Fingerprints, DNA, what?"

Amara stepped closer. "Nothing that elaborate. We just want a better peek at one section of it."

The woman's glasses slid down her nose again. "Looking for blood?"

"No," Starsky said. "I promise this will only take a minute or two."

She sighed, stood, and took the bag. "Follow me."

They walked to an open counter and she handed each of them a pair of latex gloves. They stretched them over their fingers while she recorded information off the bag into a notebook. When she finished, she donned her own gloves and wiped down the area with alcohol. She removed the belt and gently placed it on the counter, keeping her hand under the buckle as she did so.

"Don't remove it from the counter," she said. "And go easy with the buckle. No scratches please."

Amara squatted so the belt was eye level, then traced her fingers along the suspected area. "Definitely a bump there. See what you think."

Starsky moved beside her and bent down, then dragged his fingers on the belt. "Good hands. There's a ridge there for sure. Like you said, might be to support the buckle. Only one way to be certain."

The woman wriggled her nose and worked her glasses back to their proper height. "Could be a stiffener. Some manufacturers put nylon between the layers. Helps the belt last longer."

Starsky nodded. "Can you cut it open?"

"Hold on." She pulled out an alcohol swab, used it to open a drawer, then retrieved an X-ACTO knife and wiped it down also. She turned the belt on its side, sliced a three-inch section of the stitching, and pried the leather apart. "Looks like you were right."

Amara leaned over the counter and peered into the belt's new opening. "Starsky, it's a key."

The crime tech used tweezers to remove the item and drop it into a new evidence bag before handing it to Amara. The key was silver with a round head and no markings. Looked like any of a billion others out there. She turned it over and her heart jumped. A piece of green tape covered the top section. Written on the tape in black ink was *Unit 59*. She held it so Starsky could see.

"Storage unit?" he asked.

"That's what I was thinking," Amara said. She turned to the woman. "Can we get a copy of the key?"

"Take an hour or so."

"That'd be great," Starsky said. "We'll grab a bite to eat and stop back by. Sound okay, Detective?"

Amara stared at the key. Something wasn't right. She scratched her temple and shifted the weight on her legs.

"Amara?" Starsky said. "Is anything wrong?"

Was there? "No. Everything's—wait. Why would he write the unit number on there?"

"Same reason I would," the crime tech said. "So he didn't forget."

"Maybe," Amara said. "But if it is a storage unit, he'd have another key, right? It's not like he'd cut his belt open every time he went there."

Starsky crossed his arms. "Could be he only went there once and didn't need regular access to the key after that."

"True," Amara said. "But why link the key to the unit? He goes to all the trouble to hide it, why make it obvious if someone does find it? If it was me and I was worried about forgetting the unit number, I'd hide that somewhere else. Cell phone maybe. Something not so apparent. And I sure wouldn't link the key to the unit number."

"You might be overthinking this," he said.

She arched her eyebrows at him.

He held up his hands. "Or not. Got a theory?"

"Couple of them. First one is when we find this storage unit, if that's what this is, we need to have the bomb squad check everything before we go in."

Starsky nodded. "A trap. He puts the number on the key as a decoy in case it is found. I can see that."

"There's another possibility," Amara said. "We're assuming he always wore that belt, right? Wanted to keep the key with him, but didn't want anyone to know he had it. What if he wrote on the key to simplify things?"

The crime tech pushed her glasses up again. "So he'd remember the unit? We already—"

"No," Amara said. "To simplify things for us."

* * *

Amara's lunch consisted of a cold tamale from Mama's and a bottled water. Starsky downed Pringles and a Mountain Dew. They sat across from each other in the break room.

He brushed a crumb off his lip. "You're saying Dragan labeled the key so when—if—we found it, we'd know what it went to?"

"Possibly. The belt was his safety net. He knew the only way we'd see inside it is if he was dead. He wants us to find whatever that key opens."

"If that's true, why didn't he give us the name of the storage place? There are hundreds of those things around San Antonio."

She took a bite of the tamale. "Don't know. Time, maybe? In case someone got hold of the key and he wasn't dead? Give him a chance to move whatever's there?"

He turned the Pringles can upside down and finished off the chips. "You got an answer for everything?"

"Yeah," she said. "Except how you can eat that junk and still weigh about a buck-fifty."

"Jealousy does not look good on you. Besides, your tamale isn't exactly nutrition at its best."

She narrowed her eyes and fought back a smile. "Hey, my mom makes these. Back off."

"Lo siento. Looks wonderful. Really."

"It is. Want a bite?"

"Uh, no. Me and spicy food have an understanding. It won't hurt me if I don't eat it."

"Your loss. What's your plan for the key?"

"Start checking storage units, I guess. Can't do it on the clock or the LT will have my head. Fortunately, my social calendar seems to be empty for the next few forevers, so I'll hit some locations every night after work. Try the key on all the Unit 59s until I stumble on the right one. Very Cinderella, don't you think?"

She covered her mouth and giggled. "You in glass slippers. There's an image that'll turn your stomach."

"Don't judge. I have pretty feet when I shave my toes."

She coughed several times and took a long drink of water. "Don't do that to me when I'm eating. I've got to head back and get to work. This Leon Valley thing is kicking my rear. Appreciate you letting me in on this, though. You'll keep me in the loop?"

"Do I have a choice? Can't risk word getting out about my foot grooming. Cops can be a cruel bunch."

Unmotivated was putting it mildly. Amara shuffled through the eleven file folders on her desk, each representing one burglary in Leon Valley. After five minutes, she yawned and rubbed her eyes. It was like rereading a novel she'd just finished. She shoved the folders aside and pulled her laptop in front. Using the keyboard and mouse would at least require movement.

She'd taken photos with her phone at each crime scene, then uploaded them to the computer. Every room, exactly as it was when the burglary was discovered. Usually this ritual accomplished nothing more than making the homeowner feel better. With time to kill though, might as well check out her photography skills.

She scanned through the first three homes, yawned again, and stretched. The fourth house was the one with the messy daughter's bedroom. Somebody needed to teach that girl how to hang up her clothes. Compared to the girls in the previous homes—

Four houses. Four teenage girls.

From the pictures, it was clear other children lived in each house, but the four older girls each had their own room.

She opened the fifth home's photos. Three bedrooms. An oversize master with its own bathroom, one decorated with Dallas Cowboys and San Antonio Spurs posters and memorabilia, and the last one, hard to say. Generic bedspread, nothing on the walls. A computer desk with some loose change and a couple of books. A nightstand, bottom drawer opened. Inside, a pink box. Tampons.

She clicked through the remaining six homes. Four definitely had teenage girls living there. The other two might or might not, but a phone call should answer that easy enough. Even if they didn't fit the pattern, nine out of eleven did. That couldn't be a coincidence.

She pulled up a map of the school district and confirmed all the houses were in the same zone. Monroe High School, home of the Fighting Bobcats. Twenty-five hundred students. Not exactly narrowing down the suspect pool.

She punched Sergeant Norwood's extension on her phone. "Got a second?"

He walked over and pulled up a chair. "What's up?"

She recapped what she'd learned.

"Swing by the school," he said. "Find out if they all share a class or are in the same club. Cheerleading, volleyball, anything that ties them together."

"Will do. Doesn't explain why, though. The girls' rooms weren't targeted as far as we could tell."

"Find the who and we'll get the why. Talk to the parents. Have them go through their daughters' clothes again, especially bras and panties. Make sure nothing's missing."

"You thinking a perv? Using the break-ins as cover?"

He shrugged and popped his bubble gum. "Hope not, but check it out later. Hit the high school first."

"Might be quicker to get all the girls in the same room and go from there."

"Yeah, but can't do it without their parents' permission. Don't talk to the kids. If one of them's involved, I don't want a defense lawyer throwing it in our faces."

"You got it."

Norwood stood and tapped his finger on the stack of files. "Good work, Alvarez. Now bring it home."

"Thanks, Sarge. I'm on it." She slid the files and her laptop into her shoulder bag.

"Dig deep. This could be what we needed. Be nice to close this soon."

She nodded and headed for her car, nearly bumping into Starsky in the hallway.

"Just coming to see you," he said. "Got a couple of minutes?"

She frowned and shook her head. "Not really. Caught a break on a case. Why? What's up?"

"Philip Dragan. Our mystery man. Wanted to give you an update, but it's not important. I'll catch you later."

"You find something?"

"The opposite of something. Less than nothing."

"And the key?"

His eyes widened. "Didn't I tell you? We found the storage shed two days ago. Stacked high with hundred-dollar bills and dead bodies."

She swatted his arm. "Idiota. Got to run. Want me to get someone to help you find your way back to your desk?"

He grinned and peered up and down the hall. "No, I'm good. I think. Go get 'em, Alvarez."

* * *

Amara pulled into visitor parking at the high school. Philip Dragan would have to wait. She was onto something with the burglaries. She could feel it. Finally.

The school's principal assigned an aide to help her go through the computerized files. Told her to take as long as she needed and escorted her to a private room. Within minutes, the aide had accessed the records for each of the students whose homes had been burglarized.

The two unknowns were indeed girls, meaning all eleven fit the profile. Each of them either a junior or senior. Six Hispanic, four white, one African American.

Amara pulled a notepad from her bag and flipped to a clean page. "Can you see if all eleven share a class?"

"Sure. Give me a second here." She clicked the mouse a few times, then dragged her finger down the screen. "Nope."

"How about a club or sport? Maybe cheerleading?"

A few more mouse clicks. "Uh-uh. Two here, three there, but no place where all eleven are together."

"Lunchtime?"

"We go in shifts and they're on three different ones."

Amara tapped her pen on the blank page. "Same bus?"

The aide reset her search options. "Sorry, only one of them even rides the bus."

"Can you think of anything else? A time or place where all of them might be together?"

"Not here. Honestly, when they get that age they tend to leave the campus every chance they get."

Shift tactics. "Okay. Can you search and see if there are any students who share a class with all the girls?"

"I'm not sure I understand."

"Is there anyone who, at some point during the day, is in at least one class with each girl?"

The aide bit her bottom lip. "That's going to take a while. And if I include the lunch breaks in there, got to think there'd be dozens of kids. Maybe more."

Amara frowned and slid her notepad back into her bag. "Here's my card. Please let me know when you're done. I appreciate your help. Really."

The bell sounded and the noise level increased exponentially as the high schoolers changed classes. Amara stepped into the hallway and studied the sea of students. Most of them were as tall as or taller than she was and she resisted the urge to stand on tiptoe. None of the ones she saw looked like a serial burglar or hardened criminal.

They rarely did.

Amara parked outside the Rosemond residence in Leon Valley. One of the older neighborhoods around, its houses varied and the trees were mature. Not tall, just old. The newer subdivisions surrounding San Antonio and most cities in Texas were cookie cutters, with each home a minor variation of every house within a six-block radius. A gazillion acres of scrubland in all directions, so be sure to pack big homes onto tiny lots. If she ever decided to buy a house, it'd be somewhere like this.

Mr. Rosemond should be home any moment. She'd called and asked him to meet her. Go through the house again. Maybe even apologize for running out on him when Wylie was shot. Maybe. Depended on his attitude. Hopefully he'd had time to calm down.

A mail truck pulled around her and eased down the street, pausing at each house to slide today's bills and junk into each box. She'd have to make sure the postal employees were keeping their eyes open too. Out here every day, leaving mostly unwanted things at every house.

Leaving things.

A thought itched her brain. She stared at the postman as he made a U-turn and came toward her. What if—

The short beep of a horn startled her and she glanced out the back window. Mr. Rosemond stepped out of his car and raised a hand in greeting.

She grabbed her phone and exited the vehicle. "Thank you for meeting me, Mr. Rosemond."

He tapped his palm on the roof of her car. "Um, look, Detective. Sorry about last time. I don't handle stress too good, and just the thought that, well . . ."

She shook her head. "No need to apologize, sir. I understand completely. I'd be frustrated too."

"Yeah, and, uh, sorry about the guy who got shot. You know him?"

"Wylie? I do. Friend of mine."

"He doing okay?"

"Better. Thanks for asking. I wonder if we could step inside your home for a moment."

"Of course." He led the way to the front door, unlocked it, and deactivated the alarm.

"Got yourself a security system, I see. Make sure you put a sign out front and in the back. Stickers on the windows wouldn't hurt either."

"That stuff really help?"

"It doesn't hurt, and might be enough to tell someone to move on to another home."

"I'll do that. So, what are we doing here?"

"Mainly following up. Checking to see if you've discovered anything else missing."

He shook his head. "Nothing. At least not that we've found so far."

"Mr. Rosemond, I need to ask a question and I want to be as tactful as I can. You have a teenage daughter, right?"

Wrinkles appeared on his forehead. "I do, but surely you don't think she's—"

"No, sir. I wonder, though, if she's mentioned anything out of the normal."

"Like what?"

"Like maybe a favorite pair of jeans missing? Or a shirt?" She paused and made eye contact. "Or underwear? Bra or panties?"

He rubbed his hand back and forth across his mouth. "You think it was some pervert. If anyone comes near my little girl, I'll—"

"Has she mentioned anything disappearing?"

"No. Nothing. Honestly, though, do you know any teenage girls who could tell you if they were missing something like that? I mean, their closets are overflowing with clothes. Drawers too. You remember what that was like."

No, I don't. "Sure. Mind if we take a peek in her room?"

He shrugged. "Guess not, but I won't be much help. I try to stay out of there."

He escorted her down a short hallway. Two bedrooms were on the left with the master on the right. They stepped into the daughter's room and stopped just inside. Midday sun streamed through partially open blinds and lit the space. The dresser and walls were plastered with school memorabilia. A maroon cheerleader's uniform hung from the closet doorknob, and a few other items of clothing were scattered about the room. The bed was unmade and covered with pillows and two oversize teddy bears. On the nightstand, a laptop cycled through its screen saver of nature pictures.

"Anything look out of the ordinary?" Amara asked.

"Not that I can tell. What's going on? I thought you wanted to know if something else was missing."

"I do, but also want to, um, cover all the bases."

He straightened and his face flushed. "What does that mean?"

She hesitated before responding. "Maybe whoever broke in left something behind."

"You mean like dropped his wallet? We'd have found—"

"No, not like that. Can you stay right there, please? Let me check the room?"

He crossed his arms and frowned. "What are you looking for?"

"No idea. Okay if I inspect the drawers and the closet?"

He nodded.

She checked the nightstand first. Nothing out of the ordinary. She pulled it away from the wall and scanned the back, running her hand across every surface. What *was* she looking for?

The bed yielded the same results. Nothing between the mattresses. Nothing under the bed other than dirty clothes, candy wrappers, and dust bunnies.

Six drawers in the dresser, and she emptied each. Nada. She checked behind it and found two pieces of old poster board, but nothing else.

The closet came last. She stared at the area for a moment and tried to decide how to attack the clutter. The clothes were packed tight on hangers. The floor was covered in shoes. The top was buried in who knows what.

"I told work I'd be right back," Rosemond said. "Is this going to take much longer?"

She sighed. "No, sir. I'm about done. It might be better, with your permission, of course, to come back when your daughter's home?"

"I'd rather not. Let her put this behind her, you know? But if you think it's absolutely necessary?"

She glanced around the room a last time. "Yes, sir, I do. Can you turn on the ceiling fan, please?"

He flipped the wall switches. The fan slowly began rotating and picking up speed.

"Great," she said. "You can turn it off. How about the overhead lights?"

The switch clicked and the dome light under the fan came on.

She moved closer and stared upward. Her heartbeat accelerated. "That look completely lit to you? Maybe got a bulb out?"

He leaned forward and squinted up. "Yeah, I think so."

"Mind if I take a peek?'

"Hold on a sec. Got a stepladder in the coat closet. Be right back."

He returned, positioned the ladder, and handed her a lightbulb. "If you wouldn't mind while you're up there?"

"No problem." She climbed halfway up and inspected the dome before removing the center screw and handing Rosemond the glass cover. One of the two bulbs was burned out. Nothing looked out of the ordinary. She unscrewed the bulb and shook it. The wiry rattle confirmed the light's death. She screwed in the replacement and it lit up immediately.

She frowned and replaced the dome. She'd been so sure. "You can turn it off now."

From her height above the bed, she gave the room a last scan. Like she was going to spot anything from up here.

"If you're done, I really need to get back to work."

She reached up and gave the ceiling fan a gentle push, watched it make its slow circle, then stopped it and climbed up another step. "Let me take a quick look up here and then I'll get out of your way."

The tops of the fan blades and the dome light were covered in dust. Nothing had touched them in quite a while. She stifled a sneeze and made a mental note to clean hers when she got home. The three- or four-inch space below the fan was some sort of metal mesh covering the wiring and support pole for the light. She grabbed her phone and opened an app. The camera's flash lit up and she pointed the beam into the dark mesh.

Red wire, green wire, black wire, copper wire. More dust.

And a tiny black cylindrical object angled toward the bed.

Toward the bed.

"Mr. Rosemond, you're going to need to notify your work you won't be back today."

Sergeant Norwood arrived fifteen minutes after the crime scene unit. "Anything new?" he asked.

Amara sat on a leather recliner in the living room. "No, sir. Not yet. They did confirm the device is a camera and is hooked into the fan's wiring. The thing's got about a ninety-minute battery. When the light or fan is turned on, the unit not only activates but also recharges the battery. Possibly motion activated. Definitely Wi-Fi."

"Can they track the signal?"

"Already have. It's kicking off the homeowner's wireless router." She gestured toward the sofa where the homeowner sat. "Oh, I'm sorry. Sir, this is Mr. Rosemond. Mr. Rosemond, this is my boss, Sergeant Alan Norwood."

The men shook hands.

Rosemond pointed to Amara. "She's some kind of detective, Sergeant. Give her a raise, will ya?"

Norwood smiled. "She slip you a twenty to say that?"

"I'm serious. Take care of her."

"Yes, sir. We will. Detective, you said the camera had access to the home's network?"

She scooted forward in the chair. "The Wi-Fi is password protected. Whoever planted the camera either knew the code beforehand or got it from the router."

"Is that hard to do?"

"Would be for me, but according to the techs, the router has a default password from the factory. That password is separate from your Wi-Fi password. You're supposed to change it, but most people don't. Apparently, all you have to do is search for the router type and you'll get the factory password. Even easier if you use the cable company's equipment since the password is printed right on the back. Then hook up a laptop to the router and you can access everything, including the Wi-Fi password."

"And then?"

She glanced at Mr. Rosemond. "Then you can control the camera through the internet. Could be sitting on the other side of the world and watch whatever you want on your cell phone."

"Traceable?"

"I don't know. They didn't get that far yet."

He turned and stared out the front door. "Check another of the homes. Pick one."

"And if I find the same thing?"

"Then the Major Crimes Unit is going to be very busy."

* * *

In less than an hour, Amara had met two other homeowners and confirmed each had a camera installed in the teenage daughter's bedroom ceiling fan. The other break-in victims were being notified, and a patrol unit now sat parked in front of each of the homes to ensure that the location remained secure.

The crime scene techs had removed the camera at the Rosemond house by the time she returned. The news had grown worse. Not only was the camera Wi-Fi and motion-activated, it had DVR capabilities and stored data for later download. That meant whoever had put the unit in didn't have to be logged on to use the device. They could grab the video at their leisure. Easily done from any cell phone close enough to connect to the home's Wi-Fi.

The techs were confident they'd get the culprit quickly. Plenty of options to track him or her down. Serial numbers on the cameras might lead to the purchaser. Most likely they'd been bought online somewhere and shipped in bulk. Plus, some of the homeowners' routers would show information on specific dates and times the devices had been accessed from the network. That data could be used to link a suspect's cell phone or laptop to the crime. And any fingerprints on the cameras would be matched against the ones from the break-ins, so when they identified a suspect, everything would be tied into a nice package for the prosecutor.

Mr. Rosemond slumped on the couch with his head in his hands. His wife had arrived and she sat beside him, her head on his shoulder. Had to be tough finding out someone was spying on their kids like that. Anything could be on those videos, floating around the darkest regions of the web.

Sergeant Norwood leaned close. "Nice job, Alvarez."

Her stomach churned. "Doesn't feel so nice."

"They'll catch the guy soon enough. The important thing is we know now. Can't change the past, but at least it's stopped."

"It's one thing to have your house broken into. Your stuff stolen. This, though, this takes feeling violated to a different level."

Norwood nodded and remained silent for a moment. "Maybe the guy kept all the files for personal use. He's obviously somewhat tech-savvy and would know uploading anything onto the net would only make it easier to catch him."

She took a deep breath and lowered her head. "Maybe."

"We do what we can."

"Should've seen it sooner. Nothing about these burglaries made any sense, but I kept on doing the same things I always do. A little more effort and I might've figured it out earlier. Saved at least a couple of girls from this mess."

"Look at me, Alvarez."

She kept her head angled toward the floor and rolled her eyes upward. "Sir?"

"Nobody puts in more hours than you do. I've been in Property Crimes for nearly sixteen years. If you think I'd have figured it out sooner than you did, you're wrong. I'd still be logging the reports and wondering what I was missing. You go down that what-if road and there's no turning back. And you think it's bad now? Wait until you get to Homicide. Second-guess things over there and you'll be blaming yourself for someone's death. I've seen plenty of cops go through that. Not enough drugs or alcohol or therapy to get past it. You hear me?"

She nodded. "So I'm getting transferred to Homicide?"

"One day. Can't say when, but I may be able to give you a little break from your usual duties now."

"Meaning?"

"Things will be slower for a bit now that this case is out of our hands. I'll talk to Lieutenant Spelling and see if he'll agree to let you spend some time shadowing his detectives. A week maybe. Give you a chance to see if you like it as much as you think you will."

"Not sure liking it is the right way to put it, but thanks."

"No promises. One more thing. I talked to Dotson this morning. He's got pneumonia."

Her mouth dried and she steadied herself. "That doesn't sound good."

"Well, it's not the best news, but they caught it early. Fluids, antibiotics, lots of bed rest. Said he'd have to stay in the hospital longer but didn't anticipate any further complications."

"They say anything about visitors?"

He shook his head. "Didn't ask either. Try not to get him all worked up, though."

"Understood. I know he likes having company, and all we do is watch TV anyway. Hey, Sarge, can I ask you something else?"

"Shoot."

"How come you never chew your gum when we're out in the field?"

He straightened his tie and smiled. "I'm a professional, Alvarez. Don't you forget it."

Starsky bowed and extended his arm toward the empty desk. "Welcome to Homicide where our motto is 'People are dying to give us more business.'"

Amara arched her eyebrows. "Thanks, I think. Dark humor, huh? Little early in the morning for that. And I'm only here on a temporary assignment."

"Precept number one. Every person in here had to find a way to deal with this job. Some ways are better than others. Me, I try to see the jocular side of things. It's cheaper than alcohol. Just ask my ex."

"Jokes, huh? Keep working on it. You'll get there. And when I get stressed, I talk to my iguana."

Starsky inclined his head and extended his arm again. "Well then. You'll fit in just fine. And nice job on that Leon Valley mess last week. Hope they lock the kid up for a long time. Might be safer on the inside than out where those girls' fathers are."

"Last I heard the DA was pushing to try him as an adult. Otherwise, juvie, therapy, and out in two."

"They going for sex offender status?"

She shrugged. "No idea. I'm out of the loop on it and want to keep it that way."

He pursed his lips. "Can't say as I blame you. That stuff makes my skin crawl. And crimes involving children are the worst."

"You ever get called out on a case with a kid victim?"

His shoulders sagged and he nodded. "More than once. Ask my ex about that too."

"Sorry."

"Part of the job. There's no picking and choosing your cases. When it's your turn, you go."

She forced a smile. "Got it. Sorry to start off the week on a downer. So what do you want me to do? You working a case now?"

"Nope. Catching up on paperwork, but I'm on deck for the next one. Won't have to wait long. Never do. You're welcome to join me when I get the call, or you can hang out here if you'd rather. Your choice."

"Why would I want to stay here?"

"You'd be surprised at what you can learn by reviewing closed cases. They give you an idea of what we're looking for in the field. Things are different in Homicide. You'll see."

"Can't be all that different from what I was doing. Stakes are higher, of course, but investigating is investigating, right?"

He handed her a couple of folders. "Oh, to be young and naive. Precept number two. This job is about the living, not the dead. We all want justice for the victims, but a murderer knows his life is on the line. No one wants to spend the rest of their days in prison or bide their time in Huntsville waiting for the needle. He'll do whatever it takes to avoid being caught, including killing again if necessary."

"Is this the part where you tell me to trust no one?"

"You'll see. Everybody lies, either intentionally or because of their skewed point of view. The witnesses. The suspects. Even the victims sometimes. Investigating a murder isn't like anything else. Every player has their own agenda."

"Fair enough. I'll work through these this morning."

He cleared his throat. "Alvarez, last thing. I'm serious. This job will change you. Make sure you're ready for that. Find a way to separate what happens here from everything else in your life. If you can't do that, there won't *be* anything else in your life."

She kept eye contact and took a slow, deep breath. "Sounds like I'll be upping my workouts."

He raised one eyebrow. "The healthy route, huh? I considered it, but when you've already got a body like this, well . . ."

"Uh-huh. Keep telling yourself that and one day you might believe it. Listen, since I'll be here all week, any chance of taking a peek at—"

"At the Philip Dragan file? Wondered how long before you'd bring it up. No problem. Grab a blank sheet of paper and stare at it for a while. That's his file. Officially, it's a closed case. If the guy we assume shot Dragan was still alive, there'd be enough to convict him."

"I get that, but nothing on Dragan in the database? Military, NCIS, anything? And what about the key we found?"

He scratched his cheek and yawned. "We're sure the name is right. Other than that, not much. His military file is heavily redacted. Probably involved in black ops. Discharged from the Marines years ago and no trace of him until he turned up here. No record of any family. No known address. And the key? Still looking for its mate, but by itself it's not enough to warrant keeping the file open."

"So why weren't his prints in the system?"

"You tell me. Maybe the government does it for the special forces' protection. In case they're captured or something."

"Did you ask?"

He slid off the desk and into his chair. "I did. Was told no one knew why the prints weren't on file."

"You believe that?"

He rolled his eyes. "I know I look young, but come on."

"So what's your theory?"

"My theory? That the case is closed and it will stay closed. The LT made that clear."

She turned on her laptop and watched as the computer went through its start-up routine. "Oh, come on. You've got to wonder."

"I do wonder, specifically about when I can get back to my paperwork."

She pulled her lips into her mouth. "Sorry."

He sipped his coffee and spent a few moments in silence before sighing. "Mercenary."

"What?"

"Mercenary. That's my theory. His past erased."

"Um, I guess I can see that, but why would a mercenary be in San Antonio? Obviously he wasn't on vacation."

"Got nothing else yet."

"Yet?"

"Precept number three. Get to work, Alvarez."

* * *

Wylie lay in his hospital bed. A tube ran from an IV bag to his arm and dripped a steady stream of fluid. "Everybody lies, huh? Seems like a cynical way to look at things."

"I don't know," Amara said. "I can see his point. Don't trust anything that isn't supported by the evidence."

He poked at the enchilada in the Styrofoam container before him. "Then I can honestly say I trust your mother's an excellent cook."

"If the nurse asks, you didn't get the food from me."

He held out his hands. "I'd never snitch on my dealer. Been thinking, though. The doc says it'd do me good to move around more. Might get me out of here sooner."

"Yeah?"

"Well, I thought maybe I could thank your mom in person. You know, next Saturday night."

She narrowed her eyes. "No way. Not until the doctors say you're okay, and even then, it's kind of a family thing and—"

"Hey, we're family, right? Don't you want to help me get out of here?"

"You want exercise? When you're released, I'll take you to my gym. Nothing strenuous. Promise."

"Your gym got enchiladas?"

"What are you up to? Sounds like trouble."

"I'm sick of this place. Need a break, even if it's only for a few hours. Plus, it'd give me a chance to tell your mom what a fine daughter she's got."

"Uh-huh."

"Now *you're* getting cynical. Forget it. I'll stay here. Let my bed-sores fester."

She laughed and rolled her eyes. "I'll think about it. When the doc tells me you can get out for a while, we'll figure something out. No funny business, though."

"I'm a sickly old man, Alvarez. What could I possibly do?"

"That's what scares me."

He took another bite of the enchilada. "So what're you going to do?"

"I told you I'd think about it."

"Not that. The Dragan thing. Not going to leave it alone, are you?"

"Can't. Not sure what to do, but I can't abandon it."

"You think there's a connection between Dragan and Cotulla? Prove it."

"Dragan might as well not even exist, and that accident's been looked at from every possible angle, and by people with a lot more experience than me. What exactly am I supposed to prove?"

He pointed his fork at her. "That you're right and all those other people are wrong."

"You believe that?"

"Doesn't matter. Do you?"

Maybe. Probably. Yes. "Enough talk. Can we get back to the show?"

"You remember what was going on?"

"Vaguely. Mary slept with the Turkish guy and he died in her bed, so she and her mother and Anna moved him back to his room, but Daisy saw them carrying the body and now Mary knows it's her sister who's spreading the rumors."

Wylie chuckled. "I think you'll do just fine in Homicide."

"Hurry up. Maybe we can get through two episodes before I have to go."

"What's your rush? Savor the ambience. Enjoy every scene. We can watch more tomorrow."

She wiped enchilada from the corner of his mouth. "Savor the ambience? *Who are you?* And what have you done with Wylie?"

He patted his stomach. "You gonna talk or you gonna watch?"

She settled back in her chair and propped her feet on the edge of the bed. "Hit the play button, guvna."

23 **Copies of all the** files from the Cotulla accident were kept in storage with the rest of Homicide's closed cases. Most likely, the originals were stashed away in a vault somewhere in DC. The FBI's, if she had to guess. The incident had been officially classified as a mass murder since the bus driver had intentionally pulled in front of the train. The San Antonio PD was the agency of record in the case, even though the crime occurred in another county. As the scope of the tragedy had revealed itself, all parties had agreed that the SAPD had more tools and manpower, and therefore would handle the investigation for the state. Normally the Feds would've taken charge, but there was no one left to prosecute. Everyone was dead.

Amara told Starsky she planned to stay in the office all day and review old cases. She hadn't told him which ones. Hadn't needed to.

She scrutinized the dozens of banker boxes in the room. Most of the major documents had been scanned into the system and were available for her to review online, but everything else sat here. No way she wanted to sign out this much stuff, even if the clerk would let her. And toting all of it back to her desk? No thanks.

Start at the beginning. The cause of the incident. Bradley Gingham, the bus driver.

His file was surprisingly thin. She pulled the folder from the box, stopped to sign it out, then carried the paperwork upstairs. A couple of detectives sat at their desks making phone calls and scratching notes on legal pads. One of the overhead fluorescents flickered and buzzed. Other than that, the place was reasonably quiet.

She emptied the folder's contents on her desk and read the initial reports. Bradley Gingham, white male, forty-three years old. Never married, no known children. Joined the Marine Corps straight from high school, where he'd been a C-average student. Did his four-year stint, including time in the Gulf War. Raised by a single mother who died of liver cancer six months prior to the Cotulla incident. No brothers, sisters, or other known family.

They'd tried to find enough of his remains to test for drugs and alcohol but were unsuccessful. No surprise there. The combination of the collision and fireball had reduced most of the wreckage— bus, train, and human—to fragments and ashes.

Gingham left a suicide note on his dresser, a rambling diatribe covering everything from his inability to hold a job to blaming Obamacare for his mother's death to nightmares about his brief time in the military. No mention of his intention to take a busload of kids with him. Handwriting experts confirmed Gingham wrote the note.

His military record was undistinguished, but he'd received an honorable discharge. He'd served with the Seventh Marine Expeditionary Brigade, a unit that had seen extensive action in both Desert Shield and Desert Storm, but like most of the Allied forces, they'd only suffered a handful of casualties. The Iraqis were a different story. They'd died by the thousands, and Gingham doubtless had seen some of the carnage.

A list of his past jobs, at least the ones they could find, stretched nearly a full page. Grocery store, day labor, lawn service, home construction. Mechanic, liquor store, garbageman, bus driver. Second year working for the school district. Commercial driver's license was current. Never selected for random drug and alcohol testing.

A few copies of photos lay scattered among the documents. Nothing special. Pictures of government IDs mixed in with photographs of the home he shared with his mother. A couple of shots from his time in the military. Standing with some buddies beside a tank. Stretched out on a cot inside a tent with a cigarette dangling from his mouth. Like looking in a time capsule.

The report from the forensic psychologist was nearly a dozen pages long. She skimmed the first page, yawned, and flipped to the last one. The doctor's summary said Gingham's PTSD had been activated by the loss of his mother, the only stabilizing force in his life. It was likely the man had frequent breaks with reality and possibly abused drugs, though no evidence of this had been found at his home. As to whether Gingham knew the full consequences of what he was doing when he pulled the bus into the train's path, the psychologist had no opinion. Entirely possible Gingham thought he was alone on the bus.

The rest of the paperwork consisted of nothing more than snippets of the man's life. A sentence here, a paragraph there. Interviews with neighbors and coworkers and old acquaintances from school and the service, none of which shed any light on Gingham. No friends, no favorite spots. A homebody who took care of his aging mother.

Amara straightened the pile of documents. A man's whole life reduced to a few sheets of paper. The public's hatred heaped upon this worst of murderers: the child killer. He had to be insane. Had to be. No one else could do something like this.

She shuddered at the thought of the kids seeing the train. Their final second on earth one of immense fear. How could a parent ever deal with something like that? No wonder Marisa Reyes grasped at straws. Anything was better than this. And to not be able to vent your anger on the culprit? No one left to scream at? You don't get over that. Ever.

She dragged her finger through the stack and found the photos of the young Bradley Gingham in Kuwait. Where had it gone so wrong? Did he know what he was doing when he pulled in front of that freight train? Questions that would never be answered now. Not by her or anyone else. She slid the pictures into the folder and patted her hand on them.

What next? Who else was there to investigate? The train engineers? Pointless. Philip Dragan? Even if she could find more information on him, what would it accomplish? Give Mrs. Reyes some peace? Maybe, if it explained why he'd left the note on Caterina Delacruz's mom's windshield. But Homicide didn't deal with such questions.

She smoothed her fingers over the photo at the top of the stack. Half a dozen young men grinning, shirts off, cigarettes and water bottles in hand. Dwarfed by the battle tank they leaned against. One of them destined to kill a busload of kids. The rest? Who knew. Doctors or drug dealers. Truckers or teachers. CPAs or—

A very pointed nose.

She picked up the photo and held it to the light. No. Maybe? Add gray hair and a mustache? She tilted her head and squinted, then clicked her mouse a few times to pull up a picture on her monitor.

Hard to tell. Could be, but the snapshot was so old. She grabbed a blank sheet of paper and ripped off pieces to cover everything on the photo except one face. Though much younger, it was a match with the one on her computer screen.

In front of the khaki-painted tank, standing next to Bradley Gingham, his arm draped across his friend's shoulders, was Philip Dragan.

24

Starsky peered at the photo again and whistled. "That's one big coincidence."

Amara nodded. "I can't sit still. The crime lab says their equipment's not near as good as what the Feds use, so they're sending the images up to DC. Could be days before we know for sure. Maybe longer."

"Not really. You already know, don't you?"

"Yeah. Think about what that means. The double homicide, the bus driver's suicide note, everything's back in play once we get official confirmation. And if this *is* some sort of connection, a conspiracy even, what does that mean for the Cotulla accident? I mean, if it was intentional, if there's more to it than a psycho bus driver—"

He held up both hands. "Whoa, there. Slow down. You're getting ahead of yourself. Suppose the two were simply old friends? Dragan happened to be in town visiting Gingham and it triggered PTSD or whatever? Or maybe Dragan lives around here and drove to Cotulla after the incident because he recognized Gingham's name?"

She shook her head. "The Cotulla photo shows Dragan there shortly after the accident. Gingham's name hadn't been released yet."

"So he knew his old buddy drove a school bus down that way and wanted to make sure he was okay. You can come up with a dozen scenarios that don't have anything to do with a conspiracy theory. In lieu of evidence to the contrary, the official version of events will stand. For both the double homicide here in San Antonio and the accident down in Cotulla."

"So you think I'm wrong?"

He dragged a hand through his tangled red hair. "Wrong? No, but not right yet either. There's enough to keep digging. The question is whether or not you'll be allowed to—"

Her phone buzzed and she held up a finger. "Hello, Mrs. Reyes. Uh-huh. Really? Well, that's good news, I suppose. Oh, um, I'm not sure. Friends? No. I mean, I met him once but—Yeah, I can do that. Okay. A day or two? Sure. You too. Bye."

Starsky raised his eyebrows.

"Good news," Amara said. "At least I think it is. The Reyeses got approval to exhume Benjamin's body. They're moving him to the cemetery closer to their current home and going to get a DNA sample when that happens."

He exhaled loudly and stared at the floor for a moment before making eye contact. "What do you think's going to happen, Alvarez?"

"What do you mean?"

"Step back. Look at this as an outsider. What do you see?"

"I see a string of coincidences that add up to something. I just don't know what yet."

He nodded and clasped his hands in his lap. "Okay. Good. What else?"

"More questions than answers?"

"Nope. Try again. You could say that about anything. Narrow your focus. Put yourself in my shoes. What do you see?"

"Um, a shortish, attractive Hispanic detective who wants to make a name for herself?"

He laughed and ran a hand across his mouth. "Yes, but let's talk about Cotulla."

So he thinks I'm attractive? Interesting. "Okay. I see a horrible incident with a bunch of dead kids. Parents left behind to live in their grief."

"Good. I mean, not good, but correct. So, from a detective's point of view, what's the problem here?"

She rubbed her forehead.

He leaned forward. "You're personally involved, Alvarez. You have a vested interest in the outcome of the case. Right or wrong, it's going to taint everything you do."

Heat flooded her face. "That's not true. I keep everything—"

"Is Benjamin dead or alive?"

A weight hit her shoulders. "What?"

"Simple question. Is the boy dead or alive?"

Confusion flooded her mind. "I—I don't know. How could I?"

"That's what I'm saying. For me, it's easy. Benjamin's dead. The accident was investigated and resolved. I have no personal stake in the case."

"But with all this new information that's come to light, doesn't that change things?"

"There." He pointed at her and nodded. "That's what you see. Hope things aren't as we thought. But what I see is a boy in a coffin unless there's definitive proof otherwise. Yeah, I'm skeptical, but isn't that what being a detective is all about?"

She stood and placed her hands on her hips. "Of course I hope he's alive. How could I not? If there's the slightest chance—"

"Then what? We should chase after every hint of a clue, no matter how small? In a perfect world, yeah, maybe. But for a case that's already considered solved by every law enforcement agency in the country? Look, I'm not trying to discourage you. Just being realistic, that's all. You hope he's alive. Of course you do. But hope's a dangerous thing, Alvarez. It can rip you apart. Tough to go through. Tough to watch someone else go through."

"I don't care what you say. This is worth investigating."

"And I agree completely."

She crinkled her nose and tilted her head. "So all this . . . ?"

"I'm only asking you to think this through. It's fine to have theories, just don't let them get in the way of the facts."

"So what do you suggest?"

"Find the evidence. Photos won't cut it. Any shred of proof something was missed in the official investigation."

She frowned. "If Benjamin's DNA isn't in that coffin—"

"It proves nothing. His bones got mixed up. The fragments are too small. The DNA decayed. Probably a dozen other reasons. That's not what I'm worried about, though."

"No?"

"Amara, what if his DNA *is* in there? You still going to doubt the boy's dead?"

She tugged at her bottom lip, then frowned.

He stood, walked to her, and placed a hand on her shoulder. "See, *that's* what hope does to you."

The red leather squeaked as Amara leaned forward. Why did she still feel the urge to point out the chair made the noise, not her? Dr. Pritchard didn't look up from the form he'd been studying for the last few minutes.

"And you're certain she wants to go through with this?" the ME asked.

"I am. There's no talking her out of it. She wants another DNA test done."

His stomach grumbled and he glanced at his watch. "Snack time." He grabbed a bag of Cheetos from his desk, tore it open, and dumped the contents into a red plastic cup. "Would you like some? I've got another bag here. I must caution you these are the spicy ones. Flamin' Hot. Like dropping the *g* somehow makes them seem, what? Hotter? No, don't think so. More relatable? Who relates to Cheetos anyway?"

"Um, no, thank you. Not hungry."

"Suit yourself." He rummaged through his desk drawer and pulled out a thin white paper packet, ripped off the end, and slid out a pair of cheap wooden chopsticks. "Only way to eat them. Otherwise your fingers are orange and sticky all day."

"Uh-huh. Anyhow, Mrs. Reyes wondered if maybe you'd do the DNA test for her. You handled the original examinations from the accident, so we—she thought you'd already have an idea of what to expect."

"And she's aware of the chaos involved in the investigation of a scene such as the one in which her son perished?"

"If you mean does she know that there wasn't much left and it's possible the bone fragments got mixed up, then yes."

He nodded, peered into the cup, and maneuvered the chopsticks until he found the Cheeto he wanted. "Gotcha." He plopped the orange concoction into his mouth and crunched before eating two more and showing her his hands. "See? Clean as a whistle. And no."

"No?"

"No, I won't do the DNA test. She doesn't want me to."

"Yes, she does. She wanted me to ask you."

He selected his next Cheeto and examined the snack as if it were the finest sushi in San Antonio. "Keeps all that mess off your lips too. Tell her to find someone else to do the testing."

"Can I ask why?"

He pointed his chopsticks at her. "First, we don't do DNA testing here, at least at the level she will want. The need to use DNA to identify remains is not as common as one might think. The required equipment is quite expensive and we don't have the funds. We do collect the specimens, but the actual extraction work is outsourced. There's a second reason, and I bet you know what it is, Detective."

She pushed back in her seat and the leather squeaked again.

"Think about it," he said. "Tell you what. I've got six, seven Cheetos left. When they're gone, I've got to get back to work. Got a woman from New Braunfels waiting on me. Husband says she fell down the stairs. Local PD's not so sure. A couple of domestic calls in the last year. You've got seven Cheetos to figure out why I won't help. I like that. Maybe it should become a new form of time measurement. How long will it take to do the autopsy? Oh, this one will be quick, maybe three hundred Cheetos."

Ugh. A guessing game? *En serio?* She scratched her arm, then opened her mouth but had nothing to say.

He took a bite. "Six Cheetos."

"Doctor, I'm not clear on—"

"Five Cheetos. Come on, you know this. I'll give you a hint. You've already told me why I won't do the test."

She tapped her finger on her bottom lip. She'd told him? But—

"Uh-oh. Three left. I cheated and ate two. Maybe that's why they're called Cheetos?"

The only things I've even said are—oh. I'm an idiot.

"Two Cheetos."

"You can't do the DNA test because you did the original examinations."

He smiled and finished off his snack. "Care to elaborate?"

"If Mrs. Reyes suspects there's something worth looking into, it would be better if no one from the original investigation was involved this time around. Makes it easier to rule out any potential issues."

He slid the chopsticks into their paper sleeve before dropping it and the plastic cup into the trash can. "Carry her logic to its conclusion. If her child's DNA *was* misidentified, barring the extremely remote chance of an error in the process, it would have to be intentional, correct? What purpose could be served in this case by providing a false DNA match? Nothing aboveboard, certainly. Therefore, it stands to reason that if Mrs. Reyes is right, someone deliberately tampered with the sample. And since this department conducted the initial evidence collection . . . ?"

"Someone here could be involved."

He stood and pointed at himself. "Maybe even me. If we did the tests for this woman, what's to keep her from reasoning this person simply manipulated the facts once again?"

She stood and nodded. "Sorry to waste your time, Doctor. I appreciate your help. Won't bother you again."

"Bother? Of course not. I quite enjoy our little tête-à-têtes. Do keep me informed on your progress."

"You think there's something to this?"

He opened his desk drawer and reached inside. "What? No, of course not. I do, however, believe it is possible our young lady from New Braunfels met her demise prematurely. I'm extremely eager to get a peek at her hyoid. Would you like a Tic Tac?"

"Uh, no. Her hyoid?"

"New to Homicide, aren't you?" He tilted his head back and pointed to the top of his neck. "U-shaped bone here. If it's broken, could indicate strangulation, hanging, a few other things. Ask around or look it up. I'd stay and chat, but my Cheetos are gone. Have a pleasant day, Detective."

"Yeah, you too, Doc."

26 As usual on a Saturday morning, people packed the Breakfast Bodega for their weekly dose of everything from huevos rancheros to biscuits and gravy. Amara struggled to control her thoughts amid the noise. Her temporary assignment to Homicide had ended. She hated to say the week had been fun, but it was, at least in a way. The time had flown and she dreaded her return to Property Crimes on Monday. The work seemed so monotonous after the things she'd done these past several days.

Starsky had been a great mentor, even allowing her to sit in on an interrogation with a suspect. One day, that'd be her. One day soon. She'd reviewed at least a dozen closed cases and learned more than she could've dreamed. Protecting the crime scene, looking beyond the obvious for anything out of the ordinary, the unintentional deceptions of eyewitnesses. And the importance of circumstantial evidence. How the smallest things, when tied together properly, made for a compelling case against the suspect. And how sometimes, your best guess was the best you could do. Let the DA and a jury decide.

The report hadn't filtered back from DC yet, but she was confident Philip Dragan was the man in the photo next to Bradley Gingham. What that meant, no one seemed to know. She'd been told the possible connection was being "looked into" by someone to determine the relevance to either Dragan's murder or the Cotulla accident. She'd asked to be kept in the loop, and the response had been noncommittal. The whole thing reminded her of her dad's favorite movie, *Raiders of the Lost Ark*. She'd seen the film so many times she practically had it memorized. *"We've got top men working on it right now." "Who?" "Top. Men."*

Mrs. Reyes had understood and agreed with the medical examiner's decision not to do the DNA testing. It complicated matters a bit, since the laws were somewhat gray when it came to the rights of the deceased, but the Reyeses assumed a "don't ask, don't tell" policy. Depending on the results, that could change. A private company would do the testing and have answers a couple of days after retrieving the samples. The exhumation would likely take place within a week, two at the most.

And Wylie was headed home next week. His fever was gone and the pneumonia was no longer a serious threat. The doctors said he'd need to do rehab for at least a month before clearing him to return to work. He was practically giddy at the prospect of getting out of the hospital. They'd agreed to continue the *Downton Abbey*–watching parties, though. She told him the only reason she put up with the show was to keep him occupied. He was a good enough detective not to believe her.

She'd talked to his doctor and received permission for a special excursion tonight. Dinner with her family at Mama's. She'd let the topic die and he'd never brought it up again. This would be his first venture outside since the shooting, and he had no clue. She'd surprise him with the news later this afternoon.

"What's so funny?" Ronnie, the diner's weekend manager, asked.

"Nothing. Just planning my day."

"Does your day include freeing up this booth so I can get some paying customers in here?"

"Hey, I pay."

"Not full price, you don't."

She smiled and draped her arm across the back of the booth.

"It's always such a pleasure to see you, Ronnie. I think I need my coffee warmed up, if you don't mind."

He glanced around and raised his mug before sitting across from her. A waitress stopped and poured them each some coffee. He nodded his thanks and dumped sugar into the cup. "Wouldn't be a Saturday if we didn't go through our little ritual, huh?"

"Nope," she said. "Don't feel like my day's started until I've had a chance to annoy you. Highlight of my week."

He chuckled. "You need to get out more."

"No thanks. I get out plenty as it is. How's Anna?"

"Eh, same as always. Decided she wants another kid. Three's plenty, I told her. Can barely feed the ones we've got, you know?"

She sipped her coffee. "You take care of her, hear me? No way you'd ever find another woman to put up with you."

"Yeah? You an expert on relationships now? Wonderful. Tell me all about your boyfriend. Still imaginary, is he?"

"I'm waiting to find someone I'm compatible with."

He laughed and pushed his coffee cup away. "Compatible? What's that supposed to mean? You see me and Anna? She's a skinny Catholic girl from Mexico. I'm an overweight ex-Buddhist from Oregon. It wasn't exactly love at first sight, you know?"

"Not like I'm crying myself to sleep every night, and I've done the marriage thing already."

He shook his head and slid out of the seat. "Not a thing wrong with what you're doing. You don't have to prove anything to anyone. Everybody knows you're tough enough to handle life on your own. What you've got to decide is whether you *want* to do that. My two cents? Don't give up on finding someone."

She blew in her cup before taking another drink. "Therapy session over for this week?"

He knocked on the table. "Same time next Saturday?"

"Wouldn't miss it."

Amara tapped on the hospital room door and nudged it open. "You decent?"

"Depends on your definition," Wylie said. "Come on in."

He sat in the chair beside the bed, free of any tubes or other entanglements, barefoot and wearing striped pajamas.

"Well," she said. "Look at you. All dressed up and no place to go."

"Nurses made me put these on. Said they had too many complaints of me wandering the hall in my hospital gown."

She winced and shook her head. "There's an image I'll lose sleep over. Your white backside moving up and down the hall. Ugh."

"Well, there's the problem. I must've had the gown on backwards."

She snorted and leaned against the wall. "So what've you got going on tonight?"

He held up a DVD cover. "Things are about to get very interesting at the manor."

"I bet they are, but how about we get out of here for a little while?"

"You mean like the cafeteria?"

"I mean like dinner with my family. If you think you're up to the ride, that is."

He pushed on the chair's arms and stood. "Up to it? Race you to the car."

"Not so fast. Doctor says you can go only if you ride in a wheelchair. Doesn't want you ripping open his handiwork."

"No problem. But once we're out of the hospital, I don't want—"

"You'll do what I say or you'll stay here. Got it?"

"Oh, c'mon. You know how to kill a party, don't you?"

The pair made a quick stop at Wylie's for fresh clothes, then arrived at Amara's mother's house as the twilight darkened and a half-moon shone. After initial protest, Wylie plopped into his wheelchair, crossed his arms, and pouted as she bypassed the front door and pushed him into the backyard.

An oversize wooden picnic table, covered in a lacy white cloth, sat under a mesquite tree. Next to that was a card table with plastic seats circled around. A faded blue cooler and a scattering of lawn chairs, all occupied, were off to the side. Five kids hollered and chased each other through the yard. Strings of colored lights ran from the tree to the house.

Amara bent down to Wylie. "My brothers and sisters and their spouses and kids. Mom's probably in the kitchen."

One of the crowd spotted them and jumped up. "Hey, big sis. This the guy?"

"Everyone," Amara said, "this is Wylie Dotson, a friend of mine from work. Go easy on him, okay? He's old, slow, and got shot a couple of weeks ago. I'll let you introduce yourselves if you want, but don't be offended if he doesn't remember your name. Touch of Alzheimer's, I think."

Wylie started to stand and Amara planted her hands on his shoulders and shoved him back down.

"If he tries to get out of this chair," she said, "we're out of here. I'm serious, guys. No funny business." She pointed to one of the women. "Selina, you're in charge of him if I'm not out here."

The dark-haired woman stood and saluted. "*Sí, mi hermana.*"

"*Hermana?*" Wylie asked.

"Smarter, more beautiful sister."

"Uh-huh," Wylie said. "Somehow I think you embellished that a bit."

Selina took the handles of the wheelchair and rolled him over to the group. "Our visitor understands you, *sister*. Now, you go help Mama," she said. "We'll take care of your guest."

Amara narrowed her eyes. "Selina . . ."

The woman raised one hand. "Best behavior. Promise."

Wylie opened the cooler and grabbed a drink. "Best behavior? Not much of a party then, is it?"

The others laughed and Selina grinned. "I like him."

Amara rolled her eyes and shook her head. "That's because you don't know him yet."

The back screen door opened and a woman stepped into the yard with three large bowls balanced on her arms. "Aren't you going to introduce me to our guest?"

Amara took one of the bowls and inclined her head toward the group. "Mama, this is Wylie Dotson. Wylie, this is my mom, Maria."

Mama placed the food on the table, wiped her hands on her apron, and walked to her guest. "Nice to meet you, Mr. Dotson."

Wylie pushed himself up and extended his hand. "Wylie, please, ma'am. And the pleasure's all mine. I'm glad to finally meet the young lady responsible for all the food I've been stealing from your daughter."

"Sit down, Wylie," Amara said. "You know the rules."

He sank into his wheelchair. "You see how she treats me?"

Mama smiled and nodded toward Amara. "Don't take it personally. She's always been the bossy one."

The siblings laughed and chimed in with their agreement.

"If you'll excuse me," Mama said, "I've got a few things to finish up in the kitchen. Make yourself at home."

"Thank you, ma'am. Is there anything I can do to help?"

"Sí. Relax and enjoy yourself."

He toasted her with his cold drink. "Way ahead of you."

Amara stifled her grin while the others laughed. Her mother smiled and returned to the house.

Wylie scooted straighter in his wheelchair. "Your mom's a nice lady."

"Can be," Amara said, "but we've got some stories from our younger days that would—"

"Yeah," Selina said. "I can still feel the flyswatter on the back of my legs. Fastest we ever ran home."

One of the brothers shifted forward and grabbed another drink from the cooler. "What about the time I drank three Slurpees at the 7-Eleven and then put the cup back in the stack? The cashier said he was calling the cops or my mother. I begged him to let me go to jail."

Wylie angled himself closer. "So what happened?"

"The guy said the cops would just take me home in the back of a police car. Either way, my mother was going to find out. I gave him our number and Mama showed up in about ten minutes. She paid the man and asked him what the worst job at the store was." He shook his head. "Dirtiest bathrooms I ever cleaned."

Amara cleared her throat and stepped behind Wylie's wheelchair. "Let's not air our dirty laundry in public. To the table. It's about time to eat."

"What's the matter?" Selina asked. "Don't want Wylie to hear some of the things Detective Amara Alvarez did when she was growing up?"

"It's not that at all. I simply—"

"Actually," Wylie said, "I'd be quite interested in hearing those stories. My lips would be sealed, of course."

Amara playfully smacked him on the back of the head and pushed him to the end of the table. "Sealed lips. Right."

Mama brought out a huge plate of enchiladas and placed them in the center of the other dishes. She then pointed at each food and explained it to Wylie. "These are beef enchiladas, covered in cheese and a chili sauce. A little spicy. That corn on the cob is called *elote* in Mexico, and around it we have salt, lime, butter, sour cream, and cheese mayonnaise. Choose any or all of the toppings and don't be shy about it. That's guacamole, of course, and over there in the green bowl is *pozole*. It's a chicken soup with hominy and a lot of different herbs. You can top it with onion or lime or radishes. No wrong way to eat it, really."

"It all looks and smells delicious," Wylie said. "I can't thank you enough for letting me join your family this evening."

"Nonsense. You can thank me by eating your fill."

A grin spread across his face. "Now, *that* I can do."

A couple of hours later, the meal wound down. Amara and Selina chatted in the kitchen as they rinsed dishes and Tupperwared the leftovers. It'd been a good night and Wylie had, for the most part, behaved. Time to get him back to the hospital. Didn't want to wear him out.

She pushed the curtains aside and stood on tiptoe to see out the window over the sink. He was in his wheelchair under the tree next to her mother. Each of them sipped a drink and seemed to be having a good time. Wylie said something and Mama covered her mouth and laughed. Amara smiled. Nothing like these Saturday night family dinners. No matter what her week—

When did Mama change her clothes? She never wore a dress except on Sunday.

The two laughed again and Mama leaned over and placed her hand on Wylie's forearm.

Amara's eyes widened.

"Are you even listening to me?" Selina asked.

Wylie patted her mother's hand, whispered something, and the two laughed again.

Oh, no.

28

Amara shuffled into the station early Monday morning. She was in no hurry to return to her work in Property Crimes, but her stack of pending paperwork would be taller than she was by now. Plus, Norwood would have new cases waiting for her and she hated starting off behind the curve. She stood outside the door to her department and inhaled deeply.

It's all mental. Get a good attitude. Make a difference.

She pasted a smile on her face and stepped into the room. Her boss was already there and she waved at him.

He stared for a moment, then hurried toward her. "Alvarez, don't you check your voice mails?"

Her smile evaporated as quickly as her attitude. "Good morning to you too, Sergeant Norwood." She checked her phone and saw the message waiting indicator. "Sorry. When did you call?"

"Last night. You're supposed to be in a meeting that started ten minutes ago up in the chief's office. Don't blame this on me."

The chief's office? This early? "What's going on?"

"You're now eleven minutes late. Go!"

Amara trotted down the hall and up the steps. She'd met the chief once or twice, but only in passing. Ethan Johnson had been the head of the PD for almost a decade. He'd moved up the ranks quickly, and most cops liked him. Some thought he had his sights set on being mayor one day, but he denied any such aspirations, as any decent politician would. His claim of being a second nephew, twice removed, of LBJ had been refuted many times, but that didn't stop him from swearing it to be true.

The receptionist wasn't in yet, so Amara bypassed her desk and tapped on the door. No response, so she knocked louder.

"That you, Alvarez?"

"Yes, sir."

"Come on in."

She stepped into Chief Johnson's office and waited just inside the door. "I'm sorry I'm late, sir. I failed to—"

"Sit." He waved her to a seat across from his desk. "We're waiting on someone else too. A Ranger coming in from Waco. Should be here any minute."

She sat on the edge of the chair and placed her hands in her lap. "Sir, may I ask what this is about?"

He held up a Starbucks cup. "Want some coffee while we wait? Only take me a minute to make a fresh pot."

"No, thank you."

"Nice work on the Leon Valley case."

"Thank you, sir, but I had a lot of help from—"

He raised his index finger. "Never be afraid to take credit for your work, Detective. There are plenty of people who'd be happy to share in the glory, deserving or not. Humility has its time and place. Sitting in front of me isn't one of them."

"Yes, sir."

Two loud knocks echoed from the door and the Ranger stepped into the room. Late forties, wearing a white shirt, black tie, khakis, and cowboy boots. Leather belt with an oversize buckle shaped like Texas, a star-in-a-wheel Ranger badge, and a tan cattleman hat in hand. Skin slightly less leathery than the belt. Too much time in the sun. A stereotypical Texas Ranger, except this one had long blonde hair and pale red lipstick. A woman.

The chief stood and gestured to the chair beside Amara. "Ranger Colby, have a seat. Amara Alvarez, Sara Colby. That'll have to do for introductions for now. Am I correct in assuming neither of you knows why you're here?"

The women glanced at each other and nodded.

"Good. Ranger Colby, you'll receive a call sometime this morning placing you on special assignment alongside Detective Alvarez. The two of you will be based out of this facility. I'll get you an office set up later this week. In the meantime, what we're discussing stays between the people in this room, clear?"

Amara's heart raced and she squeezed her fingers into fists.

The chief continued. "Questions have arisen. You two will work together to find the answers to those questions. There may be nothing to them. In fact, you are to approach your investigation with full skepticism. As if no crime was even committed."

"Sir," the Ranger said, "what's going on?"

Chief Johnson dropped his Starbucks cup into the trash. "You two are reopening Cotulla."

Ranger Colby studied Amara and then turned to the chief. "Cotulla? As in the accident?"

Chief Johnson inclined his head toward Amara. "Detective Alvarez here made a connection that was missed—no, that's not the right word. Impossible to see the link back then. But we see it now and feel it's worthy of further investigation."

"What's changed?" the Ranger asked.

"Philip Dragan." Johnson pointed to Amara. "Give her the short version. You'll have time later to go into detail."

"Yes, sir. A man we later identified as Mr. Dragan was recently the victim of a double homicide here. Photos from the Cotulla accident scene show him there shortly after the incident occurred. He also left a cryptic note on the windshield of a car belonging to one of the Cotulla victims' parents. The school bus driver we thought was responsible for the collision had a picture of himself with his buddies in the Gulf War. One of those men looked like he could be—"

"He is," the chief said. "The man in the photo's been confirmed as Dragan. He served in the same unit as the bus driver for a brief time. So you can see why we have some questions, Ranger."

"I do. Sir, I'm not sure you have the right person, though. I know virtually nothing of Cotulla. I've only been with the Rangers for a year and a half. There are plenty of others who were around when—"

Chief Johnson held up his hand. "It's why you were chosen by your sergeant, and I agreed completely. You'll have no bias in the investigation. No opinions. No doubt she'll deny it, but even Detective Alvarez here is somewhat hopeful there's something to be found. You'll be her sounding board, as well as the link to any state resources we may require. In effect, you'll counter Alvarez's history with the people and evidence."

"Sir," Amara said, "any preconceived notions I may have will not impact the investigation. I assure you my mind is open to any and all outcomes, including the possibility there's nothing new to discover here."

The chief chuckled. "I'm not accusing you of anything, Detective. You have my full confidence. However, I wouldn't be doing my job if I didn't cover all the bases. In a situation like this, best to have more than one set of eyes. Someone from outside the force, even better."

"Sir," Ranger Colby said, "if I may ask, why the need for such secrecy?"

"Too much potential for damage. If word gets out we're taking another look at Cotulla, theories will run rampant. Everything from government conspiracies to UFOs. Won't do anyone any good, least of all the parents of those dead kids."

Amara slid back in her chair. "That's not the only reason, is it, sir?"

"Enlighten me, Alvarez."

"Cotulla was a closed case. Everything all tied up and filed away in storage boxes. If there's something new, something that changes even one little part of the incident, then there's the possibility everything we know about the accident is wrong. Everything."

The chief tapped his fingers together. "And?"

"And if everything we know about Cotulla *is* wrong, then more than one or two people must be involved. Have to be. It's too big. Death on a mass scale and for what? No terrorist claims. Nothing missing from the scene. If Cotulla was more than a nut job pulling a busload of kids in front of a train, it changes everything. And something like that would involve people with power. People who'd have the resources to know about things like a criminal investigation."

"Very good," Chief Johnson said. "But if that were true, how do you know I'm not involved?"

"We don't," Sara said.

Johnson clicked his tongue. "And that's why you're here, Ranger. You two will have complete autonomy in your investigation. Be thorough, but don't drag your feet. The longer it takes, the more likely word gets out. All the old files will be at your disposal. Recheck the evidence, and reinterview if you feel it's absolutely necessary. I'd prefer no one involved in the original investigation is contacted but understand if that can't be avoided."

Amara nodded. "Concerned about involvement from someone on the force?"

"Better to keep the investigations separate as much as possible. If we did miss something the first time around, we need to make sure it wasn't intentional. Sergeant Norwood has been told you're on special assignment. That's all he needs to know. You two will report directly to me, preferably off-site. For today, go somewhere away from here and get acquainted. Alvarez, bring her up to speed on everything you know about the case. That'll be all. And I'll remind you to discuss this with no one else unless you have my permission, understood?"

Both women yessir'd him and stood to leave.

"Sir," Ranger Colby said, "should we expect any immediate threat or danger?"

He hesitated before answering. "I'm not sure I understand your question."

"If you were us," Sara said, "would you be looking over your shoulder?"

Chief Johnson turned back to his computer. "Ask Philip Dragan."

"Probably a good idea," Amara said, "if you wait in the car. I don't want to have to explain to the Reyeses who you are."

"Agreed," Sara said. "Take your time. I can work on the laptop. If they see me, I'm a new detective training with you. Leave the car running, though. Seven in the morning and already ninety-two. Got to love Texas."

Amara dropped the air conditioner a couple of degrees. "A new detective? Yeah, no one's going to buy that unless you lose the cowboy hat. The boots too."

Sara grinned. "Not going to happen. Fought too hard to wear this getup. People should know a Ranger when they see one."

Three days since the two had been thrown together to investigate Cotulla, and this morning the body of Benjamin Reyes, or what remained of it, would be exhumed and transferred to a new cemetery. Prior to the move, DNA samples would be taken by a private company out of Illinois. Marisa Reyes had invited Amara in whatever capacity she chose to come: detective or friend. She'd decided on both.

The grave was open and a new coffin waited beside the hole. The parents stood with three men Amara didn't know, and she walked to the small group. Off to the side, two workers lingered beside a backhoe with chains attached to its boom, waiting for permission to lift the coffin from the burial vault. Marisa Reyes walked away from her husband and met Amara halfway.

The woman dabbed at her eyes with a tissue. "Thank you for coming, Detective. It means a lot."

"Of course. You doing okay?"

"This is harder than I expected. Brings up a lot of emotions I hoped were gone."

Amara hugged her. "Is there anything I can do?"

"We've run into a little bit of a situation. That taller man in the windbreaker is the parish priest. We didn't expect him to be here."

"Is that a problem?"

She sniffled and pulled a new tissue from her purse. "He's here in case we need anything. Counseling or whatever. The man in the suit is from a funeral home. He's responsible for overseeing the transfer. The other man is Mr. Logan from the DNA company. He recommended we tell the priest he's a family friend. Otherwise, there could be complications."

"Complications? Like what?"

"Um, we had to get approval from the priests in both parishes to relocate the casket. They were concerned about the sanctity of the body. Wanted to make sure the process honored that."

"And they don't know you're planning to extract DNA from the bones."

Mrs. Reyes nodded once. "But Mr. Logan said it wouldn't take long to do once he found some good, uh, candidates, he called them. A tooth, a piece of bone that's not too badly damaged, something like that. And it would be best if he could get three or four samples in case the remains did get mixed up."

"Mrs. Reyes, I don't know much about the process, but shouldn't it be done in—"

"He's taking the bones with him, Detective."

Amara's eyes widened and she brushed her hand across the beads of sweat on her upper lip. "Is that even legal?"

"I wasn't supposed to tell you, but now I don't know what to do. Mr. Logan says it's a gray area. We had to sign some papers to protect the company in case any trouble came of this. But the priest can't know. He'll never allow it, but we've come this far and I can't—won't—stop now, legal or not."

No, I don't think you will. "Does the gentleman from the funeral home know?"

"Not really. We told him we wanted a new coffin and asked if we could have a few private moments with the remains."

"And he doesn't suspect anything?"

She shook her head and stared at the ground. "He had a nephew on the bus."

The priest walked toward them and placed his arm around Mrs. Reyes. "We need to start the process if you're still certain this is what you want."

"It is. Thank you, Father. This is my friend Amara Alvarez."

"Welcome, Ms. Alvarez. I'm glad you're here. I'm sure Mrs. Reyes appreciates your support. Shall we begin?"

The three walked back to the group and stood graveside as the workers hooked the chains onto the coffin and waited for approval to lift the container from the vault. The priest said a prayer asking for God's blessing on the procedure, then nodded. The noise and fumes of the backhoe broke the quiet moment. Slowly, the casket came into view, swaying gently forward and back.

The Reyeses had opted for a full-size coffin, even though nothing more than fragments were buried. Everything appeared to be in good shape, but fading and decay were obvious. The workers placed the load on the ground beside the new casket, removed the chains, and moved away to a shady area.

"Mr. and Mrs. Reyes," the priest said, "perhaps it would be best if we all stepped inside for a few minutes and allowed this gentleman to complete the transfer."

Enzo Reyes glanced at his wife. "Father, I'd like to remain here."

"I'll go inside," Mrs. Reyes said. "Amara, will you come with me?" *So I don't have to watch a potential crime take place. Smooth.* "Of course."

"I'll stay with Enzo," Mr. Logan said.

The priest motioned toward the back of the church. "Ladies, please. I'm certain this won't take too long."

Twenty minutes later, Mr. Reyes walked into the church and sat beside his wife. "All done," he said. "They've loaded the casket onto the truck and will be leaving in a moment."

"Everything went okay?"

His eyes watered and he wiped a hand under them, then kissed her forehead. "Sí, mi amor."

Her deep breaths turned into sobs and she buried her face in his shoulder. He cradled her head and whispered in her ear.

Amara sat beside them and let the tears drip from her face. The pain never truly went away. You just learned to hide it better. Trained your mind to focus on other things. Showed how tough you were.

Pretended that Daddy's Little Girl was okay.

31 **Lunch consisted of Chick-fil-A** in the car while parked across from the Cotulla accident scene. Chicken salad for Amara and nuggets for Sara.

"Initial results by tomorrow," Amara said. "Two days for the complete workup."

"Unbelievable. Wish we could get that kind of turnaround."

"I imagine you could if the Rangers were willing to pay what the Reyeses probably did."

"Not likely." She stared out the windshield. "Hard to reconcile the photos with what's out there now. That much devastation, you'd think it'd take longer than three years to get back to normal."

"Not exactly an Eden before the accident. Scrub trees and hard dirt."

Sara dropped her empty nugget box into the bag and grabbed a folder from the back seat. "I suppose. You ready?"

Amara turned off the car and stepped outside. Her sunglasses would be working overtime today. Heat waves shimmered above the road and the dry air hung motionless. Sara adjusted her hat, walked around the vehicle, and pulled a photo from the folder.

"Bus was coming from that direction," the Ranger said. "Start there?"

The two walked across the tracks and surveyed the area.

"Anything changed since then?" Sara asked.

"The crossing gate was added. The tracks had to be replaced, of course. Part of the road too. Look around, though. Not like you'd have any trouble spotting an oncoming freight train. If the bus broke down on the tracks, the engineers would've seen it. Maybe not in time to stop, but the accident investigators are certain the impact happened at full speed or close to it. Hard to sell this as anything other than intentional."

"Especially with the suicide note."

Amara waved her hand to the left. "The train derailed right after impact. There used to be ruts down that way where the engines tore up the ground. The debris field was almost a mile. When the three tankers of propane went up, the fireball consumed everything in the area. No chance for survival."

Sara pulled her hat lower. "Perfect storm, huh? Everything that could go wrong. Did the train come through here at the same time every day?"

"Yeah. Both engineers checked out clean in the investigation. This was a one-man show. Planned or not, Gingham went out in a blaze of glory."

"What did the profilers say about him?"

Amara shrugged. "Take your pick. Plenty of things in his past you can use however you want. The suicide wouldn't have surprised anyone. The way he did it, though . . ."

"Why the kids? Any theories on that?"

"Not really. A couple of experts think he could've thought he was saving them from a life like his, full of suffering. Like he was doing them a favor. Others speculate he was so delusional he didn't even realize the kids were on the bus. Who knows?"

"And the bus was on schedule?"

Amara nodded. "Within a few minutes. Running a little late, but not enough to raise any red flags. They confirmed the timing of the last kid he picked up. Couldn't have been sitting here more than seven or eight minutes at the most."

"What about other traffic? No one saw the bus?"

"There's virtually no traffic on these roads. No one came forward to say they saw anything."

Sara stepped onto the tracks and peered south. "So the train's coming from there and Gingham hits the accelerator. Assuming the engineers had time, they'd lock up whatever brakes they had, but no way they're stopping before they hit the bus. No chance."

"None."

Sara pivoted to the north. "Impact, explosion. By the time first responders arrived, nothing to do but put out the fire."

"They held back until the hazmat teams showed up. Pretty clear no one could have survived, so they followed protocol. Couldn't be sure what was on the train and didn't want to make the situation worse. They established a perimeter to keep people away and protect the scene."

"They figure out why the tanker cars exploded? You'd think they have to be able to withstand a derailment."

"They're supposed to," Amara said, "and the Feds' reports indicated the maintenance records all checked out, but in certain situations the tankers might weaken enough to blow. There's even a special name for what happened. Don't remember it, but you can look it up back in the office if you want. Near as I understand, the derailment started a fire, which caused the liquid propane to boil and turn to gas. The tankers' metal couldn't take the pressure, so they exploded."

"Surely there's some sort of relief valve in case this happens?"

Amara shaded her eyes. "Don't remember, but we can check the file. The report had a bunch of technical jargon in it but basically said they found no evidence of anything wrong with the tanker cars or the engines."

"Everything fits, doesn't it? Nothing to say anything other than the official version happened."

Amara squatted, scooped up a handful of the dusty soil, and let the grainy dirt filter through her fingers. The dust fell nearly straight down. "Nothing other than the text to Mrs. Reyes and the coincidences with Philip Dragan."

"You buy that? The text, I mean."

"I guess we'll get our answer when the DNA results come back." Sara removed her hat and dragged her sleeve across her forehead. "Assuming the tests are positive for her son. Any other result proves nothing."

"*Correcto*, but there's still the issue with Dragan."

"Coincidental? Yes, but not criminal."

Amara smiled. "So you're my devil's advocate, huh?"

"Interesting term. You know the origin? The Catholic Church came up with it. When they consider someone for sainthood, there's a person who does everything in their power to locate evidence to prevent the canonization. Fake miracles, false testimony, anything they can find to stop it from happening. That person is called the devil's advocate."

"I'm not trying to be a saint."

Sara tilted her face toward the sky for a moment, then placed her hat back on her head. "Didn't say you were."

"We follow the evidence. When it stops, so do we."

"Agreed, but before we can follow it, we have to find it. Are you so sure it's out there?"

The energy drained from Amara's limbs. "No, I'm not."

32 **Amara drew her finger** through the dust on her desk. Rough morning. She'd gone home last night without working out, had a couple of Diet Cokes for dinner, and come to a conclusion. The Cotulla case was dead. Opinion and hope aside, nothing pointed to anything that might contradict the original investigation. She and Sara would finish up their review of the files within a day or two, but then it was over.

"You hear me?" Sara said.

"Sorry. Not enough coffee, I guess."

"I asked if you think we should put some pictures up."

Amara glanced at each of the four blank walls in their new office. Last week, this had been a storage room. The remodel must have taken less than an hour. They'd hauled most of the supplies out, except for a damaged case of toilet paper and a few unmarked bottles of a bluish liquid. A couple of old metal desks, one missing a drawer, the other with a bent leg, were supplemented with plastic chairs from the break room.

The detective shook her head. "Pictures? We'd only ruin the ambience."

"You're probably right."

"Besides, I don't think we're going to be here too long."

Sara tucked a loose strand of hair behind her ear. "No?"

"Nada. That's what we've found. If the chief called us in now and wanted a report, he'd shut us down and be right to do it. This investigation is going nowhere in a hurry."

"Somebody get up on the wrong side of the bed this morning?"

"Yeah, but for a reason. Sat up late last night talking to Larry. Ran through everything we had discovered. It was a quick and quiet conversation."

"Yeah? And did your lizard have a response?"

Amara rubbed the back of her neck. "He just shook his head."

"Smart reptile. So what's the plan, then?"

"Finish reviewing the original Cotulla files. See if there's anything that might seem suspicious with what we now know about Dragan and Gingham. If not, we close the books on this."

"And the DNA results from Benjamin Reyes?"

"Won't affect us. Whether his bones are identified or not, nothing will be proven. We stick to the evidence, and right now there's not any."

"So you're not the least bit curious about the tests?"

Amara smiled. "Dying to know."

Sara glanced at her watch. "She's late."

Marisa Reyes was to receive the DNA results this morning. She'd promised to phone Amara as soon as she had any news.

"She'll call. I'll put her on speaker, but remember, she doesn't know about you. No talking."

"No prob—"

The scraping sound of a key came from the door and the entrance swung open. A khaki-uniformed man with a mop stepped in, looked at the women, at the door, and back at the women.

Amara and Sara exchanged a glance.

"I think it's your turn," the Ranger said.

Amara pointed to her right. "They moved the supply closet to the storage room down the hall where they used to keep the file cabinets with all the blank forms. Yes, that's the same place the cleaning supplies used to be. No, I don't know why they didn't just move the file cabinets and put us in there."

The man leaned on his mop. "So where'd they move the forms?"

Sara tapped her desk. "Probably should add that to the explanation."

"We don't know where they moved the file cabinets. Oh, and yes, we have requisitioned a new lock for the door."

The man smiled and nodded. "You ladies have a nice day."

"You too," Sara said. "Spread the word, huh?"

"Will do."

Sara waited until the man left. "Maybe we should print a sign or something. Stick it to the door."

"Kind of hard to do until they get the printer hooked up."

"Yeah, but—"

Amara's phone rang and she held up a finger, took a deep breath, then hit the speaker button. "Detective Alvarez."

"Detective, it's Marisa Reyes."

"Yes, ma'am. I take it you got the results?"

"Preliminary. They said they'd email the final report no later than tomorrow night, but Benjamin's DNA wasn't in there. They compared the results to samples they took from Enzo and me. You know what that means, right?"

"Mrs. Reyes, what exactly did they say?"

"They were able to extract DNA from two of the samples."

How many fragments had they taken? Amara didn't want to know. "And?"

"The DNA was from two different people, but not Benjamin. I was right. My boy's still alive."

Amara sighed. "We warned you the fragments would be mixed. Just because neither of them was—"

"You have to admit it's suspicious though, right?"

"No, ma'am. I'm sorry, but from our perspective, it doesn't mean anything."

"Our?"

She cut her eyes toward Sara. "Our, as in the police."

"Well, to a mother, it means everything. Benjamin's bones were not in that coffin."

"Mrs. Reyes, I'll try to phrase this as gently as I can, but is that really a surprise considering what you knew going into this? If we had a complete skeleton to work with, or even just bigger bones, we could—"

"A mother knows, Detective."

Sara shook her head and frowned.

"Yes, ma'am," Amara said. "But we don't investigate based on intuition. We know for a fact Benjamin's DNA was found in some of the remains from the accident scene. There's no disputing it. The records are very clear."

"You're saying you're done with the case."

Amara planted her elbow on the desk and bent her head forward into her cupped hand. "It was never a case, Mrs. Reyes. I'm sorry. I feel like I gave you some false hope. That was never my intention. I only wanted to help."

"And you did. You listened when my own husband thought I was going crazy. This doesn't end here for me. I'll keep looking for Benjamin. I have to."

"I know you will."

"Goodbye, Detective. I won't bother you again. And thank you."

"Yes, ma'am."

Amara hung up the phone and massaged her face.

"You handled that well," Sara said.

"Doesn't feel like it. I wanted to give her closure and ended up giving her just the opposite."

"You did what you could for her. The evidence doesn't lie."

"Starsky says everyone lies."

"Okay, who's Starsky and why is he so cynical?"

"A friend in Homicide. And he's not that cynical. I think it's something he likes to say to make himself sound like one of those TV detectives. But he may be right, at least to a point. The only thing you can trust is the evidence."

"So who's lying here? Mrs. Reyes? The DNA testing company?"

Amara stood and shoved her chair under the desk. "Let's grab lunch. And no one's lying. Benjamin Reyes is dead. We'll close the loop on Philip Dragan and then we can shut this down. Get back to our real jobs."

"Not sure I can do that."

"What do you mean?"

Sara stood, planted her hands on her hips, and looked around the room. "Don't see how I could give all this up."

33 Amara bent over the women's restroom sink and splashed cold water on her face, then patted her cheeks and forehead with a paper towel. So much for her makeup, but on a day like today, the heat got what the heat wanted. Combined with the bad airflow in their makeshift office, she saw no point in fighting the inevitable. She stepped out of the bathroom and bumped into her partner.

"You want the good news or the bad news?" Sara asked.

"Good first. Always."

"They finally changed the lock on our office."

"Let me guess. They didn't leave a note telling us who had the new keys."

Sara grinned. "No wonder you're the star detective here."

"Hang out in the break room if you want. I'll go on the hunt."

Thirty-five minutes later, the duo entered their office and shivered.

Sara rubbed her arms. "Guess they got the air-conditioning fixed too."

"Lucky us. Hold on, I know how to handle this." She tore a section off the dusty toilet tissue box, stood on her plastic chair, and wedged the cardboard into half of the ceiling vent.

"Nice," Sara said. "I see you covered the section facing *your* desk."

Amara jumped down and smiled. "Really? Didn't notice."

"Uh-huh. Hey, mind if we go over the report on the railroad tankers? I want to make sure I get it clear in my head."

Amara sorted through her drawer and handed over a manila

folder. "Have at it, and good luck understanding any of the minutiae. Way too technical for my taste, not to mention most of the report is nothing but regulations being cited. Bottom line is the Feds were satisfied the railroad did everything right. No fines were assessed. There's a newspaper clipping that sums it up. Might want to start there."

Sara thumbed through the official reports and found the article. "The onboard event recorder showed the mile-long train was doing around fifty-eight miles per hour, which was within limits. Emergency brakes were applied and horn sounded prior to impact. The train had three engines with eighty-three cars, so at that speed and weight it would take more than a mile to stop after hitting the emergency brakes."

"Yep. Those kids never had a chance."

"Yeah, but doesn't it seem kind of odd that if the train was so heavy and moving that fast, it would derail after hitting a bus? Wouldn't its weight and momentum keep it on the tracks? I mean, it's not like it hit a cement truck."

Amara shrugged. "You'd think so, but check the reports. I guarantee that's covered in there somewhere."

She shuffled through the papers. "Originated in Laredo, heading to Kansas City. Nothing unusual about the load. Yada yada yada, here we go. Reason for derailment was impact with a stationary object. Inspection of rails inconclusive due to damage. Tracks outside the accident area in good repair. No evidence of human error or mechanical problems."

"Find the part about the propane tank explosions. Chemistry wasn't exactly my strong suit in school. Maybe you can make sense of it."

Sara tilted her head down and raised her eyebrows. "Don't count on it. Get your Google ready. Hmm. Look up *hematite*."

Amara searched the internet. "'A reddish-black mineral used primarily in the production of steel.'"

"Okay, so that's being shipped up from Venezuela. At some point in the derailment, the hematite gets mixed up with burning aluminum, which causes the hematite to also catch fire."

"Where'd the aluminum come from?"

Sara's lips moved as she ran her finger across the page. "Six boxcars of the stuff shipped up from Brazil. Anyway, hematite and aluminum is apparently a pretty nasty combination in a fire. The two created a thermite reaction."

"And that is . . . ?"

"Something you need to google. No idea."

Amara scanned the search results. "Burns intensely for a brief period. Temps over four thousand degrees. Creates a molten metal that eats through just about anything."

"There you go. So the thermite burns through the tanks, instantly vaporizes the liquid propane, and triggers the explosion."

"Anybody mention what the odds against all that happening were?"

Sara pouted her lips. "That's why it's called an accident. The thing that bothers me, though, is the explosion."

"What about it?"

"Why only one? Three cars, right? All of them exploded, but at exactly the same time?"

"Maybe they didn't. Does it matter?"

Sara sorted through the papers again. "Numerous 911 calls to report the blast. None of them mentioned hearing more than one boom."

"And?"

She shook her head. "Nothing. Curious, though. Even if the tankers ignited a fraction of a second apart, there'd have been more than one explosion, wouldn't there? Think about it. I can accept the explanation for what triggered the detonation, but all at precisely the same instant?"

Amara smiled and tilted her head. "That's why they call it an accident."

"I guess, but it sticks in my craw and I'm running real low on ideas. Where do we go from here?"

"Not much left, is there? Finish up the accident stuff today, work on our mysterious Mr. Dragan tomorrow, then recap with the chief. See what he thinks."

Sara picked up the top piece of paper from the folder. "I've got a good idea what he'll want to do."

Fatigue washed over Amara, and she raked her fingers through her hair. Would Homicide be like this? How did you turn loose of a case—solved or not—when you still had questions? "I'm afraid we'll be chasing our tails tomorrow. We don't have much on Philip Dragan, but I bet we have all we're going to get. Without specifics, we're dead in the water. We can throw out guesses and theories all day long, but if we can't prove any of it, we'll be shut down. Let me ask you something, Sara. Off the record. From your perspective, is there anything here?"

The Ranger sighed and swatted at a gnat. "Great. Bugs now. Anything to this? Honestly? There's enough to make it interesting for conspiracy theorists, but not enough to make it compelling to law enforcement. Yeah, there are questions I'd like to see answered, but when something this big happens, there's always going to be that. No way to tie up all the loose ends."

Amara sank back in her chair. "I don't disagree. I wanted something to be there. Not for me. For Marisa Reyes and the others. Some shred of evidence to put everything else in doubt. Anything to offer the tiniest chance the text she received might have been from her son. But there's nothing left to find. All we've got is Philip Dragan on a grassy knoll, and that's going nowhere."

"Doesn't mean we stop."

She clicked her mouse and pulled up her email. "No, it doesn't. But it does mean we . . . huh."

"Huh what?"

"Marisa Reyes forwarded me the final DNA results."

"They different from what she said?"

Amara tapped her chin. "What? Different, uh, no."

"Care to share?"

"You've seen the pictures of the kids who were on the bus, right?"

Sara's eyes narrowed. "Yeah, why?"

"Any of them look Asian to you?"

34

Sara walked behind Amara's desk and peered over her partner's shoulder. "Male, Asian parentage ninety-nine point nine nine nine percent likely. That doesn't make sense."

"Seventeen kids on that bus. Twelve Hispanic, two African American, and three Caucasian. I could pick any one of them out of a lineup."

"How does an Asian bone get mixed in with the others? Maybe the lab made a mistake?"

Amara hit the print button on her screen. An error message popped up, alerting her no printer was found. "I swear, someone's going to—"

"I'll call IT again later," Sara said.

"The lab make a mistake? Possible, but now we're sounding like Mrs. Reyes. DNA labs don't make mistakes. If they did, they'd be out of business."

"Don't want to ask her to retest the samples just to be sure?"

Amara rocked her shoulders forward to stretch her back. "That's a discussion I'm not ready for, at least not yet. Let's assume the results are valid. What does that mean? An Asian kid was on the bus? No way. And a separate morgue was set up after the accident, so no outside bones could've got mixed in. What other options are there?"

Sara returned to her seat. "This calls for boots-on-the-desk thinking. Be a lot easier with a chair that actually leaned back some."

"Take your time," Amara said, "because I'm drawing a blank. The test results *have* to be bad."

"No, they don't. They probably are, but they don't have to be. What if the child was on the bus and the parents never came forward?"

"The school never reported any other children missing."

Sara thumped her temple. "Oh, right. Well, what if the kid wasn't from around here? Maybe even already dead and someone hid the body on the bus?"

"I suppose that's an option, but certainly not a theory I'd pursue until all other possibilities were exhausted."

"Yeah, me neither. So if we stick with the test results being good, what else is there? Nothing logical. You need to think—"

Amara held up her hand, fingers splayed and palm forward. "Don't tell me to think outside the box. I hate that."

Sara smiled and rocked her boots side to side on the desktop. "I was going to tell you to use the conspiracy part of your brain. How about role-playing? You're a late-night radio host who spends her evenings chatting with truckers about aliens cutting up cows or some such. How do you explain these DNA results?"

"You're assuming aliens don't cut up cows?"

"Never, but in this case, let's leave ET and livestock out of it."

Amara blew out a stream of air. "Okay. Go back to the beginning. The text message. You have to assume—"

"Uh-uh. Not assuming anything. You're the conspiracy nut. Sell me on it. Doesn't matter whether *you* believe it, but you want that trucker from Missoula to buy into it."

"Missoula?"

"First place that popped into my mind."

Amara scrunched her nose. "Why would Missoula be—"

"Can we stay on target here?"

She grinned and took a deep breath. "Okay. Here we go. The text message proves Benjamin Reyes is still alive. The train wreck was an elaborate ruse to distract from his kidnapping, which was obviously organized by Philip Dragan for purposes as yet unknown."

"That's an impressive cover-up just to get one boy. Why Benjamin Reyes? And why not simply kidnap him? Be a lot easier."

Amara stared at the ceiling. "Something different about him. Something special. And Dragan wanted the boy but didn't want anyone else to know he had him."

"Come on," Sara said. "Nobody could be *that* special. And the timing of the accident? The explosion and fire? He wouldn't leave that to chance."

"No. The explosion is critical. It hides the evidence. Destroys and burns whatever's left of the bodies. There'd have to be a trigger. Something to force the derailment and the aftermath."

"Yeah? So how did he convince the bus driver to do it?"

"Friend of Dragan's from way back. Brainwashed to believe the government . . . the government caused his mother's death. Gave her cancer. Dragan convinces him the train collision will bring swarms of media to Cotulla and he'll be there to tell them the truth about Gingham's mom's death."

"Excellent. Now, the Asian DNA?"

"Planted by Dragan to make sure the body count was correct."

"Hmm, but wouldn't he assume they'd do DNA testing?"

"Yes. But he knew that, he thought . . . ugh. Next caller, please."

Sara pursed her lips and nodded. "You may have a second career waiting for you."

"I'm just trying to survive my first one."

"So we're back to where we started. Either that test is wrong, or the Asian bone fragment was placed there intentionally to hide something."

Amara leaned forward. "It'd have to be more than a fragment. A whole skeleton probably, or at least most of one. Only way to make sure that if DNA testing *was* done on the remains, they'd find a unique set to add to the body count."

"Why use Asian bones? Why not Hispanic?"

"Maybe Dragan didn't know they were Asian?"

"Possibly," Sara said. "But if everything else was so meticulously planned, I have to think the planting of the bones would have been too. Too many whys and what-ifs. I don't see how we can go any further until we retest the sample and rule out a lab error. That means calling Mrs. Reyes."

Amara brushed a strand of hair off her forehead. "Not yet. We need to understand the DNA testing process better. Make sure we're not missing something that would explain this."

"Wouldn't hurt, I suppose. Know anyone who can shed light on the procedure?"

"I do. I need to clear it with Chief Johnson first, but I know a guy that might be able to help. How do you feel about Tic Tacs and Cheetos?"

"Sorry to keep you waiting," Dr. Pritchard said. "Had quite the unusual autopsy going on downstairs. Didn't want to miss it. Construction worker fell three stories onto a pile of rebar. Those are the steel rods they use to reinforce concrete. Ugly situation. Multiple penetration wounds. Cause of death is easy to determine, but when we opened him up, you—"

"We don't want to take up too much of your time, Dr. Pritchard," Amara said. "This is Ranger Sara Colby. We wanted to pick your brain for a few minutes if we could."

"Pick your brain. Such a strange saying. Do you know its origin?"

Sara cut her eyes toward Amara. "Uh, no, we don't."

"Hmm. I don't either. Hold on a second." He scribbled a note, read it, added another word or two, and pushed the paper to the side. "Now then, what can I do for you ladies?"

"If you'll remember," Amara said, "I mentioned that Marisa Reyes, one of the mothers from the Cotulla accident, wanted to have DNA testing performed on her son's remains. Well, she did, and the results were a little confusing to us."

Dr. Pritchard intertwined his fingers, and wrinkles sprouted on his forehead. "Confusing? In what way?"

"Samples were taken from more than one bone fragment. The remains in the coffin were from two different individuals."

"Not surprising. We couldn't test every bone. Once we confirmed each child's DNA had been found, we separated the remains as best we could and handed them over for burial."

Amara inched forward in her seat. "Yes, sir, but the results Mrs. Reyes received included Asian DNA."

The ME smiled and leaned back. "Not unusual at all. Most people have evidence of other—"

"Virtually one hundred percent Asian."

Dr. Pritchard raised his eyebrows. "For that to be accurate, Detective, the child's genealogy would include only Asians for many generations."

"That's where we're confused," Sara said. "There were no kids on the bus who fit the profile."

"The obvious answer is the test is incorrect," the ME said. "Cross-contamination or something. Perhaps the person conducting the examination failed to follow procedures."

Amara nodded. "Sure, that was our initial reaction. We're hesitant to ask for a retest because we don't want to get Mrs. Reyes involved except as a last resort. She's been through enough. We wanted to talk to an expert first."

"You flatter me, Detective, but I'm no DNA expert. Far from it."

"Understood, but can you think of any reason, besides an invalid test, that we would get these results?"

"Only the obvious. An Asian child was on the bus that morning."

"But," Sara said, "we know that's not true, at least as far as the evidence we had prior to this. And if there *was* a child we didn't know about, chances are your tests would have picked up on it too, right? You'd have ended up with DNA that didn't match anyone."

Dr. Pritchard frowned and inclined his head toward Sara. "Very good, Ranger . . . ?"

"Colby, sir. Sara Colby."

He stared at her feet. "Understand the DNA tests we performed were specifically to determine parentage. That's standard procedure in these situations. None of the children were adopted, so we collected the parents' DNA to use as a comparison. The lab sent us the results with a summary indicating sample matched to parent. We had no need for any further information from the remains. Your boots?"

Sara pointed her toes forward. "Teju lizard skin."

Amara grimaced. "Don't let Larry hear you say that."

"I'm sorry," Dr. Pritchard said. "Who is this Larry?"

"He's my pet—can we focus on the DNA please?"

The ME nodded. "Of course. Those *are* nice boots, Miss Colby. Very becoming. Now, may I ask if either of you brought the DNA results with you?"

"No," Amara said. "Our printer's not hooked up. I can forward the email to you if that'll help?"

"Please do. I'd like to review them."

Amara used her phone to send the email to the ME. "How long will it take, Doctor? We can come back—"

"Two or three minutes," he said.

The printer whirred and spat out several pages. He handed copies to the women and scanned the paperwork before him. After a moment, he typed on his keyboard and stared at his monitor.

"Mrs. Reyes had the full test done. That's why the lab went as far as to specify ethnicity. The markers are all there."

"Markers?" Amara said.

"It's what they use to interpret the DNA. A specific gene, or perhaps even a small DNA sequence. Far beyond my ability, though I suppose with a bit of training . . ."

Amara paused a few heartbeats before speaking. "Does that mean anything as far as our problem?"

He ignored the question and stared at his monitor for several more seconds. "Interesting."

"What's that?" Sara asked.

He held up his index finger, sorted through the papers, clicked his mouse, and stared at the monitor again. "Hmm."

The women sat silently.

The ME clicked through several more screens, each time shaking his head before moving on to the next one. He scratched his bottom lip and glanced between the paper on his desk and the monitor. Finally, he clicked the mouse again and the printer shot out another page. He laid it beside the one on his desk and his eyes darted left-right as if he was watching a tennis match. "Interesting."

Amara cleared her throat. "Doctor?"

"Your Asian male's DNA is in our system."

Sara parted her lips and shook her head. "Why? Who is he?"

"According to this, Ranger Colby, he is the very Hispanic Arturo Ybarra, son of Rico and Andrea Ybarra, and he died in the Cotulla incident."

"Okay," Amara said. "You're going to have to spell that out for me. Are you saying Arturo is Asian?"

Dr. Pritchard frowned and pivoted his monitor so the women could see the screen. "No. I'm saying the DNA markers on the report you brought are an exact match for the ones we have on file. If each of the tests is accurate, then there can be no question that Arturo is Asian. However, you can see from his photo he clearly is *not* Asian."

Sara stood and paced a few steps. "One of the reports must be wrong. Some sort of glitch in the system."

"Actually," the ME said, "either both documents are wrong or both are correct. Since it would be impossible for two different testing centers to make a grievous error and yet return the identical DNA result, I submit that both must be accurate."

Amara inhaled deeply to slow her racing heartbeat. "But since we know that cannot be Arturo's DNA, whose is it? And how did someone match it to his parents? There had to be tampering somewhere in the process."

Sara rubbed her temples. "This is making my head hurt. If I understand correctly, and I doubt seriously I do, somebody intentionally switched names, DNA, bone fragments, whatever, to make it look like everything fit and all the Cotulla bodies were identified. Have I got that right?"

"I think so," Amara said. "Doctor, is there a way to confirm whether or not that really is Arturo's DNA? I need something more concrete before we go to the chief."

"Certainly," he said. "All we need are DNA samples from the parents."

Sara sat again. "But those are already in your files from the accident, right? You had to have them to match to—Oh. If one set is wrong, we can't trust any of them. For all we know, every DNA report you have is bogus."

Amara glanced at the Ranger. "Lot of work to kidnap one child, don't you think?"

"Don't. Not yet. I know where you're headed, but don't go there. Wait until we have more."

"I don't disagree," Amara said. "We get Arturo's parents' DNA tested at a different lab. It's the only way to be sure. Dr. Pritchard, can we bring the Ybarras here to obtain the samples?"

"No need," the ME said. "We have kits. They're simple to use. A cotton swab inside the cheek is all it takes. Maintain chain of custody and bring them here, then we'll forward them on to a new lab."

"Got it," Amara said. "We just need to come up with a plausible excuse for needing their DNA. Something that won't alarm them."

Sara worked her chin side to side. "Normally I'd say nothing works as good as the truth, but in this case that's probably not the best idea. I'm thoroughly confused and don't want to try to explain it to someone else."

Dr. Pritchard meshed his fingers. "Ranger Colby, let us say you provided a cheek swab for testing. I then complete the necessary paperwork and send everything off to a lab. The results are then returned to me with your specific DNA information. Now, if I followed the same procedure for each of your parents, I could unequivocally prove you are their child."

"Sure," Sara said. "Simple stuff. So why is Arturo's—"

The ME held up his index finger. "We collected and tested the DNA of the young man's parents in order to confirm his bones were among those recovered. Now, remember we could not simply segregate the bone fragments by child. Therefore, far more tests were done than needed to ensure we had at least one fragment from each victim. Still with me?"

Sara straightened in her chair and frowned. "I'm not an idiot, Doctor. You don't need to talk down to me."

His face reddened. "Miss Colby, I meant no offense. Please accept my apology. I only wanted to clarify any confusion—"

"Accepted," Sara said. "You may continue."

He swallowed hard and nodded once. "Thank you. Now, whenever a unique DNA sequence was found, the lab matched it against the markers from each set of parents. All the children were identified using the same method. And since the results we obtained for Arturo are identical to those from the Reyeses' lab, we can be assured the tests are accurate. Two different centers provided the same results."

"Which means," Sara said, "the DNA absolutely belongs to someone on that bus. The question is who. It cannot be Arturo, despite what the paperwork says."

"Wait one moment," the doctor said. He riffled through the papers again and studied another page. "I wonder . . ."

The women watched as he repeated the process of searching online, then comparing it to the page on his desk.

"I believe I've solved your dilemma, ladies. There is no need to obtain DNA samples from the Ybarras, at least not yet."

"You found something?" Amara asked.

"It might be more appropriate to say I *didn't* find something. Marisa and Enzo Reyes provided their DNA at the time of the accident so we could test for a match against their son. The lab report we received back then included a summary of their markers, as well as Benjamin's. I compared our results from Cotulla with the ones the Reyeses just received. Oddly, or perhaps not at this point, the information in our file does not match the data from the Reyeses' lab."

Amara squeezed her eyes closed. "I'm still trying to wrap my head around this."

The ME slid his notepad over and scribbled something. "I don't suppose either of you know the origin of that expression?"

"Um, no," Sara said. "But, bear with me here, the report the Reyeses received contains four DNA results: one from Enzo, one from Marisa, and two from bone fragments. One of *those* indicates an Asian child, who we know—assume—wasn't on the bus. And the ones from the Reyeses themselves are different from the ones you have on file from three years ago. That's all correct?"

"Yes, it is," Dr. Pritchard said.

Amara looked up. "What about the fourth test?"

He sorted the paperwork and found the results. "Hispanic female. And to answer your next question . . ." He clicked through several screens, alternating his view between the monitor and the printed page. "Ah. A match for Caterina Delacruz, one of the girls on the bus that day."

"Yeah," Amara said. "I know who Caterina is. She wasn't supposed to be there. Spent the night with a friend and rode to school with her."

Sara bit her lip. "Curiouser and curiouser."

"Lewis Carroll," the doctor said. "*Alice in Wonderland.*"

Sara smiled. "That one I knew."

"We don't need to see the Ybarras," Amara said. "Not yet. If we get new samples from the Reyeses, we'll be able to tell which test has their correct DNA: the one from the accident three years ago or the one from today. Once we know that, we can figure out how to proceed. Agreed?"

The others nodded.

"Fine," she said. "For now, I'd prefer this stays between the three of us."

Dr. Pritchard walked around his desk. "Certainly. If you'll wait here for a few minutes, I'll have someone bring you the testing kits. I'm intrigued by this, ladies, so please exercise all due diligence in returning the samples."

"Actually," Amara said, "I hope you don't mind, Doctor, but we'll take care of the kits."

His lips turned up at the corners. "Of course. Better if my department has no involvement. You learn quickly."

Amara stood and straightened her shirt. "No sense muddying the water any more than necessary, right?"

He tilted his head and smiled at Sara. "I understand. I do hope you'll let me know as soon as you have the results?"

"Will do," the Ranger said.

The doctor extended his hand to Sara. "I look forward to seeing your boots again, Ranger Colby."

37

Traffic on the drive to the Reyeses' house in Karnes City was light, and Amara cruised a few miles over the speed limit. In Floresville, she detoured into a CVS Pharmacy and purchased two new DNA testing kits. The San Antonio ME's office would be completely out of the loop. Plus, for an extra thirty dollars each, she could receive the results in a day. Get the tests done, overnight the kits to the lab, and wait.

The divided highway ended just before Poth and she slowed so as not to arrive before the couple had a chance to get home from work. She'd opted not to call, thinking any questions would be better answered in person. Not that she'd be able to reply to many, and any details she could share would be sparse. It'd be another two hours before the sun set, and her car's air conditioner ran at maximum to provide the artificially cool breeze they needed.

"Doing okay over there?" Amara asked. "Awful quiet."

Sara adjusted her seat belt and shifted a little. "You think he was hitting on me?"

"What? Who?"

"Dr. Pritchard. I got the feeling he was interested."

"Because of the boots? He's a bit eccentric, I think. Hard to read."

"I don't know. Seems like there was something there."

Amara raised her eyebrows and glanced at the Ranger. "The feeling go both ways?"

She brushed the rim of her hat. "He seems nice enough. Quirky, but nothing wrong with that. Not hard to look at either."

"Going to ask him out?"

"We'll see. Maybe a double date?"

Amara squeezed the steering wheel. "I don't really, I mean, I do, but . . ."

"Yeah, well, find someone. If I do go out with the doc, I'm not going alone."

"I thought you Rangers were tough. One riot, one Ranger. Or is that all just propaganda?"

Sara laughed. "We're tough, all right, but we're not stupid. If he's got some kind of foot fetish, I may need backup. Surely there's someone you've got your eyes on?"

She grinned. Foot fetish? Like claiming to shave your toes? "None that I can think of. Don't have a lot of time for dating."

"Really? I know a few guys who'd love to—"

"No, thank you. And if they're so great, why aren't *you* dating them?"

"Point taken. Tell you what. The next time you and your lizard—"

"Larry."

"The next time you and Larry are hanging out, y'all talk about it. I'm sure you can come up with one or two guys you're interested in, or at least curious about."

Could she? Did she even want to? There was Starsky, of course, but he wasn't . . . She tapped her finger on the wheel again. "I don't know. Larry's the jealous type."

"Yeah, well, until he starts buying your dinner, I say keep looking."

❉ ❉ ❉

Marisa Reyes was home by the time they arrived. Her husband, Enzo, got there twenty minutes later. Amara introduced Sara and explained they wanted to obtain DNA samples but couldn't give much other information. She emphasized the process was completely voluntary.

Mrs. Reyes was having none of it. "This has something to do with my test on the remains, doesn't it?"

Sara held her hat in her right hand and knocked it against her leg as she stood in the living room. "Ma'am, we really can't give a lot of detail at this point."

The woman stood her ground. "If you want our DNA, you're going to have to give us information. You already have a record of it anyway, don't you? From three years ago *and* on the report I just gave you? Why do you need it a third time?"

Mr. Reyes stepped forward. "Detective Alvarez, what's going on here? We are happy to help. You know that. But if this involves our son, we have a right to know what's happening."

Sara glanced at her partner, then smiled at the Reyeses. "May we sit?"

Amara answered the few questions she felt comfortable explaining. She dodged most of the dicier ones but shared enough that the couple agreed to give new samples. They knew their two sets of DNA records currently at the ME's office didn't match, and had a vague idea of what that might mean. They'd have time later to dwell on the issue and consider the possibilities.

Amara wanted to be out of there before more questions arose. She opened the first kit and asked Mrs. Reyes to scrape the inside of her cheeks with each of the three swabs. After she'd sealed them in the envelope, she unsealed the second kit and asked Mr. Reyes to do the same.

Minutes later, they were on their way back to San Antonio. A call confirmed they had until 8:30 to drop off the kits at the nearest FedEx. Plenty of time, but Amara wasn't taking any chances and flicked on her blue lights. With luck, they'd have the results by this time tomorrow. Worst case, Sunday morning.

Everything hinged on the outcome. If the samples matched the ones in the ME's office from three years ago, the investigation was over. That would mean the Asian DNA was most likely the result of a mix-up somewhere along the way.

If the results *didn't* coincide with Dr. Pritchard's . . . She added a few miles per hour to the vehicle's speed. This case could be about to explode.

38 **Amara sat with Sara** and Police Chief Johnson at a Starbucks across town from their offices. A constant stream of early Saturday morning caffeine addicts flowed in and out the door. The Breakfast Bodega would have to do without her today. She peeked again at the display of giant muffins, cookies, and scones. Starbucks should sell pancakes.

"The packages have already been delivered," Amara said. "I'm planning to call the lab to see if they can expedite the test."

"Don't," Johnson said. "I want nothing out of the ordinary done. Nothing to highlight there's anything different about those tests."

"Yes, sir," she said. "Going to be a long day."

The chief downed the last of his coffee and rapped the empty cup on the table several times. "What's on your agenda?"

Sara emptied another packet of sugar into her half-empty cup. "Thought we'd do some more digging on Philip Dragan. However the results turn out, there's still the question of his relationship with the bus driver."

"No," Johnson said. "Not yet. Take the rest of the day off. Both of you. Depending on how those tests come back, you two could get real busy. Long days with no time off. Take care of whatever you need to get done. We'll regroup here tomorrow morning. Same time. One of you touch base with Dr. Pritchard and ask him to come. Tell him to bring his files."

"I'll talk to him," Sara said.

Amara glanced at her and smiled. "I've got a ton of paperwork in the office to finish up. Once—"

The chief's eyes narrowed to slits. "What part of *take the day off* do you have trouble understanding, Detective?"

"Yes, sir. Extra time in the gym would do me good."

Johnson leaned forward. "Good work, both of you. Remember, not a word of this to anyone. The fewer who know, the better. You need anything, you come straight to me."

"Actually, sir," Sara said, "we do need something. Maybe you could have someone check on an IT issue for us? Our printer's still not hooked up."

"Simple enough. Anything else?"

Amara cleared her throat. "If the DNA results come back and this case requires more investigation, will we still be lead on it?"

The chief stood and straightened the American flag pin on his suit jacket's lapel. "Don't get ahead of yourself. As my great-uncle LBJ used to say, if we can't solve problems by ourselves, we can solve them together."

* * *

Amara pushed her workout to nearly two hours before she agreed to call it a draw with the Muay Thai bag. Her muscles ached, but she felt more refreshed than she had for days. She'd plotted her Saturday activities, ending with the usual family meal at Mama's, and resolved not to check her email until later tonight. Even if the DNA results did come in, she wouldn't know what they meant until Dr. Pritchard had a chance to compare them with his records. No sense getting all worked up over the what-if question, but the only way she'd keep her mind off it was to stay busy.

She showered, then sat in her car in the gym's parking lot. A guy about her age passed by and jogged into the building. Nice looking, in shape, and no wedding ring. She adjusted the rearview mirror and glanced at herself. Maybe her mom was right. There's no such thing as love at first sight. Stop looking for someone who doesn't exist and find a guy who makes her laugh.

Mom had told the story a hundred times since Dad passed. How the two had met at a Día de los Muertos celebration. Barely fifteen years old, he wore the traditional skeleton costume and mask and carried a handful of orange marigolds. Her face was elaborately painted and her brightly colored dress contained the outline of a rib cage.

The early November night was chilly with a gusty breeze, and he'd stopped her to offer a flower. "The problem with being a skeleton," he said, "is this cold wind cuts right through you."

Her friends rolled their eyes, but she laughed. Not a polite laugh, but one that came from deep inside. He was still making her laugh up until the day he died.

Think about it, her mother said. Don't give up because of that *imbécil*. Mom always referred to her ex as an idiot. Her brothers and sisters weren't so kind.

She rocked forward and shoved her elbows behind her to stretch her back and shoulders. Enough of that. If she found a guy, great. If not, she'd been alone this long, hadn't she?

She checked the mirror again and put the car in reverse. Still several hours of daylight left. She had time to go shopping, then have dinner with the family before wrapping up the evening at home with Larry. She'd give her boy a chance to explore the apartment while she relaxed. Maybe she'd bounce a few thoughts off him.

Like what it would mean if the DNA results didn't match Dr. Pritchard's records.

Or what it would mean if they did.

And why, when asked about double-dating with Sara, she'd paused when thinking about Starsky.

* * *

Amara parked in front of a house three doors down from her mother's. She was late and her siblings had taken all the closer spots. She hurried into the backyard and paused, confused. The kids were there, running and playing. The lights were on and lawn chairs ready. Where was everyone?

She stepped into the house and froze. Laughter in the living room. Several people talking at once. A familiar voice sounded above the others. She stepped into the room and half smiled. "Hola, everyone."

On the sofa, wedged between Mama and Selina, sat Wylie. He'd been discharged from the hospital but still had to complete several weeks of rehab before they'd clear him to return to work.

He waved to her. "Hey, there, Alvarez."

"Um, Wylie, how did—"

He nudged her sister. "Selina was kind enough to stop by my place and pick me up."

"Yeah, but—"

Her mother leaned forward on the couch. "I couldn't bear the thought of Wylie spending Saturday night alone."

"Sure. No problem. Glad he could make it. But why is everyone inside?"

Wylie tilted his head toward her mother. "I told Maria last week about your fixation with *Downton Abbey*. She said—"

"Fixation? I barely like it. I only watch to keep you company."

"Uh-huh. Anyhow, Maria wanted to see what the show was all about, and I figured, hey, why not get the whole family involved? So we're starting over with the first season. You're just in time to help me explain things."

Amara eased onto the floor and rested against the wall. The whole family? *Family?* "Oh, sure. Sounds good."

Maria smiled widely. "We're going to watch the first episode and then eat. Amara, would you please bring our guest a drink before we begin?"

This was bad. "Sí, *madre.*"

39 Amara struggled to sit still, and the double-shot espresso wasn't helping. Thirty minutes until everyone was supposed to be here. The DNA results had arrived in her email a bit after two this morning. She'd stopped by work to study the lab's reports, but nothing in the results meant anything to her. They couldn't, not until Dr. Pritchard compared them to what he had. Unable to print them out, she'd forwarded a copy to both Sara and the ME. The chief wouldn't appreciate his inbox getting cluttered with data he couldn't use.

She closed her eyes and focused on the soft jazz flowing from the ceiling speakers. She needed to slow down. Get her anticipation under control. Forget about dinner last night. And the fact Mama had asked Selina to pick up Wylie again next Saturday. If her mother was happy, good for her. Right? Keep the focus on work. Chief Johnson needed to see her confident. Cool. Logical.

The sound of traffic increased as the door opened. Sara and the ME walked in together. The Ranger came to the table while Dr. Pritchard went to the counter to place an order.

Amara held back a smile. "Morning, Sara."

"Good morning." She made eye contact, then glanced away. "I had to go to the office anyway. Asked the doc to pick me up there. Thought I'd catch a ride with him in case you and I needed to head somewhere after the meeting. Didn't want to leave my car parked here all day."

The grin couldn't hide any longer. "I didn't ask," Amara said.

"But it's strange I didn't see you there. Our office must be bigger than I thought."

Sara laughed. "You'd think I'd have the decency to at least blush, wouldn't you? When I called him yesterday to—"

Amara held up her hand and smiled. "Don't need the details. Did the doctor have an opportunity to look at the results?"

Sara placed her hat on the table and brushed a fleck off the brim. "He did but wouldn't say anything about them. Wanted to wait until we were all together."

"Any hint? Did he seem excited?"

Sara cut her eyes toward the counter. "You know Douglas. Hard to read."

"Douglas?"

"He insisted."

Amara sipped her espresso. "Of course he did. Word of advice. When the chief gets here, keep—"

"Yep. He'll be Dr. Pritchard again." She grinned and moved her hat to her knee. "So how was your day off? Get much done? You and Larry spend some quality time together?"

"Guess not. Don't see him here buying my coffee."

Sara laughed and shook her head.

"What's so funny, ladies?" The ME sat next to Sara and placed a steaming cup and a container of sugar in front of her.

"Just easing the tension," Amara said. "Care to clue us in on your findings?"

"Certainly, as soon as the chief arrives. In the meantime, why don't we—"

Chief Johnson hustled through the door and made a beeline for the table, grabbing the seat between Amara and the ME. "Not a lot of time," he said. "Let's get right to it. The DNA results come in?"

"Yes, sir," Amara said. "I forwarded the reports to Dr. Pritchard so he could review them before our meeting."

The chief turned to the ME. "And?"

"They do not match. The DNA we obtained from the Reyeses just after the Cotulla incident are different from the results in these reports."

Amara's pulse accelerated and she clamped her hands on her knees to hold them steady.

Dr. Pritchard continued. "I must assume these recent tests are accurate and the ones in our files are not."

"Why?" Chief Johnson asked.

"The chain of custody on these is unquestioned. Unless either Detective Alvarez or Sara—Ranger Colby tampered with them, which seems highly unlikely, they'd have to be valid. And two tests were performed. One on each of the parents. Shipped separately, tested separately. For neither of them to match what is in our database is alarming."

"I can assure you," Amara said, "we didn't tamper with the tests."

Johnson nodded. "Which is exactly what someone who *did* tamper with them would say. I'm confident you didn't, though if we ever need to use the information in court, the tests will have to be redone under normal procedures. Now, Doctor, if the results in your system aren't a match to these, what exactly does that mean for us? Is it possible we're simply looking at a data entry mix-up?"

The ME frowned and shrugged. "Anything is possible, except what isn't. I haven't pulled the paperwork, but I will do so to ensure they match the digitized copies in the system. Each report includes the person's name and other relevant data, so even if the forms *were* entered incorrectly, the discrepancy would be obvious. In addition, you're looking at not one, but three reports, all tied together. The two from the parents confirm the third is their child."

"And you've verified the DNA from the parents, the ones in your system, aren't random? They actually prove the third set is from their child?" the chief asked.

"I will," Pritchard said. "I don't have the expertise to do the comparison myself, but I've got an analyst who does. Won't take more than a minute or two, I'd guess."

Johnson nodded. "I know the answer, but I have to ask. Is there any way different tests could be the reason for the variance between then and now? Has technology progressed far enough—"

"No," the ME said. "Every lab uses their own format to report the results, but the tests are basically identical. Obviously, they evolve over time and I'd be surprised if in the three years since Cotulla, DNA testing hasn't improved somewhat dramatically. However, that wouldn't affect the basic picture. The genetic markers are what they are. They don't change."

"Chief, if I may?" Amara didn't wait for his response and peered at the ME. "Doctor, can you think of any scenario, outside of intentional tampering, that would account for this?"

"Assuming all is as we've said so far, I cannot."

Amara flattened her palms on the table and spread her fingers. "This can't all be for one kid. Too much involved. Train crash, switching DNA, that's major. Takes planning and money."

"Look," Johnson said, "let's cut to the chase here. We need another DNA sample from a different set of parents. Compare those to what you have on file from Cotulla. If those two also don't match, we've got a problem. A big one."

"Cut to the chase," the ME said. "Comes from the days of silent films. Some directors and screenwriters would include too much dialogue, and the studio executives insisted they cut to the chase scene. Didn't want audiences to get bored."

The chief's lips formed a straight line. "Are we boring you, Doctor?"

"Certainly not."

Johnson stared for a moment before continuing. "As far as I can tell, switching the DNA serves only one purpose: hiding the truth about the body in the coffin."

"Except," Amara said, "for Caterina Delacruz. We know for a fact her remains are there. We also know she's the only child who wasn't scheduled to be on the bus that morning."

"Doctor," Johnson said, "how quickly can you order an exhumation? Pick a set of parents, anyone except the Reyeses or Delacruzes. Let's repeat the tests and see what happens. Agreed?"

Pritchard stroked his goatee. "No, sir. At least not completely."

"No?" the chief said. "Why not?"

"Because we need to exhume them all."

40 **Amara wrapped her hands** around her espresso. Exhume all the bodies? No way to keep that quiet, and once the press got wind of the investigation, the difficulty would grow exponentially. If there was something to be found, the last thing she needed was for everyone to know they were looking.

Chief Johnson scrubbed his hand across his mouth. "Impossible. Not with what we know now. Pick one. If we find a pattern, we'll readdress this. Until then, we have to do everything possible to keep this under wraps."

Doctor Pritchard blinked several times. "No offense, Chief, but I don't report to you. My desire is to mesh our investigations, but if I feel expanding the probe is in the public's best interest, that's what I'll do."

Amara focused on the table and held her breath.

"Consider this," Johnson said. "If our investigation leaks before we've got a handle on things, how does it serve the public's interest, other than spreading rumors and affecting the families of those kids who were killed? Think about it. TV crews camped out on the porches of parents who have no idea what's going on. Being asked questions that dredge up memories they've tried to forget."

The ME smiled and tilted his head slightly. "I didn't say I'd do it. Not yet, at least. I only wanted to ensure we understood each other. Our goals are the same, for now. If that changes, I'll do whatever I think is my department's responsibility. I'll handle the next DNA tests and contact you when I have the results. Give me a couple of days, and yes, I understand the urgency, but if you don't want to sound alarms, then we need to go through normal procedures."

"Dr. Pritchard," Sara said, "is it possible to ensure no one who handled the testing three years ago does these tests? Just to eliminate any chance of, um, questions arising later?"

He nodded. "Good point, Ranger Colby. Should be simple enough to do."

"Which brings up another issue," Amara said. "As far as we know, the original tests were all in the same location twice. Once at the testing center, and before that, in the ME's office. It seems unlikely they could've been swapped at the lab. Those places get thousands of packages a day. I'm sure there's a way to do it, but I think we should focus on the local possibility first."

Dr. Pritchard stiffened. "I follow your logic, Detective, but I don't like what you're implying."

"No one does," the chief said. "But we've got to rule out any chance a person employed at your facility is involved, and I think it's best for everyone if you're not part of that investigation. If you could give us a point of contact at your department? Someone you trust?"

"I trust all my employees," the ME said.

"Of course you do," Sara said. She inched her hand toward his arm, stopping just short. "But is there someone who wasn't there three years ago? Someone with the authority to help us?"

"Karen Stovall," he said. "The deputy ME. I'll introduce you."

Sara tapped her finger on the table and smiled. "That'd be great. Thank you."

Chief Johnson pointed at Amara and Sara. "You two get with Ms. Stovall and see what you can find out. Share only what you must to get what you need. Check personnel records from that time frame. Anything suspicious turns up, dig into it quickly, but quietly. And, Doctor, I appreciate your cooperation."

Pritchard tipped his head. "And I yours, Chief."

Amara swirled her cup and stared into the remnants of her espresso. The way forward seemed clear, yet the root of a question stirred her brain. She massaged her forehead, then looked at the others. "We're forgetting something. If the DNA doesn't belong to the Cotulla kids, whose is it? There were unknown human remains in Benjamin Reyes's coffin, right? We should run the Asian DNA against the FBI's database and see if we get a hit."

Johnson nodded. "I'll take care of it. Several of our people have access to CODIS. Dr. Pritchard, any chance I can get a copy of all the DNA records from Cotulla? Might as well do them all at once."

Pritchard shook his head. "Sorry. I can give you the kids' results, but not the parents'. Since we assume the children have died, there are no privacy issues."

"Fair enough," the chief said. "Email them when you can. Now, if there's nothing else, I suggest we get to work."

The ME stood and stepped behind Sara's chair. "Ladies, if you'll return to my office, I'll introduce you to Karen Stovall. She covers for me on Sundays, so I'm certain she'll be there. Ranger Colby, perhaps you'd like to ride with me?"

* * *

Amara and Sara met with the deputy ME and asked her to walk them through the steps involved in processing and shipping DNA samples. In cases where the specimens were collected from the recently deceased, the work was done on-site, usually during the autopsy. Gathering DNA from the living was rare, but a member of their lab team handled it when necessary.

Whatever paperwork might be needed was placed in an envelope with the sample, and everything was cross-labeled with tracking numbers before the package was sealed and delivered to the mailroom. Key card security prevented unauthorized access to the area. From there, the specimen was overnighted to whichever lab currently had the bid to handle the testing.

Amara requested the personnel records of anyone with access to the mailroom at the time of the Cotulla incident. Dr. Stovall hesitated and explained she didn't want to release personal information before confirming with Dr. Pritchard, but she could provide a list of names along with their dates of employment. The two investigators agreed, with the understanding that if they needed more, Dr. Stovall would do everything possible to obtain it for them.

Sara and Amara sat in a small conference room and reviewed the data. Three people worked in the mailroom at the time of Cotulla, plus at least two dozen more with access. Any of them could've tampered with the shipments, but to do so on such a large scale would have been difficult.

"Focus on the three mailroom employees. Simplest solution's usually the best," Sara said.

Amara scanned the list of names and dates again. "And in this case, that would be, here we go, Harvey Branson. Mailroom supervisor for seven years prior to Cotulla. Quit working here the year after the incident. The other two workers are still employed."

"Want to talk to them first? See if they get nervous or remember anything unusual?"

"No. The fewer people we talk to, the better. Let's get Branson's personnel records first. See if there's anything pointing to him. I'll track down Dr. Stovall and ask her to pull his file."

Sara stood and covered her mouth as she yawned. "I'll find her. I need to stretch my legs anyway."

"Her office is across from the ME's, but I'm guessing you knew that."

The Ranger winked and grabbed her hat off the table. "Wait here, Detective. I'll be back in a few. Might take a little longer if Douglas hasn't given his okay to release personnel files to us."

"You got it. I'm going to hit the vending machines. You want anything?"

"I'm good. Thanks."

Amara wandered the hallways until she found the break room, then selected a bottled water from the Coke machine. She scanned the snacks, debating between the Cheetos and the Snickers. Either was a bad choice, but it wouldn't be the first she'd made. The Snickers won out, having convinced her the energy boost would come quicker. So would the crash. Besides, she didn't have any chopsticks.

The sound of boots on tile echoed from the doorway, and she turned to see Sara hurrying into the room, hat in one hand, manila folder in the other.

"We need to talk," the Ranger said.

"What's going on?"

"I got Branson's file. Dr. Stovall said she could give it to me without talking to her boss first."

Amara tore the end off the Snickers wrapper and took a bite. "How come?"

"Because Harvey Branson didn't quit or get fired. He was killed."

Amara closed the conference room door and sat quickly. "Killed? How? When?"

"Car crash seven months after Cotulla."

Amara slumped back in her chair. "Car crash, huh?"

"Yeah, but think about it. If Branson was involved somehow, he'd be a loose end, right? Whoever's behind whatever this is would want it taken care of. What better way than a car crash? Happens every day."

"Maybe. I mean, I feel like this whole thing is right there on the fringes. Like some great conspiracy that's got just enough semi-facts to make it plausible, but not enough to make it believable." She pasted on a huge fake smile and pantomimed in the air. "Like the hair dude on TV. Aliens. What other explanation could there be?"

Sara pursed her lips. "Hair dude?"

"Oh, come on. The guy who thinks aliens are responsible for— oh, never mind. Larry and I watch him on TV sometimes. Late night on Discovery or History or one of those other channels that used to have actual educational stuff. Forget it. Any details on the crash in his file?"

"None. Should be easy enough to get, though. A fatality requires tons of additional paperwork. I'll track it down. Not sure what jurisdiction the accident occurred in, so it may take a bit."

Amara took a bite of her Snickers. "Thanks. Let's say Branson was somehow involved. How would that work?"

"He'd need to swap the Reyeses' test kits with ones that matched the Asian DNA."

"Wouldn't have been difficult for him to switch a couple of tests, I'd think. We need a motive. I'll dig into his background and see if anything turns up. Family life, any connection to Philip Dragan, stuff like that. I'll try to get access to his bank records too. Maybe we'll get lucky and find a large cash deposit around the time of the incident."

Sara bit her finger. "Haven't been lucky so far."

Amara choked on her water. "Really? From the way our friendly medical examiner was grinning, I thought . . ."

Red tinges sprouted on Sara's tanned cheeks. "Ha-ha."

"Sorry. Trying to lighten the mood. You want to work from here or back in the office?"

"Let's head back," Sara said. "I don't think we'll need anything else here, at least not today. Too many distractions."

"Agreed. And until we know whether someone in this office is involved, I'd feel better spending as little time here as necessary. Need to say bye to anyone before we go?"

Sara packed her laptop and grinned. "Nah. He's got my number."

* * *

Amara paid a brief visit to the chief's office to discuss the need to view Harvey Branson's bank records. The man's death didn't mean it was any easier to obtain the information, especially since he'd been married. Johnson said he'd make a few phone calls but told her not to file for a warrant. Wouldn't matter anyway, because no judge would grant the request without more evidence than she had.

She spent the afternoon on her computer, digging through Harvey Branson's life. Lived in Universal City with his wife, three kids, and mother-in-law. A few hundred friends on his still-active Facebook account, some of whom kept sending him birthday greetings nearly three years after his death. No criminal record and never served in the military. Branson grew up in southeastern Missouri and moved to San Antonio straight from high school when he received an academic scholarship to Trinity University. After two years of college, he dropped out and married Louisa Martinez. Their first child was born shortly thereafter, and he'd been hired as a part-time mailroom clerk in the ME's office. Two years later, he'd worked up to supervisor, a position he held until his accident.

Louisa Branson still lived in the same home with her kids and mother. Her Facebook page was set so only friends could view it, but her oldest daughter's provided all the information she needed. Photos, dates, family events—it was all there. And nothing pointed to anything suspicious. No unexplained windfalls of cash. No mention of problems with gambling, drugs, or any other vice. To all appearances, Harvey Branson was a normal guy living a normal life. Good for him. Not for Amara.

She stretched her legs under the desk and tossed a paper clip toward Sara. "I hope you're having better luck than I am."

"Not finding anything?"

"Oh, I found plenty. Seems to have been a good husband and father. Coached his oldest daughter's T-ball team. Moved his mother-in-law into their home. Personnel file says he was a model employee. No criminal record."

Sara smiled and shook her head. "Don't you hate it when that happens?"

"So give me some good news."

"Can't. The police reports on his death don't point to anything suspicious. Branson rear-ended a broken-down semi. He was wearing his seat belt, and his air bag deployed, but didn't make much difference. His car ran up under the trailer and shaved the roof off his vehicle. The photos aren't pretty."

"They have a theory on why he hit it? Autopsy or anything?"

"No autopsy. The report says he was texting at the time of the accident. The official cause was noted as distracted driving."

Amara picked up another paper clip and unwound it into a straight line. "Who was he texting?"

"His wife. Asking her if she wanted him to pick up dinner on the way home."

"Wonder how often he did that."

Sara shrugged. "You thinking about talking to his wife?"

"No. Maybe. Quitting time, anyway. I'll mull it over tonight. You got any other ideas?"

"Still got the two guys who worked in the mailroom back then, plus everyone else who had access."

Amara bent the paper clip back into shape. "Never easy, is it?"

Sara laughed and stood. "Aliens, am I right?"

42

See me when you get in.

The note on Amara's desk was unsigned, but she knew from the scribble who'd written it. News from the chief. Six thirty and he'd still managed to beat her to the office. The man was a workhorse. No wonder he was on his third wife. She bypassed the elevator and took the stairs two at a time.

"Morning, sir."

Chief Johnson looked up from the paperwork on his desk and nodded once. "Detective. No match in CODIS for any of the DNA files Dr. Pritchard sent over. Anything new on your side?"

"The mailroom clerk? No, sir. We've gone as far as we can on him. There's nothing that—"

"Wife and three kids, right?"

How would he know that? "Yes, sir. Plus a mother-in-law who lived with them."

"Four months before Cotulla," Chief Johnson said, "Harvey Branson opened a trust fund for each of his kids. Specified the money was to be turned over when they reached twenty-one, or earlier if they needed funds for college. He put a hundred thousand cash in each account. The money was reported to the IRS as income from his mother's life insurance."

"Seems like a lot of money for an insurance policy."

The chief nodded. "Especially when you consider his mother died nearly ten years earlier."

Her morning sluggishness evaporated in an instant. "And the IRS didn't catch that?"

"Nothing to catch. The paperwork is clean. Complicated, but I'm told it's not that difficult if you know what you're doing. Fake accounts, dummy checks, that kind of thing. Takes a while and not cheap, but doable."

"So where'd the cash come from?"

He handed her a manila folder and motioned toward the door. "You investigating this or am I?"

By the time Amara arrived back in her office, Sara was waiting. The women discussed the meeting with Chief Johnson and the single sheet of paper inside the folder. A lawyer's name, three account numbers, amounts, and dates. Nothing else.

"Where do you think he got the info?" Sara said.

"Wasn't going to ask, but this is obviously under-the-table information. The chief took a chance sharing this. We can't let on to anyone that we know."

"Sure, so how do we talk to the lawyer about details we're not supposed to have?"

"We don't," Amara said. "What's the point? He'll either deny it or claim attorney-client privilege. Even with Branson dead, the lawyer's still the trustee. For all we know, the wife has no clue about the money."

"And no way to get a warrant for the lawyer's files. Can't explain to a judge that we're investigating something we're not supposed to know about."

"Let's think about this," Amara said. "Does it even matter if we go further with the information? We know the money came from somewhere other than what was reported. At this point, that's enough for me. Sí, we could start backtracking and try to discover where the cash originated, but it's not likely we'll figure it out.

It'll take someone with a lot more financial expertise than I have. Branson's our guy. That's all the confirmation we need to move on with this case."

Sara tapped her nose. "So we assume he switched the DNA samples and got paid a lot of money for it. Let someone else go back and figure out the details, including whether his death was actually a murder. All that matters are the tests Dr. Pritchard is performing. If the outcomes don't match the results in his files—and they shouldn't if our theory is correct—then this case becomes officially active."

Amara's knee bounced. "This is big, Sara. Who has three hundred thousand dollars to throw at a mailroom clerk? This *has* to be about more than Benjamin Reyes."

"You're getting ahead of yourself. One step at a time, remember?"

"Benjamin Reyes wasn't on the bus. You believe that too, don't you?"

Sara propped her boots on the desk. "Can't prove it. And even if I could, doesn't mean he's still alive."

"That's right. But with what we know now, can you prove he *was* on the bus? Can you prove *any* of those kids were on the bus?"

"Let's wait for the DNA tests before making that jump, okay?"

"Sara, if the results come back like we both think they will, we can't let this investigation go public."

The Ranger's eyes narrowed and she worked her chin to the side. "Somebody might come forward with information that'd help. But if Benjamin is still alive, if any of those kids are . . ."

"Whoever took them will kill them."

43

Amara woke to the sound of her phone vibrating on the nightstand. The LED clock's fuzzy digits cleared after she blinked the sleep from her eyes. 4:06. She groaned and flopped her hand on the nightstand until feeling returned, then checked her cell. A text from the chief. *6:00. My office.* A man of few words, unless you mentioned LBJ. He'd included Sara on the message.

Sleep another half hour or get up now? Her body begged for the former, her brain reasoned there was no point. Fifteen minutes later, she pushed herself upright and staggered to the bathroom, careful to avoid any accidental glances into the mirror. After a quick shower, a dab of lipstick, and a check on Larry, she grabbed a container of peach yogurt and a plastic spoon and headed out the door.

Sara pulled into the parking lot just behind her, and the two walked in together. They paused at the stairs, exchanged a glance, and continued on to the elevator. Three flights of steps weren't on the agenda this morning.

Chief Johnson sat at his desk, with Dr. Pritchard standing beside him whispering and pointing at some paperwork. The DNA results were back.

"Buenos días," Amara said.

Johnson motioned to the chairs but didn't speak or look up. The ME nodded and smiled at Sara, then returned to his whispering. Amara sat, then leaned forward and turned her head slightly in an attempt to hear the men's conversation. She deciphered bits and pieces, not enough to get the gist, but the tone of the discussion left little doubt. The test results did not match the originals on file.

Amara's thoughts raced. *Where do we go from here? If they think the kids weren't—*

"You want to tell them?" the chief asked Dr. Pritchard.

The ME straightened and flexed his fingers before speaking. "I opted for caution and held off on doing an exhumation. However, two days ago Karen Stovall collected DNA samples from the parents of one of the Caucasian children believed to be on the bus. She told them the state had audited our files and determined some of our data had not properly migrated to new servers. There was no reason to suspect any breach of privacy. Simply a computer glitch. In other words, she lied, and they bought the fabrication."

Sara frowned and took a heavy breath.

"Yes," Dr. Pritchard continued. "We obtained their DNA illegally. We will not use the samples for anything other than what we have thus far. In addition, we completed all paperwork with false names and Social Security numbers. There is no way the testing lab could match this DNA back to the parents. Late last night, she received the results of those tests. They do not correlate with the original data."

"Which means," the chief said, "other than the Delacruz girl, we can probably toss out all the tests from three years ago. They're bogus."

The ME shook his head. "I tend to agree, but without retesting everyone and exhuming the bodies, I'm not willing to make such an assumption."

Johnson massaged his forehead. "And if you exhume all the bodies, you're going to create a nightmare for the investigation, not to mention potentially putting lives at risk."

Pritchard dragged a chair next to Sara and sat. "You assume

the children are still alive. That may be true, but it's just as likely they are not."

Amara jerked. "What? Why would someone set up something this massive and then kill them?"

The doctor fidgeted for a heartbeat. "Are you sure you want me to answer your question? You might not like what you hear."

"I can guess," Amara said. "Clearly this was more than a kidnapping. No ransom demands. And just as obviously, huge amounts of money and planning went into this. And any hiccups in the operation, well, the culprits resolved by murder. Caterina Delacruz. Not supposed to be on the bus that morning. No plan to cover for her DNA, so they couldn't take her because we wouldn't be able to account for her body in the wreckage. They had to kill her. And Philip Dragan? Maybe he grew a conscience. Don't know what his involvement was, but he became a risk. Kill him too. Harvey Branson, the mailroom supervisor. Shortly after—"

"You suspect Harvey?" Pritchard inched forward in his chair and looked past Sara to Amara.

"We do," Sara answered.

"I knew him," the doctor said. "I can't believe—"

Chief Johnson held up his hand. "Let's move on. Dr. Pritchard, would you share your theory with them?"

"Yes, of course. Organs. The children were taken for their organs to be sold off piecemeal. There's a huge black market for healthy transplants, though it's extremely difficult to do such a thing in this country. I suspect the children were smuggled across the border into Mexico, and from there to Asia, or perhaps the Middle East."

Amara's stomach churned and she struggled to grasp the ME's theory. "I don't doubt stuff like that happens, but why here? Wouldn't it be easier to grab a bunch of kids off the street in Mexico or Guatemala or anywhere in South America? Or Africa? Why take the risk and spend the money to do it here?"

Pritchard nodded. "I had the same thought. My guess is American organs are worth more. Maybe better nutrition and hygiene. Maybe genetics. I haven't done any research into it, and I suspect even if I had, there'd be little to discover. It's a theory, Detective. Nothing more. However, it is every bit as valid as any hypothesis you may have. Lacking evidence to steer us in the right direction, one's as good as the other, no matter how much you may wish otherwise."

The chief tapped his index finger on the desk. "The investigation's moving on regardless of what's decided here. This department will work under the assumption the only confirmed deaths in Cotulla were the bus driver, the train engineers, and one child. The other bodies—fragments of bodies—were from unknown individuals, most likely dead prior to the incident. Our focus from this point forward will be to find those children, alive or not. Alvarez and Colby, I want the next steps plotted out within the hour. Report back to me then."

Amara squeezed her chair's armrests. "Sir, we don't need an hour. We have to go back to the crash scene. There had to be a transfer somewhere between there and the location where the last kid was picked up. A secluded spot where they could stage whatever equipment and vehicles they needed and get the switch done in minutes. We search there, then we head to the railroad yard. If Cotulla was intentional, they wouldn't have crossed their fingers and hoped enough damage was done to hide their actions. Had to be set up."

Sara's boots drummed on the floor and her voice rose. "Exactly. I wouldn't be surprised if the bus was rigged too. The driver could've even been dead before the impact. They wouldn't leave that to chance."

The chief peeked at his watch. "And the railroad will help how?"

"Not sure yet," Amara said. "Possible they have video footage of the train from back then, though I doubt it. We should at least be able to find out what it would take to derail the engines as well as trigger the explosion. Work our way backward from there. Maybe do a bit of research in their personnel files if they'll let us. See if anything odd happened around that time. One name. That's all we need."

Sara clasped her hands. "One name of someone who's still alive."

Johnson inclined his head toward the ME. "How about it, Doc? Give us a little time before you start digging up bodies?"

The ME crossed his arms. "Fine. I will withhold my exhumation orders, but not for long, and only with the understanding I'm kept informed of the investigation's progress."

"Absolutely," the chief said. "Wouldn't have it any other way."

Pritchard stood and frowned. "We both know that's not true, but I do appreciate the effort."

Johnson smiled and walked from behind his desk. "One more thing. Since we're assuming the rest of your data from Cotulla is not actually the DNA of the parents, we need to run it all through CODIS. A positive on any of them could be a tremendous help."

"I can understand that," the doctor said, "but I can also see how it might accomplish nothing more than devastating the parents of a dead child. Until I exhume the bodies and confirm that all my Cotulla data—notwithstanding the adults and Caterina Delacruz—is incorrect, I can't allow it. However, if you can develop a theory that would convince me it's worth the risk, I may consider providing the information. Otherwise . . ."

"What if all the bodies are from the same area?" Sara asked. "Maybe even moved through the same funeral home? That'd give us suspects to—"

Pritchard shook his head. "Highly unlikely. The remains showed no signs of decay, so all of the children would've died within the same time frame, give or take a year or two, depending on burial methods. Of course, there are numerous ways to get around the timing issue, if you plan far enough in advance. And you're assuming the children were dead when taken. We don't know that."

"No, but it's a safe bet," Sara said. "Why kill a bunch of kids at Point A just to swap them with other children at Point B? Whoever did this wasn't afraid of murder but drew the line at kids apparently."

Amara snapped her head toward Sara. "*That's* what Philip Dragan was sorry about. No kids died. None were supposed to. But then Caterina Delacruz showed up."

Chief Johnson leaned back against his desk. "Maybe. Dr. Pritchard, if you were going to do something like this, take a bunch of kids by replacing them with bodies, and having the DNA set up so no one would ever know, how would you do it?"

The ME arched his eyebrows. "You think I sit around pondering such things?"

"Don't you?" Johnson said.

"Of course I do. Part of the job, as I suspect it is for you. How would I do it? Simple. Point A is somewhere in Mexico."

Amara dragged her shoe through the dust beside the railroad tracks and watched as the wind erased the line. "Looks the same as the last time."

"Come back in ten years," Sara said. "It'll look the same then too. Trees over there might be a little taller, but that's it."

"Been here what, twenty minutes or so? And seen exactly zero vehicles pass this way. If this is what it's like in the middle of the day, has to be even more deserted early mornings."

Sara nodded. "No way this was a one-man job. Too much had to happen in too short a time."

"Yep, and there had to be people stationed down south to report on the train's progress. Wouldn't surprise me if they were ready to go for several days before the timing worked out. Which means they'd need someone at the train's next stop too. If those propane tanks were somehow rigged to blow, they wouldn't leave any evidence on them on the days they didn't go through with it."

"Aside from the people prepping everything," Sara said, "they'd need a way to get the kids out of here without being seen. I'm thinking a semi. No windows, and close enough to the interstate to jump on it and head south to the border. Not likely the truck would be checked going into Mexico, and even if it was, they'd have had someone in place to handle any problems."

Amara dragged the back of her hand across her forehead.

"Maybe I should start wearing one of those hats. Think I could pull off the look?"

Sara tugged on the brim. "I do. The Rangers could use a few more women. You really ought to consider signing up. 'Course, you'd have to be a Trooper first, but a couple of years of that under your belt, you'd be good to go."

"No thanks. Too old to start over."

She rolled her eyes. "Okay, Grandma. At least think about it when this is over. You'd like the variety. Never know what's coming next."

"Yeah, we'll see. Come on. Let's drive around and try to find a place they could've stashed a semi."

Their search didn't take long. They spotted three different possibilities within two miles of the crash scene. Each had at least one oversize metal building and an overgrown parking area with all manner of vehicles in various states of disrepair. Most likely, they had been storage sites for companies working the surrounding oil fields. One of the locations appeared to still be used on a somewhat regular basis. The other two seemed abandoned.

They stopped at each place and walked around, but as expected, nothing stood out. Three years had passed, and if any evidence had ever existed, it was long gone. Nothing here now but rust and dust.

"Come on," Amara said. "Let's head to the rail yard. Not much more to see here."

"Pull through a Whataburger on the way?"

Amara licked her lips. "Spicy ketchup? Talked me into it."

* * *

The railroad tracks ran alongside I-35 all the way south, and the drive to the Union Pacific station in Laredo took just over an hour. They'd have made the trip quicker, but Amara pulled into a rest area to dab and scrub a new ketchup stain on her shirt. They arrived shortly before three and stopped short of the guard shack.

A spur ran off the tracks and diverged into four sets a short distance ahead, each of which had boxcars and tankers sitting on them. The line they'd followed from Cotulla continued south, presumably into Mexico. No more than a handful of people seemed to work at the yard, based on the slim number of vehicles parked inside the fence.

"I hope this is the place," Sara said. "I thought it'd be bigger."

"Yeah, me too. Maybe there's another one farther south."

"Can't get much more south than this without being in Mexico. We're practically at the border now."

Amara shifted her car into drive. "Guess we'll find out soon enough."

After showing their ID, the women were directed to one of the few buildings around the tracks. Two pickup trucks sat outside the small wooden structure. Maintenance on the trains obviously took priority over repairs on the office. The windows hadn't been cleaned in a while, if ever, and the bottom of the door was splintered in several places.

Amara turned the knob and pushed, but the door stuck. She kicked the bottom as gently as she could and leaned her shoulder into it. The entrance swung open and the women stepped into the dimness. Two men stared back at them. One sat behind a desk that was covered in stacks of notebooks, the other across from him next to a half-empty bottled water dispenser. Sara glanced behind the door to ensure no one else was present.

"Can I help you?" the older man behind the desk asked. His leathery skin and crow's-feet pointed to a life in the sun.

"I hope so," Amara said. She showed her ID. "Wanted to ask a few questions about your operation if that's all right."

The man shrugged. "I'll answer if I can."

Sara moved closer. "And you are . . . ?"

"Colin Pullman. Day shift manager of the yard. That there's Pete, my number two man."

"I wonder," Amara said, "if we might speak in private?"

Pullman looked at his employee. "You in some kind of trouble, Pete?"

The man laughed and stood. "Wouldn't be the first time, and I suppose it won't be the last. I'll be in the yard if you need me."

"Good enough," the manager said. "Make sure your radio's turned on."

Sara closed the door behind Pete and leaned against it.

Amara grabbed a conical cup from the watercooler and downed the liquid in two gulps. "Hope you don't mind."

"No problem," Pullman said. "I'd offer you both chairs, but as you can see, we've only got the one Pete was using."

"That's okay," Amara said. "Long drive from San Antonio, and we're heading back when we wrap it up here. Do us good to stand a bit."

He closed the notebook in front of him and dropped it on top of one of the stacks. "What's this about? Pete really in some kind of trouble?"

"No, at least not as far as I know. Ranger Colby and I are investigating a case up north, and we have a few questions about how a railroad operates. Figured we'd take a drive down this way and see if someone here could answer them for us."

He squinted at her, then Sara, then back. "No telephones in San Antonio?"

"We thought it'd be helpful to see a rail yard."

"Uh-huh. Plenty of yards closer to San Antonio than us. This case you're looking into. It involve the UP?"

"Union Pacific?" Sara said. "Indirectly maybe."

Pullman scratched his chest. "Indirectly or not, sounds like you need to talk to Legal, not me. Not gonna jeopardize my pension. A little more than five years and I'm out."

"I understand," Amara said. "How about this? If at any point you want us to stop asking questions, we will. Don't want to get you in any trouble. Anything you can tell us would be more than we know now. It'd help us out a lot."

"Tell me about the case first, or at least how the UP's involved. It's not that I don't trust you, but in all the years I've been here, never seen the law stop by for a casual chat. Never seen 'em stop by for anything."

"Fair enough. It's an old case involving a collision at a railroad crossing. Train hit a vehicle and derailed. A few fatalities and—"

"Cotulla?" Pullman asked.

"Why would you think that?"

"Only derailment I know of in a long time. Plus the train came through here, so it makes sense you'd come by if you had questions. Plenty of other folks did back when the crash happened. What's the big mystery, though? Thought all that was closed years ago."

"It was," Amara said, "but we, um, audited the files and had a few questions. Just to close the loop on everything."

The man rubbed his palm over the stubble on his cheeks. "It was bad for everyone. The FRA—that's the Federal Railroad Administration—spent a couple of days going over the paperwork, but nothing ever came of it. They said the UP didn't have anything to do with the accident. The load was good, the train's maintenance current. Tell you what. I'll answer what I can. Have Pete show you around if you want. But I don't want any of this coming back on me. Agreed?"

Sara nodded. "As long as we don't turn up anything questionable on your part, this is all off the record. We're just here to gather information. And let's work this both ways. Whatever we ask stays in here, okay?"

Pullman gestured to the watercooler and handed Amara a dingy ceramic mug. "Do me a favor and fill it up. Then ask your questions."

45

"First off," Amara said, "you said the train came through here, right? Anything unusual happen with it?"

Pullman gulped his water. "Nope. Nothing at all. I was on shift that morning. Got to work around four, maybe a little after. Most of the cars had come up from Mexico a few days before. We staged them on some rails down south until we were ready, then pulled 'em up here and tacked five more cars on the end before we cleared it to move on."

"Does the train remain in a secured area while you're waiting to get everything together?"

"Well, yeah, pretty much. Fences and guards and stuff. Not impossible to get to them, though. A lot of the cars get tagged in places like that."

"Tagged?" Sara asked.

"Graffiti. The ones coming from Mexico are usually already covered in paint, so not much free space left."

Amara sat in the lone chair. "What kind of security do the trains have to go through to get into the country?"

"More than most cars and trucks, actually. The train, engines and all, is the property of the UP or whatever railroad is running it. Always American-owned, but Mexican law requires that their citizens operate the trains, so we hire them to handle everything down there. Once they get the train ten or fifteen feet across the border, they stop and we take over."

"How are they inspected?" Sara asked.

"You mean for smuggling? Everything is x-rayed. The train gets pulled past this tower that spits out gamma rays. Customs can see inside every car. Anything suspicious and they check it out."

Amara filled another paper cup with water and passed it to Sara. "They catch much stuff?"

Pullman nodded. "When they started the X-ray systems, inspections got a lot easier. 'Course, no telling how much still gets through. These cars sit in Mexico for a while. We've got security on them, but most of our people aren't even carrying. The cartels or somebody wants to put something on board, not a lot we can do to stop it. Once it starts heading north from down there, we try to keep the train moving until it gets on US rails. Once Customs does their thing, they hand it over to us."

"That's for the cargo," Amara said. "What about the cars themselves?"

"Whaddaya mean?"

"Anybody look them over? Make sure they're safe and haven't been tampered with in Mexico?"

"Cursory checks, mainly. We'll walk the rail looking for anything obvious. That's never been a problem, though. We baby the engines, and everything else is basically a box on wheels. Not a lot that can go wrong."

"Got it," Sara said. "What about tank cars?"

"Regs require we pull tankers out of service for a complete inspection every five or ten years, depending on what they carry. Other than that, we treat 'em the same as a boxcar. And if you're wondering, the FRA cleared the ones in Cotulla. If we'd missed anything, they'd have found it."

Sara crushed the paper cup and tossed it toward the garbage can, missing badly. She scooped the trash off the floor and dropped it in the bin. "The report we saw said the train was going almost sixty miles an hour. That seems awful fast."

"Not really," Pullman said. "Lots of flat, open land in Texas. Takes 'em a while to get to that speed. A while to stop too."

Amara pointed between herself and Sara. "We thought it was strange the train derailed after hitting the bus. It seems like something so big and heavy, well, wouldn't the momentum just shove it through? Estimates we saw said the bus weighed around ten tons, passengers and all. The train had to be a lot heavier."

Pullman chuckled. "I'd say so. That run had three SD70M engines on it, each one of them around two hundred tons. Add the freight cars to it, and there's no contest. Still, you never know. I've heard of trains derailing after hitting cows. All depends on the condition of the rails, whether the brakes are applied correctly, stuff like that."

"Got it," Amara said. She glanced at Sara, then turned back to Pullman. "I'm going to ask something that may make you, uh, uncomfortable. Remember, nothing we talk about goes beyond here. You're a smart guy. You'll figure out where I'm going with this. I'm asking you not to share it with anyone. It's vital. Agreed?"

The man hesitated, then clasped his hands on top of the desk. "What's this all about?"

Amara scooted her chair closer. "If you wanted to derail a train, how would you do it?"

Pullman hesitated and deep wrinkles appeared on his forehead. "You think Cotulla wasn't an accident?"

Sara crossed her arms. "Let's just say we're curious."

He clicked his tongue for several heartbeats. "How long have I got to get everything in place?"

Amara stood and pushed the chair toward Sara. "You mean the planning or the execution?"

"Forget the planning. How long to actually do what I need to do to get the train off the rails? Takes more than a penny on the tracks to make it happen. If I've got a day or two to set everything up, I'd do it different than I would if I only had, say, an hour or so."

Sara slid the chair back against the door and sat. "You've got ten minutes. Fifteen tops."

Pullman scratched his cheek. "And it's only me?"

"Let's say it is," Amara said.

"Access to railroad equipment?" he asked.

"No," the Ranger said.

The man shook his head. "Can't be done. Maybe if I had some dynamite to blow the rails. Even if I had a crew with me, fifteen minutes is too tight. See, the only way to guarantee a derailment would be to loosen the rails enough that they'd shift when the locomotive hit the area. Better yet, pull two or three rails completely away from the tracks. Not easy to do though, since they're bolted to the ties and welded together."

Amara frowned. "So you're telling us it's impossible for one man, or even a small crew, to do it?"

"No, I'm telling you it's extremely unlikely without the proper items."

"And what would those be?" Sara asked.

"Simplest way would be with a derailer. Probably use a couple of them just to be sure."

Amara straightened. "You're telling me there's a device built for the sole purpose of knocking trains off the tracks?"

Pullman shrugged. "Of course. We use them in situations where it makes more sense to dump a train than keep it on the rails. Say a few boxcars break loose in the yard and are heading for a main line. Better to derail them than risk a major accident."

"You got one of those things here? Can we take a look at it?"

"Yeah. I'll get Pete—"

"Any chance you could show us?" Amara said. "The fewer people involved in this, the better."

Pullman nodded and stood. "Better get you a drink before we go. It's a ways down the tracks."

The device was bright yellow, about a foot and a half long, and looked heavy. It sat low atop the rail and had a broad ridge slanting across its surface to direct the train off the track. Thick bolts secured it to the wood ties.

"Looks heavy," Amara said.

Pullman kicked the derailer with his boot. "Solid steel. That one's probably around two hundred pounds. They make movable ones that are a whole lot lighter, but for what you're talking about, I wouldn't trust a portable unit. Can't get 'em secure enough on the track for a high-speed train. They're mostly good at five miles an hour or less. Over that, you're gonna want something solid."

Sara pushed on the device with her foot. "How long would it take a couple of guys to install this thing?"

"If you do the prep work, predrill holes and all, less than ten minutes."

Amara squatted and inspected the derailer. "Think something like this would've survived the crash? If they'd found one, they'd have investigated."

"I saw the photos of Cotulla," Pullman said. "Not just the ones on the news either. Yeah, it's possible it could've survived. Would have been hard to find though, especially if you wanted to hide it. Spray-paint the thing black so it's not so obvious, and it's nothing but another chunk of steel. Everything got all mixed together. The rails, the train, the bus. Once they released the scene to the UP, we salvaged what we could from the locomotives and any cars that were still upright. We bulldozed everything else into trucks and hauled it off. We weren't looking for a derailer or anything else, as far as I know."

Amara stood and stared down the tracks. "Are these things kept in a secure area?"

"They are, but if I wanted to get one for my, uh, personal use, don't think it'd be too difficult. Any business that does a lot of shipping via rail is likely to have one or two on hand. They put them at the ends of their spurs in case a boxcar breaks loose. Wouldn't be too big a job to steal one, and they probably wouldn't even notice."

Sara removed her hat and swatted it against her leg to shake off the dust. "Any chance one was reported missing around here?"

Pullman shook his head. "Not that I know of, but I wouldn't be the one to ask. You'd need to talk to someone in security. They're in the offices down south a little ways."

Amara's phone rang and she glanced at the caller ID. Starsky. "Excuse me a minute. I need to take this."

She stepped a few yards away and turned her back to the setting sun. "Starsky. What's up?"

"Hey. How soon can you get back here?"

"Couple of hours. Something happen?"

"Yeah. We know what Dragan's key opens."

The car's headlights flashed against the squat metal buildings of the Keep-It-Cheap storage facility. Amara leaned over the steering wheel and drove slowly down the main road of the complex. She didn't bother looking at the numbers. There'd be plenty of lights and activity around the unit she sought.

Sara pointed out the windshield. "There. Flashing blues reflecting off the building."

Amara turned and eased down the long row of storage sheds. A marked patrol car switched off its overheads and passed them on its way out of the complex. Starsky's black Impala waited ahead and he stood in front of the vehicle with his hands in his pockets. Lights at the corners of each building illuminated the area, and the doors to all the storage units were closed. Whether that was good or bad, she didn't know. She parked next to the Impala, and the two women walked to Starsky.

"Glad you could make it," he said. "Just missed the bomb squad."

"They find anything?" Amara asked.

"Nope. No traps. We're good to go."

"So what's in there?"

"You're going to love this," he said. "It's unlocked. We left the unit just as we found it except for a portable light we put in there. Wanted you to see everything the way we did."

"Thanks, I think." She and Sara walked to the door, and after a glance back at Starsky, Amara lifted the metal entrance.

A few spiders scurried away and a moth dove around the light. Other than that, the unit was empty. Mostly. In the center, hanging from an overhead hook, was a dingy white nylon cord. A thin brown mailing envelope, slowly twisting in the nonexistent breeze, was attached to the end of the slender rope with a paper clip. On one side of the packet, someone had written the letters *SAPD*.

Starsky stood behind the women. "We haven't touched it yet. Didn't want to look inside the envelope until you got here."

"Such a gentleman," Sara said.

He handed Amara a pair of latex gloves. "Yeah, I get that a lot. Figured this was as much your case as mine. Probably more at this point. Detective Alvarez, would you do the honors?"

Amara stretched the gloves onto her hands. "Anybody else know what's going on here?"

"Naw," Starsky said. "Didn't even tell the LT. Don't need that kind of headache. He'll find out soon enough and read me the riot act about spending taxpayer dollars on a closed case. And as far as anyone else is concerned, this is part of an investigation into a gang murder. Called in the bomb squad because of a wire running from the lock to the inside of the shed."

"A wire?" Sara asked.

He shrugged. "Had to say something to get them here. Once I found this place, I needed an excuse to have everything checked before we did our search."

Amara approached the envelope and grasped the bottom corner, then tugged it away from the paper clip. She held the packet at arm's length while peeking inside. Three sheets of paper. She slipped them out, then dropped the envelope into an evidence bag Starsky held open for her. The portable light cast a harsh glare on the paper, and she held the pages so the others could see them as well.

The first page had very little writing, and dark smudges, finger-prints hopefully, dotted the edges and bottom.

My name is Philip Dragan. My fingerprints are below so you can verify. If you are not the police, please make sure this gets to them. They'll want it.

Amara waited until Sara and Starsky nodded, then turned to the next page.

I was as good as dead the day I left that note on the car. They couldn't let it pass. Not after the text from that boy. Sloppy. Knew it would end this way. Always does. Congrats on finding the key. My secret confession and revenge. Everything I know about this is on the next page. There have been plenty of others, but that's for later. Or never. No redemption for those. Too late. That girl tho. Shouldn't have done that. Said they wouldn't but they did. Kids aren't like the rest. They eat at you. Never go away. Make them pay. Too late for me.

Sara shifted from one foot to the other and Starsky leaned closer over Amara's shoulder. She read the final page.

Cotulla was no accident, but you know that by now. I was on security for them. Control the situation. The girl needed to be controlled. I didn't do it, but watched while they did. Watched and didn't say anything. Everything else went on plan. They took the kids. I don't know where. My guess is Mexico. They keep us compartmentalized. Smart. Don't know anyone else's name. Don't even know who they are. Wanted to make sure the kids weren't hurt. Said they needed them in perfect condition. Loaded them in a white

*semi with a red stripe on the sides near the bottom. Two cargo vans
followed it. One blue, one silver. They went south.*

*Not much more I can tell you. My pay came in cash at drop
points. Nothing electronic that could be traced. Never saw anyone.
Lots of panic when the boy sent the text. Idiot didn't secure his phone.
Sure he's in the ground now. Figured they might close up shop. Get
rid of loose ends. Me for one. That's when I wrote the note. Cried.
You believe it?*

*Got nothing left in this world. No home so don't bother looking.
Wouldn't find anything.*

*Wish I could tell you more. Really do. Find those trucks and
maybe you'll find the kids. I hope you do.*

Amara inspected the back of each page to verify nothing was
on them. "That's it. Not much, but these papers confirm what we
suspected."

"If they're authentic," Starsky said.

Sara peered up at him. "You think they're not?"

"I think there will be questions about them. But me?" He shook
his head. "This is the real thing."

Amara frowned and clenched her jaw. "You know what this
means, don't you? They'll take the investigation away from us. It's
become too big. The Feds will take over, especially if a border crossing is involved. We'll get a pat on the back and a handshake, then
be sent to our regular jobs."

"Probably," Sara said. "But think about it this way. They have
manpower and resources we can't even dream of. If the FBI or
whoever finds those kids gets them home quicker, then it's a good
thing."

"Besides," Starsky said, "don't be so sure you'll get shoved to the
background. You both know too much at this point. They'll need

your input, and once word of this gets out, things will have to move faster. The danger facing those children will ramp up exponentially. We can't handle that. Way out of our league."

"So what do we do now?" Amara asked.

Starsky glanced at his watch. "Call the chief. Let us know what he says, Detective Alvarez."

"Me? No. You found the storage unit. You should be the one—"

"No way. Your case, your call. I'm not waking him up, even for this."

Amara laughed. "No problem. I suspect it'll be an early start tomorrow."

Starsky raised his eyebrows. "Tomorrow? Don't be surprised if you don't make it home tonight. Hope you brought a change of underwear."

"Detective one-oh-one. Keep a spare set of clothes in your car and another at the office. I hope *you* have a change of underwear."

He hitched his pants up and grinned. "One word for you ladies. Commando."

Starsky wasn't far off. The chief wanted to meet in his office at 5:00 a.m. Amara had time to get home, check on Larry, and crawl into bed for a few hours' sleep before the drive in. Her call with the boss had been surprisingly short. He'd asked only one question. Whether or not she thought the note was authentic.

The parking garage was about a quarter full. Third shift had two or three hours left. She spotted Sara's car and checked the time on her dash to confirm she wasn't late. Still fifteen minutes before the meeting. Starsky's car was parked beside the Ranger's. Johnson must have decided to include him. Made sense. He knew almost as much as everyone else about the case. She jogged to the chief's office. Didn't want to be the last one there.

She was. The office was crowded as Starsky, Sara, and Dr. Pritchard stood off to the side making small talk. Chief Johnson typed on his computer while two men she didn't recognize sat across from him. One man wore a dark suit, the other khakis and a blue windbreaker with *FBI* emblazoned on the back in bright yellow.

Johnson looked up as she walked in. "Good morning, Detective. I appreciate you all coming so early. Let's move down the hall to my conference room. We'll have more space, and my admin's bringing coffee and pastries. I suspect we'll be there most of the morning, perhaps longer."

The group wandered down the hall and sank into the padded leather chairs. Chief Johnson took his spot at the head of the table.

The man in the suit introduced himself as FBI Special Agent in Charge Ricardo Garcia. The other was Assistant Special Agent in Charge Alex Berringer. Amara nodded to each and smiled. She needed to get a longer title.

The chief's administrative assistant knocked softly on the door and brought in two boxes of Starbucks coffee and an assortment of breakfast items. After arranging everything just so, she promised to check back shortly to see if anyone needed anything else and left the room. Starsky practically ran to the food.

"Don't be shy," Johnson said. "The rest of you, get something before he eats it all. This isn't the first meeting I've been in with him."

The rest of the group moseyed to the table and reviewed their options. Amara cut a slice of coffee cake into fourths and placed one section on a plate, then grabbed a banana to make herself feel better about her choice. After pouring a cup of coffee, she returned to her seat next to Starsky and glanced at his breakfast. A chocolate muffin big enough for at least two people and their dog, and some sort of egg-bacon-cheese concoction on a croissant.

"You understand," she said, "that's enough calories for the whole day. Maybe longer."

He bit into the croissant, rolled his eyes, and moaned. "You never know when you'll get to eat again. Why take chances? Besides, it's free."

"Free doesn't equal nutritious."

"You got cake."

She dropped her voice to a whisper. "Barely enough to taste."

"Maybe I have bigger taste buds," he said.

"That doesn't even make sense."

"Neither does your free versus nutritious argument. It's apples and oranges. Or muffins and bananas."

She slid her coffee cake onto his plate and peeled her banana. If she had to sacrifice to prove her point, so be it.

"Let's get started," Chief Johnson said. He addressed the FBI agents. "As I informed Special Agent Garcia last night, the San Antonio Police Department has been conducting a joint inquiry into the Cotulla accident. Together with the medical examiner's office and the Texas Rangers, we have gathered information that leads us to believe Cotulla was an intentional act designed for the sole purpose of kidnapping the children. While we have no definitive proof as of yet, it is our intention to move forward under the supposition those children are still alive. Detective Amara Alvarez has spearheaded the investigation, and I'll ask her to brief you on what we know."

Amara cleared her throat and sat straighter. It sounded like the chief was practicing for a news conference. And "spearheaded"? Gracias. "Thank you, Chief Johnson. Gentlemen, we think we know *how* they did it. What we don't know is *why* they did it."

For the next hour, she spoke without interruption while the FBI agents scribbled notes. She explained how she'd first stumbled onto the possibility that all wasn't as it seemed, and then detailed each step the team had taken to progress the investigation. Once finished, she asked Dr. Pritchard to elaborate on the DNA tests, which he did for another half hour. Before they could continue, the admin poked her head in to check on things, and the chief called for a fifteen-minute break.

When they resumed, the FBI agents fired off question after question, most centered around the DNA evidence and Philip Dragan.

"Dr. Pritchard," Agent Garcia said, "I understand the need for privacy, but we must have access to the records you have for the parents of the Cotulla victims. Since no one's run them through CODIS yet, that's critical. If by chance we do get a hit, it gives us another piece of the puzzle. If it'll make you feel better, we'll get a warrant."

"Feel better?" the ME said. "No, but a warrant would ease my concerns."

"Fine. We'll have one within the hour. We'll also want the exhumations done on the rest of the children."

"No," Amara said. "Not yet. We need—"

Chief Johnson held up his hand. "This issue has been discussed. We—meaning the SAPD—believe it's too early to risk this investigation going public. If we dig up that many bodies, there's no way to keep the news out of the press. That serves no one."

"I disagree," Agent Berringer said. "It serves us very well. For one, it confirms what you suspect. Right now, you basically have nothing more than a tease and a theory. Intriguing? Yes. Enough to get us fully involved? I'll leave that to Agent Garcia, but to have potential evidence sitting there and not look at it makes no sense."

"I tend to agree," Agent Garcia said. "Dr. Pritchard, I couldn't help but notice the chief didn't include your department in his comment regarding the exhumations. I'm curious as to your opinion on this."

The ME frowned and glanced at Sara before answering. "Gentlemen, please understand my expertise is in dealing with the deceased. As such, my views are affected by that, and that alone. Accusations have been made against one of my ex-employees. The evidence is tantalizing, but not complete. It cannot be until we retest the other bodies. I have refrained from pursuing such an action until now based on opinions I value. I have no desire to put lives at risk."

Agent Garcia extended his hand, palm up, toward the ME. "This is not a political debate, Doctor. I didn't hear your answer in there. Do we exhume or not?"

"What happens if I say yes, but not yet?"

Garcia clasped his hands. "No matter what is decided in this meeting, it's going up the ladder to Washington. They'll have the final say, and I can tell you what that will be. Those bodies will be exhumed, either by your department or by ours."

Sara leaned forward. "You can't. If those children are still alive, you'll be sentencing them to death."

"You don't know that," Berringer said. "You don't even know if they're still alive. If they are, for whatever reason they're extremely valuable to whoever took them. Too valuable to throw away."

"But in your experience," Amara said, "does getting the press involved make the job easier or more difficult?"

"The press can be very useful," Garcia said.

"Certainly can," Chief Johnson said. "But only when *you* control their information. Something like this, no way. You'll bury that town in satellite TV trucks from every major network, each looking for the big scoop. Camping out on the doorsteps of anyone they think might know anything. Rumors will be treated as fact. In this situation, we have nothing to gain and everything to lose."

"Then we're at a stalemate," Garcia said. "We'll help as much as we can, but we all know how this is going to go. DC will get those bodies exhumed and test them. If the results come back as you suspect they will, this becomes a federal case and your departments are shoved to the sidelines. That's not a threat. It's the way things work. Doctor, right or wrong, word will be that the ME's office screwed it up last time. You'll be—"

Pritchard's face flashed red as he slapped the table. "We did not screw it up."

"Fine," Garcia said. "One of your employees apparently took money in exchange for facilitating the kidnapping of a school bus full of kids. That sound better?"

The ME stood and jabbed his finger toward the FBI agents. "You come in here after we've done all the work and try to—"

"Gentlemen," Sara said. "It's a little early in the morning for a turf war, don't you think? Now, if I may make a suggestion?"

Pritchard clenched his jaw, plopped into his chair, and crossed his arms.

"Thank you," Sara said. "What if we went to the parents and told them everything we knew? Said that if word got out, the whole operation would be jeopardized? Then we exhume the bodies all at once. Do the work at night with as little fuss as possible. Dr. Pritchard, you're the expert here. Would we need all the remains or would a sample suffice?"

The ME relaxed and turned toward Sara. "Excellent question. At some point, we'd need to access everything, but for now a random sampling from each would be sufficient to confirm what we suspect. Either the DNA matches or it doesn't."

Sara smiled and nodded. "Thank you. Agent Garcia, would that work for you?"

"For now, yes. It'd give us enough to run full force with our investigation. Extra personnel, priority testing, whatever we need. Your team would be involved every step of the way. I have to caution you, though. When word gets out—and make no mistake, it will—the Bureau will want to control all aspects of the investigation, including who has access to information."

"In other words," Amara said, "we're out."

Chief Johnson shifted in his chair. "Understood and agreed. As long as our department's involvement in alerting the FBI to the case is not forgotten."

Amara took a sip of coffee. *Slick move. If things go bad, the chief can blame the FBI. If they go good, he can take credit for getting the ball rolling. LBJ would be proud.*

"I'm good with that," Garcia said. "As long as there's no foot-dragging on the exhumations. We'll take point on locating the vehicles used to transport the children south. Homeland Security will have video of all border crossings."

"Okay," Chief Johnson said. "Alvarez and Colby will handle the family notifications. Dr. Pritchard, I assume you'd like to control the exhumation process?"

"Absolutely," he said.

Amara half raised her hand. "If it turns out you do find the trucks crossing into Mexico, what then?"

Agent Berringer spoke up. "We have a working relationship with Mexican authorities. I don't foresee any issues with us being allowed to work in their country. They'll want to be involved, of course."

Amara glanced at the chief before speaking. "I have a concern with that. We don't want to tip anyone off that we're looking into Cotulla again. With the kind of planning and money it took to pull this off, there are sure to be members of their law enforcement involved."

"Detective Alvarez," Berringer said, "I've worked with my counterparts there many times. I can assure you that I trust them with my life. In fact, on more than one occasion, I have. To say you're wary of them indicates a—"

"Agent Berringer," Amara said, "I don't trust our *own* people when there's this much at stake."

"Tell you what," Garcia said. "We'll keep the investigation on this side of the border until we know more. If we find the trucks, we'll deal with it then. Now, I have a concern of my own. The trail we're chasing is more than three years old. Lots has probably happened since then. We need to catch a break. A big one."

"We caught one already," Johnson said. "Philip Dragan."

Garcia tapped his index fingers together. "True. But we still don't know the motive, and without it, none of this makes sense. Why?

Why take the kids? What makes all the effort on their part worth it? Thoughts? In your opinions, is this a rescue mission or a search for justice?"

"We've got theories," Amara said. "Plenty of them." She'd spent enough time lying in bed at night considering the possibilities. The only thing the options had in common was their conclusion. None of them had a happy ending.

48 Amara and Sara sat parked outside the home of another set of parents. Four more after this. An hour allotted at each house. They'd managed to get several done after the meeting yesterday with the FBI, and they'd finish today. At first the team considered getting everyone together and doing the notifications all at once, but Amara and Sara disagreed. Too much confusion, and a chance someone from the outside might notice that all the Cotulla parents had met. No, this needed to be done on a family-by-family basis.

They'd phoned each house to set up appointments. Told the parents they had an urgent matter to discuss but needed to do it in person. Nothing to worry about, they'd said, as if that would stop any concern.

Each notification had been eerily similar. Someone should do a case study on it. Maybe when this was all over, they would.

First came the confusion. Why were the police at their home? In a way, that was good. It meant none of the other parents had called them.

Next came the fear. Had to be bad news, didn't it? Sometimes one of the parents would ask a question. "Is it Mama?" "What's happened?" Usually they just sat silently, though. Leaning forward on the edge of their sofa or chair. Wringing their hands. Breathing fast.

Then the shock. Learning everything they thought, everything they'd been through for the last few years, might be—MIGHT

BE—completely wrong. No matter how hard they'd emphasized the fact that they weren't sure of anything, it was always the same.

Hope. In a way, the best of reactions, but also the most dangerous. Amara and Sara had given them hope, and if they had to take that away later, tell them it had all been a mistake, or worse, they'd been right but not in time . . . More than once they'd heard it. "We can't go through this again."

Lastly came the desperation. It *has* to be true. Anything to get their child back. *Anything.* They'd warned the parents against speaking to others. Got their signatures on the paperwork for the exhumation. Cautioned them again about sharing what they'd heard with anyone else, even the parents of the other kids on the bus. If word got out, nothing good could come of it.

Amara closed her eyes and inhaled deeply. "You ready?"

"Do I have a choice?" Sara asked.

"Not really. Let's get it done, though. Finish up today."

"You up for hanging out tonight? Told Douglas I'd meet him after work."

"I don't want to intrude on your . . . whatever it is."

Sara laughed and opened her door. "That's a good way to put it. And you're not intruding. Give Starsky a call and tell him to meet us. Only rule is no shop talk."

"Sounds suspiciously like a double date."

"If sitting at a restaurant and munching on nachos counts as a date for you, you really need to get out more."

Amara stepped out of the car and sighed. "You have no idea."

* * *

Sara handed Dr. Pritchard the forms. "All signed," she said. "We told them we won't notify them when we do the exhumations. Better that way."

The ME nodded and dropped the paperwork on his desk. "Everything's set up. We'll be doing most of the work over the next few nights. Minimal personnel and equipment. I expect you two will want to be present to deal with any issues that may arise?"

Amara tilted her head. "Issues?"

"Nosy neighbors and the like," Pritchard said. "Even with our precautions, this will be a noisy venture. Most of the burials occurred at the local cemetery in Cotulla, and it's surrounded by apartments and a mobile home park. That's the one that worries me. Three other locations have one body each. I don't suspect we'll have much of an issue there, but I will need to notify the proper authorities in case they get a call reporting our work."

"Okay," Amara said. "We'll handle the crowd control if it comes to that. Maybe it'd make more sense to do this during the day. More traffic, but fewer people at home."

"I don't think so," Sara said. "If we do the work in the middle of the night, it's far less likely people will see us. During the day, anyone at home is liable to just wander over and take a seat to watch."

The ME stepped toward Sara. "I agree with Ranger Colby."

Amara grinned. "Well, there's a surprise. Okay, Dr. Pritchard, you handle the notifications, but be vague. They don't need to know why, only that we have the proper approvals. I wish there was a way to avoid telling anyone else. Our risks are growing exponentially."

Sara brushed her index finger back and forth across her bottom lip. "Maybe there's a way to kill two birds with one stone."

"Interestingly enough," the ME said, "the origins of that idiom have nothing to do with—"

Sara held up her hand, palm facing the doctor, and smiled. "That's fascinating, Douglas. You'll have to fill me in later. How much notice do you need to start the exhumations?"

He frowned slightly and shrugged. "An hour to get everything rolling, then two or three hours to get everything in place. Why? What are you thinking?"

"I'm thinking I need to grab a drink and make a few phone calls. That means you're driving. You coming, Amara?"

"Yep. Got to text Starsky and let him know where to meet us. Besides, I'm curious what your plan is."

Sara's eyes brightened. "Be careful, Agent Alvarez. You know what they say." She held her palm toward Pritchard again. "Curiosity killed the cat."

       * * *

Two days later, Amara waited at the Cotulla cemetery with Sara just after sunrise. Her arms pulled her shoulders down, her legs didn't want to move, and her stomach grumbled. She'd cut short her time at Mama's last night, leaving after only one episode of *Downton Abbey*. One of her brothers had hung a bedsheet outside and worked out a way to project the show onto it so the family could eat and drink while watching. Wylie had been beyond excited, as had her mother. Looked like that relationship was moving along nicely. Her fear had moved to reluctant acceptance accompanied by bouts of anxiety over the impact of a potential breakup on Mama.

"You okay?" Sara asked.

"Yeah. Too much food last night, too little sleep, and the so-far-three-cups of coffee are making for a rough morning."

Orange mesh construction fencing ran around the perimeter of the cemetery. Tall chain-link fence panels, each covered with a heavy green tarp, blocked a smaller area from public view. Oversize portable canopies were spread throughout the worksite, obscuring the scene from the surrounding apartment buildings.

A large wooden sign stood at the front corner of the lot. An aerial photo of the cemetery covered the top half of the notice. In bold text below the picture were the words:

COTULLA CEMETERY IMPROVEMENT PROJECT
YOUR TEXAS TAX DOLLARS AT WORK

Under that, in smaller print, was an explanation that the grave sites and tombstones would not be disturbed, as well as a phone number to call if anyone had questions.

"Genius," Amara said. "Don't know what strings you pulled, but I'm impressed."

Sara smiled and crossed her arms. "Thanks, but all I did was come up with the idea. My major up in Waco did the hard work. Had to convince his contacts down at the capitol in Austin to spend the money."

"That can't have been easy. And to get it all together so quickly must've taken a miracle."

"Maybe. Don't know whose budget this is coming from, but it's cheap votes. The state reps will crow about the improvements. Probably threw some extra money into the deal to stick a play-ground somewhere too. We plant a few trees, put in a bit of sod and a sprinkler system. Maybe a few benches. We get what we need and no one's the wiser."

The rumbling echo and heavy fumes of a diesel backhoe crank-ing its engine rose above the fence. Sara tugged her hat a quarter inch lower and crinkled her nose. "Douglas says he'll need one day to get the work here done. He'll do the other three sites over the next week. Not really too big a rush since we'll be getting the DNA back on the remains here tomorrow. That'll be enough to satisfy the Feds and put any lingering doubts to rest from any of our folks too."

Amara shuffled her feet. "Assuming they come back like we expect."

"No question they will. You're not sure?"

"I am. It's just that everything's becoming so—I don't know—real, I guess."

"That's good, right?"

She sighed and walked toward the backhoe. "Depends on how it all turns out."

The next evening brought another meeting in Chief Johnson's conference room. His admin arranged a plate of deli sandwiches and a cooler of assorted drinks, then headed home. It could be a long night. Amara chose a ham and Swiss on rye, pickle, and bottled water.

"Several updates," Johnson said. "I want to make sure we're all on the same page as to how we proceed. Dr. Pritchard, mind going first?"

"The DNA tests from the Cotulla cemetery confirmed our suspicions. None of them matched what we have in our database. We still have three others to exhume and test, but at this point the results are a foregone conclusion."

The chief turned to the FBI agents. "Would the Bureau object if we held off on the remaining exhumations? No sense risking exposure if we don't need to."

Special Agent Garcia nodded. "I can sell that."

"Excellent," Johnson said. "I understand you've located the vehicles in question?"

"We found them on video," Agent Berringer said. "Crossing the border at Laredo. The footage is clear enough to see the drivers, license plates, pretty much everything on the exterior. Unfortunately, none of it did us any good. We couldn't talk to anyone in Mexico since we agreed not to yet. At least we know part of Dragan's story is accurate, though."

"Of course," Garcia said, "we have no way of knowing what, or who, was inside those vehicles. We're running the images of the drivers through our database to see if we get any hits. It's a long shot but could lead to someone. In the meantime, we're checking with other departments for any satellite surveillance that might be useful."

"How long will that take?" Sara asked.

"Not long, especially if the director gets involved. A day or two probably."

"Speaking of, anything from Washington?" Johnson asked. "They making any noise about a task force?"

Garcia glanced at his watch. "High-level meeting going on now. Don't be surprised if you see some new faces tomorrow morning."

Starsky took a bite of his dill pickle. "We need to get people in Mexico. Can't do everything from this side of the border."

"Being addressed," Berringer said.

"Good," Starsky said. "How?"

Garcia lifted the top piece of bread and inspected his sandwich. "We really can't go into that. There are, uh, sensitive issues involved."

Amara leaned back in her chair. "We came to you, remember? If you can't trust us, we might as well go our separate ways now."

Agent Berringer's lips formed a thin, straight line. "And who do you think that would hurt? You or us?"

"Whom," Dr. Pritchard said. "*Whom* do you think it would hurt. There's an easy way to know whether to use who or whom. All you need to—"

Sara touched his arm. "Thank you, Doctor. I hope we can all agree it's in everyone's best interest to work together on this, and that includes *whomever* you've got south of the border."

"We agree," Agent Garcia said, "but to be clear, the FBI has no jurisdiction in Mexico. We cannot legally operate there without specific permission from their government. The Bureau values its relationship with our counterparts in Mexico, and it would take extraordinary circumstances for us to risk damaging that rapport."

Chief Johnson eased back in his seat. "Well said. I'm going to assume Washington will opt for a task force. If so, Agent Garcia, I expect that effective tomorrow any further meetings between our departments will take place at the FBI offices here in San Antonio?"

Garcia rubbed his palms on the table. "Yes. I'll communicate with you directly. I caution you all that if a task force *is* assembled, someone from DC will be in charge, either on-site here or from Washington. There are no guarantees as to your future involvement."

"Not sure I like the sound of that," Amara said. "Even if we're there only in an advisory capacity, we can help with the local stuff. We know the families. That's got to count for something."

The senior FBI agent frowned and nodded. "It does in my book. Unfortunately, won't be my call. I can tell you this, though. No way everyone in this room gets access. One, maybe two of you. If that's the case, Chief, I assume you'll want Alvarez and Colby there?"

"Yes. I'd appreciate anything you can do to make that happen. Remind your people it'd be good to have access to all local and state resources as well as federal ones."

"Can do," Garcia said. "The good news is that if a team is assembled, they'll know everything we do when they get here. No lost time covering old ground. Agent Alvarez, Ranger Colby, if you could be at my office tomorrow morning? Say, eight? By then I'll know what the plan is, and as they say, it's easier to ask forgiveness than permission. If you're already in the room, it'll be harder to ask you to leave."

"We'll be there," Amara said. "Keep the coffee hot."

As expected, the FBI's task force arrived in San Antonio early that morning via a government jet. Half a dozen agents and three SUV-loads of equipment, with more on the way. Special Agent Garcia escorted Amara and Sara to a large open room. Folding tables and chairs were spread around the space, and every other outlet had a power strip stretching from it. Several laptops and phone chargers were already plugged in. A huge dry-erase board covered most of one wall, faded colored lines providing evidence of more than one permanent marker in its past.

The agents filtered into the room, each moving with purpose despite their lack of sleep. Garcia and Berringer mingled with the newcomers and talked business. No smiles. No laughter. These people were serious about their work. Good. The less time wasted now, the better. The two women grabbed chairs and sat along the perimeter as the task force congregated toward the front center of the room facing the whiteboard.

Garcia introduced himself to the group, then motioned for Amara and Sara to do the same. Head nods acknowledged them, then quickly turned back to the front. An older man, well-dressed, tan and in shape, with his gray hair morphing to white, stood and moved to Garcia. The two shook hands while the senior man leaned in to whisper something. Both men glanced at Amara and Sara, then resumed their private discussion. After a moment, Garcia strode toward the women and squatted.

"That's Assistant Director Davis. You can stay," he said. "But keep quiet unless you're asked a question. Give everyone a day or two to get used to you being here, okay? By then, you'll be one of us."

"Thanks," Amara said. "Appreciate it."

Garcia returned to his seat with the others. Davis removed his suit coat and draped it over a chair, then rolled up his shirtsleeves. "Welcome to Texas," he said. "First rule. Jackets are optional inside this building. When you leave this facility, you will be appropriately dressed per policy."

Every agent in the room slipped off their jacket.

Davis continued. "You all know the drill. Focus on your assignment. You need help, ask for it. Anything suspect is immediately shared with the team. No one goes off-site without signing out on the board over there. Questions so far?"

There were none.

"Good. Those ladies over there are local law enforcement. As of today, they know everything we do."

Amara pulled her lips into her mouth, stared at the floor, and crossed her arms. *Got that backward. As of today, you know everything we do.*

"For now," Davis said, "they have my approval to access all areas of the investigation. If that changes, I'll inform you. Use them as a resource, particularly on questions dealing with any of the families. Okay. Enough small talk. Before we discuss assignments, I'll remind you that you are not to speak of this investigation with anyone other than the people in this room, and never in a public environment. We need to figure out where we're going before this leaks. Every minute counts. Now, Agents Strand and Wroth, stand please."

A stocky man with a thick black mustache rose and stood next to a woman with short curly hair and oversize John Lennon glasses.

Davis gestured toward the back of the room. "For those of you who may not know these two, they'll be handling our tech. Agent

Kerilyn Strand will be lead, with Agent Tobias Wroth assisting. You two get your gear set up, then sweep the room and get the jammers operating before you do anything else. No offense, Garcia. Standard procedure whether it's our own building or not. Need to make sure no one's listening in. Once that's done, your priority is getting access to all the Mexican government's border crossing videos. Got an estimate on how long that'll take?"

The woman's lips moved as she did her internal math. "Unless they've switched systems in the last couple of months, half a day."

Davis grunted. "No way to do it quicker?"

"Sure," Agent Strand said. "We can probably be in their system within the hour. Breaking in is the easy part. Covering your tracks takes longer. If we don't do this correctly and they detect anything, they'll trace it back to us. Better to route the work through several countries first. Make it look like someone else did the snooping. Russia's pretty active right now, so they'd be our top choice. Not to mention the Mexicans may have alarms on the data. We'll have to tiptoe around until we know what we're dealing with."

"Okay," Davis said. "Half a day then. Max. Get it done and report to me when you've found the video."

The two agents yessir'd before moving to the back of the room and beginning the process of unpacking their gear.

Davis pointed to Garcia. "You've got logistics handled, right?"

"Yes, sir. Agent Berringer will coordinate all local activity. Cars, hotels, whatever we need. We also have access to helicopters and two additional small jets if needed, compliments of Ranger Colby. She's arranged for the state to move some of their assets to San Antonio. My understanding is they're parked, fueled, and ready to go with crews on standby."

"That's correct," Sara said. "Moved them over last night just in case."

Davis nodded his thanks. "Who's on Philip Dragan?"

Amara shifted in her seat. The details on how she'd obtained his name had not been shared with the FBI. They'd have figured out by now that Dragan didn't exist in the normal databases, but so far hadn't pushed the issue.

A tall, muscular agent stood. "I've got him, sir. Still a bit of a shadow, but I expect to have considerably more on him today. Waiting on the DOD to release their unredacted files. CIA's dragging their feet, but nothing unusual."

"Push it," Davis said. "If you need the director to run this up the ladder, let me know. Dragan could be the key to this whole thing. Oh, and Detective, um, Alvarez, was it? If you talk to Jeremy Winter again, tell him we said hello."

Amara pasted on her fake smile. No wonder they hadn't asked how she got Dragan's name. They already knew.

"Burkowski," Davis said, "how long before preliminary incursion plans are in place?"

Amara stiffened and glanced at Sara. Incursion? Were they planning a military operation?

A petite woman, her brunette hair cropped short, stood. "Hard to say without knowing where we might be going, but I'll have the border crossing locations set by late morning. Homeland Security will be notified of a possible operation, with specifics to come when and if needed. The hostage rescue team will hold at Quantico."

"I want two options," Davis said. "Stealth and speed."

"Can do. Speed means notifying Mexican authorities, though."

"Understood. We'll deal with that if we have to. Garcia will run point on the task force. Coordinate through him. I want every shred of information we already have reassessed. If we need to interview people again, do it, but maintain a low profile. Dig into the accident, the bus driver, everything. Find the motive. Why were those kids taken? Keep your phones on and charged. Unless you hear otherwise from me, we'll meet here at seven a.m. daily."

The group moved about the room, each member claiming their spot. Tables were quickly covered with files, computers, and phones. Subdued voices and clicking keyboards combined to form the low buzz of every office environment.

"What do we do now?" Sara asked.

"You heard the man," Amara said. "We get to work."

Amara sifted through the file again. "Davis is right. We're missing something on Dragan."

Sara tilted her head down and arched her eyebrows. "We're missing a *lot* on Dragan."

"Not what I meant. There's got to be a clue here that pushes us forward."

"I don't know," Sara said. "I've read his note a dozen times. If he knew anything else, I think he'd have told us."

"Yeah. Pretty obvious he considered the letter his deathbed confession. He'd have, um, . . ." Imbécil!

Sara leaned close. "You got something?"

"Dragan knew they'd be after him. Would've been a professional job. No loose ends, right? They wouldn't take any chances. He'd have been extra cautious. No way a random addict kills him in a street robbery."

"We already figured that, but unless you can talk your chief into letting Homicide reopen the case, it's not going anywhere. Honestly, even if they did take another look, I doubt they'd find anything different. Maybe at some point down the road when we have more names, more idea of who the players are."

Amara ran her finger along the folder's edge. "We're looking in the wrong place. Take the double homicide a step farther. Dragan's death is too neat. Short of a confession, we'll never find his killer. But whoever did murder him had to cover everything up, right? He had to kill again."

Sara closed her eyes and shook her head. "The drug addict. If he was framed for the murders, he'd have to die. Only way to make sure he couldn't say anything to confuse the situation."

"Yeah. We find his killer, we find Dragan's."

"Okay, I'll buy that, but wouldn't whoever did this make sure the scene of the addict's death was clean too?"

"Won't know until we check. Maybe they assumed no one would look too close at a druggie's OD. I think it's time to go see Starsky."

Forty minutes later, Amara stood beside the homicide detective while he sorted through the file cabinet.

"Here we go," Starsky said. "Heroin OD. Tox screen made it easy. The autopsy report said this guy was a longtime abuser. Heart and lung damage indicated heavy usage, most likely crack and—huh."

"Huh, what?"

"Lack of kidney damage indicates the subject was not a regular user of heroin."

"Which means whoever killed him didn't know him."

"Not necessarily," Starsky said. "Maybe the guy took the cash he stole and bought black tar with it. Wanted to try something new."

She placed her hands on her hips. "You don't still think this addict killed Dragan?"

"There's no evidence to the contrary. What I think isn't relevant."

She scooted closer. "It's *very* relative. I'm asking you to take another look at this man's death. See if there's anything out of place. Something that might point us to his killer."

"I could probably be talked into that. Have to rearrange my schedule, though. Do it off the clock to keep the LT out of the loop. Now that I think about it, seems like I do a lot of nonpaying work for you."

"And is that a problem?"

"Well, it *is* my toe-shaving night, but I guess I can wait another day."

Amara scrunched her face. "You know how gross that sounds, right?"

He grinned and held up one foot. "Yeah, I do."

* * *

Members of the task force filtered toward the table and perused the boxes of deli lunches and drinks. Nobody seemed eager to test the tuna salad, so Amara took one, passed on the chips, and grabbed a bottled water. Burkowski, the agent responsible for possible action inside Mexico, smiled and held out her hand.

"Pamela Burkowski, HRT assault team leader."

The woman was marginally taller than Amara, but had the presence of someone much bigger. Friendly enough, but with a sharp edge. Amara tucked the water under her arm and shook Burkowski's hand. "Detective Amara Alvarez, San Antonio PD. HRT?"

"Hostage rescue team. You in Homicide?"

Amara smiled and shook her head. "Property Crimes. And don't ask."

"Won't. Appreciate your help. Lots of times we come into situations where we're, let's just say, less than welcome."

"I'm too far down the ladder to have an ego," Amara said. "Anything to get those kids back—"

"That's your gut feeling? That they're still alive?"

Amara took a half step back. "Of course. I thought we were all assuming that."

"We may be operating under the premise, but it doesn't mean we all believe it. Please don't take offense. We're not as close to this as you are. We haven't talked to the parents or visited the graves. It hasn't become personal. From an objective view, three-plus years is a long time to go without a word. Whoever took them never had any intention of those kids ever seeing their homes again."

"Doesn't mean they're dead. There are any number of reasons to keep them alive."

Burkowski shuffled the box lunches and chose turkey and Swiss. "Of course. That's why I'm here. We're hoping we find something that lets me do my job."

"Such as?"

"Proof of life, Detective. My team doesn't go in after bodies."

Amara took a deep breath. "Well, Agent Burkowski, I hope we—"

A shout rose from Agent Strand in the back of the room. "Got it, sir. We're in."

The members of the team hurried to the oversize monitors beside her. Director Davis nudged his way to the front. "You find the truck?"

She pointed at the screen. "The truck and the vans. They'll be coming through—wait . . . now."

The group watched as the semi and two vans slowed before being waved through into Mexico.

"Nothing hinky as far as we could tell," Strand said. "They're not stopping any vehicles for a good thirty minutes before and after these went through."

Davis rubbed his chin. "So either the border guards had a time frame to let everything pass, or more likely, just another day in Mexico."

"Yes, sir. We'll clean up the video, but their technology is old. We can do screen grabs of the drivers' faces and run them through software to sharpen the images. No hits in the database on the first go-around, but we'll try again with better photos."

"Clip the video with the time stamp and email the file to me as soon as possible," Davis said. "I'll send it on and see if we had any eyes on the area. Hopefully get an idea of where the vehicles were headed. I'll request they cc you on the response. If I'm not around when they answer, start working on anything they send."

Amara watched the video cycle through again. The children were in that trailer. Scared out of their minds, or more likely, sedated and asleep. The terror would return when they awakened in their new home, wherever that might be.

More than three years since the kids had gone south. How long did it take their fear to turn to something worse? Acceptance that they were never going home.

* * *

A long afternoon bled into the evening with nothing new in the case. Everything the task force came up with merely verified the information they already had. Normally Amara would be pleased with her thoroughness, but not this time. There had to be something she'd missed. A clue pointing to the whereabouts of the kids. She'd hoped the added investigators would stumble on it quickly. Shake their heads at how incompetent the local cops were to miss such an obvious sign.

Instead, the team trickled from the room to their hotel shortly after 9:00 p.m. She wanted to stop them and ask if they could stay just a little longer, but she understood. Becoming exhausted would help no one, especially the children. A good night's rest and a fresh start in the morning were what they needed.

Besides, each of them carried their laptops with them. Likely they'd spend another couple of hours working in their rooms. Amara packed her computer in her bag and headed for the car. Larry needed some attention, then she'd scroll through everything again. Her nightly exercise in futility.

Seeking the one clue that would break the case wide open, while knowing she couldn't find something that wasn't there.

**Amara's phone rang** a little before four in the
morning. She kept her eyes closed and dragged
her hand around the nightstand until she
grasped the device. Her arm was still heavy
with sleep and she flopped it onto her chest,
then held the cell high enough to see the display. Starsky. She slid
her finger across the screen to answer the call. "What?"

"Well, good morning to you too. Planning to sleep—"

"Starsky, what do you want?"

"A bit grumpy this morning, huh? Bet I can change that."

"I swear I'll hurt you if you don't get to the point. You know I can."

"Maybe, but I think if you gave me a running start, I'd be—"

"Starsky!"

"Okay then. How soon can you be here? At the station?"

She pushed herself up onto her elbows and scooted back to lean
against the headboard. "What's happened?"

"What's happened, Detective, is you may have provided a new
lead in the Cotulla case."

* * *

Amara turned the evidence bag over and held it up to the light.
The silvery spoon inside was slightly bent, stained, and charred
along the bottom. "I don't see anything."

"Wouldn't expect you to," Starsky said. "It's not there anymore.
The tech bagged the evidence and sent it on. Besides, if *you* could
see it, so could he. We'd have caught it earlier too."

She inhaled deeply and stretched her eyelids open, then glanced up at him. He couldn't have had more than four or five hours of sleep, if that, but he looked and acted like he'd recently returned from a two-week vacation. Not fair. Her own eyes had the puffiness of someone who'd just gone several rounds with a prizefighter.

"How'd they find it?"

"I went through the evidence from the scene again. Nothing stood out. Same things we find at every OD, depending on drug of choice and their preferred usage method. This guy used a spoon to heat the black tar heroin into a liquid so he could inject the stuff. Pretty common. We found the needle too. Originally we didn't worry about testing anything. Open-and-shut case, right? Addict robs a couple of people so he can buy his next high. This time, he happened to kill them, though. The tip to Crime Stoppers, finding the gun and the drugs, it all added up to a neat package."

"Told you it was a little *too* neat."

He shrugged. "Not really. A lot of murders are tied together that easily. People aren't as smart as they think they are, although it's probably more accurate to say that we're not as stupid as they think we are. Follow the evidence and you'll find the killer. When we do, we close the books and move on."

"And you had the lab check the spoon again because . . . ?"

He poked the bag. "Too new. Most of the time they look like they've been buried for a hundred years, but you can still see silver on this one. The tech checked the spoon under the microscope and that's when he found the latex on the bottom. Too small to see unless you had really good eyes and the time to search for it."

"So your theory is what?"

"Whoever killed the addict wore gloves and burned himself when he was cooking the heroin. A tiny piece of the glove stuck, melted to the spoon, and now we're hoping there are skin cells on the latex."

"And you think *my* theories show too much hope?"

He shook his head. "Not a theory. It's fact. Okay, maybe he didn't burn himself, but there was definitely latex on the spoon. I've never seen an addict wear gloves, so it came from someone else. And if there are skin cells, there could be DNA."

She placed the back of her hand over her mouth and yawned. "And if there's DNA, we have a new lead. Useless unless it's in CODIS or we find a suspect, but still more than we had yesterday. How long before we know anything?"

"You tell me. We're holding the sample here until you can talk to your FBI buddies. They'd be able to get it processed a whole lot quicker than we could. The tech said if they brought a Rapid DNA unit here, we'd know in about an hour and a half."

"What's a Rapid DNA unit? Wait, I don't care. The FBI will know what I'm talking about?"

"I'm sure. Our tech was geeking out about the thing. Said we should get one for our lab once it's approved. I told him you'd write a check."

She glanced at her watch. "Still almost an hour before our meeting starts. I'll put in a call to Davis and give him a heads-up. Feel like grabbing a bite of breakfast after that? It's on me."

"Sounds good. Haven't had anything since a couple of Twinkies a few hours ago."

"You must be—"

"And a cinnamon roll."

"You can't be—"

"Oh, and a honey bun. Two Dr Peppers. And a bag of peanuts. I think that's all."

She rolled her eyes. "It's a wonder you're able to stand."

He patted his stomach and hitched up his pants. "Tell me about it. I'm gonna have to get a smaller belt."

Four and a half hours later, Director Davis, Amara, Sara, and an FBI DNA specialist huddled in a side room awaiting the test results. The Bureau had chartered a jet and flown in a Rapid DNA machine from Dallas. The latex contained skin cells, most of which were damaged beyond use by the heat of the spoon. Most. Enough had survived to provide DNA for analysis.

"Here we go," the specialist said. "Looks like CODIS confirms we have a match with one Daryl Spelling. His DNA is on file from—"

Amara fell back into a chair and stared ahead, aware that her mouth hung open but not caring.

Davis pointed at her. "You got something, Alvarez?"

"There's a Daryl Spelling who works here. I mean in SAPD. He's Starsky's boss. The lieutenant in charge of Homicide. This has to be a coincidence. Can't be him."

"Why not?" Sara asked. "Would explain why the investigation into Dragan's death was shut down so quickly. Plus, they'd want someone on the inside who could keep tabs on everything."

"Got a match," the specialist said. "It's definitely the same guy. His DNA is on file from a case here several years ago. Cut himself on a broken window at a murder scene. The PD had to test him so he could be excluded from the blood samples."

Davis flexed his fingers and straightened. "Do we know where Spelling is right now?"

Amara reached into her pocket and grabbed her phone. "I can find out."

"Do it without alerting anyone. Somebody go find Burkowski, and everyone else, quiet."

She dialed Starsky's number and he answered on the first ring.

"Hey, what's up? That spoon do you any good?"

"Hola. How's life in Homicide today?"

"So you're ignoring me now? I see how it is."

She tilted her head. "What're you talking about?"

"The spoon. Anything come of it?"

"Um, still waiting. Listen, wonder if I could swing by there in a few minutes. Got something I need to talk to you about."

"Ohhh, all mysterious and stuff. I like it. Have to meet in your office, though. The LT's on the warpath again. Cracking down on anything he decides is personal time while on the clock."

So he's there. "If Spelling's around, I can come by later."

"Nah. He'll be here the rest of the day probably. He's settled in with his door closed. That usually means an afternoon of paperwork for him."

"Okay. Hang out and I'll give you a call when I'm on my way. They're supposed to show up this afternoon to fix the printer hookup in my office, so if your boss leaves, let me know and we'll meet up there instead."

"You got it. Drive safe."

Drive safe? That seemed kind of, uh, personal. "Thanks. You too."

"I'm not driving, Alvarez."

Heat blasted from her cheeks to her forehead. "You know what I mean. See you in a bit." She hung up and slipped the phone back into her pocket.

"Well?" Davis said.

"Spelling's there now. Probably will be for the rest of the day."

"Okay," Davis said. "Burkowski, you go in with Alvarez and Colby. I'll park nearby and wait for your call. Don't want to set off any alarm bells. Secure his weapon—quietly—and escort him to the parking garage. I'll meet you there. Let's not make a scene. This might simply be a case of cross-contamination."

"Yes, sir," Burkowski said. "I'll get the layout of the place on the way over."

Amara glanced at the woman. Easy to see how someone could underestimate her based on size. "We'll take my car and fill you in. Sir, shouldn't we let Chief Johnson know what's going on?"

"Not yet. I'll phone him once we're there, for his benefit and ours. If Spelling bolts before we show up, I'd like to rule out the chief as informing the lieutenant. Clear?"

The women headed for Amara's car, with Sara giving an overview of Homicide's layout. Only one way into the room. Expect anywhere from twenty to forty detectives to be present. Three dozen desks, paired up back-to-back, filling the area straight ahead. Cabinets and a counter to the immediate left, file cabinets to the immediate right. Windows along the back wall, none of which opened. Chairs and small tables scattered around the right side of the room with a door leading to the supply area near the back. On the left, two offices. The first was for the sergeants to use as needed. The second was Spelling's. If he was in there, it shouldn't be a problem keeping everything quiet. And if he wasn't, they'd deal with the situation then.

They agreed Amara would go in first under the pretense of talking with Starsky. The other two would wait out of sight in the hallway for her call. If Spelling was in his office, Amara would lead, followed immediately by Sara and Burkowski. They'd briefly explain that they had a few questions for him and ask if he had a few minutes to come with them. Everything else depended on his reaction to that, but no matter what happened, they had to retrieve his weapon. From there, Chief Johnson and Director Davis could make the decisions.

The tension grew as the women approached the station. Once inside, Sara signed in Burkowski and they moved to their assigned areas. The three nodded to each other and Amara strode down the hallway and stepped into Homicide.

She paused to survey her surroundings. As expected, the room buzzed with twenty or so detectives and a couple of sergeants. Spelling's office light was on and his door was open, but she couldn't see inside from her vantage point. Starsky sat at his desk, his back to her, but there was no mistaking the unkempt red hair. She walked over, peeked in Spelling's empty office, and stood beside Starsky.

"Hey, there," she said. "Hard at it, I see."

He dropped his pen, clasped his hands behind his head, and leaned back. "Thought we were going to meet in your office."

"Changed my mind. Where's your boss?"

He craned his neck to see into Spelling's office. "The LT? Around here somewhere. Probably spying on us from the air-conditioning vent. So, what did you want to talk about? Catch a break in the case?"

She rubbed her hand across her mouth and looked around the room again. "*Que?* Oh, nothing important. It can wait."

His eyes narrowed and he lowered his voice. "What's going on, Alvarez?"

"Nothing's going on. I, uh, just needed to see if you could do something for me."

"Depends on what it is, I suppose. Is it legal?"

"Of course."

"Too bad, but I'll do it anyway."

"I need—"

"Shhh. Here he comes. Behind you. Don't turn around."

Her heartbeat accelerated and she forced herself to breathe through her nose.

"Problem, Detective?"

She turned to face Spelling. "No, sir. I was just—"

He pointed at Starsky. "I was talking to him."

"Everything's good, sir," he said. "Detective Alvarez was following up on something. All taken care of."

"Then you'll have no problem getting back to work. Need I remind you we're short-staffed? And, Alvarez, I'm quite aware of your desire to transfer into Homicide. I expect you'll need my approval to do so. Might want to remember that."

She nodded. "About the transfer, sir. I wonder if I could have a moment of your time?"

He sighed and frowned. "You on break?"

"Yes, sir."

"Fine. Two minutes, no more." He marched toward his office.

Amara bent low and loud-whispered to Starsky. "No questions. Go to the hall and get Sara. Now. Tell her we have a green light."

His mouth opened and his forehead wrinkled.

She gripped his shoulder. "Go. NOW."

54

Spelling spun his leather chair and dropped into it. "Close the door if you'd like."

"That's okay," Amara said. "I won't take much of your time."

"What can I do for you, Detective?"

Amara moved away from the door and angled herself so her peripheral vision caught the window into the office area. "You said something about me needing your approval to transfer into Homicide. Just wondering where I stood on that. I mean, if you had to make your decision today, would you allow me to move over here?"

"But I don't have to decide today. I'd have to review your file before I made the call."

"Yes, sir, but based on what you know of me . . ."

He propped his elbows on the desk and clasped his hands. "Pointless exercise. A lot of things could change between now and whenever. I've been doing this for too many years to make commitments like that."

What was taking Sara and Burkowski so long? "I see. Well, if I could ask about something else then?"

"I have a lot of work to do, so if you . . . " His brow wrinkled as two women walked into the office and closed the door. "What's going on here?"

Sara stood blocking the door. "Lieutenant Spelling, I'm Sara Colby with the Texas Rangers. This is Special Agent Burkowski with the FBI. I wonder if we could go somewhere and have a chat."

Spelling took a deep breath and pushed away from his desk.

Burkowski moved so she stood within arm's reach and placed her hand on her hip.

"Sir," Amara said, "we just want to ask a few questions. I'm certain this can be cleared up quickly."

The lieutenant frowned. "Don't treat me like a rookie, Detective. I'm not going anywhere until someone tells me what's happening here."

Amara glanced out the window to the office. Already, a crowd of detectives milled conspicuously within sight, watching without looking. "The sooner we get out of here, the better. Your name has come up in connection with an investigation we're—"

His eyes opened wide. "Cotulla? Why would my name come up? I don't know anything about it."

Amara pursed her lips. "How did you know that's what we're working on?"

"Come on," Spelling said. "Who *doesn't* know? There are no secrets in a PD."

"Sir," Burkowski said, "I need you to reach over with your left hand, retrieve your service weapon, and pass it to me. If you'll do as I ask while you're still seated, no one will see."

He spun to face her. "Listen, I don't know who you are and I don't care, but no way you're taking my gun."

Burkowski squeezed her hands into fists, her knuckles popping as if she'd fired warning shots. "You don't want to make this difficult, sir. It's simply a precautionary measure for your safety and mine."

Spelling smirked. "More for yours, I'd imagine. Why don't you back up a step or two and—"

The office door opened and nudged against Sara's back. She turned to see who was there, then turned sideways to allow the chief of police into the now-crowded room and closed the door behind him.

"Problem here?" Johnson asked.

"Not sure," Spelling said. "These *ladies* want me to accompany them but won't say more than that. Want me to hand over my gun too. That's not going to happen, sir."

The chief crossed his arms and rested against the door. "That so? Let's take this down a notch. My uncle LBJ tried to be a man of peace, and I think we'd do well to emulate him here."

Amara managed to not roll her eyes. Did he stay up at night thinking of ways to work LBJ into conversations?

"Tell you what," Johnson said. "Why don't y'all leave the lieutenant and me alone for a bit? We can all save face and still get the job done."

Spelling ran his hand over his hair. "What's going on here, Chief?"

"We'll talk about that in a minute, but not here. Too many eyes on us. This is for your benefit, Lieutenant. We can take another approach, but none of us want that. We need you to answer a couple of questions. Now then, Detective Alvarez, if you and your companions would please wait in the parking garage? We'll be along shortly."

Burkowski stiffened. "I have my orders, sir."

Johnson nodded. "And I expect you to follow them. Lieutenant Spelling, if you would please hand your service weapon to this young lady?"

"Can't do that, sir. Not without—"

The chief stepped forward, leaned over the desk, and lowered his voice. "My uncle understood that there comes a point in time when nothing works except dropping the bombs. I'm at that point, *Lieutenant.*"

Spelling clenched his jaw and breathed heavily through his nose. After several heartbeats, he slowly retrieved his gun and—keeping it below desk level so as not to be seen by his detectives—slipped the weapon to Burkowski.

Johnson straightened and smiled. "Thank you. The lieutenant and I will wait here for a few minutes, then leave together. We'll share a laugh. I might even pat him on the back. Try to undo some of the damage that's been done here this morning."

Heat flooded Amara's face. "Sir, we tried to handle this—"

"Not casting blame, Detective. For everyone's benefit, I'd like to put as much of a positive spin on this as we can. I'll wait to frisk him until we get to the parking garage."

Spelling reclined in his chair. "My detectives are good. Our little charade won't fool anyone."

Chief Johnson shrugged. "Then I suppose you should've done what these women asked instead of creating a situation."

"With all due respect, sir, if they'd marched into your office, would you—"

"Lieutenant, when someone walks into your office and you can't tell if they're *for* you or *against* you, well, you're in the wrong line of work. Best do what you're asked. Won't be any negotiating your way out of this."

"Yes, but—"

Johnson placed his palms on Spelling's desk. "You're walking out of this room with me. Now. Or you're being cuffed and led, dragged, or carried out of here by these officers. Make your decision. *With all due respect.*"

55 **Daryl Spelling sat** at the Bureau's conference room table and studied each person. Chief Johnson, FBI Assistant Director Davis, Detective Alvarez, and Ranger Colby each had a notepad in front of them and waited for him to respond. For the last few minutes he'd listened in silence as Johnson explained the details around the drug addict's death.

The lieutenant shook his head. "Sounds to me like you've already made up your minds. Maybe I should just ask for a lawyer."

Johnson tapped his pen on the table. "You can do that, but you know the drill. Makes it look like you've got something to hide."

Spelling smiled. "I've used the same line many times."

"Lieutenant," Davis said, "we need to understand why your DNA was present at the scene of Eric Messer's death. Give us a reasonable explanation and we can get on with our day."

"I told you, I have no idea who this Messer guy is. I don't hang out with drug addicts, and I wasn't there before, during, or after his death. Maybe my DNA was planted or your test was wrong. Maybe the lab screwed up and cross-contaminated it. I've been a cop for nearly thirty years. My record is *spotless*, and now you're going to toss out accusations that I'm somehow connected to this lowlife's death? Give me a break. Tell me what's really happening here. Why is the FBI involved? What's this got to do with Cotulla?"

Davis narrowed his eyes. "Who said anything about Cotulla?"

Spelling gestured toward Amara and Sara. "Why else would they be here?"

Amara glanced at the lieutenant, then turned to Johnson. "He mentioned it in his office before you came in, sir. Said that everyone knows."

Spelling shrugged. "Bring in an outsider, stick her in a separate office with Alvarez, rumors and theories start to fly. Doesn't take long to figure it out."

Davis sighed and shook his head. "We wanted to do this the easy way. Keep your name clean. We've got enough for a search warrant. One phone call and I'll have the go-ahead to start tearing your life apart. Your home, bank accounts, family, everything."

"Do what you want," the lieutenant said. "I've got nothing to hide."

"Of course not," the chief said. "You're not stupid. If you're involved, you'd have gotten rid of any evidence long ago. Moved any money offshore somewhere."

Spelling turned his hands palms up on the table. "I guess the presumption of innocence doesn't apply to this group, huh?"

"Sure it does," Johnson said. "In fact, the way I see things, you're a hundred percent correct. Your record is clean. You've always been a stellar officer. If you can't tell us anything, we might as well let you return to work while we continue the investigation."

"Finally, some common sense," Spelling said. "Appreciate it, Chief."

Johnson stood and maneuvered himself between the lieutenant and the room's exit. "Director Davis, would you please have a couple of your agents escort him back to his office? And if they could wear their FBI windbreakers while they do it?"

"I think we can manage that," Davis said.

Spelling stood and moved toward the door. "I know the way."

Johnson blocked his path. "Sit, Lieutenant. I insist. The agents who will accompany you will be here shortly."

"Unless I'm under arrest, you can't keep me here, *sir*."

"Oh, but I can. You report to me and I'm ordering you to sit and wait for your escort."

"Look," Spelling said, "if you're afraid I'm going to run, why would—"

"I don't think that at all," the chief said. "You've got nothing to hide. Said so yourself. Walking into your office with a couple of FBI agents shouldn't be an issue, should it? Of course, if you *are* somehow involved . . ."

Davis patted the table. "Might make your future a little blurry. I mean, whoever's running the operation has already shown they're willing to clean up any loose ends, right? Dragan killed and all that. A nasty business. Who knows where they've got people watching. Not a problem for anyone who isn't involved, but for someone who is, well, hope their life insurance is paid up."

Spelling laughed and crossed his arms. "You guys won't listen to anything that doesn't fit whatever conspiracy theory you're selling today. Dragan was killed because he knew something. Messer was killed to set him up for Dragan's murder. That's Hollywood stuff. You should hire a screenwriter. Don't tell me how the story ends, though. I'll wait for it on the big screen."

"No need," Johnson said. "The story ends when whoever's in charge decides it ends. Maybe they trust whoever killed Messer to keep their mouth shut. Maybe they don't. I want to believe you're not involved, Daryl. I really do. I mean, if you had anything to do with Messer's death, then you know something about that double homicide too. Ugly situation for the PD all the way around. None of us wants that."

Spelling slipped his hands into his pockets. "Told you. I've got nothing to hide. You guys do your thing. You want to come at me, not much I can do about it. Not going to lie, though. This hurts.

I've given my life to this police department and this is how I'm treated? You're supposed to have my back, not be threatening me."

Director Davis pushed his notepad away. "The threat's not from us, Lieutenant. If, as you claim, you didn't have anything to do with this, you have nothing to fear. On the other hand, if certain people see you talking to the FBI and get nervous, that's on you, not us."

Spelling pulled his lips into his mouth and breathed heavily. "Nothing I can say makes a difference. You all—"

Amara cleared her throat and straightened. "Lieutenant Spelling, Eric Messer died two days after the double homicide. The coroner said the time of death was sometime between ten and two that night. Do you remember where you were then?"

He smiled and shifted his weight on his legs. "Straight to the point, eh? I like that. No more of this dancing around. I was home all night. You can check my cell. I'll sign off on a privacy waiver too so you can access the phone company's records. See what towers I was kicking off of."

"And your wife will verify you were there?"

"She will."

Amara nodded. "Excellent. Thank you. So you won't mind if we check the phone records?"

"Not at all. Like I said, my phone was—"

"Oh, not your phone. Your wife's."

Chief Johnson arched his eyebrows and stared at her.

Spelling coughed into his fist. "My wife's? Why? What could you—"

"Somebody called Crime Stoppers that night. They wanted to be certain we found the body and the gun. It's always bothered me. Anybody who'd be in the area—who'd know where the body was—couldn't have been up to any good. I don't know. Maybe it's my time in Property Crimes, but it seems like whoever found Messer would take the drugs and the gun. Sell them, use them, whatever."

"What's that got to do with my wife?"

"Her? Nothing. But you wouldn't have been reckless enough to use your own phone. Why take any chances? Leave yours on the dresser at home to make it look like you're there. No, you'd use a different cell. Your wife's maybe. Of course, someone really smart would use a burner cell and trash the thing when they were done. Maybe they did. I'm just thinking out loud here. But now I've got it stuck in my head, and until we see the phone records, it'll eat away at me."

Benjamin's photo popped to mind. "That ever happen to you? Something gets stuck in your brain and you know the only chance you've got to get rid of it is to do everything you can to get an answer?" Wasn't that what this was all about? The itch that had been there since the first meeting with Marisa Reyes, whether she wanted to admit it or not?

Spelling moved back to his chair but remained standing. "You want to see phone records? Get a warrant."

Chief Johnson frowned and motioned toward Spelling's empty seat. "Sit down, Lieutenant. We need to talk."

56   **An hour and a** half had passed, and Spelling had done little more than imply he might or might not know something, and if he did, he might be willing to share that knowledge for the right deal. "I want to go into witness protection. Me and my wife."

Director Davis pressed his index fingers together. "I'll think about it. Depends on what you've done and how much you help us."

Johnson glared at the lieutenant. "I am not amenable to *any* deal at this point. If you've got anything to do with all this, I'll make sure—"

"This is a federal case," Spelling said. "Am I right, Director?"

Davis shrugged. "You tell me. Right now we've got a double homicide and an overdose. Those fall under local jurisdiction. Of course, we're happy to help in the investigation, but beyond that . . ."

Spelling stretched and yawned.

"Is your wife involved?" Amara asked.

The lieutenant sneered at her and pointed to the men. "And get them out of here. I talk to you two and no one else."

The chief clasped his hands and stared at the suspect for a dozen ticks of the plastic wall clock. "Here's how this works. They stay. This is their case. If that's a problem for you, fine. We arrest you, put you in general lockup, and get our warrants. I will turn this department loose on you. Your home, phones, bank accounts, computers, everything from the time your poor mama signed your birth certificate."

The lieutenant leaned back in his seat and crossed his legs. "Seems like we're at an impasse here. I need guarantees and you need information, assuming I have any. What happens next? I go back to work? Fine by me. You want to post FBI agents outside my door? Go ahead."

Davis picked up his cell phone. "Excuse me while I make a call." He dialed a number and placed the phone to his ear. "Good morning, sir. Need your help. Yes, sir. I'd like to take a look into the life of Daryl Spelling, lieutenant with the San Antonio PD. Yes, sir, possible suspect. This number would be fine. Thank you, sir. Will do." He placed the phone back on the table and nodded toward Spelling. "Please, continue."

"That supposed to impress me?" the lieutenant said. "Scare me?"

"No," Davis said. "I wanted to be certain we moved forward with or without your help. Even with a warrant, it's going to take time to go through everything. You're smart enough to know we don't have enough to charge you with anything yet. Got your DNA at the crime scene, but we can't even prove Messer was murdered. You know we can't hold you here. You want to go? Fine. Go. No FBI agents. No escort."

Chief Johnson grunted. "You'll be placed on administrative leave until this is cleared up. With pay. Don't go back to your office. If there are personal effects there that you need, we'll—"

Davis's phone dinged and he glanced at the screen. "We have our warrant. Covers your wife's possessions as well. Took a little longer than I expected. We should arrive at your house about the same time you do, Lieutenant. And Washington's already digging into your financials. If you need to make a deal, better do it soon."

Spelling clenched his jaw and pressed his palms onto the table for a moment, then his shoulders slumped and he massaged his forehead. "Send someone to pick up my wife and bring her here. If word gets out, she could be in danger. She doesn't know anything about this, but that won't matter to these people. If they think they can use her to protect themselves, they will."

Sara scratched her arm and scribbled a note. "Who are they, Lieutenant? You have names?"

"Nothing until I know my wife is safe. I want her here, in the room."

"I'll handle it," Johnson said. "Are you saying you have information that can help us with Messer's death?"

Spelling rubbed his mouth. "I'm saying I have information that can help you with a lot more than the murder of a drug addict."

**Open pizza boxes,** stacks of napkins, and paper plates lined the center of the conference table by the time Mrs. Spelling was ushered into the room. The lieutenant spent several minutes whispering to the confused woman before he took her arm and guided her to a seat beside him. He grabbed her hand, kissed the back of it, and bobbed his head repeatedly.

Amara watched without speaking. Mrs. Spelling's world was about to collapse.

The lieutenant's knee bounced rapidly and he took a deep breath. "You're recording all this, right?"

Chief Johnson nodded.

"Good," Spelling said. "It's funny. I tell suspects how much better they'll feel to get everything off their chest. Tell the truth and you'll sleep like a baby at night. Not true at all, is it? Not true." He sighed and turned to his wife. "First, I want to go on record as stating that my wife, Lilly, knows none of this. Everything I say, she'll be hearing for the first time. She is blameless in this whole thing. No matter what happens, she goes into witness protection. No charges. Agreed?"

Mrs. Spelling started to speak and he whispered to her again.

Davis nodded. "If everything you tell us is the truth as you know it, including the fact that she's not involved, we can make that happen."

"Thank you," Spelling said. He inhaled deeply and raised his chin. "Just over three years ago, I was approached with an offer. We can get into the details later, but what you'll want to know now is that no, I did not recognize the man and I've never seen him again. In exchange for information, I received regular payments into a bank account in the Caymans. I would then transfer those funds into my own account in Panama."

"We'll need those numbers," Davis said. "How much money are we talking?"

Spelling scratched his nose and glanced at his wife. "Twenty grand a month. Bonus payouts sometimes. It was for our retirement. My pension won't exactly let us live comfortably. I wanted to move somewhere we could be alone and relax. Just the two of us. An island maybe. No more homicides or traffic or stress."

The chief pushed a slice of half-eaten pizza away. "Tell us about the information they wanted."

"Didn't know at first. They said they'd tell me when the time was right. Promised me, though, that no one would be hurt. Then Cotulla happened and I got a call. They wanted me to keep them updated on the investigation. Didn't tell me why. I told them I was only on the fringe and that maybe I wasn't their guy. They didn't care. If I had to guess, they had others watching from the inside. Maybe they still do. Look, I didn't know Cotulla was going to happen. They swore no one would be hurt."

Amara glared at him. "They lied."

"Yeah," Spelling said. "They lied. But I'd already received three payments. If I didn't follow through on the deal, I was as good as dead. And I figured at that point, it didn't make any difference. There was nothing I could do to bring those people back. And a couple of months later, it was all over. Whole thing ruled an accident, and nothing I knew said otherwise."

Johnson exhaled loudly. "Why'd they come to you?"

"Not a question I wanted to ask, but if I had to guess, I'd say they knew about our medical bills. Lilly had some pretty serious health issues a while back. Insurance covered a lot but said some of it was experimental. Told us they wouldn't pay if we opted to go through with it. Nothing else was working, so we went ahead anyway. Not a tough decision at all. Who cares about money when your wife's life is at stake?" He squeezed her hand. "Anyway, the drugs worked. It's probably standard procedure and covered by insurance now, but we came out of the treatments with a mountain of debt. Before then, I'd have said no way I'd ever take cash under the table."

His wife brushed a hand under her nose. "No. We'd have found a way."

Amara shifted in her seat. Lilly Spelling's eyes were puffy, her breathing rapid, and her nose dripping. The woman saw her future disappearing.

Spelling kissed the top of his wife's head. "It's okay, baby. I'm sorry. You deserve better."

"We can get the details later," Davis said. "Right now, all I need is the location of those kids."

The lieutenant's head jerked up and he focused on the FBI director. "What kids?"

Johnson muttered a profanity. "No more games, Daryl. You want your wife to go into witness protection? You need to tell us why they took the children and where they are now."

Lilly pulled her hand away from her husband and leaned back. She stared at him, her mouth half open, and shook her head. "What are they talking about, honey?"

Spelling licked his lips and rubbed his hand over his chest. "I—I don't know. The children on the bus? They all died in the accident, right? Those kids are dead. I wish they weren't, and if I'd known that's what these people were going to do, no way. Uh-uh. Like I said, no one was supposed to get hurt. When it was all over, I figured Cotulla was some sort of giant insurance scheme."

The room grew silent except for the sound of Mrs. Spelling's sniffling. Amara glared at the lieutenant. His eyes darted left to right, and he swallowed several times as sweat beaded on his forehead. *He either doesn't know about the kids, or doesn't know that we know about them.* The question was how to determine which.

"We need more," Amara said. "You're a detective. You have to have an idea of who these people are. Even if you didn't know about the kids, you had to wonder why they went through all this. You *have* to know more."

Spelling buried his head in his hands. "Of course I wondered. Nothing I came up with made sense though, and they didn't appreciate questions. Every once in a while I'd get a call. Sort of checking in. Nothing traceable. The first time I tried to ask, I was warned. The second time, they hung up and someone else called a few minutes later. Told me it was in the best interest of myself and my wife to avoid becoming a liability. I didn't ask again."

Sara drew a question mark on her blank notepad. "Anything about their voice that might help? Any background noises?"

"No noises. The second guy I talked to, Hispanic probably. English was definitely not his first language."

Chief Johnson scowled. "How did they get word to you to kill those three people?"

Spelling's wife's eyes opened wide and she sobbed into her hands.

"Baby," the lieutenant said, "you don't have to stay."

She straightened and took several deep breaths. "Yes, I do. I need to hear all of this."

"I didn't have a choice," Spelling said. "Not by then. They'd made it clear this wasn't just about me."

Lilly pressed her folded arms across her stomach and rocked forward and back. "And you think *this* is better than death?"

He reached for her, but she pushed his hand back. "I am so sorry," he said. "You were never supposed to find out."

She studied his face for a moment. "Tell them everything you've done. Everything you know. I can't—won't—live with the thought there's something we could've done to save those children. You say you did this for us, Daryl? Then fix it."

"Baby, I—"

"Fix it, Daryl, or you'll never see me again. I'll have the divorce papers filed by this afternoon."

Spelling stared at his lap. "Okay. Okay. I knew they took the kids, but not until after the accident. You can't believe how relieved I was that they were alive. And I do know why they took them, but I don't know where."

"We're waiting," Johnson said.

Spelling crossed his arms. "Not until I see a deal, in writing. Witness protection for us."

"Let me be as clear about this as I can," Davis said. "We'll take care of your wife, but you're done. Three years you've known about those kids, and you did nothing except collect a monthly bribe. As far as I'm concerned, you'll spend the rest of your life in a federal prison. I suspect that, what with you being a dirty cop and all, you won't have to endure the rigors too long."

Lilly retrieved a tissue from her purse and wiped her nose. "No games, Daryl. You have to tell them everything."

"Mr. Spelling, you are not going into witness protection," Davis said. "The US government does not make deals with murderers. Three people, maybe more, are dead because of you."

Spelling rolled his eyes and chuckled. "You and I both know the government makes deals with murderers *every day*. You pick and choose based on what benefits you the most. Well, what could help you more than information on a bunch of missing kids? Think about it. What if word got out that the FBI could've done something but chose not to for whatever reason? How do you think the public would react?"

"And how," Johnson said, "might word get out?"

"Not from me," the lieutenant said. "I swear. Too risky for those kids. But those guys figure out you're hunting them, they'll close down shop and get rid of all the evidence."

Davis grunted. "Including you."

"Yeah, including me. But we all know that the longer this investigation goes, the more likely the news is to leak. Once that gets out, it'll explode. I wasn't kidding when I said that everyone knows Alvarez is looking into Cotulla. For all I—we—know, the clock's already ticking. Pulling me in here like this didn't help. Would've been a lot smarter to do this after hours someplace away from the office, but it's too late now. Get us the deal so we can find those children."

Davis squeezed his hands into fists several times. "First off, there is no 'we.' You're finished as a cop. I'll make some calls. But if I find out you've held out on us or lied about *anything*, I'll cancel the agreement for both you and your wife. The Bureau decides where you'll go, not you. And one way or another, when this is over, everything will go public. Your name's bound to come up. I advise that wherever you are when that happens, you stay out of sight for a very long time."

Spelling nodded and sipped his water. "Power and money. Everybody wants them. But if you've already got them, there's something far more important. You'll want to get a doctor in here before I start."

58

Dr. Douglas Pritchard carried a chair across the room, positioned it next to Sara, and sat. He studied the pizza boxes for a moment. "Where are the knives and forks?"

"Food's been there awhile," Sara said. "Room temperature."

He frowned and dropped his hands in his lap. "So no utensils?"

"Dr. Pritchard," Johnson said, "thank you for coming on such short notice. We need your help." The chief introduced the Spellings and Director Davis.

The ME clicked his tongue against the roof of his mouth. "I'm assuming this is about Cotulla?"

"It is," Johnson said. "Lieutenant, tell the doctor what you told us."

Spelling sighed and scratched his neck. "These people, they knew Cotulla looked bad. Bunch of kids killed, and for what? Guess they got spooked that someone would talk, and they were probably right. So they told us the kids were alive and being well cared for. Treated better than they were by their own families. Even gave us a hint as to why they took the children. Not sure I believe them, but I've seen enough to think it's at least plausible, if you buy into that kind of stuff."

Dr. Pritchard cocked his head. "What kind of stuff?"

"Like I said, sounds like a bunch of hocus-pocus to me, but I guess if you've got the money? Anyway, they took those kids because of DMT. You know what that is?"

Pritchard's frown deepened. "Wouldn't be much of a doctor if

284

I didn't. Dimethyltryptamine, a hallucinogenic compound found primarily in some plants in Mexico and South America, though it is possible to synthesize in the laboratory. I also know that a few Amazonian tribes use DMT in religious rituals, typically by brewing it in tea. It's illegal in most countries, and fairly rare around here, at least for now. Good enough?"

"Yeah," the lieutenant said, "but there's a whole lot more to the drug, according to the people who set up Cotulla. Supposedly it triggers special abilities. Possibly even lets you live longer. Like I said, it all sounds like something from a sci-fi movie or something."

The ME shook his head. "They've been testing DMT since the sixties. The higher the dose, the longer the hallucinations, but still no more than thirty minutes usually. If I remember correctly, the trips aren't a pleasant experience. Rapid images, geometrical patterns, that sort of thing."

"Please don't tell me they're giving this stuff to those kids," Amara said.

"No idea," Spelling said. "All I know is there's a connection between them and DMT. What that might be was never shared with me."

"And you never researched the drug yourself?" Sara asked.

"Not really. Figured it wouldn't make any difference. I mean, it's not like they were going to let me in on whatever they accomplished. I googled it, but nothing I found made much sense. Just a bunch of shady websites with people bragging about their latest high."

Dr. Pritchard scooted his chair back. "Perhaps we might take a short recess? Give me time to dig through the research material? Maybe talk to someone more qualified on the subject than I am? Off the record, of course, and with no hint as to why I need the information."

Chief Johnson glanced at his watch. "We could all use a break.

That'd give us a chance to check in with the others and see if anything new has turned up. An hour be long enough?"

The ME stood and glanced at the pizza boxes again. "Yes. And if someone would be kind enough to track down some silverware? Not those horrible plastic things either."

* * *

Several minutes late, Dr. Pritchard hurried into the conference room. "Sorry. Got tied up on a phone call. Interesting information."

"Let's get right to it," Davis said. "Any idea what the link is between DMT and the kids?"

The ME sat and scooted closer to the table. Sara pulled a ceramic plate in front of him already loaded with two slices of pizza. A silver knife, fork, and spoon sat on a cloth napkin beside the plate. He stared at the setup for a moment. "Thank you, Sa—Ranger Colby. Why the spoon?"

She shrugged. "Wanted to cover all the bases."

"Strangely enough," Pritchard said, "that saying has nothing to do with baseball, though most people assume it does. Its origins are somewhat murky, but—"

Chief Johnson coughed loudly. "Doctor, if we could continue?"

The ME nodded. "Certainly. A spoon, though? Who uses a spoon to eat pizza? I don't—"

Sara nudged him with her elbow.

Pritchard began cutting his pizza into pieces. "I talked to a friend of mine. Someone with far more experience in matters of narcotics. As it happens, there's an entire subculture devoted to DMT. Theories about extending life, talking to aliens, traveling across dimensions. All of it absolute bunk, of course, but the interesting, and substantiated, part is this: a person on a DMT trip perceives time differently. What may be in reality only two or three minutes can seem like a near eternity to the user. There are those who believe that's what happens at death when a person's life supposedly flashes before their eyes. They postulate that in its dying moments, the body unleashes a torrent of the hallucinogen. On top of that, there are currently scientists in Europe investigating a possible link between DMT and oxidative stress. Lack of oxygen. They're testing to see if DMT protects brain cells during times when oxygen is cut off to the brain."

Johnson wrote on his notepad. "And if it does?"

"It could change the way ER doctors treat patients. If a high dose of DMT could buy a patient an extra minute or two of life, countless people could be saved."

Amara caught herself staring at his pizza as he carefully cut around each pepperoni. "So what do the kids have to do with that?"

"First," the ME said, "you need a bit of background. DMT is a naturally occurring substance in humans and most other mammals. Minute quantities can be detected in the brain, but we aren't sure where it comes from. There is a theory that the pineal gland secretes the compound, but no one has proven that."

Davis scribbled a note. "The pineal gland."

Pritchard speared a pizza piece and downed it before responding. "That's a whole 'nother can of worms, as they say."

Sara poked him. "Don't."

He grinned and continued. "The pineal gland is in the center of your brain, between the two hemispheres, and is about the size of a grain of rice. It got its name because it looks kind of like a pinecone, though you'd need to squint a bit to make that connection. A lot of pseudoscience mumbo-jumbo surrounds the pineal. What we do know is that the gland has an unusually large blood flow, second only to your kidneys, in fact. For such a small organ, that's truly odd."

"Okay," the chief said, "but what does the gland do?"

Pritchard placed his fork on the table and used the spoon to chase a piece of pizza around the plate. After a few seconds, he managed to corner the bite and scoop it onto the utensil. "Too much work. That's why you don't use a spoon to eat pizza. What does the pineal do? It secretes melatonin, the substance that controls your sleep patterns. Your body triggers the gland to secrete melatonin at nighttime, or really, whenever it's dark for an extended period. And that's where the pseudoscience comes in. All kinds of bizarre theories have floated around for as long as humans have known of the pineal's existence. I figure that's what this is all about."

Amara rubbed her fingertips together and leaned forward.

The ME scanned his notes. "René Descartes studied the pineal and called it the seat of the soul. Some believe the gland originated as a third eye and evolved into its present state. All nonsense, of course, but consider this. If the pineal *does* release DMT as well as melatonin, what if you could control it? Tell it when to pump DMT into your system in large quantities?"

Sara shrugged. "You'd generate your own high. So what? Not like these people couldn't simply buy the drugs."

"You're missing it," Pritchard said. "If DMT does protect brain cells against low—or no—oxygen levels, and you could constantly produce it at will . . ."

Amara jerked upright. "Then theoretically your brain wouldn't die, even if your body did. Right?"

The ME stroked his goatee. "I'm not sure anyone's willing to make that conclusion, even the most avid supporters. But you *could* prolong the brain's life. For how long, nobody knows. Maybe enough time for a transplant. A new body but the same you. Same memories, same knowledge. The benefits would be astronomical."

"Sure," Amara said, "unless you're the donor body. Tell me that's not why they took these kids."

Pritchard shook his head. "I wouldn't think so. They'd want

someone older. Late teens maybe. By then you'd have an idea of their body type, appearance, genetic issues, all kinds of details you'd want to know before you chose someone. Too many variables with youngsters, not to mention you'd want to be able to control your environment. A child can't do that."

Sara tapped his forearm. "So why take them? If they're experimenting with this stuff, wouldn't they want someone closer to their own age?"

The ME used his fork to scoot a pizza piece onto his spoon and ate the morsel. "Before I say anything else, I must reiterate that everything I've said is pure speculation. Certainly there are those who believe in the restorative properties of DMT, but all current legitimate research indicates it's nothing more than a hallucinogen. All I've done is present one possible theory as to why those children may have been kidnapped, assuming Mr. Spelling has given us accurate information."

"I have," the lieutenant said.

"Very well," Pritchard said. "Fluoride. That's why you take kids instead of adults."

Davis wrote on his notepad, then peered at the ME. "You're going to need to clarify that."

"Fluoride accumulates in the pineal gland. In fact, there are higher concentrations of fluoride there than in your teeth and bones, and it causes the gland to calcify. Several major studies are looking into the impact of the calcification and how it affects melatonin production. I haven't seen the data, but my expert told me there's very strong evidence that excessive fluoride calcification of the pineal may cause early onset of puberty in females."

"But," Amara said, "the kids are drinking the same water the adults are. Probably using toothpaste with fluoride too. Why wouldn't they—"

"It takes years for the accumulation to be high enough to start the calcification process. Children as young as the ones in Cotulla wouldn't have the problem yet. Perhaps a slight uptick, but not enough to be an issue."

Chief Johnson stretched his arms above his head. "Quite the conspiracy theory. One thing still doesn't make sense, though. Why take American kids? Why not just grab children from a country that doesn't fluoridate their water? Seems like that'd be a whole lot easier in so many ways."

Amara blew out a stream of hot air. "How do we know they didn't?"

 **A couple of hard,** quick knocks struck the door a nanosecond before it swung open. Kerilyn Strand, the owlish-looking computer tech, leaned inside the room. "Sir, when you get a moment."

Director Davis stood and arched his back. "Whatever it is, can we do it in here?"

"Sure," she said. "Give me a few minutes to set up my equipment and I'll be ready. Got some video you'll want to see."

Amara's heart raced. "Border crossing?"

Agent Strand nodded. "And a little bit more."

"Okay," Chief Johnson said. "Let's take ten minutes. Spelling, you and your wife don't leave this room without an escort. Try it, and all deals are off, understood?"

"Yes," the lieutenant said, "but I've already told you everything I know. Shouldn't you be working on getting us out of here? And no safe houses. Too risky. If there's someone on the inside—"

"You mean besides you," Johnson said.

Spelling held out his hands, palms turned up. "The longer we're in this room, the greater the possibility that someone tracks me down. Like it or not, I'm worth more to you alive, right?"

"Chief," Amara said, "can we speak in private?"

The two moved into the hall and stood aside as Agent Wroth, the assistant computer tech, pushed a cart containing a monitor and other equipment into the conference room.

Johnson rested against the wall and crossed his arms. "What is it, Detective?"

"Put the Spellings at my apartment tonight. That'll buy us time until we figure out where to hide them long term. Easy enough to monitor the approaches to my building and secure points of entry into my place. Plus, you can have Starsky help watch them."

He frowned. "Does he know what's going on here?"

She shook her head. "Starsky's been told no more than anyone outside that room, but he's a good detective. Wouldn't be surprised if he at least had an idea of where we're headed."

The chief closed his eyes and sighed. "If this gets out, Alvarez . . ."

"Yes, sir. It could go bad in a hurry for those kids."

"Call Starsky. We'll fill him in when he gets here. I assume you two will take shifts watching the Spellings tonight? I don't want them disappearing."

"We will, but you really think they'd try to run? The lieutenant seems like he's certain his death warrant's already signed. Safest place he could be is with us."

"Don't underestimate a cop's fear of going to prison. Once he's had time to digest everything that's happened today, the lieutenant might decide he's better off on his own."

"We'll secure the apartment. He's not getting out."

"Fine. Make the call, then join us. We'll hold off for a couple of minutes until you get back. And tell Starsky to keep his mouth shut. No one needs to know where he's going. I would be curious if anyone asked, though. Could be someone we need to watch."

After phoning Starsky, Amara returned to the room, nodded to Johnson, and took her seat.

"All right," Davis said. "Agent Strand, what have you got for us?"

The woman clicked her mouse and a video played on the monitor. "You've seen this part. The trucks are crossing the border into Mexico. No luck on the screen grabs, by the way. No matches to any of the faces. Anyway, right about—hold on—now we switch to an aerial view. This is the footage I got back from your email, sir. I spliced the two videos together."

Chief Johnson rubbed his chin and leaned forward. "Satellite or drone?"

"Could be either," Davis said, "but if I had to guess, I'd go with drone, most likely skirting along our side of the border. Doubt they'd go into Mexican airspace unless they needed to for some reason. Probably just routine surveillance."

Agent Strand pointed to the monitor. "Definitely drone as you'll see when the video progresses. The farther the truck goes, the lower the viewing angle. Anyway, the vehicles continue into Nuevo Laredo but don't appear to be headed for the local airport, which is good. I can fast-forward through this part, if you'd like."

"No," the chief said. "Let it run."

The team watched as the vehicles maneuvered through the streets of Nuevo Laredo. Often, the vans were obscured by buildings, but the semi remained visible as it drove through the heavy traffic. A few larger stores, seemingly placed at random among smaller graffiti-marked shops, lined the roadway.

"We got lucky here," Strand said. "Mostly one-story buildings, and the drone's altitude keeps the truck in sight. That's César López de Lara Avenue they're on now. In just a minute, they're going to turn right on Calle Perú. That's where we lose them."

Sara bit her lip. "Any idea what's down that way?"

"More shops, residential areas, and an industrial complex. No eyes on any of it, at least that I'm aware of."

Amara gestured toward the screen as the vehicles turned and disappeared from view. "They wouldn't stop there. Too many people around. Hard to secure the area, and if they were planning to keep the kids long term, it'd be a nightmare. With all the preparation that went into this operation, they'd have chosen somewhere isolated. And if they're doing some sort of experiments, I don't know. Wouldn't they need special equipment and a more secluded location?"

"Depends," Dr. Pritchard said, "on what kind of tests. If they're simply injecting massive doses of DMT, you could do that anywhere. I'd say, however, it's highly unlikely that's what they're doing. Based on the text received by Mrs. Reyes, we suspect at least one of the children is, or at least was, still alive, and if they were giving them regular shots of DMT, that simply wouldn't be the case."

"No way," Spelling said. "With the money they had to put into this operation, no way they'd kill those kids."

"Easy enough to believe that," the ME said, "but I can think of several reasons they'd be dead. For instance, if I wanted to attempt to transplant a pineal gland, it would involve—"

Sara coughed and grabbed his arm. "Let's assume the children are still alive. If that's the case, Dr. Pritchard, care to guess what their captors might be doing?"

"If I bought into the third-eye garbage, I'd be most interested in how to stimulate DMT production within my brain. Find out if there's a way to trigger the chemical's release."

Davis dotted his legal pad several times. "And you'd do that how?"

"No idea. Before I could answer that question, I'd need time to investigate their beliefs further."

"Time," Chief Johnson said, "is something we don't have. We're throwing darts here, Doctor. Give us your best guess, and if that changes later based on new information, fine. No finger pointing."

The ME nodded. "Very well. It's an accepted fact that the pineal gland is responsible for melatonin production, and we know most of its work occurs at night. Logically, I would assume that *if* the gland also releases DMT, it may do so in the evening. Therefore, if I wanted to investigate how I might stimulate that release, I'd begin by monitoring the children while they slept. Figure out a way to measure chemical levels nonintrusively. From there, I don't know. Like I said, I'd need to research their beliefs."

Amara scooted forward so she could see around Sara. "If that's the case, you'd need someplace quiet, or at least insulated for sound."

"Yeah," Sara said. "And dark."

"Agent Strand," Davis said, "check the maps tonight. Assuming the vehicles traveled out of Nuevo Laredo, see if there's anything in their last known direction that might be a candidate. Isolated structures, abandoned warehouses, that sort of thing. Dr. Pritchard, if you'd be kind enough to do whatever you can to firm up your theories this evening?"

"Of course," the ME said. "Although it would go quicker if I had help sorting through the information. Obviously it would need to be someone familiar with this investigation."

Sara rolled her eyes. "I can help."

A series of soft knocks on the door hushed the room.

"Yes?" Davis said.

"Detective Jeremiah Peckham, San Antonio PD. Okay if I come in?"

"Get in here, Starsky," Chief Johnson said.

The redheaded detective stepped into the room and paused to get his bearings, his lips turning up a millimeter when he spotted Amara.

"We were just breaking for the evening," Johnson said. "Alvarez will fill you in on what you need to know. Did anyone ask where you were going?"

"No, sir."

"Good. Director Davis, anything else?"

"Not that I can think of. We'll reassemble here in the morning. Seven o'clock. I'm going to call DC and have the rest of Burkowski's team flown down tonight. I want them close in case we need to move quickly. Agent Strand, you and Agent Wroth will join us tomorrow with anything you find tonight. I suggest everyone get as much sleep as they can. Could be the last you see of your own beds for a while. Better bring a change of clothes or two."

The chief stood and made eye contact with Amara. "You're good to go?"

"Yes, sir."

Johnson glared at Spelling. "You try anything and any possible deal is off . . . for both of you."

The lieutenant shrugged. "Where would I go?"

Davis pulled out his cell phone. "Seven o'clock tomorrow. There's a good chance we set off alarms when we brought Mr. Spelling into this. Watch your backs out there. Anything looks suspicious, take appropriate action."

Amara gave Starsky the details he needed for now, and promised to tell him everything else when they got to her apartment. Throughout the discussion, his demeanor never changed. No sign of surprise. No shock. He asked several follow-up questions, including whether she believed Spelling had shared all he knew.

Her answer came immediately. She didn't know. There'd been little sign of any remorse, but the man seemed sincere in his desire to protect his wife . . . and himself.

The group stopped at Starsky's apartment for a few minutes while he gathered some extra clothes and toiletries. Amara refused to go to the Spellings' home due to the risk of it being watched, so they swung by a Target and she purchased a few items for them. Starsky opted to wait in the car with the couple, claiming he'd be too uncomfortable selecting panties for Mrs. Spelling.

After pulling through a local burger joint's drive-through, the group arrived at Amara's apartment.

"Don't leave anything in the car," she said. "And make sure I get all the receipts. I'm on the second floor of that building over there. This is as close a parking spot as I'll find, so follow me quickly, but don't run. Everything look good, Starsky?"

He scanned the mirrors again and casually turned around to get a better view out the back window. "Yeah. I'll bring up the rear."

The group marched across the parking lot, up the steps, and into the apartment without incident.

Amara swept her hand to the left. "Kitchen's over there. Bathroom's down the hall on the right. Two bedrooms. Mr. and Mrs. Spelling, you'll use mine. Starsky and I will hang out in here. One will sleep on the couch while the other keeps watch."

The lieutenant nodded. "Thank you, Detective. I truly app—"

"Oh," Amara said. "And I'll probably let Larry out for a while. He's harmless, so ignore him."

Mrs. Spelling's eyes widened. "Larry?"

"Larry's my iguana," she said. "Lives in the second bedroom. He's kind of big though, so some people are scared of him. I'll go get him if you'd like? Give you a chance to get acquainted."

The woman shuddered. "No, thank you."

"Got it. You'll have to leave your door open, so he might come in there, but I'll try to keep an eye on him. If he gets on the bed, don't worry about it. He won't bite unless he thinks you're a threat. Oh, and if you touch him, be sure to wash your hands afterward."

Mrs. Spelling scooted closer to her husband. "I don't think that will be an issue."

"Great," Amara said. "Make yourselves at home, but keep the curtains and windows closed. There's food and drinks in the fridge if you want any."

Starsky raised his hand. "Any Twinkies?"

Amara turned to him. "You wish. Want first or second watch?"

"Let me talk it over with Larry. See if I can convince him to take my shift."

* * *

An hour and a half later, the Spellings had retired to the bedroom. Starsky had changed into gym shorts and a faded burnt-orange T-shirt with the Longhorns logo. He and Larry were stretched out on the sofa, with the lizard nuzzled beside him and its head on his chest.

Amara raised the footrest on her recliner. "You two look cozy."

"You sure Larry isn't a dog in a lizard costume? I think he likes me."

"Yeah, I'll have to talk to him about that. He's got to get better at choosing his friends."

Muffled sounds filtered from the bedroom. Sniffling and low whispers. Mrs. Spelling would have a lot of questions. Her husband wouldn't have many answers.

Amara turned up the volume on the TV and stood. "You okay for a minute? I'm going to go put on my sweats."

Starsky stroked his finger along the ridges on Larry's head. The lizard closed his eyes until Starsky stopped rubbing, then stretched and nudged his scaly head back under his masseur's hand. "Oh yeah. We're fine."

She stared at the two for a moment, then shook her head. "Glad you two are so cozy. I'm going to go change. My gun's here on the table. When I get back, you're going to tell me how you got your nickname. Got it?"

He yawned and shifted onto his side, and Larry pressed tighter against him. "Take your time."

She switched off the lights and turned the TV's sound lower again. It took less than two minutes for her to change, but by the time she returned to the living room, Starsky's rhythmic breathing and low snores had lulled Larry to sleep.

* * *

"Starsky, wake up." Amara shook his shoulder again.

He blinked several times. "What time is it?"

"Just after midnight. We may have a problem."

He lifted his head upright, careful not to startle Larry. "The Spellings?"

"No. A visitor."

He sat up and grabbed his gun off the coffee table. "What's the situation?"

"Parking lot. Same vehicle has pulled through three times in the last hour. I don't recognize the car, and no one ever gets out. Cruises through with his lights off. Looks like only a driver, but could be someone in the back seat. Too dark to be sure."

Larry's tongue flicked and Amara set him on the floor.

"You check the balcony?"

"Yeah. All clear. Could be nothing, but . . ."

"Okay. What's the play?"

"I'm going to call for a marked unit. When he gets here, I'll have the officer phone me on my cell and have him check out the car if it comes back. At least run the plates and see if we can get any kind of ID."

Starsky stood, moved to the front window, and pulled back the curtain just far enough to see outside. "Any idea on the vehicle make?"

"Midsize four-door, black or dark blue. I'm not real good with cars."

He chuckled. "Me neither. Think we should get the Spellings up?"

She scratched her cheek. "What do you think?"

"Uh-uh. This is your op."

"Get them in the bathroom, away from windows. Better safe than sorry, right?"

"You're the boss," he said.

"I like the sound—"

A scream from the bedroom sent both officers running down the hall.

Amara flicked on the bedroom light and Starsky moved beside her. Each aimed their weapon at the bed.

Mrs. Spelling was sitting upright, her pillow pressed against her chest as a shield. Her husband lay there laughing.

Starsky sighed. "Detective Alvarez, would you kindly remove your lizard from Mrs. Spelling's bed?"

Amara handed her weapon to Starsky and lifted Larry. "Come on, big guy. Let's get you back to your own room. Starsky, kill the light. Go ahead and move the Spellings."

The lieutenant pushed himself up onto his elbows. "What's going on?"

"Nothing, probably," Starsky said. "Just want to check something out. You two need to move to the bathroom for a few minutes. Give us a chance to make sure everything's okay."

Mrs. Spelling clutched her pillow tighter. "Are we in danger?"

Amara shook her head. "A precautionary measure, that's all. But I need you to go now, please. Starsky, be right back."

She hurried and placed Larry in his cage, then scrubbed her hands and joined Starsky in the living room. "Any problems with them?"

"Nah. The LT asked for a gun, though."

"You didn't give him one, did you?"

"In case it's too dark for you to see, I'm rolling my eyes. Besides, no extras. I only had ours, and I figured you'd be wanting yours back."

She chuckled. "Keep an eye on the bathroom too. If something *is* happening, Spelling may be part of it. A rescue plan maybe."

Amara dialed the police dispatch line, identified herself, and asked for a patrol car to swing through the parking lot. The dispatcher patched her through to the officer who'd be coming by, and Amara told him about the suspicious vehicle. She didn't share any other information but did caution the policeman to be careful if he approached the car.

It took a few minutes for the patrol unit to arrive and cruise slowly through the parking lot, pausing to shine its spotlight around the area. Nothing. Amara's phone rang and she spoke to the officer again. He'd remain close to the apartment complex and she'd call if the vehicle showed up again.

Starsky peeked out the curtains. "Should we let our guests out of the bathroom?"

"Might as well. You want to lie back down too?"

He shook his head. "Awake now. Why don't you get some sleep? I'll take over."

"Too much adrenaline. I'll stretch out on the couch and rest. Keep you company."

"Before you do, mind watching the parking lot? I'll tuck in the Spellings, then I'm going to wash up. I'll scrounge up a few snacks and bring them in here."

Several minutes later, he wandered into the room empty-handed. "Pretty weak selection. No Bagel Bites, Hot Pockets, Eggos, Pizza Rolls. Don't you ever eat at home?"

"Gross," she said. "Not that kind of junk. There's some crackers and stuff in the pantry. You look in there?"

"Saw the crackers, but no Cheez Whiz. You expect me to eat them dry? Eh, get some rest. I'll hold out for breakfast. Fair warning, though. The noises you hear won't be someone kicking in the front door. My stomach's not going to be happy once it finds out we're not eating for a while."

She placed her pistol on the coffee table and snuggled into the sofa. "Don't let me fall asleep. If the car comes back, we'll need to call the officer right away."

* * *

The repeated soft taps on her shoulder slowly brought her back to the world. She scratched her stomach, yawned, burped up last night's dinner, then remembered she wasn't alone. Wonderful.

"Nice," Starsky said.

"Sorry. Forgot my manners. You weren't supposed to let me fall asleep."

"A woman's got a gun, she does what she wants."

"The car back?"

"No. All quiet in the parking lot."

"Okay. Let's swap. I'll sit up for a while and—"

"Amara, it's after five. We need to get ready to head in."

She sat up and swung her feet to the floor. "What? You were supposed to wake me so I could take another shift."

"The way you were snoring, figured you were better off catching up on your beauty sleep."

"I don't snore."

"Fair enough. It could've been my stomach talking. You want first dibs on the bathroom?"

She stood and brushed the hair out of her face. "Yeah. I'll grab a quick shower. You need to get in there before I do?"

"I'm good. I'll use the kitchen sink."

"What? Are you some sort—"

"My face. I'll use the sink to splash cold water on my face. I'm not an animal, you know."

She padded toward the restroom. "Sometimes I'm not so sure."

* * *

The meeting began promptly at seven. Burkowski joined them, and everyone appeared to be rested, though Amara suspected that by midmorning they'd all be dragging a bit. She'd explained the events from the prior evening, and all agreed that the Spellings would spend tonight in the FBI building. When asked for her gut feeling about the suspicious vehicle, she'd hesitated before finally saying she thought there was a connection with the case. Possibly someone scoping out the situation with the couple.

Agent Strand had set up a large screen in the room and used a projector to show her computer's desktop. They rewatched the border crossing video twice, then she displayed an aerial map of the area.

"They're on Highway One or Route One or whatever they call them down there," she said. "If we assume they stayed on that until they got out of Nuevo Laredo, they've got plenty of possible locations to do whatever they want."

She switched the display to a terrain view. "They could turn south and head for Monterrey, but it has the same issues as Nuevo Laredo. Worse even. Lots of traffic, lots of people. Of course, they could go through Monterrey and farther into Mexico, or down into Central America. No way to know unless there's satellite coverage that hasn't been made available. The other option would be to head west. Tons of open space, most of it flat scrubland."

"They wouldn't be there," Davis said. "No place to hide from drones or satellites. Be too easy to find them if someone went looking."

She scrolled the screen to display more land to the west. "Once you get over here, you're into hills and even a few smaller mountains. Be a lot easier to hide there."

"True," Amara said, "but wouldn't they have problems with power? Seems like they'd need plenty of electricity if they've got that many kids, plus guards, scientists, whatever. Too much for generators to handle for any length of time."

Chief Johnson inclined his head toward her. "Good point. Dr. Pritchard, any input from your research last night?"

The ME cleared his throat and tugged his tie straighter. "Ranger Colby and I spent considerable time going through the theories regarding DMT and the pineal gland. Plenty of websites discussed the merits and possibilities, but none of them were from a recognized scientific or medical organization. However, a common theme seemed to be the desire to decalcify the pineal so that one could self-induce a dimensional shift in reality through a rapid release of DMT brought about by meditation."

Several people in the room turned to Sara.

"What he means," Sara said, "is that most of the believers see this as a two-step process. Clean the pineal gland by avoiding fluoride, processed foods, certain kinds of lightbulbs, stuff like that. Depending on your age, that could take several years, but once the gland is clean, the second step is usually meditation and chanting. Supposedly, eventually you'll stumble on the right formula and be able to release DMT at will. Oh, and darkness is critical. The pineal gland responds better when your environment is pitch-black."

Amara studied the terrain map. "Can you zoom out?"

The tech scrolled her mouse wheel and raised the altitude. To the west, more mountains and hills gave way to more scrubland.

Amara sighed and rubbed her forehead. "This is so frustrating.

It's not like we're going to spot the kids in these pictures. Lieutenant, are you certain you can't remember anything else?"

Spelling shook his head. "I've told you everything I know, and I'd be surprised if anyone on this side of the border has more information than I have."

Davis nodded. "We're all frustrated. The Bureau handles kidnapping and abduction cases all the time, but not like this. We usually have clues that point us in a direction. People whose past we can dig into, or maybe we get a ransom note. If we're desperate enough, we release details to the media and offer a reward. None of that applies here."

"So what do we do?" Sara asked.

Johnson closed his eyes and leaned back in his chair. "We do the only thing we can. We keep looking."

Sara glanced at the ME and shook her head. "Like looking for a needle in a haystack."

"Actually," Amara said, "we haven't even found the haystack yet."

"Let's take fifteen minutes, folks," Davis said. "Burkowski, update us on your team when we get back."

Amara motioned to Johnson. "Talk to you for a minute, Chief? You too, Starsky."

The three assembled in the hall. "What's up?" Johnson asked.

"Probably nothing," she said. "But Spelling said something that got me thinking. Nobody this side of the border knows more about this than him. Think that's true?"

"No way to know," the chief said. "It wouldn't surprise me if it was accurate, though. A lieutenant in the police department responsible for the Cotulla investigation would be quite the coup for them. They obviously trusted him if they sent him to kill those people."

She nodded. "So maybe we can use that."

Starsky's stomach rumbled. "Sorry, not enough breakfast. Are you talking about putting Spelling in contact with whoever? He doesn't have any way to get in touch with them, remember? And even if he did, I doubt they'd still trust him. After what you saw last night, they might even be looking to get rid of him."

Amara licked her lips. "And if they are, who would they trust to do the job?"

Johnson crossed his arms and frowned. "No one from this side of the border. I see where you're going. You want to use Spelling as bait, don't you? He'll never agree to that."

"Sir," she said, "they'd send someone they trusted more than

Spelling, right? No local gang hit or anything like that. Has to be a pro. Someone they've used before. Someone they trust. And there's a good chance whoever they send has information we don't."

Starsky moved to stand beside her. "She's right, sir. And we don't need Spelling's approval. He doesn't need to know what's going on. He doesn't deserve it. We'll keep him safe and that's more than we owe him."

"And," Amara said, "Burkowski's team is here. We can use them."

"I'll think about it," Johnson said. "My main concern is Mrs. Spelling. As far as I'm concerned, she's innocent in all this. I don't want to put her in danger without her consent. And I need to talk to Director Davis if his people are going to be involved. If we do this and something goes wrong—"

Starsky's stomach grumbled again. "Be okay if Detective Alvarez and I hang out in the break room for a bit? Come up with a plan you can present to the FBI? If anything shakes loose in the meeting, you can send Ranger Colby to get us."

"Fine," Johnson said. "Don't leave the building without letting me know."

* * *

Starsky dropped his pile of vending machine loot on the table and opened his Dr Pepper. "Help yourself."

Amara looked at the cookies, potato chips, and candy bars. "It's barely eight o'clock in the morning."

"I hear ya. Popcorn too?"

Why did that suddenly sound good? "Maybe. With a Diet Coke."

"You got it."

She cleared her email while the microwave did its job.

Starsky spread paper towels over the table and emptied the bag of popcorn onto them. "You want some salt on it?"

She took a bite and shook her head. "You think this will work?"

"The trap? Don't see why not, assuming the guy you saw last night is after Spelling and not a kid looking to score drugs somewhere."

"We can't go back to the apartment. Too many civilians around."

He scooped up a handful of popcorn and shoved the kernels into his mouth. "We could go to Spelling's house. If they want to get him, seems to me that's the first place they'd look. Plus, I wouldn't be surprised if we're tailed when we leave here."

She opened her Diet Coke, took a sip, and stifled a burp.

"Let it out," Starsky said. "I've heard what you can do. Stand proud."

Her face warmed and she smiled. "I trust you'll keep that tidbit to yourself?"

He grinned. "Of course. Why would I give up a potential piece of blackmail? I mean, people would be stunned to know that Detective Amara Alvarez belches." He lowered his voice and glanced around the room. "Tell me. Do you also—"

"No, I don't. Now, can we get to work here?"

"Ready when you are. It'd help if Spelling agreed to play along, though. He's going to go through the roof if we take them to his home without telling him first. Best if we didn't have to deal with that. Besides, we'll need to get the layout of the house to firm up any plans. Spelling really needs to be on board with this."

"Yeah," she said, "but I don't think he'll play ball, and definitely not if his wife's involved. Plus, we need the shooter inside the home to prove the threat, otherwise we've got nothing."

Starsky sighed. "We could separate them. Keep her out of harm's way. Tell him this will bolster his argument for witness protection instead of prosecution."

"Maybe," Amara said. "Only one way to know. Wait here while I get the Spellings. Burkowski too. She'll need to be in on this, unless you have experience in SWAT tactics?"

"Oh yeah. I look like the SWAT type, don't I?"

Amara returned a few minutes later with the Spellings and Burkowski. Starsky explained the situation and asked the lieutenant for his cooperation.

"Nope," Spelling said. "Not for this. You want to use me as bait? I don't think so. These people are good. Way better than you are."

Burkowsi pressed her lips into a thin line and leaned toward him. "Don't bet on it."

"Listen," Spelling said. "I want to help, but not like this, and especially not if it puts my wife in danger."

Amara took a deep breath. "We didn't put her in danger, Lieutenant. You did. And now's your—"

"I said no. You need to come up with something else."

Mrs. Spelling shifted her feet. "Would capturing this man help find those missing children?"

Amara glanced at Starsky before responding. "We hope so but can't know for sure. Honestly, Mrs. Spelling, we're not even certain someone was watching us last night. But if they were, it's a safe bet they'll be back tonight."

Spelling slipped his hands into his pockets. "Which is exactly why we should stay here. You can't guarantee our safety out there."

Burkowski shrugged. "Can't guarantee your safety in here either."

The lieutenant took a half step toward her. "What's that supposed to mean?"

Mrs. Spelling placed a hand on her husband's arm. "We'll do it."

"Thank you," Amara said. "We're hopeful this is going to give us the break we need."

Spelling turned to his wife. "Honey, I don't want you involved. This is far too dangerous."

"*Involved?*" she said. "You think I'm not involved already? We'll do it, Daryl, and anything else that might help find those kids. And when they do find them and bring them home, you can talk about witness protection. But not until then."

The lieutenant rubbed his eyes. "You're sure about this, baby? We'll do whatever you want. I promise, when this is over, we'll go—"

"Daryl," his wife said, "when this is over, there *is* no more 'we.'"

63 The day dragged without any progress. The group had discussed adding personnel to the team but opted against it for now, deciding that the advantage of fresh eyes was outweighed by the increased possibility of a leak. They'd adjourned early to allow Burkowski time to meet with Davis and Johnson to review the plan for surveillance on the Spelling home.

Burkowski explained that the initial thought had been to sneak the Spellings out the back door after getting them inside, but Mrs. Spelling had shot the plan down. The woman was afraid they'd be seen and whoever might be following them would be spooked off.

The FBI team would take up positions surrounding the home as night fell. Two members were already inside the house. The lieutenant had provided the layout, and the hope was that if someone was following them, they'd make their move tonight. Any suspicious vehicles would be tracked but not stopped. No action was to be taken unless lives were in danger. The Spellings would be outfitted with Kevlar vests and secured in the guest bedroom. An agent with night-vision goggles would maintain visibility on the room's windows from a vacant home down the street. A helicopter was on standby.

"Okay," Davis said. "If the guy does show up, how are you going to make sure you don't kill him? He's not much use to us dead."

Burkowski pursed her lips like she wanted to spit. "We'll have Tasers and pepper spray, along with flashbangs and sting grenades."

Her eyes darkened. "But our main priority is our safety. If we're fired upon, we'll drop him. Two snipers, one on either side of the home, will have orders to shoot to kill, but they won't fire unless I give them clearance."

Johnson nodded. "I'll need to know as soon as there's any shooting so I can call the watch commander. The last thing we need is my guys to come roaring into a firefight."

"Agreed," Burkowski said. "My guys in there now are checking the home to be certain Spelling doesn't have any hidden firearms."

Starsky pointed to Amara. "We'll leave here a little after five with the Spellings. You'll drive as if you suspect you're being followed. Lots of turns, circle the block, that kind of stuff. I doubt we'll see anyone, but if he's watching, it's what he'd expect. Oh, and the FBI won't be tailing us. Too easy to get caught. We're on our own between here and the Spellings' residence."

Amara tapped the Glock strapped to her waist. "Shouldn't be a problem. When we get there, straight inside and lock the doors. How are we going to communicate?"

Burkowski touched her ear. "My guys will have radios."

"So we wait," Amara said, "and hope someone shows up to kill Spelling."

Starsky smiled. "I've had worse Tuesday nights."

* * *

Amara circled the block twice, pretending to check for anyone following, but in reality trying to spot the members of Burkowski's team. She was unsuccessful in both cases.

She pulled the car into the Spellings' driveway and peered at her surroundings. The ranch-style home sat in an older neighborhood with larger lots than those seen in modern subdivisions. Mature trees dotted the area, along with for-sale signs and trucks pulling trailers filled with lawn equipment. Other than a person or two checking their mailbox at the street, no one was visible.

"Get your keys out," she said. "We move directly from the vehicle into the house. Starsky, you lead the way and I'll bring up the rear. Once inside, stay away from the windows and get into the hallway. The alarm system will be off. I'll reactivate it, then join you. Questions?" She paused a heartbeat. "No? Then let's go."

The foursome moved quickly through the unfenced backyard, across a concrete patio, and into the home. The alarm beeped three times as they entered, and Amara punched in the code to activate the security system. The group moved to the hall where two FBI SWAT members waited in chairs they'd borrowed from the dining room.

"We good?" Amara asked.

"Nothing to report," one agent said. "Everyone's in position, but nothing out of the ordinary. We've got eyes on all sides of the house's exterior. If anyone comes close, we'll know."

"Great. Lieutenant, you and your wife stay here. I'm going to move through and close the curtains. If we are being watched, that's what they'd expect. After I'm done, we'll settle in for the evening. Remember, the master bathroom's off-limits. Use the hallway restroom. No windows in there."

Hours passed with no activity. The FBI agents maintained their positions in the hallway, Starsky rooted through the refrigerator for the umpteenth time, and Amara resisted the urge to peek out the curtains again. She stretched and squeezed her fingers into fists. What she wouldn't give to go a few rounds at the gym about now. The steady tension combined with the lack of movement made her muscles ache.

Sound in the hallway caught her attention and she turned toward the agents. They each leaned forward in their chairs and inclined their heads. Must be radio chatter. One held up a finger and motioned for Amara.

"One vehicle made the block twice," he said. "Same model as the one you saw last night. It's parked a few houses down. The driver's still in the car."

She squatted and kept her voice low. "What's the plan?"

"The tags came back as a rental. We hold until further notice."

Starsky moved into the hall. "What's going on?"

Amara glanced at the Spellings. The couple sat on the living room floor and stared blankly toward the TV. With the curtains and blinds closed, unless someone tossed a grenade in there, they were safe. She tugged Starsky into the master bedroom. "Suspicious vehicle parked on the street. Driver's still in it. We're waiting to see what he does."

"How long do we wait?"

"Not our call. Burkowski knows what she's doing."

He ran a hand through his hair. "Another long night."

Daryl Spelling stepped into the room. "Activity?"

Amara shook her head. "Nothing certain."

The lieutenant crossed his arms and leaned against the doorjamb. "I'm not a rookie."

Starsky tilted his head toward the street. "Vehicle parked a few doors down. Driver's still inside. Probably nothing, but they're watching it just in case."

Spelling clicked his tongue several times. "Same one as last night?"

"No way to know," Amara said. "Best thing you can do is what you're doing. Sit and let the FBI do their job. If anyone comes toward the house, we'll know about it."

"Got it," the lieutenant said. "And you'll let me know if anything changes?"

"Sure," Starsky said. "We'll let you know."

Spelling stared at him for a moment before turning and walking past the FBI agents into the living room.

"Trust him?" Amara asked.

"How can I? I do think he has his wife's best—"

A loud, high-pitched whine echoed from the rear of the house.

"The alarm system," Amara said. She ran toward the living room as the agents stood and tossed their chairs aside.

Mrs. Spelling sat on the couch and stared out the open front door. "He said he was tired of sitting. Going out to check the mail and he'd be right back. I didn't believe him, of course, especially after he kissed me."

"Amara," Starsky said. "Tell the agents what's going on. I'm going out there after him."

"Not alone, you're not."

The agents sprinted past them out the front door. Amara pulled her pistol and chased after them. As she stepped into the yard, a pinprick of light, followed immediately by a sharp crack, came from her right. "Shots fired!" She squatted and swept the area around her, fearful more shooters might be near.

Starsky moved alongside and pointed up the street. "Shot came from there. Could be a diversion. Too many friendlies around. Be sure of your target."

"You see Spelling?"

"Negative. Move back inside. We need to protect the wife. I'll cover while you—"

Tires squealed as the still-dark vehicle sped away. Two quick bursts of light brightened the night as flashbang grenades exploded. The car swerved, jumped the curb, and sideswiped a tree. The driver's door opened and a figure rolled out as the car crashed into some bushes fronting a house. A shotgun blast sounded, followed by yelling.

"Inside," Starsky said. "Move."

Amara turned and squinted against the bright light flowing from the home into the yard. She crouched and moved quickly toward the partially open door, kicking it before stepping inside and sweeping the room.

Mrs. Spelling still sat on the couch.

"You okay?" Amara asked.

Starsky moved past her so he could see down the hallway.

"Fine," the woman said. "What's happening out there?"

"No idea," Amara said. "Your husband botched the plan."

The woman's chin shook and she sniffled. "Did he, now? Perhaps that's for the best."

Starsky turned off the living room lights and waited there while Amara moved Mrs. Spelling into the hallway bathroom and stood guard outside the door. She kicked herself for not insisting on having a radio. Being in the dark, literally and figuratively, was a nightmare. She jumped as a knock on the front door broke the silence.

"It's Burkowski. I'm coming in."

Amara went into her shooting stance and waited until Starsky gave her the okay, then holstered her weapon.

"What happened?" she asked. "Is everyone all right?"

Sirens grew louder and Burkowski glanced past Amara. "We need to go. Where's Mrs. Spelling?"

Amara opened the bathroom door. "Let's go, ma'am. We have to leave."

The woman sat on the toilet's lid, her chin pressed against her chest. "My husband?"

"Not coming with us," Burkowski said. "We'll talk about it in the car, but we need to be gone when the police get here. Already too many neighbors outside. The area's not secure anymore."

Amara lowered her voice. "Anyone call Chief Johnson?"

"He knows, but not all the details. Honestly, I'm not sure *we* know everything yet. The PD is aware there are agents on the scene, though. Can you get her to the car?"

Amara walked to Mrs. Spelling and eased her hand under the woman's arm. "It'll be okay. Right now, we want to make sure everyone's safe. As soon as we get out of here, we'll find out what happened."

Mrs. Spelling shuffled through the house and waited in the laundry room until Burkowski gave them the go-ahead to exit through the garage. Amara handed the car keys to Starsky and asked him to drive, then helped the woman into the back seat of the vehicle. She reached across and buckled the seat belt for her, then hurried to the other side and slid in.

Seconds later, they were out of the neighborhood on their way back to the FBI building. Burkowski shifted in her seat to face Amara. "Why did he leave the house?"

Amara glanced at Mrs. Spelling. "Maybe we should wait and talk about—"

"No," the woman said. "He's dead, isn't he?"

Burkowski nodded. "High-caliber rifle round. Too much power for the Kevlar vest. I'm sorry."

Amara took Mrs. Spelling's hand in hers and squeezed. "I'm sorry too."

The woman took a deep breath. "I knew he was going to do it. I could see it on his face."

"Maybe," Amara said, "this was his way of resolving everything. Trying to make it up to you."

"Maybe. Did they catch the man who shot him?"

Burkowski turned farther around in her seat. "Actually, it was a woman. And yes, we caught her. She's injured, but not seriously. They're clearing her at the hospital before they bring her in."

Starsky looked in the rearview mirror and made eye contact with Amara. "Anyone on your team hurt?" he asked.

"No," Burkowski said. "For an operation that went bad so quickly, we were lucky. If the shooter had decided to go after us instead of trying to get out of there, it could've turned out a whole lot different."

Amara tilted her head back. "You know what this means. They'll find out we've got the shooter. If they weren't closing down shop before, they will be now. We're running out of time."

* * *

The team returned to the conference room, with Mrs. Spelling retiring to a cot in a vacant office. Director Davis was already there, as were Ranger Colby and the ME. Chief Johnson and two agents waited at the hospital for the shooter to be released. So far, the woman had said nothing. Her fingerprints and photo had been taken and sent to the FBI and CIA for database searches. If she was in the system, they'd know soon enough.

"What happened out there?" Davis asked.

Burkowski recapped the events while her boss listened intently.

Davis sighed. "This is going to be all over the morning news. We need a cover story. Nothing elaborate. Just something to buy us time."

"Sir," Amara said, "with all due respect, no matter what we say, whoever sent the shooter will know it's not true."

"Yes, but the press won't. We don't need any distractions. If they start digging now, it'll only make things worse."

Starsky stifled a yawn. "Once word gets out that Spelling's dead, rumors are going to be flying around the department. Won't be long before someone puts two and two together. The FBI takes him out of his office a couple of days ago, and last night he dies in a firefight."

"We can use that," Amara said. "Say he'd been working with the Bureau on a case. Gang related or something. He pretended to be on the take to get intel on their operation. Last night was a meet that went bad and the shooter got spooked."

"I can work with that," Davis said. "I'll get Johnson to release a few vague details. Say Lieutenant Spelling died as a hero and the investigation is ongoing. We'll hold a joint press conference later today to discuss the case further, though naturally we won't have much to share. Anything to drag this out as long as possible. In the meantime, we need—"

His phone rang and he glanced at the screen before holding up a finger and answering. "Davis. Yeah. Okay. Uh-huh. Uh-huh. Shoot it to my email now. All of it. Yeah. Okay. Call me if anything changes."

"Finally some good news," Davis said. "We have an ID on our shooter. Louisa Gonzales. Mexican citizen. Well-known to authorities on both sides of the border for her work with the cartels. Most likely used one of their tunnels to get into the country. The bad news is that with her rep, she's probably not going to give us much information. She'll be more afraid of whoever sent her than she will be of us."

"So are we any better off than we were before tonight?" Amara asked.

Davis shrugged. "Don't know. I'd say there's a possibility we're in a *worse* situation. Whatever operation those people have going, it's being shut down. Hopefully, they'll move it to a new site. Otherwise . . ."

"Otherwise," Amara said, "those kids are dead."

**The team huddled** in the conference room to discuss the recent events and plot a way forward. The tension had ratcheted up after Spelling's death, and Amara couldn't keep her knees from bouncing. Whoever these people were, there was no longer any doubt that they were deadly serious about protecting their secrets. If the kids hadn't already been moved or killed, they would be soon.

Chief Johnson clicked his pen repeatedly. "Nothing out of the shooter yet?"

Davis shook his head. "She's not talking, and we need to assume she's not going to. I made a call to DC and told them to get in touch with Mexican authorities and see what they have on her. Didn't figure we had much to lose at this point."

Sara inched forward in her seat. "Nothing on her that might help? ID? Bus ticket?"

"No," Davis said. "Nothing at the rental car agency either. Her cell phone's a burner and Agent Strand is digging into it now. If there's anything there, she'll find it. And I'm pulling the rest of the team back here. If something breaks, I want them close."

Starsky stood and paced his side of the table. "What if we offered the shooter immunity?"

Johnson arched his eyebrows. "Immunity for shooting a cop? I don't think so."

Amara placed her hands on her knees to slow the bouncing. "No one would have to know. Spelling could still be a hero. Look, he knew what he was doing when he walked out that door. Right now, he's dead for nothing. If the shooter gives us information, at least the lieutenant did something to help. It's not like he doesn't have culpability in all this."

The chief knocked his fist on the table. "As long as I'm in charge of this department, no cop killer is getting immunity. If word ever leaked, every officer out there would be at risk. Culpable or not, Spelling was still a cop when he died. I will not send that message."

The FBI director rubbed his eyebrows. "Let me think about it. I can always take the case federal and make the decision ours."

Johnson pivoted to face Davis. "No way. Whether you take the case or not, the shooter's not getting off. She pays for Spelling's death."

"We'll see," Davis said. "No point discussing it until we have nowhere else to go, though. Besides, not likely she's going to talk even if we do offer her a deal."

Dr. Pritchard tilted his head. "When exactly do you determine we have nowhere else to go? From an outsider's perspective, last night's operation accomplished nothing more than getting a man killed."

Burkowski clenched her fists and glared at him.

Sara's mouth dropped open and she leaned away from the ME. "Tact's not your strong suit, you know that?"

"Perhaps, but the facts are the facts. What did we gain?"

Davis waved his hand in the air. "It's all right, Ranger Colby. The doctor may be correct from today's view, but unfortunately, we can't operate that way. We ran the op in the hopes of gaining information, and it went bad. Happens far more often than we'd like, but we do still have the cell phone. It may provide a clue."

Burkowski breathed heavily. "If it'd help, I'd be happy to bring the doctor along on our next operation. Let him see that things rarely go as planned when dealing with *live* people."

"We're all on edge today," Davis said. "Understandably so, but it accomplishes nothing. Burkowski, how's your team?"

She shrugged. "Disappointed we lost a friendly, but otherwise okay. They're resting now. I told them we might be back in action soon, so sleep while they can."

"Good," Davis said. "Tell them I appreciate their work, and don't sweat the friendly. Nothing they could do about that. In the meantime, let's focus on—"

Amara jumped as the door burst open. Agent Strand, followed by Agent Wroth, hurried into the room. She carried an armful of gadgets and eased them onto the end of the table, then opened her laptop. Her assistant moved the projector and screen into position.

"Got something?" Davis asked.

Strand glanced at him while she typed on her keyboard. "Want the technical version or just the basics?"

"Basics. You can try to explain the technical voodoo to me later."

"Okay. We were able to crack the shooter's cell and get some information. No texts or voice mails, only other phone numbers. All calls were short, less than a minute."

Amara rubbed her hands together. "Any calls made last night?"

"No, and our assumption is that all the calls are to and from other burners, or even personal phones that are wiped on a regular basis. Simple to do in Mexico since their system's a lot looser than ours. One thing stays the same, though. Doesn't matter what phone you have—if you use it, you're pinging off cell towers, and those can be tracked."

Davis steepled his fingers. "What did you find?"

She clicked the mouse a couple of times and pointed at the

screen. "Monclova, Mexico. She placed four calls to different phone numbers from there a few days ago. If the shooter contacted people in the same area, we may have our location. Agent Wroth is working on a hack into their cell network. If any of the other four phones are still active, we may be able to locate them."

Johnson shifted in his seat. "Excellent. What do we know about the town?"

The tech centered the screen on the city and scrolled in until words popped into view. She clicked on the town's name. "Two hundred thousand people. Primary industry is steel production."

The chief walked to the coffeepot and poured himself another cup. "They'd certainly have plenty of power available there."

Sara squinted at the map. "What are the black areas south of the city?"

The view shifted and zoomed in. "Those are the steel plants. Black because of the coal, I'd guess."

"Coal?" Amara said. "Are there mines around there?"

The tech scrolled in closer and moved the view over the mountains. Several roads ran into the hills, each dead-ending at clusters of small buildings. "Yep. Half a dozen of them at least. Makes sense. Build the steel plants near the mines."

Amara flicked her bottom lip. "Be plenty dark in one of those mines, wouldn't it? Access to electrical power too."

Starsky jangled the keys and coins in his pocket. "It'd have to be an abandoned one, though. Too many people around otherwise, and it would sure be quiet in there."

"I confess," Dr. Pritchard said, "that I am somewhat ignorant concerning the aspects of mining. Would there be enough space to accommodate the research requirements? Large, clean rooms, for instance?"

"I'd think so," Davis said. "And from a security standpoint, you couldn't choose a better location. Isolated, easy to spot anyone headed toward you, and only one way into the complex. It's ideal."

"I'll make a call," Davis said. "One way or another, we'll get eyes on those mines and see what's there."

Johnson nodded once. "Won't be able to get a peek inside them, but maybe we'll spot something out of place."

"How long to get everything set up?" Amara asked.

"Depends," Davis said, "on a lot of things. Whether a satellite's close enough or we need to send a drone. If it's a drone, do we notify Mexican authorities? And do any other departments have assets on the ground who might be able to assist? Assuming we get approval, best-case scenario is four to six hours before we can get a look at the area. Two or three days at worst. If we could get anything out of the shooter, that might help."

"Might?" Sara asked.

"Yes," Davis said. "We'd still need time to confirm her information before taking any action. She's not exactly a reliable informant."

Amara exhaled a long, slow breath. "Two or three days? Might as well be months. If the children are in Monclova, their captors will have time to move them, or worse. We'll never see those kids again."

"Sir," Burkowski said, "do we still have choppers on standby?"

"We do," the chief said. "A couple of them, one of ours and one of the state's."

Burkowski shifted her chin to one side. "Understood, but that won't work. If we have to go into Mexico in a hurry, I need military-grade hardware. Something big enough to carry my whole team and our equipment."

Davis typed on his phone. "We'll see what our options are, but let's hope it's not necessary. Flying military helicopters into Mexico would require an awful lot of clearance from authorities on both sides. We'd have to get the State Department involved and—"

"With all due respect, sir," Burkowski said, "that decision needs to be made now, and with as few people involved as possible." She stiffened. "If we go in heavy and they know we're coming, it'll be a bloodbath, for us and whoever they're holding."

He nodded. "I hear your concerns and I'll talk to the director to get the ball rolling. We need better intel, though. The decision will end up at the White House, and without more evidence, I can't see us getting approval to violate Mexico's airspace. Even if we could verify those children are there, I'm not sure we'd get the go-ahead."

"Understood," she said. "Light a fire, sir."

 **Davis stood.** "I'm going to make some calls and see if I can expedite things. Burkowski, start formulating your plans. Assume your destination will be one of the coal mines."

Dr. Pritchard pushed away from the table. "If you have need of me, I'll be at my office. I'm afraid I have quite a bit of paperwork to catch up on."

"Perhaps," Sara said, "we could arrange for someone to bring the paperwork to you here?"

The ME frowned. "I suppose that would be possible, but I really don't see how my presence here would contribute anything."

"Douglas," Sara said, "I think we should all stay close. Time is short, and if we do need you, well, it'd be better if you were here."

Amara nodded. Smart. Keep him close to eliminate any suspicion if something goes wrong on the op. "I agree. If it's not too much trouble, Doctor, would you mind staying?"

"Of course not," the ME said. "I didn't want to be in the way, but if you think you may need me, who am I to argue?"

Davis placed his hand on the doorknob. "I'll be back shortly. Chief Johnson, would you mind taking over while I'm gone?"

The chief's eyes narrowed and he rubbed the back of his neck. Clearly the man didn't view Director Davis as being in charge. "Take your time," he said. "I've got this. Agent Strand, let's have another look at those coal mines. Any way to know how old those images are?"

"No, sir. If you think it's important, I could find out, but it might take a while."

Johnson shook his head. "No. It's not like they've moved the mines. We'll wait for the real-time view and see if we can spot any new roads. I'd assume they'd be using an abandoned mine if one was available. Anyone disagree?"

Starsky cleared his throat. "They'd have to weigh the advantage of complete isolation over the disadvantage of making traffic to and from the place more obvious. I don't know anything about mines, but I've seen enough *Scooby-Doo* episodes to know if a place is supposed to be vacant and it's not, people will find out."

Amara half frowned and raised her eyebrows. Scooby-Doo? She braced herself for the chief's reaction.

"Explain," Johnson said. "But leave out the cartoons."

"Okay," Starsky said. "If the place is supposed to be empty, any sign of activity will be noticed. Cars going to and from. Power being used. There'd be no way to completely isolate the facility unless everything ran on generators and no one ever came or went. That's highly unlikely. In an occupied mine, I'd think traffic would easily blend in, and the excess power usage probably wouldn't even be noticed."

"True," Amara said. "But in a working mine, you'd need to be isolated within the structure. Wouldn't that create the same issue, not to mention the fact you'd have to build the thing while all those people were around? I mean, the workers would start to question what's behind the door they're not allowed to enter, right?"

Starsky puffed his cheeks side to side. "Yep. Either way, unless you're a James Bond villain and can build your base on an island, it's a roll of the dice. If it was me, I'd go for the option with the fewest people involved. The abandoned mine."

Chief Johnson squinted at Starsky, then turned. "Agent Burkowski, if you—"

"Just Burkowski, sir, if you don't mind. Kind of got used to it in the military."

Amara smiled at her. She'd never seen anyone as comfortable with themselves. The woman knew who she was and what she was capable of.

"Fine," Johnson said. "Burkowski, from a security standpoint, which would you choose?"

"Easy," she said. "The abandoned mine. Far easier to control. So much so that if it was me, I'd go as far as to set up a dummy mine if I had to. Call the site a test location or whatever."

Amara rocked forward and rested her forearms on the table. "A dummy location. Covers both angles. Nobody questions activity there and you maintain security. I like it. Agent Strand, can you find out who owns those mines?"

"Should be simple enough."

Chief Johnson scooted forward in his chair. "What're you thinking, Detective?"

"Dummy location, abandoned mine, whatever. It's going to be on the books. The power company, the steel company, somewhere. We get into those records—I assume you can do that, Agent?"

Strand switched off her laptop's link to the projector and began typing. "Wouldn't be much of a hacker if I couldn't."

"Okay," Amara said. "We get into their ledgers and search for anything different. Something like high power costs with no income credited back to the location. If money's changing hands, there's a record of it somewhere. They have to be able to cover their tracks in case someone questions what's going on. The fewer people who know what's happening, the better, right? So they'd want to make the operation look as legit as possible."

Sara pointed at her. "Right. So to the electric company, it's just another coal mine or whatever. No one there would question it.

We need to get a forensic accountant in here, though. A good one, and quickly."

"If I may," Dr. Pritchard said. "We are still assuming these children were taken for medical experimentation, correct?"

Chief Johnson nodded. "That's the working theory."

"Yes," the ME said. "If that is the case, why bother with all this nonsense about coal mines and steel companies and what have you? Why not simply build what you need? Design your research facility and construct it in the mountains, then tell people whatever you'd like. Stick a giant satellite dish on top and inform the locals you're searching for extraterrestrials or some such nonsense."

The room quieted for several clock ticks.

Starsky pursed his lips. "Call the place a government research facility. It's isolated, but out in the open. No secrets to hide. Investigate aliens or global warming or why the sky is blue. Spin the wheel and pick one. Then put the icing on the cake by sectioning off part of the location and busing in school kids now and then for tours. Genius."

"Thank you," Dr. Pritchard said.

Starsky leaned around Amara. "I didn't mean—forget it. Nice job."

"Agent Strand," Johnson said, "can you check for any government research facilities in the area?"

The woman grunted, clicked her mouse, and resumed her typing.

Director Davis stepped back into the room. "Well, we've lit a match in DC. The State Department is in the loop, and they're going ballistic. We've got the okay for a satellite, but absolutely no drones without Mexican government approval. Problem is, CIA says no satellite coverage for at least two days. Low priority."

Amara squeezed her fists. "Low priority? What could possibly be more important than a bunch of missing kids?"

Davis frowned and shook his head. "According to them, plenty. Look, it's easy enough to sit in here and demand resources, but the truth is that State and the CIA have to balance our needs with their own problems."

Johnson rubbed his palms on the table. "FBI drones?"

"None are designed to operate over long distances for increased times," Davis said. "I asked my boss to take this to the White House and see if we can get approval to bypass State and run military drones over the area. It's a shot in the dark, but next year's an election year. The president will want credit if we rescue the children and, maybe more importantly, if the op goes badly he'll want to show he tried everything, including bending the rules, to find them."

Starsky scratched the sparse whiskers on his cheeks. "So once again we hurry up and wait. No different from any other investigation, I suppose."

"Hey," Agent Strand said. "Not surprisingly, Mexico's not exactly covered in research installations, at least ones operated by the government. Maybe I should add in private facilities too?"

Johnson swiveled his chair. "Stick to government for now. Fewer questions from the local authorities and general public, I'd expect. Any possibilities near Monclova?"

"One." An aerial image popped onto the big screen, and she circled her mouse arrow around the mountains and coal mines. "Here's where we were looking earlier. If you continue higher and a little to the southeast, you'll come to the National Institute for Geological Research. According to their website, the organization's goal is to seek new methods to extract Mexico's natural minerals and ores without damaging the environment. Been operational since 2002. Not open to the public."

Amara stared at the image. "Looks small. No way to zoom in closer?"

"Nope. What you see is what I've got."

"Okay," Davis said. "If it's been up and running for so long, it's probably a legitimate government facility, or at least started out that way. Agent Strand, does anything on the shooter's phone link her or the cell to this building?"

She focused on the ceiling and moved her lips for a few seconds. "Nothing direct. The listed number for the facility wasn't in her call log. That'd be too easy. Once Agent Wroth's able to hack into their cell system, we may know more. Standard procedure would be for everyone to destroy their phone if someone gets caught. If they didn't, I can use that."

"How?" Johnson said.

"If any of the cells still have the battery in them, we can check their network for any pings. All phones do it now. Cell towers, Wi-Fi, GPS. If we get a hit, we can triangulate the phone's position."

Amara bit her bottom lip. "How close to the actual location can you get?"

"Depends on what's around. The more things the phone's pinging on, the better the location. If it's only one cell tower, could be a huge area. Two or three towers, throw in GPS, I can get within fifty feet. Wi-Fi, even closer."

"Do it," Davis said. "How long?"

"An hour or less, depending on how hard it is to get past the encryptions into the cell tower system."

"If it'd help," the director said, "I can get the NSA to send—"

"Sir, please don't insult us." Strand scooped up her laptop and stood to leave.

Davis smiled. "We'll wait to hear from you two. Burkowski, you're on deck. How do you get in there without starting a firefight?"

"With the intel we've got now? We don't."

Director Davis shook his head. "We're not going in without more intel. Just asking for your initial thoughts."

"Depending on the terrain," Burkowski said, "choppers drop us off on the backside of the mountain and we come in from there. Even then, I'm not sure we won't be seen. Have to do it at night and cut the power to the facility when we're ready to breach."

Dr. Pritchard shook his head. "Can't do that. If there's some sort of experimentation occurring, removing the electricity might be catastrophic to any test subjects."

"Plus," Sara said, "they've probably got backup generators. Cutting the power might warn them you're there."

Burkowski studied her fingernails for a moment. "Is it safe to assume that no matter what we learn in the next few hours, I still won't have any idea what's inside the building?"

"Yes," Davis said. "You'll be going in blind."

"Sir," she said. "I can deal with going in blind. What I can't handle is being trapped in a foreign country. Whether we find something inside or not, once we kick in the door, all bets are off. We'll go at night, but if civilians are around—real scientists, say—people are going to die. Getting in might be the easy part."

"Understood. The choppers will remain in proximity and arrive on your recall. They'll bring you back the same way you went in."

"Fair enough. Need room for my team, our gear, and twenty or so civilians."

"Twenty?" Amara asked.

Burkowski shrugged. "I'm assuming you'll want some of the bad guys too. Hard to question them if they're still in Mexico."

Chief Johnson scratched his nose and sighed. "Just so we're all on the same page, we're talking about illegally crossing the border into a sovereign nation, staging a hostage rescue mission on a government-owned facility that may or may not have anything to do with the children from Cotulla, then kidnapping Mexican citizens and bringing them back here. That about sum it up?"

Starsky smiled. "Well, when you put it that way, it doesn't sound so bad."

Davis stood and arched his back. "We need more. No way this op gets approved as is."

Amara tapped some information into her cell phone. "We're acting like Monclova is on the other side of the world. It's less than a six-hour drive from here. Let me go. I can get there late tonight and check out the place in the morning."

Johnson frowned. "I don't think—"

"I'm going," Amara said. "I look the part and I speak the language. A Mexican ID would make things easier, though. And I'll need a vehicle with Mexican tags. Nothing nice."

"Easy enough," Davis said.

Starsky fidgeted in his chair. "I'm going with you. It's too dangerous to go alone."

Amara stared at him. "No offense, but a pasty white guy with fiery red hair doesn't exactly blend in."

"Pasty? You couldn't say pale?"

"Sorry," she said. "But one little woman isn't quite as conspicuous."

"Plus," Starsky said, "I'm a little intimidating, right? People might be put off by my size. Not speak as freely."

Amara pulled both lips into her mouth and nodded. "Exactly."

"No," Johnson said. "I won't allow it. You'd be too far from any backup. Too risky."

"I appreciate your concern," she said, "but unless you plan to lock me up, I'm going. We'll do it off the clock if you want. No liability for the department."

"I'm not worried about—"

"Let her go," Burkowski said.

The chief glared at the woman. "She's my responsibility, not yours."

Burkowski squeezed her fists and popped her knuckles, then stared at Amara. "Alvarez can handle it. No one else in this room is qualified. Let her go."

Amara nodded once to Burkowski, then lifted her chin and turned to her boss. "I can do this, sir. I *want* to do it."

The chief doodled circles on the table with his finger for a moment, then sighed. "I'm not signing off without details. What's your plan, Alvarez?"

"Plan? I'm going to walk in their front door."

* * *

Amara drove the rickety car up the rutted mountain road. The vehicle coughed and sputtered as it protested the steep incline. Twice, pickup trucks packed with miners barreled past her as the employees hurried to work. A layer of coal dust coated the landscape and added to the bleakness of the early Saturday morning.

The drive to Monclova had been uneventful, though she'd stopped about an hour into Mexico to recover her pistol from its hiding spot in the trunk and strap it to her waist. Her phone remained back in San Antonio and she'd purchased a prepaid cell at a gas station. A quick call to Starsky to make sure the GPS tracker sewn into the waistband of her jeans was working, and she'd ceased all communication. After a restless night at a cheap motel, she'd skipped a shower, bundled her hair in a bandanna, and headed for the Geological Research facility.

The aerial photo had shown the entrance to the installation was via a dirt road accessed beyond La Esmeralda mine. Signs pointed the way to the entrance, and she slowed to dodge the slew of vehicles moving about, then continued past the mine onto a narrow lane barely wide enough for her car.

The road before this one had only *seemed* bumpy. She bounced from hole to hole, scrunching her neck to keep from banging her head on the roof. If she met a vehicle coming toward her, someone was going to have to pull awfully close to the mountain's edge.

After nearly thirty minutes of the abuse, she rounded a sharp curve and spotted the research facility above her on the right. It'd take another fifteen or twenty minutes to get there, and anyone in the building had a perfect view down at her. If they were looking, they knew she was coming.

She took a deep breath and maintained her pace. Undercover work was new to her, and her greatest fear was slipping into English. The team had agreed that her cover story would be simple and believable. She needed a job.

She'd been fired from the steel mill for coming in late one day, though the true story was she'd slapped her supervisor after he'd grabbed her backside one too many times. The company blacklisted her at the mines, so she'd driven up the rest of the way to see if they had any jobs available. She could work days, nights, weekends, whenever they needed her. Plus, she had reliable transportation.

The parking lot, unpaved, of course, was small. Three cars were there, each seeming to be in the same condition as her own. A small sign indicated this was a geological research facility and no visitors were allowed. The building itself badly needed a fresh coat of paint. The road trailed around the far side of the squat white building, and she stopped the car where she could get a look that way.

She smoothed her baggy shirt and ensured her weapon remained concealed, then stepped out of her vehicle. She bent and stared into the mirror on the door, pretending to primp while surveying her surroundings. Satisfied, she stood and took a step toward the entrance. Cameras were perched high on each corner of the structure, out of place for such a dilapidated building.

She'd taken three steps when the building's door opened and a man walked outside toward her. He wore a white dress shirt, tie, and dark slacks. His black-framed glasses were too big for his face, and his oversize smile struck her as something he practiced in front of a mirror.

"Can I help you?" he said.

"Good morning. I came to apply for a job."

The man shook his head. "I'm sorry, but we have nothing. Our budget is very strict."

"Yes, but I lost my job at the steel plant and the coal mines won't hire me. My mama is sick and needs medicine. Even if it's only one day—"

"Nothing. We have not hired for many years, and when we do, the government will send someone. I'm sorry you drove up here."

Amara crossed her arms, frowned, and leaned against the car. "Could I go inside and use your restroom? It is a long and bumpy ride back down."

The man glanced behind him. "We are not allowed to let anyone inside unless they work here. You understand. Regulations and all."

"Señor, I promise not to touch anything."

"No, I'm sorry. I could get in a lot of trouble."

She walked closer and looked at his ID badge. "Geraldo, por favor. I don't want to squat outside."

He hesitated and peeked toward the building again. "Let me go—"

The front door cracked open, then another man poked his head outside and spoke in a gruff voice. "I need your assistance."

Geraldo sighed and held his palms up. "I must return to my duties. Enjoy your day, señora."

"I understand," she said. "Would it be okay if I went to the side of the building? I hate to stop on the road. Too dangerous, you see?"

"Do it quickly, then you must leave. I don't want to be reported to my boss."

Amara smiled and rubbed Geraldo's arm. "Gracias."

He wiped the back of his hand across his mustache, grinned, and hurried inside. Wonderful. There must be cameras on that side too. Amara maintained her expression and walked around the corner of the building. After a few more steps, she stopped and surveyed the area. As expected, cameras were mounted on this side as well.

The things I do for this job. She moved as close to the wall as she could and pressed her right side against the building. She tugged her shirt lower, unfastened her pants, and squatted, reasonably confident her weapon, as well as her privates, were out of sight. *Please don't let this show up on YouTube.*

She walked away from the facility to gain a better view of the area behind the building. Certain she was being watched, she stretched and meandered twenty feet, then planted her hands on her hips and stared out at the scenery. Low mountains flowed to the horizon. A few lazy birds, vultures maybe, drifted in the clear sky. The wind, hot and dry even at this altitude, maintained a steady breeze.

This was taking too long. She shaded her eyes and slowly turned. The space behind the building was much larger than the front parking lot. Rusted 55-gallon drums. A truck that looked like it'd been abandoned decades ago. Broken pallets. Nothing out of place, but she could only see part of the area, and she hadn't come this far to leave without answers. The confrontation on her arrival was suspicious, but not nearly enough to warrant action. She had to get a closer—

"Señora, you must go now." Geraldo rounded the front corner of the building.

Amara pointed at the old pickup. "The truck, do you want to sell it? My uncle—"

"Por favor. Go now."

She turned her back to him and took half a dozen steps toward the rusted truck. "He can tow it and then sell it for scrap. He'd give you a good price."

His voice grew louder and heavier as he ran toward her and grabbed her arm. "Señora!"

She stopped and turned back toward him. "No? Okay. But if you change your mind, will—"

He pulled her toward her car, opened the door, and maneuvered her inside. "I have work to do. We have no jobs for you. Please do not come back."

"Sí, Geraldo. Gracias, and I hope I didn't cause any problems."

He closed the car door, stepped back, and pasted on his smile again. "No, no problems. Adiós, señora."

She returned his smile, cranked her vehicle, and backed away from the research facility. Geraldo stared as she drove off, a trail of dust kicking up behind her. She had a feeling he'd be watching for a long time. None of that mattered right now. She needed to get somewhere and make a phone call. She'd seen enough to know what was behind the building.

It wasn't the large concrete pad that frightened her. It could've been built for government helicopters to fly to and from the area. The smattering of cars parked back there didn't scare her either. All newer and high-end, they could belong to the researchers. Not likely, but plausible enough.

It was what she'd glimpsed beyond those things that terrified her. The briefest view of something big and yellow.

A school bus, its windows painted black.

68 Amara's call to the team had been tense. She'd pulled over at the bottom of the mountain and phoned San Antonio. From here, she should be able to spot the bus if it came down. Other roads snaked away from the coal mines she'd passed, but all were smaller. If they were leaving the area, they'd have to come by her. She hoped.

She'd finished her report and Davis insisted on going over everything again. He grilled her on the man she'd spoken with, Geraldo Tejada, and told Agent Strand to dig up whatever she could on the guy. Amara had to go into every detail about how she'd managed to get a peek behind the building. Johnson had complimented her on her quick thinking. She had a feeling Starsky might not be so generous when she saw him next. Davis questioned how she knew the concrete slab was a helicopter pad, and she'd conceded she couldn't be sure, but it looked about the right size, sat away from the facility, and a paved path ran between the two.

Most of the focus was on the school bus. Was she *certain* that's what she'd seen? Could it have been simply a way to shuttle employees to and from town? Maybe they used it for extra storage? Yes, yes, yes. She offered to drive back up and try to get a better look but advised strongly against it. All agreed a repeat trip would be too risky. Her visit might have already spooked them, if they were even there to begin with.

Finally, Davis was satisfied enough to contact his boss. They needed a drone above the site, and they needed it now. The call had ended with agreement to dial back after twenty minutes.

When they'd reconnected, Davis said an emergency meeting was taking place at the White House with the directors of the FBI and CIA, and the secretary of state would attend via a secured phone link from his hotel in Germany. The ETA on the drone, if approved, would be two hours or less. The okay for a rescue mission would take much longer, and the president was insistent that no action would occur without first informing Mexican authorities.

Johnson wanted Amara to head back across the border, but she refused. Someone had to watch for the school bus. Once the drone arrived, maybe. But not now. If they moved the children and no one was there to see it, the game would be over.

Sweat soaked her back as the vinyl seats heated in the afternoon sun. Naturally, the car's air-conditioning didn't work. She should probably move to a new location. Several small shops lined the streets and a crowd stood at a bus stop fifty feet away. Too many people could have spotted her and wondered why she'd been here so long. Did the research facility have employees in town watching comings and goings? But if she moved, she'd lose visibility of the road for a minute or two. Not worth the risk.

She stepped out of the car and walked into a shop, careful to stay near the large front windows. She bought two bottles of water, a bag of chips, and a pork empanada. Her stomach would not be happy, but the choices were limited.

Back in her car, she took a bite of the greasy pastry and dropped the rest back in the sack. Enough of that. Mama's cooking put it to shame. She'd miss dinner tonight, but had at least remembered to call yesterday and tell her she had to work. Her mother had said something about getting her nails done today. As far as Amara could remember, it'd been years since Mama had a manicure. Wylie must be coming for dinner again.

The bottled water, though not chilled, was refreshing. She chugged it for several seconds, then screwed the cap back on and stared out the windshield. At the top of that mountain, a group of kids might be waiting for someone to come. Or maybe they'd given up hope long ago. Her heartbeat accelerated. She was likely within minutes of Benjamin and the other children. What must they have suffered?

Her ringing phone jarred her. "Hola."

"Alvarez. It's Davis. We have the green light. Should have eyes on the target shortly. As soon as we do, you're to return."

She nodded. His words were vague enough that on the remote chance anyone was listening, nothing would be revealed. "Got it. I'll wait for . . ."

A filthy police car, its driver's-side door badly dented, slowly crept down the street in front of her. Third time she'd seen the vehicle this morning.

"Alvarez, everything okay?"

She hit the speakerphone button, then placed the phone in her lap and started the car. "Yeah. Need to relocate."

"Problem?"

"Don't think so. Some of the locals looking too familiar."

"Play it safe. Head out now. Nothing's going to happen within the next couple of hours. By then, we'll have—"

"Hold on," Amara said. The police car pulled to a stop next to the road heading down the mountain. Two officers stepped out of the vehicle, relaxed against the hood, and lit cigarettes. Moments later, a second squad car and a black Lexus joined them.

"What's going on there, Alvarez?"

"Not sure. Two cop cars parked at the road coming down from

the research facility. Third vehicle, a Lexus, joined them, but I can't see inside. I don't like this."

"I'm putting you on speaker. There. The usual team's in the room. Describe what you see again."

She scrunched lower in her seat. "Normal traffic going up and down the mountain. Three vehicles just parked where the road comes out and merges into town. Two police cars with a pair of cops in each. A third car, Lexus sedan, black with tinted windows, is there too. No one getting in or out of it. Looks like they're all waiting for something."

"Alvarez, this is Johnson. Are you in any danger in your current position?"

"No, at least I don't think so. They don't seem to be jittery. No sign they see me, or if they do, that I'm a threat. How long before the drone gets here?"

"An hour at least," Davis said. "Can you maintain surveillance?"

"Yeah, but if I pull around, I can read the tags on the Lexus. Maybe see inside through the windshield."

"Negative," Johnson said. "Too dangerous. Anything suspicious is liable to speed up any plans they have and make everything worse. Hold where you are unless you're in danger."

"Sir," Starsky said. "Shouldn't we get help on the way?"

"Can't," Davis said. "No clearance to move Burkowski's team into Mexico. We've got no agents close to Alvarez, and alerting the Mexican authorities is more of a risk than I'm willing to take now. If something *is* happening, we already know local law enforcement is in on it, or at least some of them are, and without knowing who we can trust, we'll be—"

"Whatever you're going to do, do it now," Amara said. "I'm looking at two—no, three school buses coming down the mountain."

"Three of them?" Johnson said. "Can you tell if there are people inside?"

"No," Amara said. "The windows are blacked out. I can see through the windshield, but there's a divider between the driver and the rest of the bus. Hold on . . . okay. The cops are back in their cars. Must be an escort. I'll tail them, but you guys need to send me some help in a hurry."

"We're working on it," Davis said. "Stay as far back as you can. Shouldn't be too hard to spot the buses from a distance."

Starsky's voice cracked. "What if they split up?"

"They haven't yet," Amara said. "They all took a left turn. One cop in front, the other in the back, with the Lexus trailing all of them. I'm pulling out now. Won't be able to keep the phone on much longer, though. I want to save battery power in case this goes on all day."

"We gave you a charger for the car," Johnson said.

She peeked at her watch. "Yeah, but you didn't give me a car with a working cigarette lighter. How long before you can do something?"

"These things take time, Detective," Davis said. "This could be a diversion. We need to make sure they're not—"

"Sir"—Amara pounded the steering wheel—"we're not going to be any more certain than we are right now, short of looking inside those buses and that research facility."

"My team is ready," Burkowski said. "We can be at Lackland

in fifteen minutes. The aircrew can plot their path while we're on the way."

"Uh-uh," Davis said. "Not without White House approval."

Amara's jaw ached as she mashed her teeth together. "We could be minutes away from losing these kids forever."

"Sir," Burkowski said. "The targets are in the open. There's no better time to strike. We've trained for this exact situation. Kids held hostage on a school bus. Give us our shot."

"Not true," Davis said. "School buses don't have blacked-out windows. You'd still be going into an unknown situation. Too many variables."

"Maybe," she said, "but one thing's certain. Every minute my team sits here increases the chances we won't be able to effect a rescue. If we were in Mexico, we'd at least have options. Right now, we've got nothing."

"She's right," Johnson said. "If we had drone coverage, I'd say we could hold off. Wait and see where they're going. But you've got one of my people hanging on a limb out there, and I don't like it. We need to get her help. Now."

Amara took a deep breath and picked up the phone. "We're heading south on Harold R. Pape Boulevard. Big road, you shouldn't have a problem finding it. Lots of traffic. I'll hang back as far as I can, but what do I do if the buses split up?"

"The Lexus," Sara said. "If it stays with any of them, I'd stick with it."

"Agreed," Davis said. "You're our eyes until we get—"

"She's not trained for this," Johnson said. "This is far beyond the scope of a local PD. Your department needs to get off its—"

"You can argue about this all day if you want"—Amara clenched the steering wheel—"but I've got to turn the phone off. I'll call back in thirty minutes if you think anything will have changed by then."

"Detective," Davis said, "by then we'll have drone coverage. That'll give us more information to work with. If you feel you're in danger, back off. The worst thing that could happen now is for us to lose you."

Amara bit her bottom lip. "No, sir, that's not the worst thing that could happen."

"We hear you," Johnson said. "Call back in thirty. Stay safe."

70

Amara trailed the convoy for several miles beyond the city limits. Traffic thinned as the
surrounding buildings became smaller and
more spread out. After ten minutes, they
drove through another populated area that tapered off quickly
into open land. On the horizon, low mountains shimmered in the
heat waves.

She slowed as the group pulled off the road to the right and
stopped behind a gas station, amid dozens of other large vehicles
strewn around the property. Semis and charter buses and farm
equipment parked as if a tornado had dropped them at random.

They could be planning to transfer the kids to something less
visible. She needed to follow them behind the building, but it was
too dangerous. Not for her, but for any children who might be on
those buses. If someone from the research facility recognized her,
there'd be no talking her way out of trouble, and the kids would
pay the price.

Nothing beyond the gas station except dirt and brush as far as
she could see. Amara took a quick left turn down a gravel road,
drove a hundred feet or so, then turned the car around. She thought
about raising the hood and pretending she'd broken down but
feared someone might stop and try to help.

From her vantage point, she could see most of the last bus and the Lexus. That'd have to do. A figure stepped out of the driver's seat of the car and moved out of her sight. She glanced at her watch. Twenty-three minutes since she'd talked to the team. Close enough.

"Alvarez," Davis said. "You're early. Something happen?"

"We've stopped. Not sure what's going on." She gave the details on where they were.

"Okay. We'll have a drone overhead within a few. Once we do, you're to back off and return to the States."

Amara traced her finger in the dust on the dashboard. "What's the plan, sir?"

"Still being developed. Burkowski's team is at Lackland and waiting for the okay to move. They can be airborne within two minutes of presidential approval."

"Detective," Chief Johnson said. "Listen closely. When the drone's there, you turn around. Understood? No heroics."

"Yes, sir. No heroics. What's the ETA on approval from the White House?"

"Unknown," Davis said. "State Department is still insisting we don't move without approval from Mexican authorities. Too little evidence showing American lives are at risk."

"And the drone will solve that problem how?"

"Once we get photos of the passengers, we'll match them to the missing kids from Cotulla. That should be enough to convince them."

"Yes, sir, but what if you don't get those pictures? What if they transfer those kids inside a garage or something?"

"Then we'll deal with the situation then."

Too much left to chance. "Sir, when is the drone going to be here?"

"Five minutes or less. Just got to route it down from Monclova."

She started her car and put it in drive. "Make sure it has its cameras turned on."

"Wait. Amara . . ."

His shaking voice made her heart jump. "Hey, Starsky."

"You can't—"

She switched the phone off and drove toward the gas station.

71 **Amara eased her vehicle** across the four-lane road and onto the gas station's lot. All eight pumps had cars parked beside them, and she idled past to the side of the building. There were no painted lines to indicate any designated parking area, so she crept as far forward as she dared and came to a stop between two eighteen-wheelers.

From here, she could see the Lexus and most of the last two buses. No activity was visible, though people straggled past from other vehicles parked farther out in the lot. Truck drivers mostly, but a few families and at least one load of charter bus patrons also moved back and forth. Restrooms, food, and an opportunity to stretch their legs waited inside the building.

No way to tell if anyone else was in the Lexus. She'd have to chance it and hope if there was someone inside, they wouldn't know her car. A deep breath, then *three, two, one.* She accelerated behind the group of vehicles into the back lot and parked between the charter bus and another semi. Her hands shook and she wiped her palms on her jeans, then turned to peer out the back window. No one came after her. Yet.

She forced herself to slow her breathing, then stepped out of the car and strode toward the gas station. Head tilted down, eyes scanning left-right. *Move fast.*

Both police cars sat at the front of the line. No sign of movement there. She walked between the first and second school buses. On the right, the rear windows were blackened. On the left, one man sat in the driver's seat while another stood beside him. A divider blocked her view of the back of the bus. She didn't recognize the driver, but the other man's profile looked vaguely familiar, like she'd—

Geraldo. From the research center. He'd know her clothes. Her car. Her face. She kept her pace and stepped into the crowded market. Bathrooms to the right, cashiers to the left. Food and gadgets for drivers in the middle.

She moved close to a rack of candy bars and stood on tiptoe to see over the display. Four men, two of them cops, lingered off to the left and watched as a woman loaded food into three cardboard boxes. Lunch for the people on the buses. One of the men wore a suit. Must be the Lexus driver. If he'd been at the research facility during her visit, he might be able to identify her from the surveillance cameras.

She ducked and moved toward the right. If the man spotted her, there was nowhere to run. She inched along the ends of the rows until she was on the opposite side of the store. Once they finished, the men would exit through the door away from her. She could wait until they were in the bus and . . .

And what? Nothing would've changed. The drone, if it was there, would only see four men. Not enough to prove anything.

Think.

She squatted and pretended to peruse the items in front of her. Giant-sized drink mugs. Air fresheners. Small tools. Phone chargers. Nothing to help her get—

Tools. She scanned the selection. There.

A screwdriver. Short and thin, like the kind you'd use to remove screws from electronics. Not much, but something.

She couldn't buy it, though. Too risky. The cashiers were on the same side of the market as the men.

She checked the ceiling and walls for security cameras. None.

You can do this. Her heart pounded in her ears and she ground her teeth. *Come on, Amara. Children in danger mere yards away and you're worried about shoplifting?* She bit her bottom lip and lifted two plastic packs off the shelf, each holding a screwdriver. A woman came around the corner and moved slowly toward her. Amara frowned, stood, and studied each tool intently as if trying to decide.

The woman scooted past her and to the next row. Amara squatted again and ripped open one of the packs, slicing her finger on the sharp plastic in the process. Blood oozed from the wound, and she squeezed her thumb against the cut, then slipped the screwdriver into her jeans. She stood and glanced around, but no one paid any attention.

The four men seemed to be finishing their business. Three of them each held a cardboard box, while the best-dressed among them talked with the woman and sorted through some money. They'd be leaving any second.

She tucked her chin and hurried back the way she came, stepped outside the building, and peeked at the sky. *Por favor, Dios, let there be a drone up there.*

She slipped the screwdriver from her pocket, palmed it, and moved toward the third bus.

72 **The plan was simple.** Grip the screwdriver in her right hand and stab the tool into the inside of the front tire on the passenger side. Leave it there and keep moving. Should create a slow leak, forcing the bus—and convoy hopefully—to stop somewhere down the road. Or maybe the puncture would deflate the tire immediately. Either way, they'd have to move the kids to another vehicle, and the drone should spot everything.

Sweat soaked her shirt as she moved closer. She cut her eyes toward the driver. He was kicked back, his feet on the steering wheel, while another man leaned against the dash. So far, so good.

She slowed her pace so it wouldn't be too obvious when she paused to use the screwdriver. For once, her stature served her well. She might have to hunch over a little, but the tire's top was almost the perfect height for her plan. A few more steps and she'd be there.

Stab hard. Protect your hand in case the screwdriver breaks. Only one shot at this, so make it count.

She was close enough now to touch the bus and peeked behind her to ensure no one was watching. If this worked, Davis and his team would have to—

"I know you."

She jerked to a stop and stared at the source of the voice.

Geraldo. *Stay calm.*

The man scratched his face and tilted his head. "This morning. At the facility. What are you doing here?"

She opened her eyes wide and smiled. "Oh, sí. I stopped for some lunch. My home is not far from—"

"What do you have in your hand?" He stepped forward and reached for her arm.

"What, this? It's only a—" She planted her feet and swung her left fist at his chin, landing the hook and dropping Geraldo to one knee. A quick kick to his sternum sent him onto his back. She glanced through the bus windshield in time to see the two men heading for the door.

She reached and plunged the screwdriver into the tire far enough back that it would remain unseen. Maybe.

Geraldo rolled to his side, and she kicked at him again, this time more like a frightened girl than a trained officer.

The men rounded the front of the bus and one of them moved toward her. "What's going on?"

Amara pointed at Geraldo. "This man, he grabbed my, my . . ." She brushed away a tear.

The bus driver laughed. "He picked the wrong señorita, eh?"

The other man bent down to Geraldo. "Come on. Get up. If he sees you like this, we'll all be in trouble."

"Tell your friend he's lucky," Amara said. "I didn't kick him where I should have. Next time I will." She lifted her chin and took a step toward her car. Another couple of seconds and she could turn behind that eighteen-wheeler and then dart to her car.

A hand grabbed her ankle. "No," Geraldo said. "She's lying. I saw her at—"

Amara kicked at him and screamed. "You touch me again? You learn nothing?" She jerked her leg away and spat beside Geraldo before backing toward her vehicle.

One of the men grabbed her arm. "I'm sorry, señorita, but perhaps it would be best if you waited until we could clear this up."

She frowned. "I have no time for this. Let me go, or I will call the police."

The man smiled. "The police? There are two officers in the market. We will bring them."

"No," Amara said. "That is not necessary. I believe your friend has learned his lesson."

Geraldo rolled onto his knees. "I'm telling you, I know her. Don't let her leave."

She lunged toward him again, but the man gripped her tighter. If she didn't get out of here, she was as good as dead. Worse, they might do something to the kids if they found out who she really was. She couldn't let that happen.

She jerked her right leg backward and up between the legs of the man holding her. He grunted and released her, but his friend grabbed her before she could turn. Geraldo stumbled to his feet, shuffled to them, and punched her in the stomach.

She bent forward, certain she was going to throw up.

A slap rocked her face to the side and her vision blurred.

If she could get to her gun, she had a chance to take one or two of them with her.

"Enough," a voice said. "That will be quite enough."

She spat blood onto the ground and squinted. Mr. Lexus.

"This is not how we treat our guests." He grabbed her hair and tilted her face upward so he could see it better. "You are a long way from home, Detective Alvarez."

73   **Amara tried to lean** forward, but the restraint held her in place. At least they'd put her seat belt on too. No blindfold or gag, though that probably wasn't good news. They weren't worried about what she saw. Her hands were tied behind her and had grown numb several miles ago.

When they'd taken her, she'd been forced to climb into the back seat and change into filthy jeans and a ragged T-shirt. If they knew about the GPS tracker, they said nothing. Either way, her old clothes—and best chance of being rescued—now rested inside a rusty 55-gallon trash barrel at the back of the parking lot.

While she'd donned her new outfit, Mr. Lexus carried on a lengthy phone discussion outside, complete with broad hand gestures and rapid head movements. No doubt she was the topic of conversation. When he'd finished his call, he'd insisted she ride up front with him. Keep him company on the drive. Give him a chance to work on his English.

"Are you enjoying your stay in our beautiful country, Detective? Or may I call you Amara?"

She stared out the windshield at the bus. No indication of a tire going flat. If Davis was right, a drone would be watching them now. They wanted evidence of Americans being held against their will. Well, here she was. She'd given it to them. Not the way she'd planned, but maybe enough to jump-start the powers in DC.

Mr. Lexus glanced at her. "You do not want to talk? I am sure you have many questions."

She pursed her lips, shifting in her seat to try to take pressure off her arms.

A corner of his mouth dipped lower and he shook his head. "Your government is not the only one with technology. Your visit to our facility did not go without notice. Or perhaps we received a communication from someone on your team? Ranger Colby? How well do you know her? Or your friend, how do you say it, Starsky?"

No way. None of the team would've turned her in. She didn't know the FBI agents well, but Director Davis wouldn't have risked using any personnel he didn't trust.

The man angled toward her and lowered his voice. "Or one of the FBI people maybe? You'd be surprised at how little money it takes."

"Yeah?" she said. "How much did it take for you?"

He smiled and revealed gleaming white teeth, though one of the front ones was chipped. "So she finally speaks. I will tell you. I am paid a considerable sum—for Mexico. Maybe not so much in the States. Enough for my family to live well. Certainly more than an American detective makes."

"Your family must be proud."

He shrugged. "I tell them the truth. I work for a private security firm."

"Do you tell them you kidnap children?"

He glanced at her. "I do no such thing. I protect the interests of the firm's clients."

She shook her head. "Whatever helps you sleep at night. You know what's going on, yet choose to ignore it. You have your own kids, right? What if someone—"

He held up a hand. "This is not the movies, Detective. I will not be influenced by your speech. We both have jobs to do. Based on the current situation, I would have to say I have performed my duties better than you have performed yours. Would you agree?"

She gritted her teeth. Yes, but only because of her stupidity and recklessness. "Where are we going?"

"An interesting question. You assume *we* are going somewhere."

"Fine. Where are the buses going?"

His laugh ended in a harsh cough. "So this is the part where I tell you the whole story? Who we are? What we do? Where our secret hideout is? This is not a James Bond movie, Detective Alvarez. Whatever your future may hold, you will not hear such information from me. My employers would not be pleased."

A series of beeps sounded and he held his cell phone to his ear. "Yes? You are certain? Have traffic blocked in both directions. Do it quickly. Follow outdoors protocol. Leave someone to take care of it and bring it to the rendezvous. We may need it." He slipped the phone back into his pocket and cut his eyes toward her.

"Problem?" she asked.

He slowed as the convoy pulled to the side of the road. "No problem. Slight delay. We will remain in the car."

"Can I stretch my legs? Just for a minute? This isn't the most comfortable position to sit in."

"We will remain in the car."

As the vehicle came to a stop, one of the police cars sped back the way they'd come, its lights flashing and siren blaring. Amara pressed the side of her head against the window. *They don't want anyone to see what they're doing. Have to be transferring the kids to another bus.*

Mr. Lexus grabbed her arm and yanked her upright. "Nothing for you to see there."

After several minutes, no traffic passed the convoy. The cops must be in position. She leaned to the right as much as she dared.

Nothing. From this angle, they could transfer elephants between the vehicles and she wouldn't see them. If anything was happening, at least the drone would have a view.

Movement up ahead grabbed her attention. Two figures ran from the bus into the dusty field. Kids. A boy, then a taller girl. Each wearing dark, wraparound sunglasses. Long-sleeved shirts and jeans.

A man stepped into view. Geraldo. He smiled and stared at the kids for a moment before chasing after them.

Mr. Lexus clicked his tongue. "So you get to see after all. Watch closely and observe how we handle such things."

After a moment, the kids paused and turned back toward the vehicles. The shorter figure now ran after the other. Amara's heart froze at the sound echoing across the field.

Laughter.

The children weren't trying to escape.

They were playing.

74 **After two and a** half more hours of steady driving and multiple turns, the vehicles took a sharp right off what passed for the main road and headed down a wide path. The pair of buses ahead kicked up so much dust Amara couldn't see more than fifty or sixty feet to the side. Barren landscape, spotty brush, flat land.

The Lexus bounced in a hole and she squeezed her knees together. Should've hit the restroom back at the gas station. The buses must have bathrooms built into them. No way a group of kids could go that long.

She tried to piece together what might be happening back in the States. If the drone had seen everything, surely a plan was in motion. And they had to be aware there were youngsters involved, though whether they were American kids was an unknown. Still, with all the effort given to protect the children from the sun—and public view—it had to lend credence to their theory.

Whether the State Department signed off on an operation or not, the White House had too much information to claim plausible deniability. They'd have to act or risk the consequences if things went south for the children. She harbored no illusions about her own fate.

Mr. Lexus squinted and leaned toward the windshield. "We will be there soon. Someone is going to have to wash my car tonight."

"Don't suppose you'd care to tell me where 'there' is?"

"Does it really matter?"

She drew her lips into her mouth. "Make it easier for me to re-create the situation at my debriefing back in the States."

He chuckled and rubbed his palm along the top of the steering wheel. "*Optimista*, eh? Look around. What do you see? Nothing. A person, if they are not careful, could disappear out here. Never be found."

"Guess I'll have to be careful then."

"Sí. There are many dangers, señorita. One never knows which day will be their last."

"Sometimes they do," she said. "Like whoever let the boy send the text message to his mother. They had to know there was a price to pay."

The man wrinkled his forehead. "That is true. Even an idiota would know such an error could not be allowed to pass without punishment."

Her pulse quickened. "And the boy? What happened to him?"

He pursed his lips and tapped his finger on the steering wheel. "Enough talk. When we arrive, you will speak to no one. If you try, you will be gagged and blindfolded. You will be secured in a room. There is a mattress, so you may sleep if you wish. We will leave early in the morning. We have much distance before us."

"Please tell me there's a bathroom."

"*Baño*? Sí, there is one. I imagine it is not up to your standards. A word of advice. Watch for the scorpions."

"Wonderful."

He chuckled and pointed ahead. "One of my men forgot to take a flashlight to the baño. He learned some areas of the body are more tender than others. You could hear his screams for miles."

They continued the drive in silence for another half hour before pulling behind an old building that was little more than a shack. The structure's rusted tin roof and decaying wooden support beams didn't bode well for whatever was inside. Several 55-gallon drums, darkened and full of holes, waited to burn more trash. A couple of ancient pieces of road construction equipment were huddled together off to the side. The first bus crept forward and slowed beside a large round cylinder elevated six or seven feet off the ground.

Gasoline. Diesel maybe. What did school buses use? She frowned and studied the building again. What did it matter what kind of fuel they used? If her situation didn't improve soon, she could end up in one of the fire drums.

She inclined her head toward the dilapidated structure. "Everybody going to sleep in there? Doesn't look very big."

"No," Mr. Lexus said. "We will have the place to ourselves and a guard or two. Everyone else will remain on the buses. It is much more comfortable there. I will give you a tour of your temporary home, but you would like to use the restroom first, no?"

"Very much so."

He walked around the car, opened her door, and helped her stand. "I am going to untie your hands. As long as you behave, I will leave them free while we are here. Take another look around you. There is nowhere to run. One of my men will hold my car keys. We will have a man patrolling all night. If you try to escape, I cannot guarantee that my men will continue to be gentlemen."

She turned her back to him and held her hands out so he could untie them. "Like you said, where am I going to go? Now, if you would show me to the restroom?"

He grabbed a box of tissues from the car and handed it to her, then smiled and swept his arm across the landscape. "Take your pick. Snakes are rare, but like I said, watch for the scorpions. Do you need an escort?"

"I can manage." She strode toward the largest soon-to-be-tumble-weed she could find, did a quick scan for anything that might bite or sting, and blew out a stream of air as relief washed over her. The buses blocked her view of most of the building, but Mr. Lexus leaned against his car, glancing her way every few seconds. At least he had the courtesy not to stare.

The dusky-orange sky was cloudless and a quarter-moon had started its climb. It'd be dark soon. If she was going to do anything, she'd better figure it out fast. She stood and walked slowly back to the building.

Mr. Lexus nodded and retrieved the box of tissues. "I hope you found our facilities to be acceptable?"

She ignored him and watched the second school bus pull to the gas pump.

"Come," he said. "I will show you to your bedroom. One of my men will bring you food and water shortly."

The two walked along the side of the building. Amara used her peripheral vision to inspect the walls for loose panels or holes. Everything appeared sturdy enough, but a good kick would prob-ably bring down most of the structure. The problem remained, though. Even if she did get out, where was she going?

They rounded the corner and her heart leaped into her throat. A long strip of land appeared to have been cleared of brush and smoothed.

A runway.

Were they planning to fly the children out of the country? Or was this just a refueling point for the buses? Or were they sending someone to pick her up? Why?

If they put those kids on a plane, there'd be no saving them.

They could be anywhere in Central or South America within hours. Even if the US government tracked the plane to its destination, the resources to take action wouldn't be in place.

She couldn't allow that to happen.

Not while she still lived.

75 **Amara pressed her back** against the wall of the tiny bedroom in the front corner of the derelict building. There'd be no sleeping tonight. She sat on a musty mattress so thin it didn't protect her from the hardness of the plywood floor. A holey, dirty blanket was wadded beside her. Though there were no windows, she felt the darkness settle across the region. No sound other than the occasional cough outside her locked door. No crickets, birds, or traffic noises. Too quiet.

Hope Starsky thinks to check in on Larry. The lizard could easily go two or three days without food but would need his water refilled. *Has to be past midnight by now. Dinner at Mama's would be breaking up. Wonder if Wylie went tonight. Hope so, though I'd never tell him.*

Her family. That's what she'd miss the most.

Come morning or whenever the airplane arrived, she'd make her move, whatever that might be. Rush a guard and grab a weapon. Sprint to the plane and shoot out the tires so it couldn't take off. Force them to keep the kids here a little longer. Great plan if she was filming an action movie. In real life, she'd be dead before she got to the first guard.

Her part in this was all but over. The buses and plane would head on to wherever without her. What value could she possibly have to her captors? She certainly wouldn't be the first cop they'd killed. Mr. Lexus would get the nod to take care of her.

But not like this. If they wanted her dead, they'd have to work for it.

She stood and stretched. Going out the door was not an option. If she caught the guard by surprise, she could take care of him, but not without making a racket. She'd have to find another way out, then formulate a plan.

The Lexus wasn't an option. No way to know where the keys were. The construction equipment wouldn't work either. Even if she knew how to start the machines, the noise would wake everyone. What was left? Running? Where could she go that they wouldn't find her?

And even if she escaped, so what? There was still the problem of the potential airplane. Stopping it from flying the children out of Mexico was the priority, and she couldn't do that if she wasn't here.

She moved to the wall opposite the door and pushed her foot along the bottom. The tin panel bowed outward. A swift, hard kick would pop it off the wooden beam easily enough. Too loud. She'd have to sit and apply increasing pressure with her heel.

An image of a scorpion flashed through her mind, and she scooted her foot side to side before sitting. She wedged her palms on the floor behind her, leaned back, and placed the sole of her shoe against the wall. She took a deep breath and held it, listening for any activity that might signal a guard's approach.

Nothing except a low hum. In the distance and getting closer. Had to be the third bus.

She straightened and rubbed her hands together. She could use the noise of the bus to cover her kicks against the wall. The vehicle's arrival might even pull some attention away from the area.

Muffled voices from outside dribbled into her room. A couple of guards stood inches from her on the other side of the wall, and she inched closer to try to make out what they were saying.

One of the men was eager to get back to bed. The other attempted to convince his partner to go ahead and start his shift early. What difference would thirty minutes make?

The noise grew closer now, and speckles of light flashed through seams in the wall as the bus turned behind the other vehicles. After a moment, the engine shut off and all was quiet again. One of the men murmured that he was going back to bed. The other spat a profanity. Both laughed and silence fell again.

Amara scooted back into position to press against the wall. She closed her eyes and waited for anything to indicate the guard had moved. Nothing. No way to know if he was on the other side of the world or standing inches away.

A low grunt answered the question. He was still there. Maybe if she tried another wall, she could—

What was that? A shuffling sound, then two taps on her wall.

She froze, certain her heartbeat could be heard by the guard.

Another series of taps, then a low voice.

"Detective Amara Alvarez. Are you in there?"

76

Amara squeezed her hands into fists. That voice. The question came again.

"Detective Amara Alvarez, are you in there?"

Amara placed her mouth a millimeter from the wall. "Burkowski?"

"Yes. How many guards inside?"

How? Even if the drone had followed them, how had—

"How many guards?" Burkowski's repeated whisper came with added urgency.

"One," Amara said. "I think. Right outside my door."

"Can you distract him?"

Amara stood and flexed her legs. "Be my pleasure."

"Ten seconds, then go. And keep it as quiet as possible."

Amara counted to eight, then tapped on the door. "Hey. Baño, por favor."

A key rattled in the lock and the door pushed open. The guard shined his flashlight in the room and stepped inside. His right hand held a gun pointed in her general direction.

"Tissues?" she asked.

He sighed, shook his head, and gestured out the doorway. "Hurry up."

A floorboard creaked somewhere close, and he glanced back. "Who is there?"

It was all Amara needed. Her roundhouse kick landed solidly on the back of the guard's head. He collapsed to the ground and she planted her foot on his wrist before grabbing his gun. The man moaned and tried to push himself onto his knees, but she buried another kick into his gut. He gasped for air and she hammered the butt of the pistol against the side of his skull. He crumpled, probably unconscious, maybe dead. She didn't care either way.

A smallish figure stood in the doorway, silhouetted by a dim glow somewhere behind her. "Turn off the light. And remind me to stay on your good side."

"Sorry, Burkowski. I've got some anger issues to work out," Amara said.

"Looks like you just did."

She stood and checked the gun. Full magazine and one in the chamber. "I'm only getting started."

Burkowski held up her hand. "Uh-uh. Wait here. Make sure your friend there stays down."

"If you think I'm—"

"My team's trained for these situations. We know each other. Work together every day. Hate to be blunt, but we don't need you mucking it up. We're going to hit the buses with flashbangs before we storm them. You don't fit into the equation. Want to help those kids? Stay here."

She glanced at the prone figure at her feet. "Can I hit him again if he moves?"

Burkowski touched a finger to her ear. "Roger that. Stand by. Alvarez, stay in this room and keep low. Should all be over in a couple of minutes. I'll come get you when we've secured the targets."

"Be careful, Burkowski. There are kids out there."

The woman turned and disappeared into the darkness. Amara squatted near the guard and peered out the door.

All over in a few minutes? It seemed so sudden, but so long in coming. Her legs ached and her shoulders sagged. Exhaustion was winning out over adrenaline. She took a deep breath and rocked forward on her toes. In seconds, people just outside this building would be dead.

Please, God. Protect the kids.

On cue, the sound of breaking glass was immediately followed by several loud bursts. Screaming and gunfire continued for another fifteen or twenty seconds, then only a few shouts.

American shouts.

Amara checked her captive again before inching outside the room. She sidled toward the front door, careful to keep the unconscious guard in her line of sight.

A single shot rang out from behind the building and she ducked. More yelling, then silence.

Not knowing was torture. With nothing to tie up the guard, she couldn't leave him. He didn't seem too heavy though, so if she dragged him, she might be able to keep him close enough to watch in case he came to.

The front door opened and Amara raised her weapon.

"Easy," Burkowski said. "Good to go."

"The kids?"

"Confused, scared, but not injured. One of my men took a bullet in the arm, but he'll be okay."

"The others?"

Burkowski shrugged. "Four dead, three close to it, and three more uninjured. Not sure which category your guy there falls in."

"How did you find us? The drone?"

"Pretty simple, actually. We had eyes on you back at the gas station, and when they grabbed you, we hoped it was enough to green-light the mission. But Kerilyn really brought it home. After that, there was—"

"Kerilyn?"

"Agent Strand. She saw the guy in the Lexus on his phone. Did her magic and tracked down his number. After that, we listened in on every call he made or received. That's how we knew about the bus with the flat tire. You have something to do with that?"

Amara licked her lips and smiled. "Yeah. Remind me to send some pesos to the gas station. I owe them for a screwdriver."

Burkowski chuckled. "The phone conversations gave the White House the push they needed to override State. Someone made the call to Mexico to tell them we were coming. Had to wait while their people secured the bus and took it off the main road, but everything else went to plan."

"You make it sound easy."

"I've been on harder."

"I'm sure. Can I see the children?"

"Yeah, but no questions about their captivity please. We have people back in the States ready to handle everything."

Amara walked outside, then paused. "What's the plan to get us home?"

"Sun will be up soon. Be a shame to waste that nice runway out there."

"Burkowski, I can't thank you enough. I swear, I thought it was over for me. And the children, well, I . . ."

The FBI agent moved toward the prone guard. "Go see your kids, Alvarez."

77 **Faint trails of pink** crept into the eastern sky as Amara walked around the building. The FBI team had herded the children into the last bus, away from the violence of the first two vehicles. Several agents milled about, their weapons still out. Near the construction equipment, three men sat on the ground, their hands secured behind them. Amara shined her flashlight on their faces. Two she didn't recognize. The third was Mr. Lexus.

Next to them, one of the FBI agents knelt beside the wounded Mexicans. None of the three moved. Sedated or dead. Those who had been killed outright must still be wherever they'd fallen.

She walked to the last bus and waited as the guard contacted Burkowski. He tapped on the door and the man inside swung it open. The divider was closed, blocking the view to the back, but not the sound. Crying and coughing. She handed her gun to the agent, took a deep breath, and opened the door.

The interior lights were on, illuminating the section. A pair of closet-sized structures blocked the rear exit. Bathrooms probably. Carpeting covered the floor, and a large TV screen filled the wall directly behind the driver. Three columns of individual airplane-like chairs occupied most of the space. She counted twelve rows of seats. Enough for thirty-six people. At least one child was in each.

The weeping shrank to sniffles as they all stared at her. Forty-five, maybe fifty children. She gritted her teeth and brushed her hand under her eyes. Where had they all come from? Hispanic. Black. Asian. White. Some appeared to be as young as four or five. Others as old as teenagers.

"It's going to be okay," she said. Many of the kids would be suffering from Stockholm syndrome. They'd grown to see their captors as friends. Family even. And they'd just watched some of them die.

She swallowed hard and tried to smile. "Is Benjamin here? Benjamin Reyes?"

No one responded.

She moved down one of the aisles and looked at each child. It'd been over three years. Would he have changed so much she wouldn't recognize him? Halfway down the bus, a girl, Hispanic, eight or nine years old, made eye contact. She could be any of the Cotulla girls.

"Hi, sweetie," Amara said. "Do you know Benjamin?"

The girl nodded.

Amara squeezed the back of the seat and squatted beside the child. "Is he with you?"

"He had to leave."

Leave? When? Where? No questions, Burkowski had said. "It's okay, sweetheart. Do you know where he went?"

The girl bit her upper lip and glanced around the bus.

Amara took the child's hand in her own. "No one's going to hurt you. You can talk to me."

"They said Benjamin did a bad thing and we couldn't say goodbye. That's what they always say."

They always say? They. Who were *they*? If these people hurt Benjamin or any of the kids, she'd find them. Wealthy or not, powerful or not, she'd get to them. Then *they* would learn the hard way who *she* was.

She smiled and kissed the girl on her forehead. "Thank you."

The child dragged the back of her hand under her nose. "Where are we going now?"

"*A casa.* We're going home."

EPILOGUE

Amara stared at the packed parking lot. Ten days since she'd returned to the States, and the case was still being untangled. Forty-eight children recovered, including sixteen from Cotulla. All except Benjamin Reyes. He'd come home in the cargo hold of an aircraft. In exchange for protection, Mr. Lexus had given up the location of the boy's body. Eight other children buried near him still waited to be identified.

Mexican authorities had wanted to hold all the rescued kids until their nationalities could be confirmed, but Amara and Burkowski overrode their wishes. Director Davis sent a plane large enough to carry them all and told the State Department to work it out. So far, the investigation indicated that all the children except the Cotulla group were from Mexico or Central America.

An FBI crime scene unit was still working inside the fake geological research center in Mexico. Based on interviews with the children, as well as the Bureau's investigation, Spelling's information about the kidnappers' desire to learn more about DMT appeared to be accurate. The facility housed dozens of isolation chambers, each of which blocked all light and sound from the outside world. Medical equipment, most of it state of the art, was everywhere. A play area, dining room, and kitchen occupied much of the space. Amara chose not to dwell on the operating room they'd found.

By and large, the children were in good health physically but still appeared confused much of the time. Therapists and counselors would be working for years to help the kids acclimate to their new environment. Scientists had requested access to the children in order to study everything from the impact of removing fluoride to whether actual progress was made in DMT research. Thus far, every family had denied their requests.

Theories about who had taken the kids ran the gamut from the Illuminati to the one-percenters to the US government. Whoever they were, they'd covered their tracks quickly. A joint American-Mexican task force was working to unravel the mystery. She doubted the group would ever find an answer.

"Ready?"

Starsky's voice startled her. "Yeah. Ready."

He placed his hand on hers. "You don't have to do this, you know."

She nodded. "I know, but I want to."

They exited the car and walked toward the church. The service would begin in a few minutes, but the pair moved slowly.

Inside, hundreds of candles flickered along the front. Ornate bouquets lined both sides. Several large photographs were propped on easels, including Amara's favorite. The one still in her desk. A six-year-old boy. Strands of dark brown hair drooping across his forehead, almost reaching his jet-black eyes. A dab of blue face paint covering his nose and cat whiskers drawn around his mouth.

No seats were available, so they stood along the back wall.

Marisa and Enzo Reyes sat on the front pew, surrounded by family members.

Amara pulled a tissue from her pocket and patted her eyes. What must they be going through? To have been so close, and now having to deal with their son's death again. The boy was a hero. He had to understand what would happen. Forty-eight children were free because of him. Did knowing that make it any easier for his parents?

The priest entered and spoke to the family before moving beside the casket. Marisa Reyes turned and scanned the crowded room. So many people. All there to offer comfort. To say thank you.

Mrs. Reyes spotted the two detectives, stood, and walked down the aisle toward them. Tears streamed down Amara's face, and Starsky squeezed her arm.

Marisa hugged her, and Amara whispered in her ear. "Lo siento. I'm so sorry."

The woman shook her head. "No. Por favor, no. Please, Amara. Sit with us. Benjamin would insist."

Amara sniffled and glanced at Starsky. Water pooled in his eyes, and his bottom lip quivered.

She took his hand and gave it a quick squeeze, then turned and followed Benjamin's mother.

Read on for a sneak peek from
TOM THREADGILL'S NEXT THRILLING STORY

The teenage boy drifted his third loop around the water park's lazy river, bouncing off other inner tubes like slow-motion bumper cars. Ahead, a family held hands to link their four floats together as they meandered through the twists and turns of the attraction. The distance between the boy and family dwindled until he caught up, and his left leg, dangling over the tube and into the water, brushed against the back of the mother's head. She jerked, turned to see who'd bumped her, and screamed.

A normal reaction for most people when they spot a dead body.

"Turn off the video, please," Amara said.

Dr. Douglas Pritchard, the medical examiner for Bexar County, which included San Antonio and, when requested, the surrounding areas, clicked his mouse, and the recording paused. "I requested the footage from the Cannonball Water Park after doing the young man's autopsy. I trust it will be useful in your investigation, Detective Alvarez?"

Her investigation? Was Zachary Coleman going to be her first case? Finally? After the Feds took control of the ongoing probe into the Cotulla aftermath, she'd been granted a transfer from Property Crimes to Homicide. The entirety of her first month in the new department had consisted of reviewing old files, shadowing other detectives as they worked, and trying to locate a desk to call her own. Her boss, Lieutenant Rico Segura, told her on three occasions that he'd find a home for her soon, but his voice had a distinct "whenever you ask, I push it back a week" vibe to it. Every morning, she toted her belongings to any open spot she could find and arranged her makeshift office. When the LT hollered her name an hour ago, she figured he'd finally found her a permanent workspace. She was wrong.

He'd been sitting behind his desk, an unlit cigar hanging from his mouth. Each morning he pulled a new stogie from his drawer and planted it between his teeth. By the end of the day, most of the cigar would be gone, whether from absorption or chewing or swallowing or spitting or . . . she'd managed to restrain a shudder.

He'd told her to get to the ME's office ASAP and find out what Pritchard's got. Suspicious death. See if it's worth investigating.

After a quick yessir, she'd hurried over and caught the doctor between autopsies and meetings. Douglas Pritchard worked with her on Cotulla, and at the time he'd been dating Sara Colby, a Texas Ranger who'd also been involved in the inquiry. The two were no longer together, a fact Amara knew from her increasingly infrequent conversations with the woman.

The ME cleared his throat. "Detective?"

"Sorry." She shifted in the red leather armchair. "Yes, the security video will be helpful if we move forward with an investigation. At this point, that doesn't seem likely. When the tox screenings come back, the department may take another look, but I haven't seen anything yet that points to murder."

He scanned his desktop. "How's Sara? Do you two speak often?"

"Um, last I heard she was doing well."

He shuffled through a stack of file folders. "So that's a no?"

"We talk on occasion. She's fine."

"Give her my best, would you?" He looked up and stroked his goatee. "Now that's an interesting saying, isn't it? My best. My best what? Intentions? Makes no sense. Wishes? I suppose that might work under the right circumstances, but I—"

"You have more evidence to substantiate your suspicions regarding the death?"

He nodded. "Zachary Bryce Coleman, seventeen-year-old Caucasian male. I have his file ready to, um, it's right, well . . ." He moved his hand in a circle over his desk twice, then pounced on a folder. "Here we go. The young man expired in rather peculiar circumstances."

"Yeah, I saw the story on the news."

He shrugged. "Perhaps. I'm afraid I don't spend much time watching television." He dragged his finger down a sheet of paper. "The death transpired two days ago. Exceptionally hot, if you'll recall. The decedent and a group of friends planned to spend the day at the water park. Have you ever been there, Detective?"

"Uh, no. Not that I recall."

He tilted his head. "Is that something you'd forget? Of course, if you visited before the age of three, it's unlikely you'd remember, and recent studies regarding Freud's childhood amnesia theory indicate that most events occurring before a child reaches seven or eight fade as—"

"No," she said. "I've never been there. You were saying the victim and his friends wanted to spend the day at the water park?"

"Yes, along with thousands of others. Alcohol isn't allowed, but easy enough to smuggle in apparently. The deceased had a blood-alcohol content of point-zero-zero-eight. Our initial theory was the combination of excessive temperatures and alcohol consumption led to a heatstroke. The autopsy, however, showed no signs of petechiae hemorrhages or—"

"English, please."

"There was no indication of bleeding in the membranes surrounding some of the body's organs. No congestion in the lungs or swelling in the brain. None of the symptoms we'd typically identify in a heatstroke victim. And before you ask, alcohol poisoning would exhibit many of these same indications, and others also which weren't detected during autopsy."

She planted her elbows on the chair's armrests and leaned forward. "How did he die, then?"

"We don't know. It will be four to six weeks before the toxicology tests are completed, but as of now, the cause of death is undetermined."

"But you told Lieutenant Segura it was suspicious. Just because you don't know how he died doesn't mean it's a potential homicide."

He slid a large photograph toward her. "Take a look at this. That's from one of the water park's security cameras."

The cropped photo focused on Zachary Coleman, though numerous people were visible in the water around him.

Amara glanced at the doctor. "Is he alive or dead here?"

"Hard to tell, isn't it?"

She grunted and turned back to the picture. The deeply tanned victim wore only a bathing suit and floated on a large yellow inner tube. His head was tilted backward and his arms were spread to the sides. Each hand, palms up, was tucked under one of the inner tube's handles. His knees were propped over the edge and his feet dangled in the water. The right foot appeared to be pressed against the side wall of the waterway as he slowly circled along the river. He looked like any other teenager relaxing on a hot day.

"Now here is a photo from the autopsy," Dr. Pritchard said. He passed her another picture.

"These are his wrists?" she asked.

"Yes. Although it may not be clear in the image, sand was embedded on the backsides of both wrists. We did not see that anywhere else on the body."

Amara compared the two pictures. "So you think what? Maybe his wrists rubbed against the inner tube and the sand got pressed into his skin?"

"Unlikely, but a possibility. Some sand granules were subcutaneous. Under the skin."

"Interesting. How do *you* think the sand got smashed in there?"

"I've given it some thought. It's possible he was pinned to the ground, and in the struggle to free himself, the sand could have become embedded. Imagine someone sitting on his chest and planting his knees on the victim's wrists. Unfortunately, there is no bruising to substantiate the theory, but I believe it's one alternative."

She scratched her eyebrow and squinted at the pictures again. "Uh-huh. Got any earlier video of him at the park?"

He smiled and steepled his fingers. "A bit beyond the scope of my investigation. That's why you're here."

She scooted back in her chair and crossed her legs. "I get why you think this could be suspicious, but is it enough? I mean, shouldn't we wait for the tox report? Trust me, I'd love to look into this, but so far you haven't said anything that makes me believe it might be a homicide."

"I thought not." He pulled another photo from the folder and used his pen to circle an area before passing it over. "Tell me what you see."

She held the picture higher and inspected the circled area. "The right foot. I assume that's your hand flexing the toes downward?"

"It is."

After a few long seconds, she shook her head. "Looks like maybe a little scrape on the knuckle on his big toe?"

"Exactly. Compare that to the first photograph. I believe the abrasion occurred when his foot contacted the painted concrete wall of the attraction. But no sign of any blood. A wound like that wouldn't have bled necessarily, but microscopically I would expect to see traces of burst capillaries near the skin. I did notice ruptured capillaries on his wrists, but there were none here."

"Uh-huh. And that's because . . . ?"

"His heart wasn't beating, Detective. I'm certain he was already dead when he went in the water."

Tom Threadgill is a full-time author and a member of the International Thriller Writers (ITW) and American Christian Fiction Writers (ACFW). He is currently on the suspense/thriller publishing board for LPC Books, a division of Iron Stream Media, and lives with his wife in rural Tennessee.

CONNECT WITH

TOM THREADGILL

- SMART SUSPENSE -

TOMTHREADGILL.COM

 TomThreadgill.author

 Tom_Threadgill

Printed in the United States
By Bookmasters